CU00833551

Attempting Deception

A Priest's Tale, book one

Lindsay Llewellyn

First edition published Feedaread 2012
This edition copyright © 2014 Lindsay Llewellyn
All rights reserved.
ISBN:
ISBN-13:978-1496036285
ISBN-10:149603628X

DEDICATION

A great number of people by now have suffered the collateral damage of living in proximity of a novel in formation.

This book is dedicated to all those living and working alongside the self-obsessed and unreasonable, such as I am.

CONTENTS

Prologue

The princess sat alone in her bedchamber and ran her fingers over the scars around her mouth. She hadn't seen her own face for years, shunning mirrors of all kinds even as her father shunned her. It wasn't so much the scars themselves she loathed, though they were bad enough — the badly disguised disgust they caused was enough to make anyone weep. No, rather, she hid from the isolation they stood for. Her scars were a closely guarded secret. Few, very few, ever looked her in the eye. Fewer still got to keep their tongues afterward.

There was a loneliness in this that she had never successfully explained. She believed her true self was hidden deep within — and yet she yearned to find herself in the eyes of another.

Even her father would not look at her, would not talk to her these days, locked up as he was with his men of war — and Lord Reath, of course, always him. It was Reath who had concocted the myth of her curse to cover her shame and Reath who kept her hidden. But the king knew it was her fault, this 'curse', this impotence she had placed on the royal line by her own folly. She was sure he hated her for it.

So she sat in her tower, resigned, she believed, to the fate life had laid out for her. A fairy-tale princess, cursed with ugliness, whom no prince would ever dream of rescuing.

Chapter 1

It was time, again.

I left my books at my desk and entered the temple. Around me, the statues knelt in their endless vigil, worshipping Re'a, beloved of the Creator. In many ways they were more friends to me than their originals in the village. I patted Karl absently on his wooden head and brushed the dust off Abitha's carved shoulder. Karl, naturally, was in the centre of Holy Re'a's gaze, his square jaw highlighted by the fall of shadow across his face. Abitha, hair braided and knotted by skilled woodwork, was next to her apprentice (who really ought to come and give the pair of them a wipe down). The whole temple was silent save the sound of my footsteps as I wove through the Statues of Intent to stand before my god and light the candles for our prayers.

Candles lit, I stepped around Re'a to the bell-rope that hung behind her. In theory, the tolling of the temple bell called the village to prayer, or at least to mindfulness of Re'a's mercy. I had seen no evidence that it did. Perhaps if the war ever came closer the bell might be attended but, just now, the war seemed no more than a cause of higher taxes. I muttered to myself and took the worn rope in my hands. Moving half a ton of bronze evenly on the end of a rope was a skill that had taken practice to master, and I'd had *lots* of practice. Ever since I was old enough to judge the rhythm, I had rung that bell for the call to prayer, three times every day. In a routine almost as familiar as breathing, I pulled hard on the rope, feeling the weight shift sluggishly above me until it began tolling.

Dreamily I swung the rope, counting softly under my breath. On the fourth toll of three, there was a soft crack above me and I faltered. The chiming immediately lost its rhythm, and the steady toll became a jarring assault on the ears while the rope flopped and flailed about at my feet.

If only, if *only* I had stopped then, and had the tower checked! Had I stopped, the rest of my life would have gone on as it always had. Saen, the sun, the Law-Giver, forbids sorcery — including the arts of presage — but if I could go back and warn myself … no matter. As relentlessly as the need to take the next breath, my own life's pattern drove me to take hold of the rope once more and pull hard to bring the bell back under my control — and to begin the end.

I heard a snap, loud and sharp. It was answered by a litany of creaks and groans and something in the belfry screamed. With a curse, I threw myself backwards as the rope became sickeningly slack in my hands. The bell dropped, chased by its wheel and struts, which strew about like sticks in a child's game. It stopped at the lip of the tower and balanced there a moment, as if it had simply desired a change of view. Creaking softly, the rope swung below, most of its length now looped on the floor. Carefully — so carefully — I extracted my foot from its coils. The lopsided bell, so horribly close to me, leered, as if laughing at my sudden loss of dignity, sat in a heap as I was. The temple space was silent once more and I dared to hope that was it.

I released the breath I had been holding and thanked Re'a for her mercy,

and her bell threw itself at me.

Frantically, I rolled out of the way as the whole bell tower collapsed inwards, landing like an autumn bonfire over the now misshapen bell. Blessed Lady! I thought the noise alone would kill me! I hugged the floor in terror, prostrate in a mockery of devotion, while it seemed to me that the entire world fell about me.

Moments later, the temple was still again. I spat out the grit, wiped my eyes and nose, and panted my relief. The temple still stood, and so might I.

Saen shone through the new hole in the roof as if blessing the ruin.

I began to swear again, but lost the words in a fit of coughing. Like some sort of theophany, the dust that had been coating so many of the statues had risen to meet the falling debris to create a great cloud filling the temple. Saen's light shone through the motes, lending a terrible beauty that I comprehensively failed to enjoy.

My hands were shaking and my skull ringing with the sound of the falling bell, but duty and habit still called every bit as powerfully as the force that had pushed the bell down. As soon as I was sure I was still alive and whole, I forced myself up from where I lay. It wasn't far to the feet of Re'a, mercifully. With my scarf over my mouth, I dropped to my knees, leaned my face into the dust and said the hour, slowly and with much more coughing.

Duty done I got to my feet once again and viewed the destruction.

"It's alright!" I called to the folk who were waiting outside.

It was right that they should have waited for me to finish my prayers, but I was feeling wobbly and teary now. It was time to hand the problem of the ruined tower over to someone else, at least for a bit.

Still no one came in so I tottered over to the door and opened it wide.

Outside stood not a soul. Not one. No one had noticed. I had known that the tolling went unheeded, but altogether unnoticed?

Or perhaps, a monstrous voice whispered in my heart, *they did notice and did not care.*

I stared dully at the empty hillside a moment longer before turning to the little stand of wash water by the door to wipe off the worst of the dust. Anything could have happened up here — broken leg, split head — I might even have been attacked for all they knew and I would have been all alone. I sniffed with self-pity.

"It's alright," I repeated to myself, pathetically.

The sound of my voice singularly failed, in the dust and ruins, to echo as it ought to have done. I sniffed, coughed and swore yet again.

It isn't fair! Here I sit day and night, praying for their unworthy souls and they can't be bothered *to come and see how I am. It is patently obvious that disaster has befallen me!*

Obviously — obviously — it was not that I was indignant for *me*, but for my Lady. In snubbing me, her daughter, her representative, they snubbed *her* and it was my *duty* to point this out to them. I nodded to myself. They needed to be told it was their duty to fix my — or rather, Holy Re'a's — temple.

I stomped back to my rooms, changed into boots (the exercise significantly slowed by a tendency to stab my foot at the boot), grabbed my cloak, untangled it from the hook on only the second attempt, and set off down the hill full of — wholly righteous — ire.

When I reached the village smithy, I found Karl taking instructions on a new set of hinges for Ruid's door. The blacksmith was red-faced from his forge. Though he was the one taking instruction, he stood arms folded, shoulders square. Ruid, by contrast, smaller and fatter, was sweating rivers in his woollen shirt and his beard dripped. As he stood there listening to Ruid, the smug, self-satisfied look on Karl's face did nothing to improve my temper.

He wouldn't be looking so smug if his *roof had just fallen on him.*

I coughed and the blacksmith glanced over. When he saw me, he looked me up and down as though I were an unsatisfactory ewe at market. I could not help but feel the contrast. Even burnt and sweaty in a leather apron, Karl managed to look groomed. I had left my scarf behind and my braids were still full of dust, my shirts and skirts likewise covered. My boots were old and I had long since given up on stockings.

Stupid, stupid! I thought.

I thought too late that ten minutes straightening my appearance before I had come down would have been ten minutes well spent. Once again I had come to lock horns with Karl half-set and ill prepared. It was by no means the first time we had fought. Once he had even called me a priestess — a priest*ess!* — quite deliberately, too. Even the W'shten know it is only the handmaids of their heathen gods who call themselves priestesses. Those who mediate the full humanity of Re'a are simply 'priest', and of course Karl knew it. He was always unfailingly rude and arrogant towards me. I needed all the armour I could gather and, arriving thus dishevelled, I had abandoned a crucial piece, losing ground before I began. I ground my teeth and tried to reassert myself.

"Where in the world have you been?" I hissed.

Karl smirked.

"Not in whatever pit you've just been rolling in, that's for sure, Kayt'an Sahn."

I side-stepped his scorn, self-conscious, and tried a new tack.

"Do you pay any heed to your Lady's temple, smith? Or does nothing beyond your own little world have any significance?"

I was shaking again and it occurred to me, belatedly, that perhaps this was not the perfect time to resolve this. My head still hammered with the sound of the falling bell and I was beginning to feel sick. I was rattled, I realised, and not — perhaps — as reasonable as I might be. Almost certainly, I would have backed down then, if that unspeakable man hadn't laughed — *laughed*!

"Saahni," he said, laughing in my face even while he addressed me with the title of my priesthood, "go back to your little temple and your prayers. I have man's work to attend to."

He glanced back at Ruid and they both smirked. I felt a familiar fire burn in the pit of my belly. How *dare* they! '*Man's work*' indeed! The heat spread to my cheeks, and my fists clenched into tight knots, nails biting into my palms. Shoulders squared and chin high, I closed the little gap between Karl and me.

"Well your 'man's work' clearly renders you deaf and stupid," I snarled. "The tower bell fell down *while I was ringing it* — nearly killing me, I might add — but *you*," I stabbed a finger in his direction, "can't notice anything beyond the end of your — overly big — fat nose."

I was shrill by the end of it, and even I was aware the nose gibe was a cheap one, but I was struggling under my disadvantage.

Damn, I look a mess!

By this time a small crowd had gathered around the smithy, drawn by my strident tones. I ignored them.

Karl rolled one shoulder in a studied gesture of indifference, turning slightly to include his growing audience.

"I hardly see how this concerns me, Saahni. The temple is your concern. If you don't maintain a thing, it falls down." He sneered triumphantly, "Maybe you should pray a little less and do a little more."

For a moment I simply stood and fumed. He had — as always — missed the point. I did *plenty*. Anyone would have told you how busy I was. I just wasn't a carpenter. Besides, I barely managed to buy the candles on the temple income and if I didn't sweeten the moon with my work as a healer I'd starve. (*Not that they'd care*.) How was I supposed to pay for all that needed doing? *Besides,* there was supposed to be a partnership between temple and village. That was the how it had always been; that was how it worked. I looked after their souls; they looked after me. All this and a dozen more damning arguments presented themselves to me. What I said was,

"I cannot possibly fix it on my own!"

It sounded too pathetic for words. My legs started trembling again and I could feel tears rising. *Next time*, I promised myself, *I will stop and eat before I try to take on Karl*. Like a wolf, the blacksmith pounced on my weakness. He turned his back to me, though I saw him glance at our audience, and quipped,

"Now then, Saahni, where is your faith? I'm sure the Blessed Re'a will lend her aid."

I heard a snigger behind me and my wrath lifted me up out of my reason and into high dudgeon. I turned to the sniggerer and his fellows.

"You fat, idle cattle!" I stamped my foot. "You do nothing all day but eat and scratch out a living. Do any of you look beyond your noses? Eh?" I pointed a long, dusty finger at Enrith. "Do any of you think of the *Pit* that awaits the slattern and the drunkard?

"Holy Re'a loves you all better than her own self, but even she — of Blessed Name — cannot help anyone who turns their back on her like you do!" I could see their eyes hardening from sneaky amusement to dislike, but, O Lady! I couldn't stop myself. "You creep from one bed to another — don't think I don't know! — and then think that a smart statue in front of Re'a is all it takes to make it right with Saen." I stamped my foot again. "You're all fools! Empty, godless fools — no better than heathens! You've no discipline, no soul and no charity — no, not for things that won't come back to you."

On and on I berated them. I waved my finger at them some more and probably stamped my foot often — I may even have shaken my fist. When I had finished, I was breathless. I looked at their carefully blank faces and — unusually — felt a qualm or two about my rhetoric. Even then, I think, I knew I had gone too far.

Karl, rot his stockings — and if he can afford to buy stockings at Ephatha I'm sure he'd hardly notice the money needed to repair the tower — kept his back to me the whole time. When I had finished he turned, not to me but to the villagers standing round.

"Well, then, Saahni, it seems we're a hopeless cause." There was more snickering, louder this time and somehow colder. "If we're so unacceptable to Re'a then what good our money or labour could be, I cannot think." He preened, revelling in the shocked admiration of his peers. "I would hate, Saahni, to taint your Lady's temple with the devotions of *heathens*."

I wanted to spit, but if I wanted any help, I belatedly realised, I had to try to win the villagers back round. Struggling to gather some sort of calm, I turned to them and said,

"This is an opportunity for you to show your love for Re'a. She loves you so much she died for you! Now is a chance for you to restore her temple to its glory so that our Ladlas celebrations can be really splendid."

I gave them all a cheery and supportive smile. At least that was my intention. The smile died on my face when Karl (may he rot among the Dark Wyrms for all eternity) opened his *fat* mouth and said,

"If your precious lady loves us so much, Saahni, I'm sure she'd *much* rather her children spent their efforts on their own village than use them for only *her* gain."

I think — I fear — I did spit this time. There is only so much a woman can take, after all. I could barely breathe for indignation. His self-satisfaction was palpable. How dare he? How *dare* he speak so? I waited for someone to speak, for someone to say something about how they needed me, needed my Lady who shields them from the wrath of Farock Rha and comforts them in their affliction. No one said a word. They just waited, bright eyed and hungry like children watching cockerels fight. So I opened my mouth and — Blessed Lady forgive me — I said,

"Then you are cursed," and I spat on the floor again for emphasis. "Since you have abandoned Re'a in her need, she will forsake you in yours. The day is surely coming when you will call on her and she will not hear you. You have silenced her bell and her bell will not warn you when disaster comes. You will find yourselves judged by Farock Rha and found wanting."

I paused to draw breath and then hissed, "You will pay for your apostasy in blood."

Then gathering my cloak around me I stormed off, back up the hill.

I went back to the temple and tidied up as best I could. I was fine, of course. It was the dust that was making my eyes water and my nose run, that was all. I wiped the statues and the pricket stands, and shook out the rugs. I swept the earthen floor. As darkness began to fall, I dragged out the fallen rubble, taking a route around the edge of the temple to save as much of the floor as possible. Then, I dusted the statues and swept the floor again. After that I went to examine the fallen bell. It sat in its own little crater, far too heavy for me to move on my own. I marched up to it and kicked it.

Then I went and sat on my bed and wept until I slept.

I slept and dreamt the whole world was falling on me, and somehow I was falling with it: falling and fragmenting as I fell.

Chapter 2

Ladlastide approached and I was still alone. For a whole month after the bell had fallen not a soul set foot in the temple except me.

So I prayed alone with a hole in the roof and a bell in the floor. The bell was a little slumped now: with spring coming in wet, the rain had softened the floor under it. It looked a little drunk but — try as I might — I still could not shift the damn thing.

I had hoped that if I only waited, Karl and the others would come crawling for their place in the celebrations. The winter was ending and the folk down the hill would want to bless the spring, surely? But, kneeling on my own among the statues, I feared this Ladlas would be a sorry affair. As things stood, these wooden companions would be be the only ones at the Great Wedding Feast.

Still, while my prayers as a priest were spurned, I had a living to earn. One may scorn a priest and take the gamble, but few will turn their back on a healer for long — even if they did refuse to enter the temple itself. Hathil was more experienced than I, for sure, but she travelled further afield and — believe it or not — had a sharper tongue than I. The day-to-day physical care of the village tended to fall to me. So, on the day the village died, it was as a healer that I set out that morning.

Fris'an was expecting her first and was sick with nerves as much as the pregnancy. Her mother had died at the birth of Fris'an's little sister so my patient had cousins coming from Ephatha to help her. Hopefully, I would come away with some cheese for my dinner.

I was just shouldering my bag when the temple door banged open, and framed in the doorway stood a thoroughly dishevelled man.

"Quick!" he said, "The bell!"

It took a moment or two of bewildered stare, on my part, before I solved the problem. This, clearly, was one of Fris'an's cousins. They must have arranged a signal with Hathil. Alarm gripped me. Was the baby already stirring? It was far too early! Foolish family — to have arranged such a signal without consulting me — and without seeing to the bell! Well, if the time was now, it was too late.

"There is nothing to be done now." I frowned at the young man who, while I had been thinking, had strode into the temple and now stood, aghast, looking at the fallen bell. "We had best get to her side as soon as possible. I'll need motherwort, yellow fin ... "

I headed back to my rooms, muttering to myself. To my surprise the stranger followed. He was, I noticed, more than merely unkempt. Sweat spiked his cropped hair, and he was drawn and pale-lipped. He laboured at his breathing and, this close, I could smell the sweat on him.

"What happened to your bell, priest?"

"Saahni," I said, sharply.

Since the row with Karl I had lost much of the dignity of my priesthood: this last shred, my title, the title of my teacher and those who would come after me in Re'a's service, that I would *not* lose. The man simply snorted.

"What, by all the Dark Lord's spawn, happened here?"

"Did Fris'an not say?" I asked, surprised. "The bell tower fell down, last moon."

"Last *moon*? Saen's balls, woman — "

"Saahni."

It was a point of principle now.

He made a noise half snort, half shout.

"Why did no one fix it?!" He spun on his heels to stare into the temple, before turning back to me, white-faced. Words started tumbling out of his mouth, running together in his urgency. *"*The W'shten are coming and folk are going to be scattered about in their homes and fields and every place in between. They're going to be cut down where they stand! *Why is there no bell?!"*

He was practically screaming by the end.

I was astonished. Who was this man and who did he think he was? Where had he come from? It was becoming increasingly unlikely that he was Fris'an's cousin, but the W'shten were miles away at Ttaroc's border. The man must be a lunatic. I eyed him nervously. Certainly he was wild enough.

"Come," I said, "have some tea and calm down."

The wild man's hands dropped to his sides and, for a moment, I thought the lunatic had listened to me. I felt, not smug, of course — holy people are not smug — but a little pleased with myself. But, no. The look in his eye was incredulous, not wondering. He shouldered past me into my rooms.

"Who in the nine hells do you think you are?!" I demanded.

Bobbing in the deranged man's wake, I watched speechless as he marched over to my cooking pots. The trespasser — the *thief* — snatched up a pot and a spoon, barged past me *again,* and on back into the temple.

"Hey!" I called, but he was already out the door and careering down the hill.

I could hear him banging at the pot and shouting wildly, and I frowned. The man might be dangerous. I hoped the villagers did not hurt him when they eventually subdued him, but he was clearly out of his mind. It was possible, I thought, that he might be a refugee from the east. Few came this far west; most stayed amongst their own, joining the King's army — men and women alike — to try and fight the invaders off. Those who did flee westwards rarely came much past the River Arwn. Perhaps this poor man's mind was addled by the fighting and he had fled and kept fleeing. Then, as I stood in the doorway and watched the stranger running down into the village, the cold thought crept across my mind: *What if he's right? What if the W'shten* are *coming?*

I went outside and climbed up the steps to the roof. I tutted as I stepped onto the roof; I had to stop using the roof as a place for anything that had no other home. It would need clearing before the feast. Over my shoulder I could see the lunatic waving my spoon in the air as the villagers began to approach him. Karl, I noticed, had not left his forge. With one foot, I pushed out of the way the pot for melting candle stubs and crossed to the eastern side of the temple, expecting to see Talishead snug in its hollow in the distance.

What I saw was smoke and fire.

Horror held me paralysed for a moment — then I was heading back down the stairs and down the hill as fast as my legs could carry me.

Some of the villagers looked up as I approached, but most were gathered round the visitor. His audience was incredulous and slightly amused, but even I could see the passing frowns and shuffling feet that hinted at an undercurrent of alarm.

"Hi! Hi!" I called breathlessly as I reached them. "It's true!"

Ra'an and his lads were nearest the stranger and looked most worried, but they had relatives in Talishead. As usual, Talin stood slightly behind the immaculate Abitha who viewed the speaker with a tight-lipped mouth and with dusty hands on hips. It always touched me how well Abitha cared for her young apprentices; she seemed to have so much time for them. As I spoke, the pair turned to me as one, Talin resting a slender hand on his mistress' arm.

"Karl," I called.

He wielded the hammer for the village. No sense in trying to get any decision without him.

"Karl!"

I saw him speak to his boy who came out to us.

"Karl says, he can't just drop everything or the work will be spoiled."

I hissed out a sigh through clenched teeth. The man was insufferable.

"Karl!" I shouted, keeping my shoulders turned to the spoon-wielder. I needed everyone to hear. "Talishead is ablaze!"

Finally the stubborn man put down the tools of his trade and turned, a frown on his heavy face. He came out of the smithy.

"Maybe there's been an accident," he said, doubtfully.

"No, *no!*" cried the stranger.

I began to fear for this man's health. Really, the way veins were jumping around in his neck and temple, a fit might be imminent if he did not calm down. Why should he care so much about the actions of a village full of strangers? If he was so frightened, why did he not just run on?

"Look — listen to me," he urged. "There's not enough of you to fight and you're not trained. You have no weapons. You *must* hide. There's no more time for talk, you *must* come with me to the woods."

He gestured to the woodlands by the River Tharret, west of the village.

"But why would Yr's men come here?" said Talin. "It's just a little village. There are no soldiers here."

"You're out of your mind," Abitha agreed.

I really thought the man was going to do himself an injury. His temple pulsed with the rhythm of his frustration and his colour was dangerously high.

"Perhaps we should send a runner just in case," I suggested. "In the meantime we can hide as this man says. If the fires are just an accident, the runner can offer our help. If not, he can come back to warn us. Either way, we'll know what's going on."

"What, and all the while this runner trots to Talishead and back we cower in the woods like rabbits? I see no reason here for our fires to grow cold as a day's work is lost." Karl spat. "I know, Kayt'an Sahn, that you don't count the hours save for your *prayers*," he sneered that last word as though it were something shameful, "but some of us earn our bread."

The stranger finally exploded. He dropped my pot and spoon, and punched Karl hard in the mouth before grabbing him by his apron and shaking him.

"Even the priest has more sense than you." He shook Karl again. "What's half a day's labour against your *life*?"

He pushed Karl away. Karl, oblivious to his bleeding lip, started back at his attacker, but the stranger had already turned away.

"Wait!" I called. "Let us at least gather those who will come."

The stranger threw his hands out to his sides, as if to gather the wind in his arms.

"Do as you will," he said, dropping his hands and striding away.

Those in his path stepped back out of his way as though they feared infection.

I turned to the others and bit my lip. Now and again I think before I speak. This was one of those rare moments. Having thought, I tried desperately not to speak at all. *Let someone else do the talking*, was the thought.

It was a good one — but only if someone else did say something. No one uttered a word. I looked at Karl's face and I wondered what it would have cost me to go and make peace after our fight. If I had swallowed my pride, and rebuilt the bridges I had burnt, he might at least have listened to me now. Instead, I had sat in my resentful vigil on the hilltop. The moon had waned and waxed again, and I had succeeded only in rendering myself and my god irrelevant to the village and objectionable to the village smith. I looked around the others to see if anyone else would speak, but one by one they lowered their eyes.

With nothing to lose, I tried once more.

"We could still send a runner to Talishead, even if we don't hide. To see what happened."

Karl stared at me.

"Are you offering, S*aahni*?"

It was far more likely, surely, that the stranger was deranged and the fire an accidental one. It was a couple of hours walking to get to Talishead. If the stranger had seen the W'shten attack there, then he could not be far ahead of the soldiers, if indeed they were coming this way. It seemed to me far more likely that — if there were W'shten soldiers — they must have gone another way, or they would be here by now. *Wouldn't they?* If — *if* — Talishead had been attacked, an organised alarm ought to be sent to the king. Either way, our neighbours needed help, for certain. Still I hesitated. A cowardly voice urged that, if they *were* coming this way, I had no desire to meet them on the road.

"Or is it beneath your dignity to raise a sweat for the village you tell me you serve?"

I will not say I had no choice — there is always a choice — but of the two unpalatable options — namely take the road to Talishead and risk meeting an army or stay and receive the brunt of Karl's disdain — one was a distant possibility whilst the other stared me in face.

"I'll get a bag together," I said.

Karl turned away from me, red faced, his split lip swelling rapidly. I took the opportunity to catch Abitha's ear on my way past.

"Try and get Fris'an out — take her for a walk or something. As many others as you can — no?"

She eyed me darkly for a moment and curled her lip, turning her back on me without a word.

The journey back up the hill was a lonely one, and I entered the stillness of the temple with a heavy heart. I dared not take the time to pray for Re'a's blessing but only nodded my head in her direction as I passed. As I did, I fired off a quick prayer.

Blessed Re'a, Saviour of the World, have mercy on me.

I collected my water skin and some biscuits, and picked up my bag on the way out. Its contents were basic, but the people of Talishead — if I got that far — would need all the salves I could supply if those fires had caught them unaware. Slinging the bag over my shoulder, I left the temple again, pausing just for a moment to look down at the little village tucked in against the River Tharret. There was more than just a hill climb between village and temple, and had been as long as I could remember. It was no co-incidence that nearly all temples were built a little apart from the village: nobody wants their gods too close.

Not for the first time, I wished I had held on to my mother's womb just a few hours longer.

Still, time was of the essence, so I set off resolutely eastwards.

Chapter 3

I crossed the rolling scrub-land to meet up with the road to the east, and headed down it at a good pace. I did not often leave the village — my ministry as a priest was exclusively within the bounds of my own village. Even when I was acting as a healer, it was tactful not to travel without Hathil. Also, of course — in theory at least — my work as a healer took second place to my duties in the temple. So, despite the circumstances, it was good to stride out. I pushed the possible W'shten invasion back into the land of fantasy. Talishead had had a disastrous-looking fire and I was heading there to offer the help of Harset. I dropped my chin and increased my stride, enjoying the pull at the backs of my legs and the light wind on my face. My bag was light, and the further I travelled without meeting any foreign army, the lighter my heart became.

At length, my lungs began to burn and I slowed my pace. I took out my water bottle and a biscuit, and ate and drank as I walked. The birds were singing and sheep grazed on the rise of the hill. The prospect of encountering marauding hordes so far from the border was ridiculous. I wiped biscuity hands on my skirt and snorted at myself. That stranger had really had me going. Just this once Karl had been right: the man was a lunatic. Surely, I would have met the soldiers by now if they were coming. Relief made me stop and laugh. I stepped off the road and sank to my knees, pulling out my beads. I would to offer thanks to Re'a for our continued preservation.

I had few precious possessions but my prayer-beads were among them. They were a gift from my mother, shortly after I had left home. If I closed my eyes I could picture the scene still: my mother close enough to touch, yet Amtil's hand on my shoulder putting her forever out of reach. I had felt so homesick, standing there, conscious with a child's perspicacity that in my mother's uncertainty something was forever broken.

The beads were beautiful: each painted a different colour and the apex bright yellow — Saen's colour. My teacher, Amtil Sahn, had thanked my mother for them and then shown her the door.

Much of the paint was rubbed off now, through constant use. Even today I could not hold them without a touch of sadness, but they brought peace, too, through years of daily use.

Among my thanks to Re'a for her goodness to humanity, and to the people of Harset in particular, I snuck in a little petition that perhaps now Karl would see the value of restoring her bell. Next time, after all, it might not be a lunatic.

A distant sound filtered in through my prayers: horses, lots of horses — the W'shten soldiers! Unbidden, half-heard conversations rose to the surface of my mind: people who thought I could not hear, talking about the 'unspeakable' things the W'shten did to the priests of the Holy Three. My gut felt as though I had swallowed a stone, and my heart seemed to swell to fill my whole chest. The possibilities of 'unspeakable' filled my universe.

They were coming.

Frantically, I scanned the hillside for somewhere to hide. Not far off, down the hill a little from where I clung to the earth, there was a small gorse bush — but was it big enough? I scrambled down and frantically dug into the underside of the bush. The gorse pulled at my clothes and my hair and dug into my face and fingers but I was driven on and in, pulling it around me to hide.

I started to pray again, less articulate, more desperate. *Please don't let them see me, please don't let them see me, O Re'a, please don't let them see me.* The horses thundered past and I closed my eyes, unable to shake the conviction that they would feel me looking. Even once I was behind them, still I did not look up. *O Re'a, Holy Lady, please don't let them see me.* The sound of hooves dimmed and I guessed that the road had taken them around the hill and out of sight, but still I did not look up. After what seemed like hours, or even days, the horses' thunder died away. They hadn't stopped, hadn't seen me.

The backwash of fear hit me and I began to cry, hugging the thorn bush to me and weeping my relief and terror.

The sound of my own voice filled my memory: *The day will come when you will call on her and she will not hear you. You have silenced her bell and her bell will not warn you when disaster comes,* I'd said. *You will pay for your apostasy in blood.*

Amtil used to say that Re'a punishes people by giving them what they ask for. Now Re'a had cursed my temper and hardness of heart by fulfilling my curse. I leaned my forehead on the rough bark of the gorse and wallowed in self-pity. Amtil had placed me in her stead to stand, for the people of Harset, as Re'a. I was nothing like Re'a. I was selfish, hot-headed and arrogant. I had abandoned her people and now … my heart stopped, smothered with the weight of my imagination, with what might be waiting for me when I got back to Harset. I tried to bury my face in the bark of the bush and lost myself to misery.

Eventually, my own bodily needs forced me to dig my way out of the gorse. I retreated backwards, awkwardly, more aware of the pricking and scratching of the gorse now I was no longer in fear for my life. It took more time than I would have liked — given the urgent signals my body was giving me — but, eventually, I was free to sort myself out.

Returning to the road, I half-considered not returning home. It would be better, perhaps, not to see my own village burning, not to find the bodies. I told myself Talishead still needed me. I thought of a thousand reasons for heading away from the soldiers and from what they might be doing to my own people. *Sweet Re'a, have mercy on them*. Fris'an , I thought, remembering the heavily pregnant woman, had she played it safe and left for the woods? Was she, perhaps, even now being cut down by whey-faced heathens: her baby dying even before it drew breath?

I did not want to see. I did not want to know.

Then, I snorted at myself. I could add cowardice to my many faults. I knew where my duty lay. I *must* return and do what I could for the wounded who depended on me. My stomach tightened so much I thought I would heave. None but I could send the dead on their way. None but I would be there with the skills to help the wounded. I pushed my fingers into my braids before brushing down my skirts and starting off after the horses, with a heavy heart and dragging feet.

As I walked, I wondered again about the stranger who had come to warn us. How had he got so far ahead of those horses? Why had the W'shten spent so long in Talishead? (There was a possible answer to that I could not bring myself to think about.) Who *was* he and why did he care so much? I did not know the folk of Talishead well but I did not even recognise his face. Where, then, had he come from?

Hope flickered. Perhaps, I thought, perhaps after all he was wrong. Perhaps the fires were a coincidence. Perhaps the horses were our soldiers, passing through. I had not *seen* them; they might not be Yr's men. I clutched at this straw. Perhaps I *should* first go back towards Talishead to find out what had happened. I stopped and chewed my lip. If Karl was not struck down by W'shten soldiers, he would sneer unbearably at my failure even to get as far as the neighbouring village. My own lip curled in response. I was most assuredly a coward. I kept on plodding back to Harset.

Eventually, the road curved and I saw my temple on the hill, to the right of the setting sun. Between Saen and Re'a, between sun and temple, I could see smoke rising like incense. *Odd, how it makes my eyes sting and water even from this distance.*

Telling myself I needed bandages, that I should approach the village obliquely, in case soldiers were still there, telling myself anything that would postpone seeing what — who — lay in that smoke, I veered off up the hill. I was bedraggled and weary and in need of the comfort of my home. I needed to wash my hands before I attended the wounded, I thought, pleased to find another excuse. Not even when I saw that that the door to the temple had been kicked in, did I consider that the temple provided an excellent vantage point. Anyone who wanted to see what was going on and who was coming would be hard pushed to find a better place. My brain was addled with tiredness and worry and I stepped into the temple looking only for Re'a's blessing. I was in every way unprepared for the arm that snaked round my waist pinning my arms to my side. The hand that reached under my chin, wrenching my head up and around until I felt the tendons in my neck scream, was equally surprising.

There was a pause, and a cold voice to my right asked,

"Well, what are you waiting for?"

Another voice, rougher, as though the journey through the throat and past tongue and teeth had been a long and arduous one, answered close to my ear,

"Saen's balls, Reath, she's a priest."

"Superstitious, Challawin? Afraid Saen might strike you down on his bride's behalf?"

The voice by my ear sighed and — unbearably — the hand around my jaw tightened further. I could feel the full length of the tendons in my neck, count every bone between skull and shoulder. I could not think of anything to do or say (I was not even confident that I *could* speak).

A third man entered the temple, I saw his dark hair out of the corner of my eye. *(Dark? How many W'shten are dark?)* His coat brushed my leg on his way past.

"It's done."

His voice was as dry as the Dark Lord's pit.

The grip on my jaw tightened some more. My breath hissed out between my teeth, but still I could find no words, no sound that would bring meaning to this sudden attack. Challawin made a sort of explosive sigh and pushed me violently away from him. I tripped and fell on my face.

"This is sickening, Reath, I can't do it any more. Tell me how *this* serves my country."

"It's not your *country* that pays you, it's your king, or had you forgotten whom you serve?"

As my brain tried hard to catch up with events, I began to wonder how it was, if these men were rampaging W'shten, that they were speaking the king's own Ttarcine. I even found the space to wonder where I had heard Challawin's voice before. My frazzled mind flapped about, failing to grapple with any problem, seeking distraction from the growing sensation of my elbow in my own ribs. A row raged above me, but I dared not move to ease the pain, for fear of drawing their attention back to me. My whole world began to revolve around my elbow, the yawning pit it was digging in my ribcage, and my urgent desire not to be noticed. The voices of the three men faded into my periphery. I heard Reath talking about saving lives but somehow I had lost interest. Challawin replied and he was angry now — familiar in his anger. My fingers were becoming numb. The third man spoke and I was lifted up by the hair. I found the voice to complain, but only wordlessly. The fingers of my left hand woke up with the hot pin pricks of restored sensation.

"I'll do it," Challawin said, "but not in a temple."

Reath tutted and the third voice volunteered,

"I'll come and hold your hand, Hal, shall I?"

I was dragged back out into the fading light, round the side of the temple.

How nice, I'm to die just next to my bedroom.

Challawin spoke again.

"I'm letting her go, Hazzor."

Hazzor stepped round to face Challawin. His hair, I saw, was not as dark as I had thought, but still much darker than I had expected any W'shten to be. He was short, too, not the towering monster of my mother's tales. With his small beard and long jacket, he looked about as foreign as Ruid. Ruid, though, could not have put so much energy into so little movement.

"Those villagers will have died for nothing," he said, "if this priest runs off and tells people that it was the king's own men that did this."

I felt sick. The king? Gayton had done this? My head spun — though that could just as likely have been a combination of fear and weariness.

"She's a priest without a village, now," Challawin replied. Now, I really felt sick. How many had died? "Who'll listen to her? It's her word against the king's." I felt him lean in towards Hazzor, his breath against the side of my face. "Hazzor, I can't do this. Not like this."

"Then I shall."

I heard the sound of metal on metal as Hazzor pulled a knife from its sheath. As I stared at it, I heard the sound repeated behind me.

"Don't be a fool, Hal."

At last I found the voice to speak.

"Why?" I said, almost tonelessly.

Hazzor would not quite look at me; he spoke to the man behind me.

"Hal, If you carry like this you're going to have to kill *one* of us. Even if you manage to kill me, you don't think Reath's going to let you run into the sunset with this woman do you? He'll hunt you down."

"You could say I killed her. You could say you killed her. Reath's not going to come to look and no one is going to believe *her.*"

"So when she starts running round the countryside spreading rumours of the king's ruthlessness, what's Reath going to do then?"

"No one could know it was her."

"She's a *priest,* Hal. How many priests has this village got? How many priests are there, running round away from their village?"

"We could both run," he said, urgently, "Haz, it doesn't have to come to this."

Challawin, behind me, sounded increasingly desperate, his agitation putting him neatly in line with another memory.

Even through the fog of my fear, I knew who he was or at least where I had last seen him: angry, desperate, turning his back on the village in disgust. I spoke again, though this time my question was not quite the same.

"*Why?*"

Challawin let go of my hair and gave me a push.

"Run," he said.

I staggered and nearly fell. Something in my brain flared up and I turned. I had been shoved, shouted at and sneered at. I had hiked more than half way to Talishead and been terrified, then come home again only to have my head half wrenched from my shoulders. I had been shoved around some more, pulled by the hair, in fact, and ignored.

I had had enough.

My temper burned through my stupor and I said, through gritted teeth,

"No."

At last both men looked at me.

"What in the nine hells is going on?" I exclaimed. "You, H.. Kallawin," I stumbled slightly over his name, but rallied, "You come into my village all frantic to empty it, so that — what? So that your own army, *my* king's army, can ride through and ... and ..." I stoked the furnace of indignation again before the enormity of it overwhelmed me, "and *then* along comes your band of thugs who kill — what? Who? *Everyone?*"

The sheer awfulness of it danced in front of me again, accompanied by the treacherous thought, *this is your doing, Kayt'an, your curse*. I turned, snarling, from the thought.

"And you do all this in the name of the King?! How? How can our king order such a thing? And..."

I noticed — mid-rant — that both men were doing a very good impression of two small boys caught red-handed. For a moment, I thought it was me that had inspired the look and my conceit swelled. Then I realised they were looking over my shoulder.

I turned to see an elegant man, dressed in the soft fabrics of court, standing observing us with a wry expression on his lean face.

"Well, well," said Reath.

Chapter 4

From the look on the two men's faces you would have thought Reath was the Dark Lord himself, but Reath appeared to have eyes only for me (though I learnt later that what Reath appeared to be doing was no guarantee of anything). His expression reminded me of Amtil Sahn when she used visit my mother when I was small.

"How is she coming along, Talith? Is she ready yet?" Amtil would ask, and always Mother would reply,

"Not yet, Saahni, not yet, she's still too little, surely."

I blinked, and returned to the present.

"You are a fascinating woman, Saahni. I can see why dear Challawin has been having difficulty killing you."

He turned his diamond eyes on Challawin who shrank, noticeably. He looked like a mouse, cornered by a snake, hoping against hope, if he only looks small enough, the snake might move on in search of a better meal. Reath returned his attention to me.

"How many civilians would stop and argue with death to find out the truth?"

My brief flare of anger had been doused by the fear of the other two men, so I just shrugged. Reath seemed moderately disappointed.

"So then, Saahni, do you still want to know?"

I forced my chin up, and answered,

"I'd like to know what makes a king turn on his own people like this, yes."

Reath turned from me.

"Challawin, tell the men to camp a league south of here, in the Hethron valley." His voice dropped a couple more degrees and became positively icy. "Wait for me there."

Challawin, looking like a condemned man, turned and fled. The aristocrat, for such I took him to be, turned to me again.

"Why don't you make your guests some supper, Saahni, and we can talk."

I considered mentioning that I had not yet kept the hour or that I had intended to use the dusk to hunt for my supper, but decided I could take a death-wish too far. In a daze, I returned to the temple, climbing over the door on the way to my rooms. They were just as I had left them, but it was as if these were some other woman's rooms. The woman who lived here was a simple priest whose days consisted of prayer, study and tending the sick. I was another creature, steeped in fear and guilt, whose day had been full of violence. I did not belong here. I shook myself out of the reverie, and began to prepare what I had for this strange man who had followed me in.

While I made supper, Reath reclined on my skins, leaning against the wall, and talked about the war. All the while he talked, his body looked as though he was only a step away from sleep, but his eyes were wychi-bright and never left me. I am certain neither a twitch of finger or face escaped him. Not a man to be taken by surprise.

He talked of the strange nature of our land: a long thin nation sandwiched between the mountains and the sea. He told me of the difficulty of holding together the people of these Western Reaches — a hill country of pasture, mostly, with woodland and some mines along the northern border — and those of the rich arable land of the Eastern Territories. He told me of the vast mineral resources of the land to the north-east of Ttaroc, the Ga'ared Heights. While I waited for the broth to heat, I heard how our king, Gayton, was considered weak by his neighbours. He had few allies and his only daughter Ttarah seemed so unlikely to marry (poor hideous thing that she was) that he had no obvious heir. Our neighbours in Ga'ared owed fealty to the W'shten and the kings of Shteriv. Reath explained that the regular raids from Ga'ared into our border-lands had last provoked the farmers to fight back. Villages had been razed. King Gayton not only had the excuse he needed to go to war but he had homeless and grieving people willing to sign up for vengeance and bread. He told me how the Western Reaches had still taken little notice of the war. It was too far away and the raiding from the Ga'ared Heights had never concerned them. What did they care who held the Ga'ared?

I handed Reath his food and he said no more, seeming to apply himself wholly to his supper, his long fingers dealing daintily with the basic fare I had provided. I thought about his words, and about the smoke on the horizon. I imagined our decimated village was Talishead and what Karl would have said if he had thought the W'shten really were here after all, looting and burning and killing. I thought of Challawin's desperate attempt to empty Harset. Of course, there could be no witnesses that the soldiers looting and burning were our own and not Yr's.

I sat down and looked at the dish of leftovers before me, but my mouth was dry and full of the taste of bile. Both physically and emotionally I was all out. If I didn't eat soon I would either faint or be sick.

It does not matter terribly: I will not be hungry for long.

The dead do not usually have much appetite.

"You should eat, Saahni, this is surprisingly palatable."

"I'm not hungry."

"Still, you should eat. You'll be travelling for many days. You can't start on an empty stomach."

"Travelling?"

I was trying to be resigned to my death, but did I really need to travel first?

"Can't you guess? I'm disappointed, Saahni. Still, you're very tired, I can see. You've had a lot to take in.

"Yes, travelling. I need you to, spread the word — you're a priest, you should be good at that. Tell the people of the Western Reaches what you have seen."

I had rallied a bit since Challawin had told me to run, but now that the crisis was over I was sinking back into a daze. I simply did not think I could take in any more.

"You want me," I said slowly, "to tell everyone I can that ... that the king is poking his people with a big sharp stick in the hope they'll join the attack on the W'shten?"

The elegant gentleman looked saddened.

"Really Saahni, you disappoint me again. Perhaps I shall have to kill you after all. You have seen the W'shten forces destroy your village, pillage your farms and murder your neighbours."

Ah.

Of their own accord, my fingers curled into fists. The feel of my nails digging into the palm of my hands was calling to me from far away.

"No," I stared into the abyss, "I haven't."

"I tell you, Kayt'an Sahn, your life depends on that being what you saw. If you run around the country telling any other tale I will have you arrested, tortured and publicly executed as a traitor to His Majesty."

I closed my eyes.

"No," I said.

"I thought Saen forbids suicide."

"He also forbids lying. I do my best to live in his light, Re'a knows, but in this case I won't be killing myself — you will."

I was so tired. I wished he would kill me and be done.

Reath put his plate aside and steepled his fingers. He sighed.

"You know if Yr wins this war he will not allow your temples to stand," he cast a pointed look through the wall towards the fallen bell, "even as much as they do."

I fixed my eyes on my fists curled in my lap and tried to focus on the pain in my hands. They were starting to ache, too, holding the tension. I opened them out and felt the release. I knew I was angry, far far away, but I was too tired, too wrung out.

"I will not serve Re'a by spreading a gross lie. She would not seek to preserve herself at the expense of her husband's oaths."

Reath smiled and shook his head.

"I'm not speaking to the Blessed Re'a, I'm talking to you. You are risking not just your life but — if Yr wins — the lives of all her servants."

I, too, shook my head. Numbers were becoming meaningless.

"I've already killed a whole village," I said miserably, "I can't see that it makes any difference to me now."

Reath's eyebrows rose and it was a while before he spoke.

"So," he said. He sounded, not angry, but bored. "Now, I know why you are so unmoved by the prospect of death. I thought you were courageous, with a searching mind. I see now that you are just a coward. Well."

I returned my eyes to my hands. My nails were dirty, I noticed. I should not have prepared food with my hands in such a state. I began to pick them clean, and then stopped. It was not as if it mattered anymore. Having examined the backs of my hands more thoroughly than I had in my life, I turned my hands over and stared at the palms, tracing the circles marked there, and wondered, not for the first time, if my fingers were over long. Reath still did not speak. I glanced up to see those diamond eyes fixed on my face. My attention fled back to the safety of my hands.

At last Reath spoke, slowly.

"What a great creature you are, that the world moves on your action or inaction. I had no idea that Re'a was so powerful."

The slight to my goddess provoked me. I looked up into Reath's calculating eye. I lifted my chin.

"Re'a is Saen's wife, Saen is Farock Rha's Son, Farock Rha is all in all. Do *you* have the ear of the First Cause? Because, if so, you could surely end this war with a word."

"As I recall Farock Rha condemned Re'a to be hung to die on the Tree, but let's move away from sophistry. You are not to blame for this village's destruction. The whole village is not dead, by the way, only the witnesses. The survivors will, of course, have to move, there are not enough of them, I think, to sustain a village here. Harsett, in that sense, is no more.

"I have heard Challawin's report. The villagers refused to heed his warning. You did all you could to persuade them, I understand. You are not to blame."

I made an attempt to upset his composure.

"What about the king who commanded this? What about *you*?"

Reath nodded calmly,

"Yes, you can fairly say we share a part of the blame."

"A. Part."

I repeated the words dully. The anger I felt was still too far away to be of use. Somehow this man who seemed half courtier, half assassin was hypnotising me.

"A part, yes. They were warned. They were foolish."

With his words, the guilt that had been bubbling under the surface since I had first seen the fires in Talishead, came rushing up to overwhelm me.

"If I'd not destroyed my influence," I urged, "If I'd got the bell fixed ..." My voice started to defy me so I stopped talking while I got it back under control. I spoke into my lap. "If I had been a better priest they would still be alive."

I felt naked in front of this murdering politician but I was too drained to hold up any barriers. Tears started to run down my cheeks. *O Re'a*, I thought, *forgive me.*

Reath said only "Tcha!" in obvious disgust and called through the doorway,

"Hazzor!"

Hazzor must have been just inside the temple for he was in the doorway immediately, face carefully blank.

"Take this priest out and kill her. I was thoroughly mistaken in her."

I boggled, astonished. I looked up, outraged, though I could not quite tell you why.

With the grace of a cat, Reath stood up and looked down his narrow nose at me.

"I'm sorry. Did you expect what? Pity? Admiration?" His tone became sneeringly high pitched. "Poor little priestess feels bad about her neighbours' stupid arrogance. Isn't she sad, poor girl, isn't she pious, isn't she *humble*."

My mouth hung open. This was not what I expected. I did not expect pity — well not really — but, yes, I thought, I *am* pious. I had just poured out my heart to this man, shown him how deeply affected I was by my own error, *shown him* my humility. But Reath stood over me, a picture of contempt, and I was utterly baffled by it.

Then, suddenly, I saw myself through his eyes. I was more concerned with the state of my soul than I was the lost lives of Karl, Ra'an, Abitha, Talin and Essin, Fris'an, perhaps, and her unborn child. So many were dead and here I was, sitting in my own little pit of self-loathing, feeling sorry for myself.

I stood up to go with Hazzor. The world would not be any poorer without me.

"Oh sit down!"

I sat. My inquisitor walked over to the chest where I kept my herbs and all the equipment of my craft. Smoothly, he opened it and pulled out my ribbon stick and twisted it between his fingers.

"Are you any good?" he asked, again with that measuring look in his eye. "Clearly you're useless as a priest, especially now your village — who held you in such small regard — is dead, but are you any good with this?"

I shrugged, already tired of looking up and aware of Hazzor's sardonic gaze from the doorway. Reath used the ribbon stick to point at me, one beautifully booted foot resting on the lip of my medicine trunk.

"You, Saahni, want redemption, and I, as it happens, need a healer. I have had an unexpected — and inconvenient — vacancy in the team I am building. Even though you're not what I'd hoped for, I'm prepared to offer you a deal."

"A deal," I repeated, woodenly.

It seemed the most sensible conversation I managed this evening was when I parroted Reath's words back to him.

"You don't like my methods. You are not, I'll confess, the only one, but they are driven by the King's need to find soldiers to fight in a war he is — to be frank — losing. If you can help me put a halt to this war, I can call a halt to the ravages of our mock-W'shten raiding band. The killing stops and you can find meaning for your own inadequacies."

If the man was not such a cold, calculating creature, I would suspect him of being smug. It took a moment for it to dawn on me that he was asking me to work for him. I gaped. It had been a long, long, *long* day and I had been in fear for my life for too much of it. I just wanted to go to bed. I said so.

Reath threw my ribbon stick at me, which I fumbled and dropped.

"Go to bed then. In the morning Hazzor, here, will take you to the inn in Marrett where I am gathering some people. Pack to be about a month on the road and take your medical supplies with you. I'll meet you there.

I barely noticed him leave. I crawled over to my bed and fell into oblivion at last.

Chapter 5

I was climbing a great hill. It was like the one I habitually climbed to the temple but seemed steeper and emptier. Where was everyone? It was vital I got to the summit in time but my legs felt like lead and would not move properly. Amtil Sahn was waiting for me at the top. I could hear her calling for me but I was going nowhere.

She called, "Saahni! Saahni!"

She sounded cross, which was normal, but I couldn't fathom why she was calling me as if I were a priest. Re'a willing it would be years yet before I took her place in the temple.

"Saahni!" she called again.

She spoke to me but I could not make sense of her words. I was failing her. I struggled to climb the hill, to reach her, to hear her.

Suddenly, there was a hand on my arm, shaking me, dragging me back. I fell and clung to the ground, but that was worse still: clumps of earth came up in my hands, dripping blood. I moaned in horror and was released. Freed, I ran and ran — yet always the summit was out of reach.

"Sahnithi! Sahnithi!" I called, using the old, familiar title, "I'm coming!"

Suddenly she stood before me.

"You are unclean," she said to me, and threw a bucket of water over me.

Gasping, I awoke. I swore vigorously and turned to my assailant.

"Saen's Ball's, Saahni," Hazzor said, "I thought I'd never wake you. I could have been Yr himself with a set of Ashi cymbals and you'd have known nothing about it."

He chuckled briefly at his own vision, but I was unimpressed.

"Why, by all that's beautiful, would Yr enter a temple of Re'a at all?"

I ached abominably. I pushed the heels of my hands into my eyes and tried to persuade them to focus. As I did so, memories from yesterday rose from the murk of my sleep. They leered at me, lewd in their ugliness. Re'a teaches us that we have nothing to fear from evil; if we hold fast to Saen's light, even death is not to be feared. But these memories would be part of me forever now. I could not guess for how long they would be part of my morning awakening. I thought of my family, my friends. Which of them, I wondered, were still alive? My stomach knotted dreadfully and I wanted to heave. I began to ask, but lost my nerve. Coward that I was, I did not want to know that my mother, sister, father, brothers, playmates were dead. I hid my face in my hands and curled into a ball. It was too awful.

Hazzor was having none of it. He threw a rag in my direction.

"Here. Dry yourself and get packing."

With no better plan, I took the rag and dried myself off as best I could; doing my best to restore my braids into some kind of order. I reviewed all my earthly possessions. I had never left my village overnight before. I did not know where to start. I looked across at Hazzor, leaning nonchalantly in the doorway. He was not as dark as I had thought yesterday, his hair the colour of honey. His eyes were a cold grey — not like the icy blue of Reath's, but hardly warm. I had never seen a man wear his jacket that long before either — almost as long as some women's skirts. I wondered where he was from. I was willing to bet my meagre store of shreknas that it was not Ephatha. Not, of course, that I would gamble ... I returned my mind to its task.

"Most people find getting up and picking things up helps," said Hazzor.

Clearly, a self-proclaimed wit of some sort. Perhaps that was why he travelled so far from home.

I raised a shoulder in a half-shrug.

"What do I need?"

"How should I know? I'm not a healer."

Healer, well, I could start there.

"I'll need the chest," I said, pointing through the doorway to my medicine chest that lay in the living room.

"That *chest*?" He nearly looked animated. "Saahni, you can only take what you can carry."

I was unimpressed. If I was to be conscripted into this, I was not going ill-equipped.

"Reath said he wants me for a healer. To heal, I need the contents of that chest. Someone will have to help me."

Hazzor looked down at me and spoke as if I were a slightly stupid child.

"Listen, Saahni. Reath's collecting a small team. That means a team of specialists, experts. Everyone will be carrying their own equipment." He looked over his shoulder at the chest behind him and sighed. "OK,

Saahni, think about it. You're being sent on one of Reath's missions so you'll need things to treat wounds, broken bones, poisons, perhaps. You might need your own poisons — "

"I don't keep poisons!"

Hazzor nodded, and then cocked his head like a wychi watching an interesting mouse.

"What about L'thoren's flower?"

"That's a tonic for a weak heart," I said impatiently.

"And if you give it to a healthy man?" He shook his head at my expression. "Bring medicines that could be dangerous, then: sedatives, hallucinogens," he finished his sentence with a shrug.

"I'll not cause harm." I said emphatically, "I am a priest of Re'a."

Again, Hazzor nodded, but I was beginning to think that this nod meant, *You're talking nonsense.*

"A fine priest. Your temple's a ruin and most of your people are dead. There is no village to support you and only this broken barn of a place to worship your goddess."

I was beginning to feel got at, so I said, defensively,

"My goddess is alive and well."

"And she has plenty of priests. Reath's got you on his hook now. Don't be so quick to assume what you will and won't do for him. Pack the poisons."

I sat on my bed and felt sick. Not only was my way of life being swept away, but this man was telling me that my identity would follow. If a woman cannot tell what she might do, she does not, surely, know who she is. Saen's commands are absolutes and, if I could not be sure of holding to them, I was dead even to myself. Better to die and wake in Re'a's arms, than to fade away into some faithless stranger. I opened my mouth to speak, and shut it again. Hazzor's expression became curiously blank and he stared over my head at the wall behind me.

"Do you think that in my worst nightmares I believed, even last moon, that I would be capable of murdering the greater part of a village of my own countrymen? Each step is so simple, so small: *so reasonable*. Every day you can see the way back and then, suddenly, a door shuts behind you and you've become a monster.

"You've made the decision not to die. Now your soul belongs to Reath."

His eye returned to mine and he smiled, briefly, and turned away.

I stopped him.

"You make him sound like the Dark Lord."

Still facing away from me, the man shrugged and walked out the room. My stomach tightened further. *I am a priest of Re'a*, I said to myself, and repeated it once more for emphasis. Since I had been weaned, I was schooled in the life of Re'a, in the precepts of Saen, in the holiness of Farock Rha. I bit my lip and raised my chin. *I am better than this. I* will *not lose myself.* Challawin had refused Reath's orders to kill me. If a heathen like that could draw a line — albeit perhaps after untold murders, but still — if he had found the strength of purpose, then surely so could I.

Briefly, I considered what else I was capable of, namely continuing rows with a whole village for a month at a time leaving my folk bereft of priestly counsel when they most needed it. A great pit of doubt and guilt and grief opened up before me and I tottered at its brink.

Hazzor re-entered, pack in hand. He threw the bag at me.

"No time for day dreaming," he said. "Pack!"

My fingers traced the pattern of trees and circles on the door frame. This temple had been my home almost as long as I could remember. The night it had become my life sat fresh in my memory. I had knelt by Amtil as she lay in her bed, that was my bed now … had been my bed, until now.

She fought for breath while I held her hand, wiping her forehead, gently pushing her salt-and-pepper hair out of her eyes. I had sought frantically for something I could do for her, something I could make better.

"Sahnithi," I had said, the intimate title catching in my throat, "can I make you some more tea? Some broth perhaps?" She had shaken her head, wearily. "Some sugar bread then? I'm sure we've still got some. Perhaps Enrith has some," I babbled.

All Hathil's teaching on sitting with the dying, and all Amtil's teaching on death and its beauty, were lost to me. I sat watching my mentor, my second mother, die.

"Please, Sahnithi," even now I needed her to help me, "there must be something I can do for you?"

It was too soon, far too soon. I should have had years yet of being mentored, being the disciple, told what to do. It was not *fair*. Amtil had squeezed my hand, but shook her head. She hauled in another breath and whispered,

"It's time, Kayt'an."

Feebly, she had coughed and the effort, small though it was, was enough to leave her prone. My heart climbed into my mouth. I steeled myself to reach over and close her eyes but, at last, Amtil had blinked. She sucked in another painful lungful of air.

"We're both frightened."

Again, the coughing; again, the exhausted stillness. I was ashamed of myself.

"Shhhh," I had said, placing my lips in the circles on her hand, "Shhh, Sahnithi. Re'a will walk with both of us."

Tears ran treacherously down my face and a vile part of me railed like a spoilt child. *I* had wanted the words of comfort. *I* had wanted to be cared for still. I had not *wanted* to be the priest — but Amtil had already nodded, weakly.

I put my forehead in the palm of her hand and fought back tears that threatened to drown me.

At first light I left her side to keep the hour. When I had returned, she was dead.

Heaving great wrenching sobs, as though I were trying somehow to vomit up my grief, I had crawled into the bed with my dead friend. Terrified of the moment I should know her to be cold, I wrapped my arms around her as if somehow I could have been able to keep her warm. When my tears finally exhausted themselves, I had uncurled my right hand, hoping against hope that I could go home to my family.

Re'a had agreed with her servant, and not with me. In the centre of my palm were the interlinking circles of the Three, still red, marking me as her priest.

I had been sick.

Chapter 6

We walked. We walked and walked and walked. Hazzor was not good company. Not cheering company, anyhow, and my insistence on saying the hours did not, apparently, improve his temper. Then, too, I found it difficult to look him in the eye (*how many had he killed: who had he killed?*) which didn't help the conversation. Damn him! Whatever he said, I was still a priest dedicated to remembering, morning, noon and night, Re'a's goodness and thanking her for all that she has done for us. They could kill my flock and they could take me away from the temple but they would not stop me being a priest. *It is*, I thought angrily, *what I* am*, even* who I am*. Deep inside I feared what it would mean if I stopped. I had my thread box and my candle and my flint-box. Dawn and dusk and midday, I laid my face in the dust and worshipped Saen the source of Life, and blessed his Holy Bride, Re'a. All the while Hazzor stood to the side and huffed, arms folded, and each time he huffed I became increasingly pointed in my prayers. As we walked together, I thought about Challawin's antagonism and Reath's contempt and wondered what could possibly provoke such a negative reaction. After all, I thought, as Hazzor and I walked in single file through the scrubland and woods and into the forests that hid the River Arwn, after all, the law of the Three is love.

I glared at Hazzor's back.

On the third evening, when I looked up from saying the hour to see him whittling sticks with rather more vigour than strictly necessary, I finally asked,

"Why does it bother you so much when I pray?"

Hazzor shrugged. A thing he did a lot, I had come to notice.

"Not so much, Saahni," he answered, "but it does take a good hour, maybe two, off the day's walk."

I raised my eyebrows in what I considered a measured response.

"Surely, not so much."

Hazzor went back to his whittling in the half-light.

"We start later, finish earlier and stop longer at midday."

I tutted and rolled my eyes. Not perhaps the most diplomatic step, but, really, the man was exaggerating ridiculously. When Hazzor merely shrugged again, I clarified,

"It can't make that much difference."

"We could look to being in Marrett tomorrow, were it not for this."

Oooh, I thought, *12 hours earlier.* So I said,

"Does it really matter that we'll be there the morning after instead?"

Hazzor said nothing, just went on whittling. I sighed out between my teeth in a hissing noise, breathed in again and said,

"When I pray, I enfold us in Re'a's love."

Hazzor's grey eyes widened and his nostrils actually flared over his moustache. He threw the stick down and surged to his feet.

"When you pray you waste our time to no purpose

except the practice of your own self-righteousness," Hazzor snapped.

My mouth fell open. Self-righteous? I realised I was sitting there like a renwit, so I pulled myself together. I opened my mouth, purposefully this time, but failed to find any useful words, so I shut it again.

I became conscious of doing a fair impression of a fish. By now, Hazzor had had the grace to drop his gaze and was busy with the fastening of his jacket. His eyes flicked up to me.

"Sorry, Saahni," he said.

I was nearly tall enough to be eye to eye, so I too stood and drew myself to my full height. I was so cross my eyes were nearly slits.

"*Saahni* is a title that confers respect, Hazzor, so there is clearly little point in you using it."

Hazzor's face closed like the mouth of an ishet over its young, and I cursed. I needed a bell around my neck, like those who have the rotting disease. I poisoned everything I touched. I was, I decided, the worst priest ever.

The rest of the evening was awkward, to say the least. Hazzor silently served up the rabbit he had prepared and I, to my shame, dared not speak the words of blessing and only nodded my thanks. It was a miserable, silent meal. As soon as it was cleared I lay down to sleep, though it was far too early. It was that or sit looking at my lap or else at the man I had insulted for forcing him to answer a question I had asked him.

But, really, the man was insufferable. *'Practising my own self-righteousness'*! I huffed and turned on to my side, and found myself looking at *him*, so I turned again, staring up into the trees. *I* was the one who woke every morning with the weight of my own failure while he was clearly so thick skinned and *stupid* that the knowledge of his own murders scarcely seemed to touch him! *He sneers at my piety, absolutely certain that my faith is unanswered, while he condemns* me *as narrow minded. Self-righteous, indeed!* I fell asleep turning over in my mind exactly how righteous I was.

I dreamt. I was back on the temple hill, though the temple was not there. I was on my knees facing the spot where Re'a ought to stand. Around me were the villagers' Statues of Intent, smashed and broken. In every case, I knew, the heads were intact but the faces were gone. These faceless fragments were calling to me for help, but I did not turn to them. I remained prostrate before an image that was not there. I put my hands over my ears to block out their calls as I tried desperately to hear my goddess.

"Guide me, Blessed Re'a!" I called out, "Where are you?"

On and on went the dream, remorselessly, as I called for my goddess and fended off the ghosts of the people she had given into my care. Eventually, the hill was empty. All the ghosts faded away and I was left on the hill with no god and no people. No comfort of any sort, in fact.

I spent the night weeping on an empty hilltop.

I woke well before dawn and to the now familiar pit of guilt and grief was added the knowledge that my old life had gone for ever. I would never again be that person. The only thing I could hope for was that this new person I was becoming could be someone I would recognise, and of whom I would not be ashamed. After all, I thought, I had never wanted to be a priest in the first place. How much was I still bound by the decision made by Amtil and confirmed by Re'a? I ran my thumb across my palm in the dark. If I no longer had any flock, was I still a priest? There was a time — less than a tennight ago — when I thought I would have given my eye teeth to be relieved of that burden, but it turned out I had been a priest too long to let go easily. I should have felt light hearted, liberated. Instead, I felt sickened, lost. I thought of Re'a being led from death to life by her beloved Saen. *Re'a*, I prayed, *Saviour of the world, guide me*.

I heard Hazzor beginning to move. My brilliance at burning bridges was not matched by a comparable skill in building them. Still, every child has to start somewhere. I cleared my throat,

"Shall I make breakfast?"

In the half-light I could see Hazzor rolling up his sleeping mat.

"You have your prayers to say," the honorific was violent in its unspoken presence. "The less delay the better."

I sat up and paid undue attention to smoothing down the fabric of my skirts.

"I was thinking, umm," I cleared my throat again. "Perhaps I could pray while we walked. It's not unheard of. The Reader Gherin …"

Hazzor was clearly waiting for something more immediately relevant. He began to strap his mat to the bottom of his bag, merely glancing in my direction.

"But, umm, breakfast," I sounded like an idiot, but this was so close to an apology it was painful, "I thought breakfast was definitely needed now."

Hazzor stood up with his usual grace.

"I'll fetch water," was all he said.

I had seen what I thought was a bird's nest in the trees above us. Once Hazzor had left the small clearing in which we were camped, I girded my skirts and circled my chosen tree. I was glad Hazzor had not stayed to witness an exercise I had not tried for years. Even as a child I spent very little time climbing trees, but I had been very much lighter and more agile then, not to mention a different shape. I didn't expect this to be a graceful enterprise and an audience would not have helped. Nonetheless, I was going to need an easy climb.

Saen was merciful. A badger-fox had been looking for grubs. It wasn't much but it was a foothold. I took a couple of preparatory hops and launched myself upwards to a knot in the trunk about shoulder height. As I heaved myself up, my skirts became loose again. I swore and hugged the tree as I tried to tuck the hem back into the waistband but to no avail. *Please, Holy Re'a, keep the man away until I am down again.* A huff and two puffs enabled a desperate scrabble to the first branch. I skinned my knuckles and caught my hair and clothes in the branches. My hair, in fact, was rapidly beginning to resemble the very thing I was after. Eventually, I was stable on the lowest branch. What had seemed a simple plan was alot more difficult than I remembered, but at least I had finished the hardest part. The tree stretched away from me like a badly constructed ladder. I reached up and across and stepped up on to the next branch, which swayed alarmingly as I put my weight on it but, after a moment, I was confident all was well. Heartened, I swung my left foot around to a branch that would enable me to reach the nest. Only once my weight was transferred did I realise I had trodden on my hem. I dithered. It would probably be alright, as long as my right foot was free of my skirts I should be able to free myself. As I hung there, uncommitted to either branch, *something* walked over my hand. I squawked like a startled chicken and snatched my hand away. Launching back towards the tree in a desperate attempt not to fall, I reached up with my — as yet undefiled — hand to grab a new branch.

The sound of the fabric of my skirt tearing lasted considerably longer than my relief at not falling. I swore. Again. Both feet now on the same branch, I clung to the tree and swore fluently and at length. Vengefully, I wiped on my damaged skirts the hand that had been spidered or beetled or whatever, and swore some more.

"She will be a priest, Hathil, and such language does not become a priest of Re'a."

Hathil and Amtil had been nose to nose, chalk and cheese. Hathil was a big woman with a generously sized body and a smile to match; Amtil, a little bird of a woman, somehow still managed to look down on Hathil. My teacher in the healing arts had remained calm.

"She is a competent healer, Saahni, with time she will be very good. She'll need a cool head, and some cathartic vocabulary vents the panic."

Amtil snorted.

"What keeps a cool head is *prayer* and the knowledge that Re'a leads us all by the hand if we'll only trust her. Never forget, Hathil, you are only teaching her a passing trade until she can take my place. Re'a does not want a priest with the tongue of a Hethin whore."

Well, apparently, Re'a had wanted such a priest because, despite every disciplinary action Amtil could think of, my language remained decidedly blue and the Lady had still chosen me.

Priest or not, I *was* stuck halfway up a tree and swearing was not going to get me breakfast.

I took a firm hold on the tree with both hands and shook my foot free. I closed my eyes, breathed in — *Re'a, Saviour of the world* — and breathed out — *guide me*. With newly opened eyes — prayerful eyes, mind — I checked my feet. They were still were they ought to be, and the nest was almost in reach. (*Breathe in, breathe out*). If I shuffled carefully sideways, I ought to be able to reach the eggs. Heart banging against my teeth, I sent my hands ahead and slowly, carefully, stepped out away from the trunk of the tree. A stray twig scratched my cheek and evoked another curse — it really stung! This, I thought, was All Hazzor's Fault. I hoped he choked on his eggs. (*Breathe in, shuffle a foot along*) *Saviour of the World* (*breathe out, shuffle the other foot*) *guide me. OK, carefully now.* I reached up and took the nest.

"If you drop the eggs down to me, you — "

Hazzor got no further as, with a startled yell, I lost my precarious footing altogether. Abandoning the nest, I grabbed frantically at the branch above me, but too late. The small of my back hit the place my feet had occupied moments earlier. The nest lead the way, tumbling down the tree. I vaguely heard Hazzor's curse but my mind was fully occupied. The reaching fingers of the tree gave me a last farewell as I dropped to the ground like an over ambitious toad.

I hated Hazzor.

A scarred hand reached down to me to pull me to my feet. Painfully, I stood. Hazzor handed me a wren's egg. On the ground, I saw the broken remains of the nest lying in sticky egg-goo.

"Next time, Saahni, you pray, and I'll fetch the breakfast. I'm confident it will be quicker."

Hazzor went back to the river. While he was gone, I removed layers of shirts and vests, and carefully applied salves to my scratches and the really very sore, scraped bruise on my back. I checked my ribs as well, not having had the chance since I ground my elbow into them. When the spy returned shortly after with a couple of trout, I was dressed again and had turned to my knee. Flustered, I flicked my skirts back over my legs but, without looking up from cooking the fish, Hazzor simply asked if I could walk. Wincing, I straightened out my leg. I had twisted it slightly when I had landed and walloped it on a root when I had fallen. It hurt. All the same, I nodded carefully and asserted it was fine.

My companion gave me a measured look.

"You look like shit."

I opened my mouth to deliver a stinging response and then closed it again. My hand went to my hair and my eyes dropped to the tear and the snags in my skirt. My face, I knew, was scratched and probably pale. He probably had a point. More, not only had I made breakfast take over an hour of the morning, but I was not going to be moving very fast or very far with my knee as it was. My attempt to make up with this man had meant we probably were not going to make it to Marrett until well after the Ladlas feast. I was kidding myself. We would be lucky to get there before H'mariq. I could not think of anything I could usefully say.

Hazzor simply handed me my breakfast. As we ate, he outlined his plan. He intended, he said, to go ahead to the *Nimble Sheep* in Marrett, tell the landlord we were on our way, pick up a mount on Reath's bill, and come back for me. He reckoned he could get me to Marrett about a day later than we would have got there anyway.

I sat with my back against a tree (not the one that had been my nemesis, I was avoiding that one) and stared at the spy. He had grumped and sulked about my taking a couple of hours — so he said — out of each day's walk and yet, when I so comprehensibly crippled our progress, the man barely blinked. Re'a bless him, though, he still could not resist exaggerating. When I was fit we would not have got there before the following day. How was Hazzor going to get there and back, and there again in a day and a half or so? I mentioned this and he said something about moving quicker on his own.

"You said I was only adding an hour or two to the journey each day," I said, trying to find a crack in the man's self confidence somewhere, Re'a forgive me.

The spy shrugged his narrow shoulders, inevitably, and replied,

"I was taking into account how much slower we were moving anyway."

I took, I thought, this further blow to my self-confidence on the chin. Each time I thought I had reached rock bottom and seen myself clearly I discovered, no, in fact, it was just a ledge: there was a whole new chasm below me. I was arrogant, cowardly, selfish, self-righteous and now also, apparently, ridiculously slow.

"Oh," I said, and nodded a bit. "I see."

Hazzor carried on, apparently oblivious to my discomfort.

"Did I see you still had bread and cheese left?" I nodded. "Good," he said. "I'll be back tonight. Stay here."

The woods were full of who-knows-what, and who, and who-knows-what possible delays were waiting for this man in Marrett, so I asked,

"What if you're not back then?"

Hazzor licked his fingers clean.

"Wait for me until I am."

"But what if you don't come back?"

Hazzor brushed the crumbs of his breakfast off his lap.

"Wait for me until I do."

He got up, dropped the detritus of his breakfast into a pile with mine, shouldered his pack, nodded a farewell and, like that, was gone.

Chapter 7

I collected up the breakfast remains and only then realised I had no spade with which to bury them. I sighed and lurched off to abandon them at a suitable distance from the camp. Each step hurt and with my hands full of rubbish I could not use the trees I was passing for support. (I was starting to take a dim view of trees.) Quickly, I decided I did not need to take it that far, and I shoved the fishy leftovers under a bush for some rat or fox to enjoy. It would be fine, I thought. I wiped my hands on the bracken and hissed with pain as I stood again.

"Right," I said to myself and turned to stagger back to the fire.

I mended my skirt as best I could and ordered my hair again. For many hours, I just sat and stared into the flames and thought about war. Ours had been rumbling on for a couple of years now, but it had always seemed so distant to me. It was a land-grab, obviously; the Eastern Reaches not only grew enough grain for Ttaroc, they sold much of it to W'shten. Yr, the W'shten king, presumably thought it was cheaper to take the land than to buy the bread. I couldn't see how. So many lives lost! Briefly, the dead of my village fell into the shadow of all the many dead to Yr's greed. I knew my goddess grieved for Ttarcine and W'shten alike, but my heart ached chiefly for my own friends and neighbours. I badly wanted to hate Reath. What did he want with me?

Holy Re'a, have mercy on me.

It was not long, however, before the flames began to sink lower and become a mere flickering amongst the wood Hazzor had gathered while I had been saying the evening hour. I felt completely useless, completely adrift. Five days ago I had been sitting at home in the temple merely worrying about Fris'an's lying in, and stewing over the Ladlas preparations and now — so many, many dead! And only five days ago! It was only three more days until the feast. I was so uprooted, it felt unreal to think of it. I ought to be decorating the temple by now, co-ordinating the offerings of boughs and spring flowers, getting people to gather the feast, getting Karl to pick a Re'a and a Saen, and the dancers. The liturgies of preparation should be sung. It was the highlight of my year. I loved Ladlas, the sun himself coming down to woo the holy maiden pure. I sighed and poked the dying fire. The slightly hysterical thought crossed my mind that I could do it all here in the clearing. The trees could be my temple decorated with ... with ... leaves? flowers? feathers? I snorted at the idea, but carried on with the fantasy. I could sing the liturgies, I thought, and act the parts. The feast would be tricky, but if I cut the bread and cheese into small pieces it could *look* pretty, maybe? I laughed at myself, weakly.

Then I thought in all seriousness, I *could* sing the liturgies. I turned the idea over in my mind. According to Hazzor we should be in Marrett for Ladlas. It would be possible to go to the temple there. The priest might let me assist, as I used to assist Amtil. If I sang the liturgies now, I would be ready. A part of me that had been starving for the last five days — or even perhaps since the row with Karl — seized on the idea with a vigour that nearly frightened me. It was only a semblance of the person I had been for so much of my life, but I had lost so much, a semblance was enough.

I fed the fire, got out my candle and lit it from the flames. I could not kneel, so I lay prostrate before the light. With my face in the dust of our creation, I began to sing the story of Saen's birth from the heart of Faroch Rha. The words were as familiar as my own tongue, and I lost myself in the weaving of them. So lost was I, that the first I knew that I was no longer alone was the blade against my neck and the soft voice in my ear. It was a strange accent, slow and undulating, that said,

"Make a move, darlin', and I'll separate your pretty head from your body."

Jerked from my devotions, my mind exploded in a red mist. His horribly patronising tone, compounded by the lack of respect, made the rude awakening doubly outrageous. I was probably all the angrier because of the row with Hazzor, still hot and sore in my memory. So quick was I to leap to anger, in fact, that I failed to take in the full import of what the stranger had actually said. I moved.

A boot between my shoulders halted me. The blade pressed closer against my throat.

The soft voice spoke again, slower and if possible softer, as though he were speaking to a child.

"I meant what I said, sweetheart."

I was apoplectic. I snarled into the ground,

"And I mean what I say when I say that you are an arrogant, unprincipled *heathen* for whom the Dark Lord's pit will clearly be a welcome distraction given what must be the empty godlessness of your present existence." I drew breath, heedless of the grass and earth I drew into my mouth. "Get your knife off my neck and leave me to my prayers before I curse you properly." I spat out grass and mud. "And if you have anything further to say to me, you can address me — as you ought — as Saahni, or waste your breath."

I drew in another breath, more carefully this time, and with a discipline that Amtil would have been proud of — or maybe not, given the circumstances — I returned to my chants.

"Haenid's tits," the soft voice swore, sounding surprised as much as outraged.

The foot came off my back and a second voice, lighter and distinctly amused said,

"Well, you can't complain, Abe, she's not moving."

I applied myself to ignoring them and concentrating on Holy Things.

Perhaps, I thought, by sunset they'll be gone.

No. As I finished the liturgy I opened my eyes and ears again and heard voices either side of me.

"I think she's finally finished," said one.

"Hother's Scrot, I was beginning to wonder if she is even human," said the heathen.

Now that I had had time to calm down, I had time also to wonder if I had been entirely prudent. It was becoming doubtful whether I would ever again go more than a couple of days without being in fear of my life. I closed my eyes again and debated if it was safe to move. A third voice, that somehow hinted at dark corners and sharp edges, added lightly,

"Do you think she's stuck?"

In truth I was so stiff I was not sure I could move, but I was stung into replying,

"You told me not to move."

"Aya, that was then, darlin'," the insufferable heathen answered, "but Thorn will be back any minute with something for the pot, and we figured, sweeting, that you were the one to cook it for us, you having done nothing but lie there all day."

If there had been any distance between me and the earth I would have spat. As it was, I ground my teeth. I neither moved nor spoke. It was bad enough when folk addressed me without my due title, but at least even Challawin used ordinary civility. 'Darlin',' however, and 'sweetheart' were beyond the pale. There was a line to be drawn. Part of my brain screamed that I was mad but the events of the last few days, I think, had severely damaged my instinct for self-preservation.

There was a pause and the softly spoken alien added,

"Did no one ever teach you, sweetheart, that it's rude not to answer when a one is speaking to you?"

Where *was* he from? I had never heard so many strange accents before. This one was unlike anything I had ever heard, even among the summer traders. I heard leather creak as someone moved. A hand came down to rest in the periphery of my vision while the other grabbed the back of my hair painfully. What was this urge everyone seemed to have to pull my hair? It was like being a little girl again. I liked it no better now than then. Once again I was lifted up by my hair as I scrabbled to get my feet back under me. This new stranger brought my face up to his and, as my joints complained at the sudden movement, I saw the man was very, very fair — almost white, in fact: W'shten! He saw my eyes widen and his mouth curled in a sneer.

"Perhaps it falls to me to educate you, love."

The other two — nose to nose as I was with the W'shten I could not see them — sniggered.

Fear jumped up and down and screamed at me, but pride and anger still had the upper hand. I was torn between sticking to my initial line of stubborn deafness and pointing out to this infuriating man the inadequacies he laboured under. Never able to keep silent for long, I decided this W'shten was certainly stupid. More, since the W'shten have different (that is, false) gods, he was probably ignorant too.

I said,

"Let me start the education, then. It is customary to address a priest of Re'a as 'Saahni'; not to do so is rude. If you find the word too difficult for your W'shten tongue," he pulled my hair tighter still, but I carried on recklessly, "you can at least refrain from using any false endearments. To address any woman whom you are not courting as though she were a lover is exceptionally rude, and I shall not converse with anyone unable to manage basic courtesy."

My heart was beating so hard and fast I thought it was going to crack a rib. My knee was screaming and I was beginning to fear losing my entire head of hair, but I was *not* going to be bullied by this barbarian. I hardened my eyes and — as best I could without being scalped — raised my chin and tried not to wobble as I favoured my sore knee.

The W'shten's eyebrows rose. Then, he flashed shiny white teeth and laughed merrily. It was a jolly, deep laugh, backed up by a good sized ribcage and not, apparently, hindered by the leather armour he wore. The other two joined in with equal evidence of joy. I was still insulted and frightened but I relaxed a little. Things could not be too bad if people were laughing. The W'shten let go of my hair and turned to his fellows they all shared his merriment. I put my hands to my scalp and smiled wanly. What a jolly bunch.

Without warning, the pale man turned suddenly and I found myself back on the ground with my ears ringing and half my face on fire. I gasped and blinked, curling up around my hurt, and listened to their laughter. I clutched my jaw, unsure if it still worked.

"What, by all the Dark Wyrms of Shael, is going on?"

A new figure had entered the clearing. I was not prepared to unfold yet but I thought the voice was a woman's.

"Abe's just teaching the priest some manners."

The speaker snickered and I heard a tut and the thud of something hitting the ground not far from me.

"Stop mucking about, Ranyl, and cook these, will you, before I waste away."

"Nay, Thorn," Ranyl replied, "Abe says the priest is cook tonight."

There was more suppressed chortling. I did not hear her move but, suddenly, there were slender fingers gripping my tender jaw. I could not help hissing in protest. She — it was a she — turned my face to hers. I found myself wishing that someone, just someone, would refrain from hauling me about like a rag doll. She looked at me through narrowed eyes. I wondered how she had got the scar that ran along her jaw.

Suddenly, the four of them forgot about me and turned, all of them, weapons in their hands.

A familiar dry voice said,

"If you'd been spending less time priest-bating and more time with your eyes and ears open I'd have not got as close as I did before you noticed."

Hazzor gave a dismissive snort. The bandits relaxed, and Abe strode over, arms wide to clasp the little spy in a bear hug. Hazzor neatly side-stepped him with a flick of his coat.

"I think Reath's lost his grip." He turned to me. "I didn't think it was possible for you to look worse, Saahni."

He walked over to me and offered me his hand to pull me up. I astonished myself with how pleased I was to see his dry smile. He held on until I was steady before returning his attention to Abe.

"You're late."

Chapter 8

Abe grinned merrily at me,

"We were distracted by your pretty priest."

It was the second time he had called me pretty. I scowled. I was convinced it was ironic. It was not an adjective that had ever been applied to me before. Perhaps in this clown's mind it just meant, 'wearing skirts'. Hazzor's eyes narrowed slightly.

"Is there anyone you've not slowed down, Sahnithi?" The affectionate term made me blink in surprise. "Saen's boots, priest, with you involved, the war will have ended by itself before Reath can get his plan off the ground."

I was tired and sore and — now I seemed to be safe again — decidedly wobbly, so I just said childishly,

"They started it."

Abe laughed, white teeth flashing in the firelight. What a cheery soul. I hated him. He thumped me on the back so vigorously Hazzor had to steady me again. He smirked.

"You must forgive me, *Sahnithi*, love," the wretched heathen had not failed to use the intimate title. I rolled my eyes. "I didn't know you were one of Reath's. You should have said."

I drew breath to retaliate and then, suddenly, I could not be bothered. It had been another very long day.

"You didn't ask," was all I managed.

I limped away from him and flopped by the fire with a sigh. An intelligent man would have considered the conversation over. Abe — may the Dark Lord's Wyrms consume him for all eternity — followed and sat down next to me. He rested his hand on the ground behind me and leaned towards me until I glared a glare once learned from Hathil. He flashed his nasty teeth around in apparent delight and sat up straighter. In his slow drawl he said,

"I should introduce you, Sahnithi, pet, to my team."

I closed my eyes. I supposed it worked as a compromise but that did not mean I had to like it.

Abe continued, it seemed, oblivious.

"This here is Axyl."

Abe gestured in the direction of the big man sitting the other side of the fire. He nodded back at me. He had the classic colouring of a Ttarcine, not white-blonde like the W'shten. He made the big outlander look like a stripling. Flat-faced and scarred, he was not a pretty sight, but his pleasure in the introduction seemed amiable enough.

"He's named for the axe he carries," said Abe. "Don't expect much from him in the way of conversation, and try not to stand to close too him in a brawl, he's been known to get a bit carried away.

"Over there is Ranyl."

Ranyl barely glanced my way. He was off at the edge of the clearing, skinning rabbits. Thorn stood close by, arms crossed. Ranyl was small; smaller than Hazzor and darker, too. Sharp-faced, he did not look like a man whose usual outlook was happy.

"Not a man you'll see coming, girl,"

("Saahni," I corrected, automatically. Hazzor smiled into his beard.)

"So try not to get stroppy with him," Abe continued as if I had not spoken. "He's not like me — keeps things deep, if you know what I mean." Those wretched teeth did another round of his audience. "Last but by no means least, there's my lovely Thorn."

Unlike any Ttarcine woman I had ever met, Thorn had sheared off her hair close to her scalp. Given the amount of time I had spent being dragged about by the hair, over the last few days, I could appreciate the wisdom. Bright eyed, she flashed me a smile. I found myself thinking she should eat more: there was nothing of her. She was all bone and sinew.

"She can put an arrow through a wren's eye at 300 paces."

He gave my back another hearty pat for no reason I could discern, and called to Ranyl,

"Ranyl, I'm starving over here. I think Axyl's considering eating the priest."

Everyone except Ranyl and I laughed merrily. Ranyl managed a sarcastic smirk. I worked my neck and jaw.

I took in the four of them. Two burly, two slight; three men, one woman; three Ttarcine, one — I was confident only one — W'shten: all wearing leather armour and bearing weapons, all quite clearly hard as nails.

"You're bandits," I said.

Abe looked outraged.

"Nay, beautiful Sahnithi, not bandits, no! We're simply friends travelling together, these three noble souls sheltering a refugee under their wings." He tried, and failed, to look vulnerable. I felt my eyebrow twitch. "From time to time, the people we meet take exception to us," he leered at me, "and we find ourselves the richer for it." The sunny smile shone out again, "We are victims, I assure you, of prejudice and mistrust, but we merely take ... compensation for our injury."

"Not from all."

Hazzor rejoined us at the fire. Unnoticed, he must have returned to the woods and brought back a mule he had left out of sight.

Abe made an open handed gesture at Hazzor.

"How was I to know the grandma with her horses was one of Reath's people? That was underhand, surely, buck."

Inevitably, Hazzor merely shrugged. Thorn winked at me from across the clearing.

"You should have seen it, Saahni," she said, "the four of us pinned down by a woman old enough to be my *mother's* mother."

Abe continued to grin merrily. I decided that if I never saw another tooth as long as I lived, it would be too soon. Thorn came and joined us. She ladled out the tea that had been brewing on the fire, and passed me a cup. The tea was hot and bitter and reassuring: the continuation of some small part of my world. I breathed in its fragrance.

"She was a scary lady," the archer said.

Takes one to know one, I thought. Thorn shook her head.

"And now we work for the king. I never thought I'd see the day."

My head ached abominably. I sipped gratefully at the tea. I noticed Thorn was giving me that piercing gaze again. She was waiting, and I realised the others were also. I shrugged and with a sideways glance at Hazzor I muttered something about healing skills. Thorn smiled.

"You are not a very good advert for your talents, Saahni."

I cleared my throat.

"I've been busy."

Thorn's smile broadened. I found my own mouth twitching in response.

"It is a difficult thing," said Thorn, "priest and healer. So many duties, so little time."

She chuckled. It was a deep, rich chuckle and very infectious. Underneath all the hurt and guilt and pride and anger, I found a laugh rising for the first time in ... how long? I forgot myself and began to laugh at the sheer lunacy of it all, and Thorn laughed with me. The other bandits laughed — even Ranyl — and, to my astonishment, when the rabbit was served I had a good meal. For the first time since Challawin had climbed that hill, I found myself relaxing and letting go. I listened as Abe and his comrades told increasingly outrageous tales, while Hazzor looked on with a wry smile.

"But you, sweet Sahnithi," said Abe after the last of the meat had been sucked from the bones, "how come you to be saying your prayers out in these forests?"

I looked away. I was happy for the first time, well, for the first time, really since Amtil had died. I did not want to retrace my steps into darkness.

Something in my face must have resonated with Ranyl, for he said,

"Come, Saahni, it's time for the tales to turn darker."

His narrow face developed a hint of a smile,

"I cooked, Saahni, you tell."

I looked round the fire and saw four sets of eyes, waiting. Hazzor was carefully examining his cuffs.

"Well, then," I said, and paused.

As I opened my mouth to tell my tale, my heart swelled to breaking point. Why was I here? Because everyone I knew was dead. Probably. Sat in the firelight, I stood at the edge of a deep ravine. One step further, I knew, and I would plunge into the abyss and not all Hazzor's heartless pragmatism would ever draw me back. I needed to tell a different story: one further away. I drew a deep breath.

"Once upon a time there was an old priest of Re'a who still had not chosen an acolyte to succeed her. Many had offered themselves but she had found each one wanting. This one was too stupid, that one lacking in piety; this was one too frivolous, that one joyless. The entire village pestered her to take a disciple, fearing they would be left without a priest when the old priest died, but she remained adamant that she would not be rushed.

"Then, one day, word came to the priest that a baby had been born with her hair already the colour of Saen's light, born in the hour of the sun god's great strength. This child, said the priest, was born to serve Saen's bride, born to love the sun and its light and life, *born* to be a priest. So, from the baby's first hour, the priest took a hand in her rearing and, as soon as the child was old enough to learn to read, she left her home and went to live at the temple."

I remember the day, still. I remember my mother trying not to cry and my father telling me how proud he was. I remember being in awe of the stern little priest and not wanting to leave my mother to live with the ramrod-straight woman. I remember the long lonely walk through the village and up the hill to the temple with not a word spoken to me.

My life from then on had been set apart from the other children of the village as Amtil set out to create me in her own image. I was taught to read and write, taught the stories of our salvation, taught the liturgies, taught the meaning of the temple seasons, taught the rites of passage, taught the hours. There was little time to play and very little time with my peers, but over time I saw in the old priest a great affection for me and, in return, I began to love her as a second mother.

"The child grew up clever and pious and, at first, the priest congratulated herself on the wisdom of taking a child from the cradle to train as a priest. At length, though, she began to worry that the child, taken apart from village life at such a tender age, had little or no sympathy for the daily needs and concerns of the people who were to be her flock."

My cheeks still burn when I remember the day Amtil caught me calling my mother stupid. My sister, Anid, had spilt the oil and my mother had dipped her fingers in it and flicked some at the threshold 'to keep the Dark Lord out'. With shame I still remember the sneer with which I had asked my own mother how it was that Re'a had not thought to use oil to keep the Dark Lord at bay. What a pity she had died a traitor's death, I had scoffed, when all she'd needed was a little oil. I had lifted my chin and called her a stupid old woman.

Some sixth sense had caused me to turn and see Amtil standing in the doorway looking like thunder. That journey from my parents' home to the temple had also been in silence.

"So the old priest apprenticed her young acolyte to the local healer in the hope that some practical service might open the girl's heart to the daily frailties of the people around her. The healer reached into the fledgling priest and found her childhood. For the next ten years, the healer schooled her pupil in the arts of medicine, midwifery and surgery, but the old priest's disciple still spent her nights in the temple."

Hathil had been a horrible shock: she was everything Amtil was not. She was earthy and hearty, stout and busty. She was always laughing and never beat around the bush. On my first day, instructed though I was to mine for gold not grit, I grew steadily more thin-lipped and superior. Schooled in piety, I was outraged when she called me a sanctimonious prude who would put a lemon to shame. Then she sent me into the brambles to gather therith.

Amtil and Hathil had had little love for each other, poles apart as they were, but they both cared deeply for me and I loved them both. Hathil saw my priesthood as something far off, seeing my training as a healer to have more immediate worth. Amtil, once I showed proficiency, saw my craft simply as a temporary source of income, saving the village from having to pay to feed two mouths.

"Then one day a new king was crowned who declared redundant the ancient duty of each community to support its temple. Offerings to the gods, he said, should be freewill offerings and a temple tax was against the spirit of Re'a's self-sacrificial love."

It had been a year of a bad harvest and the people had been struggling to feed their own families. Released from their obligation to the temple, the people had given very little and no one, least of all Amtil, had begrudged them the food they needed. The following year had been bountiful but somehow the difference did not translate into freewill offerings for the temple, and so it continued, year after year. Gayton had argued that if the temples served the people better they would have a better income but, for established priests like Amtil, this was a foreign language. The living from my work tending the sick had to support both of us. Hathil gave me as much to do as she could, to help out. For a long time I was so busy with my work as a healer and my duties in the temple that I did not notice how ill Amtil had become.

"When the old priest died, she took with her the villagers' sense of duty to the temple."

Unbidden, I recalled the final row with Karl, my own stubborn pride, the slaughter of the village and the long night with Reath. My throat tightened. I drew breath carefully.

"In the end they no longer had much need for a priest and Reath recruited the young priest as a healer for the team he was putting together."

When the others realised my tale was done, there was silence for another moment or two. Then Axyl spoke directly to me for the first time.

"Saahni, you're a terrible story-teller. Don't do it."

There was another pause and I thought Ranyl was choking.

"Ranyl?" I said, and he gave a great whooping guffaw.

Needless to say, the four of them were folded up in an instant. I tottered on the brink of indignation, hurt that the naked revelation of my history was so rejected. Hazzor caught my eye and raised an eyebrow. I shook my head and smiled. My bag, I noticed, had been turned over but my cloak was still nearby. I curled up in it while the bandits laughed.

My days were not getting any shorter.

Chapter 9

I woke, as usual, in the darkness before dawn. Everything *ached*. I gave thanks to Re'a that I would not have to walk today but I did not relish the idea of a day on a mule either. I sat up slowly and applied salves as best I could. I thought if I moved quickly there ought to be time to say the hour before everyone was ready to go; a party of six must surely take longer to decamp than just two.

Apparently, I was wrong. Five pairs of hands, all experienced travellers, can in fact clear a camp astonishingly quickly and efficiently. Axyl practically picked me up and dropped me on the mule, and the whole party was moving well before full light. Breakfast was passed round and eaten as we went, which I thought nigh-on ungodly. Sheepishly, I began to realise just how much Hazzor had altered his pace to match mine. Avoiding his eye, I returned to the study of the rings on my palm that occupied so much of my time lately.

Why does Re'a take her priests and mark them in honour of the Three? What is the point of it? I ran my thumb across my palm anew, as if somewhere in the marks I would find the answer, any answer, to the question that haunted me: *Who am I now?*

Panic began to swell within me. I missed Amtil

like a thread from my soul; she had been so calm, so solid, so *sure*. She, I knew, had loved Ladlastide. True, she delighted in having the whole village run to her beck and call, but the romantic capture of the great god's heart by the holy maiden was her favourite tale.

I turned my mind to the approaching feast. Whoever I was, the marriage of Saen and Re'a was a glory, a wonder to be embraced. Heaven wedded to earth. I looked ahead to Marrett and to the feast of Ladlas on the morrow. If I could assist in the feast... the thirst for something of my old self reawakened after yesterday's violence, and I began to sing. I have always loved the chants of the second day — the tale of Re'a's birth and childhood, the tale of Saen's courtship. I lifted heart and voice, and the beauty of it all lifted me.

Ranyl asked Hazzor to gag me. Thankfully, I was not the only one Hazzor routinely ignored. Thorn said if she had known Reath was conscripting them as acolytes she would have refused whatever the consequences. I ignored both of them — and the others, who were no more respectful — and closed my ears to their chatter. True, I muted my tone a little but, once more, I lost myself in words so much older than I.

From time to time I surfaced a little, to accept a drink or a bite to eat. I also watched as the scenery shifted rapidly once we had crossed the River Arwn. We left the woods and forests behind us and entered farmland. It was not the smallholdings I was used to but great rolling fields of arable cultivation. My eyes ached, as though they were being stretched from their sockets, the horizon was so far away! I shut my eyes and focused on the chants, not so much to ignore the view as to forget the muscles in my legs and rear, and the pain in my knee and back.

Sweet Re'a have mercy!

The village of Marrett, when we finally came to it that evening, was smaller than I had hoped. It owed the inn chiefly to river traffic. A small town, indeed, but with more than its share of vagrants, it seemed. I saw several families hunched together in corners and alleyways, and the town had an overstretched feel to it. We were now within reach of the war's effects.

The six of us attracted little attention as we entered the town, to my surprise. I said as much to Thorn, who shrugged. It was Ranyl who remarked that in a town so full of strangers, a few more made little difference. I wondered how the place could manage so many extra mouths to feed and Abe told me that the king's men came regularly to Marrett for army 'volunteers'. Hungry, homeless men and women were easy recruits. I avoided looking at Hazzor.

When we got to the *Nimble Sheep,* Abe and the others went in whilst Hazzor led the mule and me around the corner to the stable attached to the inn. We found a stable-hand waiting for us. He was a small lad but sleek and self-satisfied. I guessed the inn was doing well from the movement of people — especially if they got regular business from the king's men. The boy grumbled about the extra work until Hazzor tossed him a Shrekna. The lad caught the coin neatly and it vanished swiftly. With the coin in his pocket, he became all attendant helpfulness so, as Hazzor helped me down, I asked him which way to the temple. After a day on that mule, I felt like I had been given another beating. I was thinking longingly of dinner and bed, but the temple bell was ringing and I knew I needed to introduce myself. If I waited until tomorrow morning the priest would already have her hands full and would not welcome an interloper. As it was, I knew there was a good chance she would reject me. Priests do not travel, so a priest so far from home would arouse suspicions I would find hard to lay to rest, but I *needed* this. After six days of being pushed, punched, terrified and disorientated, I yearned for a touchstone. Had I been livelier, I think I would have been tense with nerves, but I was so tired, I was merely following my instincts: homing in like an injured badger-fox to its earth. The Ladlas rites started in earnest in the morning and, if I was to be part of them, I had to be at the temple that day.

I winced and swore as I got down and felt the full effect of the ground's pull on my bruised and battered muscles. Hazzor kept his grip on my elbow as the boy left and at first I thought it was just kindness. More fool me. He led me out of the stable, inexorably, in the opposite direction to the temple. When I protested he said,

"You cannot go, Saahni."

I tried to stop so I could look him square in the eye with the full effect of my outrage but the man was neither stopping nor letting go. It had the choice between hobbling along with him or being dragged along the ground. I had to make do with hissing angrily,

"What do you mean I *cannot* go? I must go."

"There is no obligation."

You would think we were discussing the weather.

"I am a *priest*."

I made another vain attempt to regain control of my arm. Hazzor's lip curled slightly.

"Really? I don't think any of us had noticed." I practically spat, but before I could reply to his wit, he continued, "You have no duty in Marrett."

My righteous indignation lost something in my limp and the small squeak of pain as I misplaced my foot and jolted my back. Lost something, but was not altogether lost.

"I have a duty to Re'a."

Missing not a step, Hazzor merely said,

"Tcha!"

It was the kind of 'tcha' that, in a normal person, might be accompanied by a rolling of the eyes, but I neither saw nor looked to see if Hazzor rolled his. I just said (perhaps a little sulkily),

"I disoblige no one but myself."

Hazzor dragged me into the alley between the stable and the inn and spun me round to face him.

"You are a priest with no village, how much do you think you'll stand out? What kind of questions do you think they'll start asking about the people you're travelling with? Just how memorable do you think we'll become?"

"No."

I am not sure what I was rejecting. He was right. A roaming priest stands out like a tame wychi, but I had been holding on to this chance to be *me* like a mother clings to her ailing infant. I was not just going to say goodbye and walk away.

"No," I repeated, "I will not."

Will not lose to this, will not give up: will not abandon my own self, and become some other person. I took deep, careful breaths to try to curb the hot tears of indignation that were threatening. The thought of the sacred rites taking place somewhere I was not, began to unravel me.

"I will not give up who I *am*."

Hazzor's face, incredibly, became even more impassive and I held up my hand, my marked hand, partly in display and partly to ward off his offense.

"I know, I do see that when we're on the move, there are more urgent priorities than the ... life I'm used to. But tonight, Hazzor, tonight, surely I am not needed for anything. Tomorrow is the feast of Ladlas, Hazzor, Hazzor, surely you must see?" I repeated his name, as if the simple repetition of his identity could link him to mine. "Hazzor, a healer is what I do; a priest is what I *am*."

I dropped my hand back to my side and, for a moment, I thought I saw a look of pity behind those grey eyes. So I was utterly unprepared to be grabbed by my shirt-front and slammed back against the wall.

"We are at *war*," he snarled.

I was astonished by his vehemence. Once again, the lack of the honorific was like a thunderclap in the air between us.

"Look around you. The temple will be full, not because the people of Marrett are particularly devout but because this place is full of people who have no other shelter — "

"Then the priest will need my help."

Hazzor rode over my interjection as if I had not spoken.

"And Marrett is far from the teeth of this war but even then your Harset is nothing, a pale shade of what is visited on the villages of the Eastern Territories — "

"*Pale?*"

"Pale. We did not rape. We did not mutilate. We did not sow the fields with salt — we did our best..."

Hazzor drew in a ragged breath and, for the first time, I got a glimpse of what his role in those dreadful mummeries had cost him. It did not, however, make me like him any more. He continued more quietly,

"We did our best to create the effect of war with as little of its violence as possible."

His lips thinned and he shoved me against the wall again. I fought to keep my balance.

"We are trying to stop a war and you want to risk everything for what?"

I opened my mouth to speak, to defend myself, to justify myself, but Hazzor answered his own question.

"For your own precious *identity*."

Again, he shoved me against the wall and this time my head banged against the wooden frame behind me and I bit my tongue. As he walked away, I slid to the floor and wrapped my hands around my head, fighting back the tears that relentlessly rolled down my face.

It was not long before I heard footsteps heading my way. I kept my head down. The streets were full of people huddled in doorways. I saw no reason why I should attract attention. My heart sank when I heard a soft, W'shten accent exclaim,

"Sahnithi, sweeting, you look all done in, pet."

I really had thought it could not get worse, but somehow it always could.

"Thorn's paid for baths for you and her. She's taken quite a shine to you and who can blame her?" I could feel the wink, even curled up as I was. "Haenid's blood, though, darlin', you look like you need it. Hurry up, mind, Fendrick says he'll not hold dinner long."

I heard the creak of his armour and I looked up to see Abe offering me his hand. Wearily, I took it and he pulled me effortlessly to my feet in one smooth motion. Without so much as a "by your leave" he pulled my arm round his neck and wrapped his arm under mine. Cheek to cheek, nearly, he appeared to ignore my wobbling lip and red rimmed eyes, and, leering at me, said,

"If you like, hun', I'll help you bathe."

Chapter 10

I love baths. I love the warmth and I love the languor. I love the feeling of being in a little bath-world bubble in which nothing needs to be done, no decisions made. No one can talk to me or ask for me. Baths are a rare taste of heaven. On this occasion, after five days of travelling, I also relished being clean again. I stewed in the hot water and felt my aches and pains melt into the bath.

For a long time, I simply lay there, a body in a comfortable place, but inevitably, eventually, tired and beleaguered as I was, my mind betrayed me. Slowly, it started spiralling around and around the memories that haunted me and I sank into the darkness. There, I found the monster of self-loathing waiting for me. My blissful inactivity became a trap as the dragon's many heads snarled and snapped at me.

You are pathetic <the monster curled its lip>

You are useless <the beast sneered>

You failed your village <it roared at me and I cowered>

You are so self-absorbed that even the destruction of your own village is a source of self pity instead of grief for the dead <the monster snarled and snapped>

You did not stay even to bury the dead <the beast fed on my gut>

You are not able to keep the feast <the creature tore at my heart>

You are useless to your village, useless to your new fellows — a burden only <the beast smacked its lips>

You cannot even make breakfast or *keep the hours* <the thing bared its teeth>

Tears rolled down my cheeks but I could not stop myself re-walking the well-trod labyrinth. The assault continued:

Your prayers are only a nuisance to your companions <cracking of bone, sucking of marrow>

Your self-pity is pathetic and self-centred <the monster laughed as it fed on me>

I drew a deep breath and washed my face. I found myself back in my childhood when I had banged on Amtil's door in the middle of the night. I had stood there in my night gown, hammering and sobbing until she had let me in. Red eyed and half-mad with tiredness, I had demanded,

"Why should I care if Re'a loves me?"

The little priest had sighed and led me into her living room. She had sat me down on her skins and begun to warm some milk for me.

"Why should you not care?" the sleep-filled priest had countered, eventually.

"But if Re'a loves everyone, what is her love *worth*? She loves murderers and thieves and vagabonds and liars," I had agonised. "What does it matter if she also loves me?"

Amtil had been bewildered by the question but she had also sat with me for hours while I had sobbed in an agony of self doubt. She had patted my hand and stroked my head, and spoken soothingly of what

Re'a's love had cost her; told me that even if it were only me that had needed her, she would still have died for me, still loved me. But, I had been consumed by the need to be special, by that child's need to be somebody's *best* friend, which perhaps we never quite lose. That night, I had eventually given up and crawled back to bed, defeated by tiredness rather than comforted. Amtil never had answered my question to my satisfaction but for years it had not mattered. For years, I had been special: Hathil's star pupil, Harset's child acolyte and then the village priest. The moment I was stripped of my role, it seemed, I found the old question roaring back: *how do I prove my worth? What makes me special?*

I breathed in deeply — *Re'a, Saviour of the world* — I breathed out — *guide me*.

I lay in the bath and let the prayers enter my bloodstream.

After a little while, my stomach rumbled and I remembered Fenrick's threat not to hold dinner. Reluctantly, I rose from the bath and dried myself. The herbs I had put in the bath had added their potency to the hot water, and I felt considerably better: not yet ready to skip like a lamb, but better than I had been. I applied fresh salves to the aches and bruises, and felt half-way human as I went back down the corridor to my room.

To my surprise my own clothes were not where I had left them. In their place were new clothes, more like Thorn's than my own. Gone were the layers of thin, worn fabric and in their place were hardy clothes of new wool and linen with — were they leather breeches? No, when I put them on they were longer than breeches. There was only one skirt: a split skirt, made of heavy wool, which was knee length. I held it up and raised my eyebrows. The shirts simply replaced my own, but being better quality, there were fewer of them. I picked up one of the boots that had replaced mine — oh it was wonderfully soft and lined.

I tried to be a little bit outraged at this high handed approach to my costume, but failed. It was undeniable, these clothes were far better made and far more practical for life on the road and indeed in ditches or (and the memory pricked my battered pride) up trees. I stroked the soft woollen lining of the jerkin that Hazzor — surely Hazzor — had provided. I had never seen so many pockets — inside and out — on a garment. The arms, curiously, were only loosely attached. A design, I discovered, which gave me great freedom of movement. The stitching alone must have taken an age. Perhaps not Hazzor, then. This had been ordered days ago. This must be Reath's work.

Stiffly, I dressed and shook my head in wonder at how well these new clothes fitted. I marvelled at the memory and eye for detail Reath must have and, strangely, I began to fear the man more than I had before. I saw a glimpse of his ability to plot and manipulate, and I wondered what he had planned for us. Doubting that I had time to re-braid my hair without losing my dinner, I simply pulled it back behind my head in a knot. As I left the room, I caught sight of my reflection in the bronze mirror on the wall. I did not recognise myself.

Disconcerted, I hobbled downstairs to the private room Reath had hired for us. I paused on the threshold. Across the table from each other were Abe and Ranyl, playing dice, their bowls pushed aside, empty. As I watched, Ranyl threw his dice and Abe thumped the table in disgust. Ranyl lent back in triumph, arm hooked over the back of the chair, thin lips curled. Abe pushed his bench back, looked up and saw me. He turned to Ranyl.

"Now, Ranyl, my heart's brother, we'll have to finish this another day, the girls are here."

I never saw Ranyl's reaction to this sudden end of a game he was clearly winning, for I had turned in surprise. Thorn stood behind me and I had not heard so much as a rustle or a footfall. She slapped my arm in a hearty sort of way, barely noticing that she had made me jump like a startled deer.

"A bath and fresh clothes and I feel a new woman, no?" she said with satisfaction.

Before I could stammer my thanks for her generosity Abe, obviously, was unable to resist the opening she had left.

He patted his thigh with a wink,

"Well, there's only one way to find out, love."

Thorn flashed me a grin and sauntered slowly over to where he sat, while Ranyl gave a whistle. She put one booted foot up next to Abe, then, as his grin began to widen further (Re'a, but I hated those teeth), Thorn neatly kicked over the bench in a single motion. As the bandit sat, sprawled on the floor, she answered him,

"I dunno, Abe," and she pouted like a tavern wench, "what do you think?"

Abe roared with laughter and rolled swiftly to his feet.

"No," he said, kissing her soundly on the lips, "same harridan as ever."

They were, all three of them, laughing now — at least for once it was not at my expense — but I was unsure whether to join in. I stood there uncertain, then jumped once more as a voice spoke gruffly at my shoulder.

"Move, will you, if you're not going in."

I turned to see the mountain that was Axyl looming behind me. What was it about these people that they could all creak at will, when they wanted to be noticed, but even the biggest of them moved like wraiths when it suited them?

"If you're not hungry, I am." He towered over me and shouted, "House!"

I put a protesting finger in my ear and a hand out for pause.

"I'm moving, I'm moving."

I limped over to the table and chose a chair across from Abe and Thorn.

Ranyl eyed me and there was a shadow of a smile on his saturnine face as he tilted his head like a bird.

"Well, priest," he said, "maybe all healers should be beaten before you need them to work. Gives a man confidence to see one heal herself."

I opened my mouth to make a pious response but did a double take. It had been a while since I had spent time with Hathil but I knew her response. In a new spirit of daring, I gave it.

"You should pay me, then, for the demonstration."

Thorn gave a little whoop and thumped the table. I smiled, enjoying the moment of friendship.

Ranyl had not finished.

"What, Saahni, in kind?"

Abe reached forward and patted Ranyl's hand, still holding the dice as it was, and said,

"Aye, but Ranyl, my buck, I know how much it hurts you to pay for anything, so this debt I'll gladly take from you," and the white teeth flashed again.

Indignation and outrage flashed in my heart, but I bit my lip. This was play, I reminded myself — something I had yearned for as a child; something I had never had much of. *Do. Not. Spoil. It. Now.* I tapped the table with a finger, as if in thought, and looked up.

"Bandit," I said, "you could not afford me."

"She needs playmates, companions." I was hid behind the door and Hathil thought she was speaking to Amtil in private. "She is too serious, Saahni, too wrapped up in herself and her god."

As usual the two of them were standing eye to eye. As usual, Amtil was tight lipped in disapproval.

"She was up to her hips in ox dung! What kind of example is that?"

As usual Hathil, hands on hips, was doing a fair impression of a charging heifer.

"She was making friends."

"She does not need friends. When she is priest in my place, she will have no friends."

"No? And why's that? I don't recall any great edict from Saen banning friendship."

"Do not mock!"

"Get off your great high horse! I am not mocking. Everyone needs friends."

"Chasing 'friendship' is what distracts us from what we need to do. She will have Re'a. Our Lady is all she needs. Re'a is a friend to everyone, comforter to the afflicted — "

"Balls, Saahni!" Amtil's eyebrows had disappeared up, almost beyond her hairline. "Left as she is, Kayt'an will become a loveless prig with nothing to give to anyone. You know that, that's why you gave her to me in the first place."

"I wanted you to teach her compassion, not waste her time playing foolish, filthy games."

"She *needs* to play in the shit from time to time."

Well, Hathil, here I am, playing.

And I can hear Amtil's disapproval, even from her grave.

The evening broke up early and I followed Thorn down the rambling corridors to our corner of the inn. At my doorway she paused to say goodnight. The moonlight lit her profile and she seemed suddenly fragile.

"Thorn," I asked, suddenly bold, "why do you do this?" Into her puzzled expression I went on, "Why do you live this life?"

She smiled and leaned a graceful arm against the wall. She seemed to study her hand for a moment before saying simply,

"It's not a very original story."

Part of me was dying of curiosity but I simply brushed my new skirts, and muttered something about not wanting to pry. Thorn gave a little bark of laughter and came nearer to lean her shoulder against the doorframe.

"I am the seventh of eight siblings to survive infancy and the only girl. By the time I was old enough to wed my father had established himself and looked for me to marry well."

"He chose for you?"

"He did." The archer smiled, but it was not a wholly happy smile. "Unfortunately, for my father, his choice had a younger, far less eligible, brother," she looked up at me and smiled, "a much more handsome man."

She gazed into the past and seemed to forget me altogether. I began to think she was altogether lost so I asked,

"What was he like?"

"Like?" She shook her head but her eyes were still focused long ago. "I've mostly forgotten." From the look on her face I didn't believe her. She looked like she remembered well. "The long and the short of it is that we ran away together."

Indignation brewed in my breast.

"But he abandoned you?!"

Finally, Thorn saw me and she chuckled.

"I'm sorry to confess to you Saahni, no. We were several weeks on the run, you see, living as best we could. Evrh — my beaux — took the first opportunity to settle down that was offered: life in the hill country among the sheep, a farm hand." Thorn rested her shorn head on the doorpost. She met my eyes with a look I could not quite read, full of sadness but somehow also laughter. "I'd got used to living by my wits but he, well, he wanted an ordered life. I expect he has little sheepherder children by now."

She smiled again, wryly, and then laughed at my expression. I had assumed only disaster could bring people to this. I had never dreamed anyone could *choose* this life over home and family. I failed to stop myself look disapprovingly at the archer who laughed again.

"Goodnight, Saahni," she said.

Chapter 11

The next morning, in grey dawn light, I woke and rolled out of bed to try to be active before the morning's bleakness surfaced. Years and years of training, and habit, meant I had lit my candle and was already prostrate before the ghosts awoke. It was the feast of Ladlas, and I was not singing the morning chants, not readying Saen and the maidens to their parts: I would not be greeting the spring. My family, perhaps, my friends — such as I had — my neighbours, would never do so again. Desperately, I lay my heart before my goddess and begged her for grace, for mercy, for amnesia even. Then, I placed my face in the dust and prayed for strength.

That pale shade of my duty done, I dressed in my new clothes, but returned my hair to its customary braids before heading downstairs for breakfast.

I was the last down. Already in the snug were the four bandits, as well as Hazzor, Reath and another man I did not know. The latter was an unremarkable man, save for his hair which was the colour of carrots and curled like a sheep's fleece. I caught myself staring and hastily crossed the room.

The bandits were surprised to see me that was clear. Needless to say, it was Abe that voiced it.

"Sahnithi, love, my surprise in seeing you is

matched only by my joy. I thought you followers of Re'a were off celebrating a wedding, no? Don't tell me you had such a good time last night you've forsworn yourself for our company?"

The pale man gave another of his horrible grins and then, strangely, winced.

Thorn reached out a hand.

"Are you alright, Saahni?"

I shrugged and nodded, sick at heart. In answer to their puzzlement, Hazzor tossed a pair of gloves across the table to me. Slowly, I picked them up and put them on, hiding the circles on my palm. The fingers were left uncovered for the main part as were the backs of the hands. Ranyl sneered,

"There's no way you'll pass her off as an archer."

Reath lifted his cool eyes and examined Ranyl for a good minute before he spoke. To Ranyl's credit, he hid any discomfort well. I would have been ready to drop through the floor by the time Reath spoke.

"Who says we're trying to pass her off as anything?"

Ranyl bared his yellow teeth in a mock smile.

"Listen, Reath, I know you've got the others eating out of your hand, but I'm just along for the ride. Remember that. The priest is clearly gagging to go and grovel in the temple and now you're covering her tattoos with archer's gloves and dressing her in short skirts and a jerkin. But I'm just saying, you can paint 'archer' in big letters across her chest, she still won't look like one."

There's only ever so much I can take of being treated like a thing, so I clicked my hands in front of Ranyl's face.

"I'm actually sitting here, you know," I pointed out.

Reath's eye's glinted, I think, but all he said was,

"I believe Seneit will be in shortly."

I was not surprised when, within moments, the serving wench arrived with a tray of cold meats and biscuits. Her face was closed and she looked none of us in the eye. Muttering only something about being back with drinks, she was about to leave when I asked if I could have milk. She half turned her face to Reath — but even then did not look the master spy in the eye — and when he nodded she left. I turned to Abe, surprised that something in a skirt had been in the same room with him without any smiles, winks, leers or any, in fact, acknowledgement of her sex or his. I raised an eyebrow and he feigned innocence — all gestures and endearments but no conviction. Ranyl gave the closest thing I had seen yet to a proper smile.

"He tried it last night when she brought his dinner," he said smugly. "The charming Abernast was actually silenced."

I was gobsmacked.

"Sweet Re'a!" I leaned forward, "What did she say?"

Abe shifted uncomfortably.

"I'd prefer not to talk about it," he muttered, "and, lovely Sahnithi, you'll not mention it either if you've any charity in you."

Failing any test of self-control Amtil might have set me, I could not refrain from glancing back at Ranyl, whose satisfaction was palpable.

"Suffice it to say, Saahni, that his family jewels were threatened in terms that brooked," for a moment I thought he was actually going to grin, "no measure of doubt."

I flicked my eyes to Thorn.

"Don't look at me, I wasn't there, but I'm equally astonished."

The girl, Seneit, returned with drinks and placed each on the table with extreme care as if she was trying very hard not to smash it down. When she put my milk in front of me, I could almost feel the distaste radiating off her.

Uncomfortable starting a conversation with Reath, I decided that Hazzor was definitely the lesser of two evils. I caught his eye,

"She seems to hate us."

Hazzor took a pull from his drink.

"She does."

I should not have been taken aback by his apparent indifference, but nevertheless I was.

"Why?" I asked.

"Because she's not stupid."

Before I could think of anything sensible to say in response, the stranger in the corner coughed. Reath leaned back with an open gesture and said,

"My apologies. Kayt'an Sahn, may I present the mage Fryn'gh."

He was, for all-the-world, a gentleman introducing two courtiers. I stared at Fryn'gh — if that was his name, which I doubted — in disgust and disdain.

He smiled at me. (What was this fashion for smiling wantonly?)

"A pleasure, madam."

Of course, he had been sat in the corner digesting the fact that I was a priest of Re'a and — I was sure — composing some show of indifference. ('Madam' indeed!) I, on the other hand, was thrown into conversation with the creature still all shock and bile. Instinctively I responded,

"Saahni," and then to Reath, "A *mage*?"

Bleurgh! Even the feel of the word on my tongue was hateful.

Hazzor grimaced.

"Please, Fryn'gh, do us all a favour and call the priest 'Saahni'."

Abe — rot his socks — had recovered his composure and put an arm around the ginger wizard-creature. He leaned in and spoke quietly into Fryn'gh's ear. Fryn'gh pulled away and turned wide-eyed to look back at the burly bandit who, inevitably, smiled sunnily.

The so-called mage turned back to me and his upper lip curled, briefly.

"My apologies, *Saahni*," he said, though he sounded more like he was sorry for what he had eaten than for anything he had said, "I hadn't realised a title meant so much to you."

Put like that, it sounded somewhat grubby; trust a wizard to twist the truth of a thing. Still, I was surprised at Abe. I glanced at the grinning renwit who — urgh! — pressed both hands to his heart and sighed. Perhaps he needed to prove something after Seneit's assault.

I supposed I needed to be gracious in response. The attention of the room was directed solely at me. I cleared my throat.

"Well," I said, "I'm sure that a man such as yourself must have more urgent things to think about than courtesy." (The terrible punishments set aside for the likes of him by Farock Rha, for example). I smiled sweetly — or at least it was meant to be sweetly. "Please don't let such little things trouble you, sir. Speak as you feel able."

Fryn'gh lurched forward in his seat towards me. I thought for a moment I may have lit a wick too many, and be in for another beating, but Reath merely held one finger slightly raised and the whole table was back, as it were, in his hand. He made a circular motion with that same finger.

"You should all eat before Seneit loses patience and comes in to clear your breakfast away before you're done. She's done it before."

He steepled his fingers together and raised his eyebrows.

"Kayt'an Sahn, Fryn'gh," he looked pointedly at each of us in turn, "do try and get along. I need the skills of both of you to make this work but, if you hinder this team with your bickering, you will have to be replaced."

I did not like the look in his eye, not at all. The dreadful man smiled charmingly and went on,

"The seven of you need to make your way to the little village of Dar Tor." Abe practically spasmed. "Do you have something to add, Abernast?"

Abe stuffed some ham in his mouth and waved a fork in denial, so Reath continued,

"Do try not to draw attention to yourselves. I suggest you stay off the roads and out of the villages along the way, no? It really is a glorious season to be travelling. I understand the fens are at their best in the spring. The bird life along the Tuq is quite astonishing, really it is. Once you get to Dar Tor, head for the farm to the north east. The woman, Heanah, will be waiting for you. She'll fill you in."

Fryn'gh frowned.

"I still don't see the need to have a priest along. I mean," and he snorted with *the* most annoying laugh, "It's not as if we're expecting Re'a to bless the war effort surely?"

He snorted again, clearly quite carried away by his own wit.

Reath leaned back from the table a little and studied the wizard. After a pause long enough to make us all uncomfortable — even the mage, and I thought they were all immune to any human decency — the master spy answered,

"Kayt'an Sahn is a talented healer." He looked me up and down. "A walking testament to her skills."

Ranyl looked briefly uncomfortable. I could almost hear him wondering if last night the spy had been nearer than we had guessed.

The mage was undaunted.

"I know several mages who could heal a man in minutes so you'd never know he'd been injured."

Reath cocked his head.

"True, but I've known several men die from a mage's healing. That and I can't afford the time it takes to sleep off such a cure. Magic healing is spectacular but I don't like to rely on it. You, however, sir, are quite another matter."

Fryn'gh preened. I tried to resist the urge to compete but failed, so I asked a question; one I hoped would make me seem dispassionate and inquiring (and not hopelessly biased, like *some*.)

"How is it that the W'shten aren't coming further west," I asked, brightly, "if they're causing so much havoc here?"

To my gall, Reath merely got up from the table.

"Well," he announced, "Onwards and upwards, as the king is so fond of telling me."

He smiled briefly, brushed imaginary fluff (I assume it was imaginary) off his sleeve, nodded to the rest of us, and left. I sat with my mouth hanging open. I had hoped to impress the courtier; instead, the accursed creature of the Dark Lord's arts leaned back in his chair with his hand flat on the table and addressed me, patronisingly.

"The W'shten are hoping to exacerbate the divide that already exists between east and west in Ttaroc. By holding back from the west, they're hoping to create resentment in the east. I wouldn't be surprised if they've already put out feelers to some nobles in Gayton's court — somebody willing to rule a province under Yr. If the Eastern Territories secede, Yr can then starve Gayton into submission just like his father did the Ga'ared."

I hated to encourage the man, but one more question would not change anything.

"And are they likely to?"

The mage shrugged.

"You've seen them."

His green eyes met mine and I saw amusement in them.

"You find this funny!"

Fryn'gh stood.

"Gayton has been strutting around like no one could touch him. He's a spoilt boy-king, with no idea of politics, trying to out-think the son of one of the most devious dynasties in the Circle Sea. I'm astonished anyone's actually trying in this war." He made a dismissive gesture. "The only reason Lord Reath could persuade me along is that the Tower is a little ... claustrophobic, right now."

I leaned back, triumphant.

"You mean even you're own kind don't like you?"

Ranyl actually laughed. Well, it was more of a snicker, really. He whispered theatrically to Axyl,

"Do you think we could sell tickets?"

Fryn'gh turned his back and walked stiffly to the door. Astonishing! Was there nothing remarkable about the man aside from his hair? Neither tall nor short — he was middling height, middling build, perhaps a little pale but he was neither unfavoured nor handsome. Not particularly fast, either, because before he reached the door Abe had also stood.

"Hey now, buck, not so fast!"

Abe came to stand behind me, which disturbed me a little, especially when he put his white hands on my shoulders.

"Now, I know she might just possibly be the most annoying woman that ever suckled on Haenid's tits."

"I — " I managed, before Abe's hands tightened alarmingly.

"*But* we've all got to share the same air 'til this thing is done, sonney,"

I saw the heretic twitch, *Ha!* I thought, *see how you like it!*

The bandit's tone became so soft and sweet I could have spread it on the bread I was still eating. (Not eating just then, of course, on account of having a bandit's hands round my neck, nearly).

"So, you go and take a quick walk, now, if you like, and when you come back, you're both going to play nice, yes?"

Abe — may the unspeakable wyrms feed on his tongue — shook me back a forth a few times so my head, whether I willed it or no, nodded.

The wizard sighed and scratched his chin (neither square nor weak, of course, nor bearded, but clean shaven and … chin-shaped). He lifted his head in a kind of half nod and made a vaguely positive 'hnnmm' sound. Then he sneered and left the room.

"That went well," growled Axyl.

Interlude

The princess stood at her balcony and looked across the city. Below her was the beauty of the palace gardens, green with new growth. If she listened she could hear the fountains playing.

Far across the city was a little pool, fed from a stinking stream, where long ago, lost and angry, she had met Laeni. Princess Ttarah had had a lovely time playing truant with the beggar-child Laeni. They had paddled in the pool, laughing and splashing, and Laeni had shared her meagre meal with the princess. Ttarah had promised endless friendship and had trotted home, reconciled in her own heart to the parents who had bid her to stay within the palace on that fine day.

It was a pity, thought the princess, that they had not thought to mention the sickness that had been seen in the lower town.

When Ttarah had fallen ill, it was not the pain of his daughter that sent King Gayton running. He ran, not to his physician, but to the master of his spies. He had needed his shame covered: his only daughter had caught a vile, disfiguring, slum-dwellers' disease. While the princess had screamed with pain, the King's Man had wrapped a web of deceit around her. He ensured that none would associated the king's *disfigured daughter with the sewers and filth that bred the firepox.*

Ttarah wondered if the pool was still there; wondered if Laeni still lived.

She wondered how many had spotted then what was whispered now.

Her father was mad.

Chapter 12

After breakfast, we were quickly on the move. Hazzor had apparently done the shopping the night before. He gave me leave (and money) to visit the local herbalist to fill some gaps in my stock, on the promise that I would remember we were on an urgent mission and that I would keep my palms hidden.

The herbalist was an old man with crooked hands. Greeting him, I bit my tongue against a blessing, as such, and simply wished him a blessed Ladlas. The old man simply nodded. *Oh, Holy Lady, how I want to be in your temple this morning!* He must have blessed me in turn, for before I could lose myself in melancholy yet again, the herbalist gestured at his goods and I was mercifully, pitifully, distracted.

Oh! I nearly lost myself in the smells and textures. There were herbs and seeds and stamens and bark and roots and anything else I could ask for. I rubbed the scent off some catmint leaves and sniffed, appreciatively. The old man nodded. I asked for some thyme and ginger, Haenid's heart, Collinsonia, nettle, mustard, therith, lavender, black dock root, gentian bark — I paused for a heart beat then asked for wolfsbane and alvia.

The old man wrapped each selection awkwardly.

It is always uncomfortable starting a conversation

about a chronic problem — as priest or as healer — but I have never been any good at keeping my peace. Holding my tongue on the blessing was about the extent of my self-control; refraining from giving a medical opinion as well was beyond my powers.

"Have you any wolf's heart?" I asked.

He smiled and beckoned. I leaned forward. He picked up a packet hidden out of sight and held it out of reach.

"It's very good for the crippling of joints, did you know?"

At last the man spoke.

"It's not my stock."

I bit my lip. I had been given money to stock up but Hazzor had not actually said it was *only* for the mission.

"How many have you?"

He showed me, and I examined the funds I had left. Well, I thought, it would do my knee a lot of good too and Hathil always said Re'a blesses the healer that takes time for them that can't pay you. I bought the wolf's heart and gave the old man two. The smile I got in return cheered me no end.

There, I told myself, all this nonsense about losing myself. I smiled smugly; it would take more than a bunch of rowdy bandits and a self-satisfied mage to distract me from my calling.

I walked on with a spring in my step.

Well, I would have done, if it had not hurt.

The bandits were still waiting patiently when I returned to the *Nimble Sheep*. They were even content to wait, once I had hoved into view, until I had actually drawn level with them, before they shouldered their packs. Abe gave his usual over-familiar greeting and the others nodded at me, Thorn with a smile. The four bandits were armed to the teeth under their coats and Thorn had her fearsome bow on her back. Strangely, Hazzor also had a bow.

"I said he'd never make an archer of you, but he's determined," muttered Ranyl to me as I caught up with the group.

I shook my head puzzled.

"But I'm supposed to be the healer," I answered quietly. "Why do I need pretend another role?"

"No pretence, Saahni."

Hazzor passed me the bow. Ranyl and I exchanged the glance of co-conspirators caught out.

"There was a bow in your rooms back in Harset. Reath wants to make you as useful as possible. Hopefully, we'll have little need for your healing skills for most of the trip."

Ranyl's mouth twitched.

"He means none of the rest of us," he whispered to me for everyone to hear.

Thorn patted me on the shoulder. I had bound my knee as tight as I could with my new wolf's heart and it was pretty comfortable but I was under no illusions what a day's walking would do. Fryn'gh was leaning against the wall of the inn, feigning indifference again. Was that discomfort I read in his expression? If so, I felt a moment's sympathy. It was uncomfortable hiding what we were. I had dressed in a priest's skirts for five years now, long enough for these short skirts and the stiff jerkin to feel strange. I wondered how long Fryn'gh had been wearing his robes. He seemed about my age. The students of magic start wearing their robes, I had heard, as soon as they start their studies. That would mean Fryn'gh had been dressed for his chosen — I felt my lip curl a little even in my sympathy — calling for about fifteen years. My mind

followed my lip. *Tcha! What am I thinking?*
We set off eastwards.

The first day travelling together was unremarkable. Fryn'gh and I dropped to the back, and bickered on and off. The four bandits continued with their seemingly unending banter. Their target would move around, sometimes one of us sometimes another. I envied them their easy friendship but my only natural ally in the group, the only other non-adventurer, was a more natural enemy and neither of us was prepared to let go of centuries of wrangling between Temple and Tower. Hazzor seemed content at the edge. Even Ranyl was more talkative, giving as-good-as-he-got in the ribbing that went round.

The spy, I now realised, had set a gentle pace (by his standards) and he gave me plenty of opportunities to stop and rest but still my knee became progressively more painful as the day wore on. On one such rest, I sat massaging the wretched joint, cursing all things arboreal. Hazzor stood impassively by and asked me how I did. I shrugged, and then felt it was surly. The man was due some acknowledgement of his consideration. I thanked him, awkwardly.

"Don't thank me for anything, Saahni. If necessary, we'll leave you behind, if this knee doesn't sort itself out soon." He turned his shoulders to include the rest and said, "Two more minutes."

Marvellous! It was good to know I was among cheerful company. I shook my head in puzzlement at the man and hurriedly re-bandaged the knee and got gracelessly to my feet.

By the end of the day, I was limping badly but still just about keeping up. While the others made camp in the lea of a lone oak, I flopped down and drew my beads from my pocket. The wizard, I noticed, was muttering to himself. I lit the candle with a surreptitious glance at Hazzor, shielding the flame with my hand as I prayed. I offered my day to my goddess, and found myself giving thanks for it. True, it had been hard but no one had actually hit me — a red letter day, lately — and I had enjoyed the repartee of the bandits. Abe had continued to be his usual overly familiar self but he had taken perhaps more than his fair share of being the brunt of the others' humour. Also, for once, I had little to upbraid myself for. There is little room for sin when all your thought goes into putting one foot in front of the other. I had, perhaps, been a little rude to Fryn'gh but, surely, he had been too provoking for words! The creature was so smug and convinced of his own rectitude. I prayed for his soul and, with more ardour, for the people I had left behind me. I prayed for Re'a to guide me through the days ahead. The grey skies above us were oppressive, so I prayed for a change in the weather.

Have I mentioned the old adage that Re'a punishes people by giving them what they have asked for?

That night, I dreamt of the temple again. Still Re'a was not there. Instead, I stood by the fallen bell and looked up at a blood red sky. Blood dripped down from the broken rafters and into my face. The more I tried to wipe it away, the more it fell but I could not move away, could not leave the beginning of my shame.

The blood was surprisingly cold.

I opened my eyes to see Axyl stoically trying to keep the fire going as rain fell through the branches of the tree in big heavy dollops. It was several hours before dawn so I tried to hide from the rain under my new cloak. I was torn between blessing Reath for providing me with a cloak of such thick wool and cursing him for putting me under this godforsaken tree at the wrong end of Ttaroc. Through the dense cloud cover it was hard to tell when Saen might approach, bringing with him the new day. I guessed earlier rather than later, and tried in vain to light my little candle. I spoke the words I was duty bound to offer but my heart was far from thankful, very far.

With difficulty, I got the wolf's heart bound around my knee without getting it, or the bandages, wet. I disappeared under my cloak, making it a kind of tent, though this left my back exposed to the rain. I sighed and stood wriggling my shoulders unhappily as I swung the cloak back round. *Blurgh!* I tested my gammy leg and found it uncertain, as if the leg was not sure whether or not it could take my weight. Otherwise, it was in surprisingly good form. I tried putting all my weight on it: not a good idea. I gasped and staggered, reeling.

The others were all shouldering their packs.

"When you've finished practising for a travelling tumbler, Saahni," remarked Hazzor with his usual charm, "you might want to roll up your mat before it floats away."

I swore and turned swiftly.

Stupid, stupid, stupid!

In the rain, they split my pack among them and Axyl, without a by-your-leave, threw me over his shoulder. Nobody said a word. I bit my lip in frustration. I felt twice the fool — for twisting the knee anew and for being slung over the barbarian's shoulder like an old sack. Three times the fool — for injuring myself in the first place. I wanted to howl like a baby and sulk. Instead, I had to strive for what little dignity and grace I could find, bottom in the air, while everyone else carried my things as well as their own.

We had been following a path that barely warranted the name — a raised point between fields along which beasts of burden had been led to their work in times of peace — which was rapidly turning into slurry. I could hear Fryn'gh cursing as he slipped and slid but Axyl, despite his size and load, thankfully never missed a step. None of the bandits did, from what I could see. Their only concession to the rain was that the banter was less frequent.

After a couple of hours of being bounced on Axyl's shoulder, the rain had soaked through my cloak and jerkin and started to drip down between my shoulder blades and run up my neck. As the rainwater curled round my jaw and started to fill my ears I beat my hands in the small of the giant's back.

"Axyl? Axyl, put me down, now!" I said to the wet wool that was starting to chafe my cheek. "I'm sure my leg is fine now?" I couldn't keep the uncertainty out of my voice, but I pushed on, "I'll walk, really, I'm fine."

Axyl said not a word but the wizard seemed to have the attention of the group as he, and everyone around him, started swearing. Not being able to see was vexing.

"What's going on?"

Hazzor dropped back to be level with me and said,

"Fryn'gh has managed not only to slip and fall, but to take Ranyl with him. If I were Fryn'gh I'd watch my back for a good while." There was a pause. "And what happens, Saahni, when you also slip in the mud?"

Ranyl was cursing up and down, and Fryn'gh was apologising, profusely, whilst at the same time managing to complain about the state of his trousers. Abe cheerfully reminded him it would have been worse had he been in skirts.

"Can I at least have this conversation the right way up?" I asked with some acerbity.

Axyl put me down and I, gingerly, tested the strength of my leg. My eyes were filled with the sight of an extremely muddy Fryn'gh. No misfortune, I thought, came unmixed. I smiled. He caught my eye and marched over to where Hazzor and I stood.

"This is foolish beyond measure," he huffed. "For how long are we all going to have to carry this perverse priest's effects?"

(*Perverse priest?* I almost swallowed my tongue in outrage. I avenged myself in my heart, watching the mage fidget as he tried to sort out the discomfort of his sodden trousers.)

Abe strolled over. How did such a man manage to stroll in this weather? He threw a friendly arm around the wizard.

"Ah, my sunny buck, I feel your frustration, I do, I really do." The rogue flashed his teeth about in a cheery smile, "But, in this weather, the little priest has no choice."

"*Little* priest?!"

Everyone, inevitably, ignored me. Hazzor simply asked,

"Do you have another solution, Fryn'gh?"

Fryn'gh nodded, vigorously.

"It's not my thing," he answered, "but I have some basic healing skills. A twisted knee should be no trouble." Hazzor opened his mouth to object but Fryn'gh continued, "I know, I know, she'll have to sleep it off, but it'd only be a very little work for her body to do — It's just reducing swelling — and you're carrying her anyway."

"Now wait a *minute!*"

The thought of magic working on my body was nauseating. Hazzor just measured me up and down with a calculating eye. I could not help but notice the other bandits, listening in, were also looking speculative.

"It'd be perfectly straightforward. Just a minor healing spell. The body knows what to do; I just have to accelerate it."

"No!" I looked around in vain for allies but found none. "It's ungodly! An abomination!"

Hazzor wiped the rain from his face. Fryn'gh pushed his case, may he rot in the Pit for all time,

"She'll only sleep for a couple of hours, I swear."

Hazzor nodded.

"Do it."

"No!" I was shouting and nearly crying, "No, I'll be fine!"

Please, I thought, please do not taint me with the vile touch of it. I stepped forward and grimaced. It hurt. I lied with a bright smile,

"See. Fine."

Fryn'gh stepped towards me and I thought I was going to be sick. I stepped sideways — right into Axyl who promptly wrapped his tree trunk arms around me. I decided my current strategy was not working so I tried a new tack. In a burst of originality I shouted,

"No!"

Fryn'gh smiled, patronisingly, and told me to relax. It was only a little magic, he said, nothing to make a fuss about. *Only a little magic? Might as well say 'only a little plague'.* The wizard crouched down to reach for my knee. I kicked him in the face. (Axyl helpfully taking the weight off my lame leg.) I had the brief satisfaction of seeing the mage sat on his rump in the mud again before there was a flash of movement in the corner of my eye. My jaw exploded and I fell into darkness.

Chapter 13

I woke rested, warm and dry, and very, very hungry. There was something niggling me, some memory of wrongness, but my mind was mostly gripped by the hunger in my belly. I opened my eyes and looked up at the thatch. It seemed a fair way off. I listened to the rain beating down. I had been punched again, I thought. This time, though, my jaw felt fine. My head felt fine. No aches, no pain. There was only the hollowness of my fast. Something smelt good. I surfaced some more and heard Hazzor speaking. He sounded annoyed, I thought idly.

"... a couple of hours? For how long is she going to sleep?"

"I don't know — I don't understand, Hazzor," said Fryn'gh. "It was just a twisted knee."

Fryn'gh. I seethed. *How dare he*? *How* dare *he*?!

Unusually, my anger was crowded out by gnawing hunger and the growing realisation that I was free from the aches and pains I had been carrying since Challawin had arrived in my village — oh, a lifetime ago. All those little nicks and scratches, the lingering stiffness in my neck, the bruised back and the tenderness that ought to be in my jaw. My head by rights — I knew from recent experience — ought to be doing a fair impression of Karl's anvil. And my leg.

Blessed Re'a, my leg felt wonderful! I luxuriated in the absence of pain for a moment until the emptiness in my stomach became its own pain.

I sat up and my eyes were filled with the sight of a pot of broth bubbling in the hearth. A fleeting thought wondered where we were, but the scent of broth almost shut down my reason and I scrambled over to the fire with unseemly haste. Without a word of greeting to my travelling companions, I simply asked, "Bowls?"

As soon as Thorn put a dish in my hand I dipped it into the pot and, without bothering to find a spoon, I lifted the bowl to my mouth and drank the broth, scalding lips and throat without regard. As soon as it was empty, I refilled and drank again, heedless of the mess dripping down my chin and wrists. Wordlessly, Ranyl handed me a hunk of bread and I tore into it ravenously. Fryn'gh cleared his throat.

"Did I mention she'd be hungry when she woke?"

I did not sleep well that night. Like the invalid that has slept all day, it took me hours to achieve so much as a doze. My bolted meal sat heavily in my stomach and my mind fretted over this new taint.

The ghosts of folk who had fled this home of theirs, for fear of the W'shten, seemed to linger around me. The place had clearly been looted by troops — chairs and dishes broken, cupboards open — but there was no real sign of violence. Hazzor had, apparently, decided the rain was making the cross country routes impassable with Fryn'gh and me in the party and difficult even for the others. He had moved to the roads and hoped the rain would help cloak us from sight. They had found the abandoned village and seized the opportunity to be dry and warm. I gathered that Fryn'gh had dried us all with his arts.

Magic! Amtil had always said that magic was a direct challenge to Farock Rha, a defiance of the precepts of Saen and a rejection of the healing of Re'a. She said the Dark Lord lurked behind all magic, and within all magic lay his snares. It was an abomination; a blight on the face of the earth. You only had to look at poor Princess Ttarah to see what it could do. Hapless thing still a child, and her beauty stolen from her by a malcontent of a mage. I sighed at the tragedy, for a moment, before returning to my own grievance.

I tossed and turned. What was magic? Had it passed through me — healed me and left — or was it now part of my healed body? I stared up at the thatch. Ah, but it felt good not to hurt anymore.

Another sigh gustily fled me, and I wished I could follow it.

Ranyl threw a boot at me and told me to shut up and lie still. I bit my lip and listened to the others breathing — a gruntling susurration behind the rhythm of the rain beating on the roof. *Re'a, saviour of the world, guide me.* I matched my breathing to that of my companions.

I must have slept, I think. Certainly my thoughts became disjointed in that fashion particular to the shadow-lands. When I woke, still foggy, it was with a taste of bitter dreams in my mouth. The morning was still dark but I was restless. Despite the rain I conceived the urge to get some fresh air, some time to myself. Never, since I had left my parents' home, had I spent so much time in any kind of group and, rain or no rain, I wanted some solitude.

I got up with all the stealth I had learnt sneaking past teachers to play truant, and reached the door in what I thought was silence. I inched the door open carefully and slunk outside. As I turned to close the door, I found a ghost was already in the space behind me. With a gasp, I started backwards into the rain and Hazzor stepped forward and closed the door behind him. I could almost hear his eyebrows rise as he waited in the dark for me to speak. For a moment, I considered playing him at his own game and smiled wryly at the thought. We both knew who would speak first.

"I'm just going for a walk."

"In the dark. On your own."

The bland statements dripped incredulity.

"In the dark, on my own, yes," I snapped.

Re'a wept, the man was infuriating!

"With W'shten all around." I shrugged and he continued, "Is there no part of this that's causing you concern?"

"There's no one here but us." I sighed, "I won't go far."

I looked round. The moon was bright enough to give some light through the clouds. Not much but enough for me to see something of the village around me in the dark before dawn.

"Look, the temple is just there. Let me say the hour in a temple and I'll come straight back."

Hazzor made a dismissive noise, something between a sigh and a 'tcha'. I thought I saw a shrug of his narrow shoulders as he opened the door again and disappeared, as though he had never been there. For a moment, I wondered if he had been only a ghost of my imaginings.

I set out towards the temple, glorying in stretching my legs and walking easily for the first time in some four days. Even given it was so early, the village was eerily quiet. There were no dogs, no horses, no early risers: the place was dead but for the rain that fell with unwearying persistence. There was, of course, no high place for Re'a in these flat fields but, with the usual discomfort that surrounds holy things, Re'a's house was at the edge of the village, a little distance from the houses. It stood, forlorn and empty. I sniffed. What was that smell?

Shaking away the oddity, I turned to the temple. I had a flash of déjà vu, pushing open a door that was already swinging on one hinge. Inside, the temple had been assaulted. It was my first clear view of how much the W'shten hate Re'a. The Statues of Intent had been attacked vigorously with — an axe, was it? Many of them were now headless and/or dismembered. All of them were scarred with hatchet marks. Most had been kicked over. It was like seeing an attack on the village itself. (Thoughts of what might have happened to my own neighbours rose up and leered at me. I pushed them away.) Re'a's statue was missing. They must have killed a dog or something and used the blood to paint slogans on the walls and splattered it about the room. The door to the priest's quarters had been kicked in but I did not go in; that was private space. The priest's broom, though, was lying near to where she must have left it. I cleared a space with it among the dust and wood chippings. The pricket stand was gone but, on a whim, I went back outside and up the stairs to the roof. There were her candles, buckets, rushes and all the bits and bobs that could not be kept in the sacred space, and that she did not want to keep in her rooms. I found some candle stubs and took them back down.

I looked around the chaos of the temple with the candles in my hand. How were the daughters of Re'a to fight such fierce opponents? We were horribly unprepared: Re'a taught only peace and acceptance.

Early one morning, when I was still a child, Amtil had been reflecting on Re'a's Holy Sacrifice and I had broken across her to say,

"Sahnithi, Hathil says all life is a battle. She says we have to fight just to stand still."

Actually, I had rebuked her as only a child on the cusp of adulthood can. She had destroyed a wasps' nest near her home with efficient ruthlessness and I had been outraged. She had puffed up like a retta fish and lectured me at length. We fought against everything, she said, against injury and disease, against lawlessness and even against one another. She had said even our birth was a battle and death very often was. She had said if Saen had wanted us to live in harmony, he should have made us differently. Naturally, I was keen to put this view to Amtil at my earliest opportunity.

Amtil had given me her victory smile. It was a smile she reserved for when she was confident she was unassailable. It was a kind smile, very loving, but also very smug.

"I remember, Kayt'an, when you were still very little, I heard you shouting in the night. I found you curled up at the foot of your bed, under the covers, struggling to be free. I peeled the covers from you and you launched yourself at me. What a state you were in! When you had calmed enough to talk to me, I asked you what the matter was and you said, Kayt'an — do you remember? — 'the bed was attacking me, Sahnithi, I couldn't get out'." I had remembered, and I had shifted uncomfortably. I felt silly now, but the fear had been real, then. "We are all lost, Kayt'an, and we all strike out at the world around us. We have lost sight of our light, lost our way, and in the darkness we have lost ourselves in fear. The answer, Kayt'an, is not to fight, but to fix our eyes on Saen."

"But, if we stare at the sun, we go blind."

I had felt a little smug myself. Amtil had tutted.

"How often, Kayt'an, have you flinched from the sunlight when I've opened the shutters in the morning?"

I remember rolling my eyes at this. Amtil continued,

"When we live in darkness, the sun does blind us. The bright light hurts our weakened eyes. The answer is not to shrink back into the darkness but to bare the pain as best we can. It will get easier."

"And wasp stings help me see the light," I had said, mockingly.

"Why should your comfort be more important than their life?"

I was not prepared to let it go that easily.

"Hathil knew of a woman who was killed by wasp stings."

Her throat had filled and she had died, wild eyed and frantic. The tale had not helped my charity towards wasps in general.

"I know a man who died in the closet. Should we close our bowels for fear of death?"

Amtil had shaken her head, knowingly.

"Death comes to all of us eventually, Kayt'an. It is senseless to run in fear of it."

She had come nearer and sat beside me.

"Kayt'an, daughter, Re'a loves us more than life, and Saen loves us because he loves her. Farock Rha has given all things into his hand. There is no need to worry. All will be well. We just have to learn to trust the gods for our protection, and walk with Re'a into death when our time comes."

I nodded to myself. Re'a had called me, made me her priest. I would trust her. I would trust Saen's providence.

That morning, I knelt among the ruined statues, closed my eyes and imagined I was home. I lit the candles and sang the hour like I had not since I had been saying the hour on my own.

When I stood up and turned to leave the place, I had a spring in my step that was not just down to the wizard's repair. Despite the destruction around me, I felt revived. I smiled and stepped around the door to the path outside.

Hazzor was waiting outside. I pulled a face of exaggerated disbelief, opening my eyes wide and tilting my head.

"It's barely dawn! Yes, I took a little longer, but I started early. Hazzor, really, I know you don't love Re'a but –"

"We've got a problem, Saahni."

"Oh."

I reviewed my immediate assumption, and conceded I had been harsh. I started to apologise but the spy carried right on.

"While you were praying," I could hear the effort he put into keeping the word neutral, "Ranyl went scouting. There's a trap waiting for us at the crossroads."

"A trap?" I had no idea how to make an intelligent contribution to this conversation but I did my best. "What kind of trap?"

Hazzor actually put his hands in the pockets of his long coat, and then produced his shrug.

"Woman, baby, broken cart," he said cryptically. "Disappointingly unimaginative, but we need to move carefully. Come."

I started to head back towards the house we had slept in. Automatically heading past Hazzor, back the way he had come. To my surprise, he grabbed my arm.

"Not that way," he said.

I shook my arm free.

"Don't be ridiculous, Hazzor. It makes no difference which way round I go."

Before he could argue or take action to stop me, I had skipped round the building. I smiled to myself. Funny, only a handful of days with a gammy leg, but I was finding every easy movement wonderful. I heard the spy curse behind me just before I saw why he had not wanted me to come this way round the temple.

I am familiar with corpses. Ever since childhood, I have helped lay them out for burial. Most have been simply sad; some have taken work to make them presentable for the Feast. I have stitched wounds closed and worked to give a semblance of peace to faces tense with their final pain.

Nothing could prepare me for this.

The priest had not run with the others. She must have stayed with her temple. The W'shten had found her. It had not been a dog they had killed to provide paint for their work. They had clearly taken their time with her, and then left her for scavengers. My eyes filled with colours that did not belong, with the terror in her one eye still showing. My nose and mouth clogged with the smell of blood and piss and rotting flesh. I made a move to straighten her limbs but the sight and smell of her, and my imagination, overwhelmed my reflexes and I turned and vomited.

Strong hands led me back out of sight of the corpse and I was handed a handkerchief, which I pressed to my mouth.

"Just once, Saahni, it would be nice if you did as I asked. Come."

I tried to stop retching long enough to protest but the best I could manage was a mewling noise like a sick cat. The soulless spy started to lead me away. I rallied my resistance. She should not be left in the street to rot. I managed a deep breath. (*By the Dark Lord's Wyrms, would that smell never leave my nose?*)

"We must bury her," I managed.

Hazzor stood square to me.

"I'm sorry, Saahni. We have not the time," he stopped my interjection with an impatient gesture, "and more importantly we can't risk it. The odds are strong they'll be watching the corpse. If we bury her they'll know someone's here and come looking."

I felt I should find a further objection. The nameless priest had not run from the W'shten. (*Yes,* said a voice deep within, *and see what happened to her.*) She was a sister priest. I should not abandon her ruined corpse. (The same voice drew pictures in my mind of what preparing that same corpse for burial might mean. My gut spasmed again.) Hazzor spoke more gently this time.

"Come, Saahni, we have problems of our own."

Chapter 14

So it was that I found myself, newly healed, newly revived, newly horrified, peering round the corner of an abandoned building, looking at a woman sat in the mud in the rain. She was holding some sort of bundle. I had thought it a baby but Abe was adamant it was not.

"If it's a baby, Sahnithi, pet, it's not well," he had whispered.

Thorn nodded.

"It has not moved nor has she paid it any mind in all the time we've been here," she said.

"But it's only just dawn." I looked between the two of them — two poised hawks, sharp and focused. "If it's a trap she must have been there all night?"

Neither of them answered, their attention was fixed on the woman and her cart. Even Axyl, whom I normally dismissed as big but harmless, even he had an air about him that made me eye him cautiously. Fryn'gh had lost his composure and was chewing his nails compulsively and muttering under his breath. I was far too pius to take pleasure in the swollen nose he sported — a legacy, I could only assume, of the kick I gave him — but a lesser person might have done. I smiled to myself. *Teach him to force himself on people.*

Only Hazzor seemed the same, in the light of the threat that apparently lurked in the road ahead of us. Self-contained and inscrutable, he was not even looking at the trap. He was waiting for Ranyl to return. I gave up looking for conversation or enlightenment, and composed my soul to patience.

At least my cloak was still keeping off the rain, but my calves were beginning to complain about remaining crouched for so long. I sighed. It would be so nice to be warm and safe and comfortable for more than half an hour at a time. I looked at the crops growing either side of the road and wondered who would harvest them.

Out of nowhere a hand closed over my mouth, muffling my strangled squawk as Ranyl spoke softly, just behind me.

"Two archers in the barn to the north there."

He released my face and I gave him a dirty look. Something distantly related to a smile crossed his dark face. Hazzor simply nodded.

"Did you leave them?"

"Of course."

The spy nodded again. Without taking his eyes off the cart, Abe said,

"Rush them?"

"They're too far."

"The priest and I can pin them down."

This last was Thorn. I blinked. What did she think I was capable of?

"We don't know what or who they've got hidden by the cart." The spy looked speculatively at Fryn'gh. "One mage is all they need to turn the tables on us."

"Shabby outfit like that's not going to have a mage," Ranyl sneered.

"Underestimating your opponent is becoming a habit, Ranyl."

"Can we go round them?"

Again, my contribution was ignored. I bit my lip with frustration but, for once, managed to exercise self-control and stay quiet, if a little sulky. Abe had now joined Hazzor, both of them looking at the wizard, intently.

"What we need, my lad, is a decoy."

"My thoughts exactly."

The next hour was fraught. Ranyl went back to kill the archers before they even knew he was there. Thorn and I took their place. When we saw Abe, Axyl and Ranyl leave the village, we fired at them. As Abe tripped and fell, the woman by the cart pulled a pair of blades out of the bundle she had been holding and started running towards Axyl followed by four others. Thorn had predicted, rightly, that we had the count of three to shoot at the five attacking bandits. The woman dropped but I still had not fired when the remaining bandits had reached Axyl and discovered he was an illusion. Thorn had time to fire again and, even through the murk, another fell, but then our own people were too close for another shot to be safe.

It took the real Abe and Axyl — with Hazzor — longer than they had hoped to intercept the wagon bandits. 'Our' bandits had been slow leaving for some reason, and the wagon bandits were faster than Abe had reckoned. They had changed direction, as Hazzor had feared, and started running towards the barn, heading for Thorn and me. I leaned out to see better but Thorn pulled me back with a hiss. Ranyl was out there somewhere, I knew, and we depended on him to cut off the foe before they reached us. My stomach was in knots. Two ambushers turned at the fence, to fend off Abe and the others, while the quicker continued to the barn.

Where was Ranyl?

Thorn bade me stay where I was and left our perch in the barn loft. I watched from the window while Abe, Axyl and Hazzor closed in on two of the bandits. The third disappeared into the village. I looked to see where the first bandit, the woman, should have been lying in the road. Should have been, but wasn't. My eyes widened, and I looked around for Thorn, who was no longer by my side.

I chewed my lip. It would be alright, I thought. Both Thorn and Ranyl were hunting Fleet Foot and, at the fence, it was three to two in our favour. I looked back out the window. The five bandits were fighting fiercely. I had yet to spot the woman. Where could she have got to? Thorn shot her! Surely? Did she not? I lent out of the window

and looked the pretend-mother in the eye.

"Re'a wept!"

I threw myself backwards and sat on the floor with my jaw hanging near my knees. *How*? I thought. Then, *What do I do*? The obvious answer was to pick up my bow again and shoot the woman — again. But, there was a world of difference between firing arrows at some figures in the distance and killing someone up close, someone whose eyes you can see.

She is going to kill me.

I shuffled backwards on my bottom. There was a small wake of straw gathering behind me. My breath was coming fast and shallow, and I thought my heart was going to climb out of my chest.

I may have whimpered a bit.

The window filled with the dreadful woman. Frozen in the moment, I found myself taking in each detail. Her skin was tanned, with brown eyes and hair, and a wide mouth. Those eyes were narrowed and her lips were drawn in pain. I sat and watched as she climbed through the window. Her skirts — a disguise, I supposed — were torn and sticking to her thigh where a dark stain surrounded the arrow shaft, which still protruded. The woman's stamina, I thought, watching her fight on despite her obvious pain, must have been considerable. I stared at the twin blades she drew from her belt. I admired them less.

She stared at the bodies of her comrades in the corner.

"You'll pay for that," she said, matter-of-factly. "Where are the rest of you?"

It occurred to me, belatedly, that I could have pushed her through the hatch.

"Re'a, Saviour of the world..." I muttered.

Why is my life more important than her life? I did not think I would have time to answer. She knelt and placed a blade to my throat. I reflected that my pain-free existence was not going to last even half a day. Although, of course, death is the end of all pain. I could feel hysteria rising.

"Where?" the bandit repeated.

I opened and shut my mouth a couple of times before managing to say,

"That wound'll go bad."

The pretend-mother frowned but she did not plunge her knife into my throat, so I continued,

"If you let me, I can remove the arrow and bind the wound."

I smiled reassuringly. I did not feel reassured. She did not look as though she needed reassurance.

In fact, she looked rather surprised.

As she fell to the floor Thorn said,

" 'If you let me, I can remove the arrow and bind the wound?' Saahni, what were you thinking?"

She wiped her knife on the dead woman and casually searched the body. Several blades of various types later, she slung her bow back on to her back and helped me to my feet.

"Let's go," she said.

Outside Ranyl was waiting.

"Job done," he said.

By the time we reached Abe and Axyl, the last bandit was lying in the mud.

"Shooting fish in a barrel," Ranyl smirked.

"Where's Hazzor?"

Thorn was looking round while Ranyl searched the dead bandit's corpse. Ranyl jerked his head back to where we had started.

"Gone to dig the mage out of his hiding place," he said with a sneer.

Having looted what he fancied from the fallen man, Ranyl set off with Thorn — limping slightly, I noticed with a frown — presumably to plunder the last body. My bag was back where we had spent the night.

"I'll go back and get my bag," I said. "Did anyone else leave their things there?" Abe looked at me pityingly.

"Saahnithi, darlin', never leave your bag behind."

I stomped off. 'Saahnithi, darling, never leave your bag behind,' I muttered. Patronising whey-faced heathen. I heard a shout behind me but took no notice. I was too busy complaining about sarcastic archers, ginger cowards, war-mongering kings, and anyone else I could think of to blame for anything. Not least on my list were be-whiskered spies who caused me to leave my bag behind. Be-whiskered spies, I reminded myself, who had probably killed my friends and neighbours. I kicked a stone and bit my lip as a wave of grief and anger threatened. I just wanted to go home, but I could not even find the house I'd slept in last night. I kicked another stone and scowled at myself. In the end, I retraced my steps to the temple, with a view to finding my way by tracking my nocturnal path back.

As I reached the temple, I paused in my recriminations for just a moment to touch the wall of the building. I rested my face against its cool surface and prayed for the priest lying on the other side. In my quiet, I heard horses — not many — and voices. At this distance, I could not hear the words but the rhythm was lilting, like Abe's. I swore. Two minutes peace — was it so much to ask for?

I ran back to the house, choosing speed over stealth. The door had been left open. I scuttled in, rolled up my bed with more haste than tidiness, and collected my bag. With my bow over one shoulder and a badly packed bag over the other, I scurried back through the empty streets to where I thought the others would be.

My route was not direct but it was better than the journey out — urgency focusing my mind, thank Re'a, rather than muddling it in panic. I found the others gathered behind the wall from which, earlier, we had watched the woman and her cart. Fryn'gh stood a little aside looking sick. Abe, Thorn and Hazzor were huddled together and Axyl and Ranyl were clearly looking for me. Ranyl saw me first.

"Where in the bloody balls have you been?"

I blinked and wondered whether to point out that his question made no real sense. I took in his pale face, with an expression grimmer than usual, matched by Axyl's worried frown. Then, I saw that Abe and Thorn were not huddled *with* Hazzor, but *over* him.

"W'shten," I simply said, feeling *déjà vu* with an

horrible sense of ill-boding, "I think," I clarified. "I heard horses and voices beyond the temple."

Ranyl nearly exploded.

"What in the nine hells were you doing at the temple? Haenid's tits, woman!"

"Saahni," I said, reflexively, but with little conviction in the face of Ranyl's rage.

Ranyl took an angry step towards me and I backed off rapidly.

"I was lost," I said, plaintively.

I could hear Hazzor swearing fluently.

"Reath must be mad," Ranyl continued, "to saddle us with two of the most useless scuts in Ttaroc!"

Despite Ranyl's anger, I found myself paying more attention to Hazzor. His voice sounded strained and neither Abernast nor Thorn had taken their eyes off him in all the time I had been there. Neither had I had any silly comments from the eternally quipping W'shten.

"What's wrong with Hazzor?" I asked.

By way of answer, Abe moved aside. A small part of my mind regarded his grey face and the blood on his hands and cuffs. I was already moving in to help before I had fully taken in Hazzor's pallor and the wound in his side. Someone had undone his coat and torn the spy's shirt to plug the wound but the cloth was already red and there was a scarlet trail running down to his belt.

"Re'a's blood!"

My bag was off my shoulder even as I knelt down beside the bleeding man.

"What happened?"

"Fryn'gh stabbed him."

These were Thorn's first words since I had arrived.

"What?!"

I turned to look at the outcast wizard. He was positively green. He ran his hands through his sheep's fleece and looked at me helplessly.

"I didn't mean to."

I believed him. He looked awful, though not, of course, as bad as Hazzor. Heedless of the rain, I started pulling apart my pack to get to my bandages, which I had stupidly put at the bottom. *Fool! Fool! Daughter of a fool!* I knelt in the mud and started to clean the cut, the rain doing most of my work for me.

"Stupid fish-brain was hiding behind that barrel. Thought Hazzor was one of our friends over there and lashed out before he looked." Thorn snorted. "Heaven help us, what with one offering to mend the enemy and the other stabbing our own people, we're never going to make it in one piece."

I flushed even as I concentrated on the damage done to the little spy — there was nothing to him, lying helpless in the mud.

Abe put a hand on my shoulder,

"Wait up, little priest, did you say W'shten?"

Hazzor's injury had pushed them from my mind but the picture of my battered sister flashed before me, and I looked up anxiously.

"I heard them," I said, "on the other side of the village."

At a gesture from Abe, the wiry thief was gone.

"We have to move him," I said, not needing to clarify who.

It was Axyl who suggested the barn, on the basis that it was easiest to defend and hard to burn us out in this weather. It was also him who picked up the fallen spy, as gently as a mother gathering up her infant, but still the wounded man stifled a cry of pain. Ranyl was back before we moved and confirmed the presence of half a dozen mounted W'shten scouting through the village. He thought they were a small raiding party, sent to harry any corners of resistance. He figured they were also just looking for shelter.

"But, if they choose the same house," he warned, "or find our dead friends, they can't help but know that we're here and we're armed."

Chapter 15

We slunk back to the barn, and on the way I discovered that this was, apparently, H'th Iriq — a village so close to the border that it had been variously Ga'ared, Ttarcine and W'shten. Unfortunately for them they were currently Ttarcine.

Axyl and Abe pulled the dead bandits up from the street into the barn loft, and closed the hatch after us. Ranyl left us to tidy up as best we could without alerting the W'shten. Fryn'gh had dried off the others but I had refused, remaining righteously damp. By the time Hazzor had been laid out for me to work on, he had fainted. I cleaned and stitched and bandaged as best I could, anointing the gash with Hathil's finest concoctions.

Frowning and tight lipped, the pale outlander joined me.

"Well?" he asked.

I looked up and nodded with desperate optimism.

"It's a clean cut and there's nothing essential damaged but," I paused and wiped my forehead anxiously.

"But he needs rest."

I nodded.

"What about you?" I asked, tentatively, and then when Abe only shrugged, "I am supposed to be the healer, you know."

With a waggled eyebrow and an innuendo, the W'shten submitted to my ministrations. He had several bruises, which I anointed with lavender, and a long, thin wound down his arm that I poked, and decided could be cleaned and left.

Ranyl joined us and I turned to him.

"I need to bind that ankle."

The little thief actually looked surprised.

"How do you know it's my ankle?"

"You'd be moving differently if it were your knee or hip."

He pulled a face and sat to remove his boot.

"They shouldn't find the bodies," he said, "as long as they're not actually looking — but I couldn't get to the house." He shook his head. "They'll almost certainly know we've been here, it's just a matter of how hard they search."

The bandits exchanged looks. Unusually, it was Axyl who spoke first.

"I say we don't wait for them to start looking."

Ranyl flashed his yellow teeth. It was more like a dog baring his fangs than a smile.

"Nothing like stabbing a man in the back for making sure he never sees you."

I finished anointing and bandaging Ranyl's ankle and then wrapped my arms around my waist. Fryn'gh too, I could see, was wide eyed and white knuckled, watching four killers. For that was what they were, I thought. Gone were the easy, jocular adventurers. Here stood four people whose standard answer to a problem was to dispatch it.

"Can't we just hide?" I whispered.

Once again I was ignored. I tried again, louder

"We can't just kill everyone who threatens us."

"Sssh," Abe dismissed me. "Ranyl?"

Ranyl, now booted and standing once more, tested his ankle and grinned like a fox.

"I'll need the mage. And Thorn, she's quiet."

Thorn nodded but the mage jumped up from where he had been crouched in the corner.

"Me? No!" he squawked.

Almost without appearing to move, the dark man had crossed the loft and had a thin dagger pressed against the wizard's throat. I found it in me to be sorry for him as Ranyl whispered softly in his ear. Fryn'gh licked his lips repeatedly while he listened and when the thief had finished, the mage nodded carefully. Ranyl's mouth curled slightly at one corner and he put the knife away.

"Re'a, have mercy," I whispered.

"I doubt it." Hazzor was awake. "Abe," he called, faintly, and when the big man turned in answer, "we need to talk."

"Later, buck," was the reply, with a brief flash of teeth. "Ready?" he asked the assassination party, who all nodded with varying degrees of enthusiasm. "Right then, I'll keep watch downstairs. Axyl, you babysit the priest. Saahni?" I looked up into eyes like flint. "If that man dies I'll tie you up for the W'shten to find."

Which was unfair, I thought, seeing as I had done my best *and* it was not me who had stabbed him in the first place. I crossed my arms sullenly and raised an eyebrow, in what I hoped was a sarcastic manner, as the bandits trouped out, bearing the wizard with them. I was left with Hazzor and Axyl — neither of whom were chatty — and a pile of, thankfully, silent corpses.

I made a pillow for the spy and got him as comfortable as I could. I wanted to make up a tincture for him but there was nowhere to light a fire. The fire would have helped fend off the chills, too, which often follow an injury like his. I bit my lip and looked at the dead bandits in the corner. They were going to be a problem, too. Even if the others did succeed in killing these W'shten outriders, there would be others. As long as we were hidden here, we could not afford to leave corpses lying around to be found but neither could we share a room with them for long. I sighed. We could not afford to move Hazzor either.

Chewing my lip some more, I covered Reath's agent with my cloak.

"I'm not an invalid, Saahni."

"Yes you are. Here," I said reaching into my bag, "chew on this."

"What is it?"

"It's a mild narcotic."

The spy made his strange snorty cough and pushed the root away.

"Put it away, I need my wits about me."

"It'll ease the pain."

"Pain is good. It tells you you're still alive." I just tutted. "What's that you're doing?" he asked.

"I'm crushing some gentian bark."

"What for?"

I raised my eyebrows.

"Surely you should be conserving your strength, not interrogating me."

Hazzor frowned,

"What's it *for*?"

I tsked.

"It keeps the wound clean."

"But you've cleaned the cut. Dammit, you were poking around long enough!"

"Will you stop second guessing me!" He completely failed to look apologetic. "Without a fire to brew this, I need to crush it and it'll take me ages. I might as well prepare it now."

I sighed again. The spy stared at the ceiling.

"Abernast knows he's going to have to leave me here. It might take a day or two before he acts on it but I know I can't travel, and you don't have time to wait for me to be well enough."

"You'll die."

"Everyone dies."

I tucked the cloak around him again to save having to answer. He closed his eyes and I moved away to avoid disturbing him. I certainly did not move because he had disturbed me — of course not! A wall provided a convenient prop while I listened for the others. All I heard was the sound of rain. My legs decided they had done enough, for a while, so I sank to the floor and hugged my knees, staring at the sleeping man. Lost in thought, I chewed my lip.

It occurred to me that while he probably did not count me as his friend, I was beginning to count him as mine. Unreasonably, I was starting to divide him in my mind. I was hiving off the man who had killed my kith and kin so coldly, as if that were a stranger, another Hazzor I did not know. Bloody-minded and ruthless, this man, *this* Hazzor had been a constant and stable companion while all else fell apart around me. I had come to depend on him. Also, while I did not know what Reath had planned — and this increasingly nagged at me — I was confident that he had not sent Hazzor simply because the little spy had nothing better to do. Losing him would surely materially damage the chances of us achieving Reath's goal.

Reath, what have you planned for us? This journey had happened to me: choosing me, rather than

I, it. It was, perhaps, a chance to stop the war, to save lives — save temples too. (The dead priest flashed again before my mind.) If I had had a true choice, would I have come? Would I have risked so much, of my own will, for an unknown goal?

I prodded an idea. Did the end *ever* justify the means? Reath clearly thought if the end was important enough it justified any means. I thought of my destroyed village, and closed my eyes for a moment. Who got to say which was the greater good? The blessed Re'a believed the lives and the sanctity of the human race were worth her own. But ours was not self-sacrifice. *We* were sacrificed by Reath to save a lie. I thought of the bandits killed because they threatened our life, and of the W'shten, hunted even as I sat. *Who are we to think our lives more valuable than another's*?

I stared at Hazzor. It came down to this. If I could not get him mobile, he would die and I really did not want him to die. What means were justified by his life?

I thought about the mage. If we boosted Hazzor's healing with magic, we might save his life. My lip was getting sore. I grabbed a braid and chewed that instead. It had been years since I had last resorted to chewing my hair.

Magic was wrong. Undoubtedly, it was. It denied Saen's sovereignty. But, I told myself, Fryn'gh has already set out irrevocably on that path, I would never convince him that his life's ambition was dust and ashes. What, then, was lost if I asked him to perform magic? Was my spiritual integrity more important than Hazzor's life?

I laughed out loud. Axyl turned his head, surprised, but I took no notice. *My spiritual integrity* — because I was doing so well at spiritual purity, wasn't I? I shook my head, laughing again, bitterly.

"You alright, Saahni?" asked Axyl, clearly worried that I was beginning to lose what fragile grip on sanity I still had.

In amongst the pride and anger, cowardice and doubt, encouraging an established mage to use magic on a man who had no objection to magic was barely any kind of sin, I thought, let alone one to give me any concern.

Then I remembered that Ranyl had dragged the said mage off to kill W'shten. I groaned and dropped my head onto my knees.

Axyl nodded.

"I'm hungry too."

I waited anxiously for the others to return. The rain was keeping most of the likely insects away from the dead bodies in the corner but it would not be long in this weather before we would be able to smell them. I was very worried about contagion.

I had said the midday hour and Saen was well past his zenith by the time I heard voices below. Casting a glance at the impassive Axyl, I crawled over to the hatch and peered down at the returning members of our team. Ranyl was looking darkly satisfied, Thorn and Abe, sharp and dangerous, and the mage was yet decidedly green about the gills. For a moment, I was worried — perhaps he *was* ill. Then, he looked up and saw me. He squared his shoulders and lifted his chin. I smiled, disparagingly. If he was still worried about what I thought, he was merely having a bad day. I thought of Hazzor behind me.

A very bad day.

Axyl leaned over the hole.

"Any luck?"

Ranyl gave a fierce grin, closer to a snarl.

"He almost looks feral," I muttered.

Axyl pulled me from the ladder and held me back for a moment.

"Hear me, Kayt'an Sahn. Ranyl's a dangerous man. There's something missing," he tapped his temple, "here. Your life, your death," he shook his head, "it's all one to him. They say he slit the throat of his own sister's son to prove a point. He's not right. Never forget it."

I don't think, in all my time with Abe's bandits, I have ever heard Axyl say even half as many words before or since.

I waited for the three bandits to climb up into the loft before I scrambled down, muttering to Thorn something about a call of nature. As I reached the ground, I heard Abe talking about his 'natural call' and scowled. I grabbed the wizard's arm.

"We need to talk."

I could taste bile at the prospect. Fryn'gh raised an eyebrow and tried to look superior.

"Well, *Saahni*?"

I realised I had left my cloak upstairs with the spy and looked doubtfully out at the rain.

"Next door," I said.

The rain had eased again to a drizzle so I was only slightly wetter when I got to the shed beside the barn. The mage followed more slowly and pointedly dried himself. I felt the hairs on the back of my neck stand up at the proximity of his magic. There was not a lot of room. There were broken barrels and boxes scattered willy-nilly: a picture of vandalism. I sat on a box that had escaped and looked at my hands, not wanting to look Fryn'gh in the eye. I had no doubt he was pulling a supercilious face. Pish! I smoothed out the wet woollen skirt and considered how to begin. Really, I had had plenty of time to think about this. I bit my lip anew. The wizard ran out of patience.

"Well?" he said again.

I plunged in.

"Hazzor is going to die."

I looked up. To my surprise, the mage looked horrified. Clearly, he had had no idea. I outlined Hazzor's prediction that we would have to leave him. I did not need to explain the rest. His stubble was showing red against his pale face.

"What would you have me do, Saahni?"

He placed the emphasis on 'you'. He surely could not guess what I was about to ask of him.

"You can heal him."

The mage looked at me as though I had grown a second head.

"Are you out of your sanctimonious little mind?"

"Sanctimonious?" I answered, outraged. "You hypocritical puffed up bag of wind! Don't think I haven't noticed you looking down your nose at me!"

"Really, priest? I wasn't aware you noticed anything not written in your precious book of lies and fairy tales."

The conversation descended, from this point, for a good five minutes while we traded insults. Neither of us realised how loud we had become. Not until the door of our shed opened, suddenly.

As one the pair of us turned to face the intruder, wide-eyed and grey-faced. We both had to look up to the face of the armed warrior standing there. His eyebrows rose steadily as he observed us there. United now in discomfiture, the mage and I stood like naughty children and waited for the drubbing that was predicted in the barbarian's face.

"Do you want us all killed?" We both shook our heads. "Maybe you've both had enough of life?" Again we shook our heads, dolefully. Axyl nodded slowly. "Well then." He sniffed. "Abe wants you, Saahni."

I nodded, chastened, but I delayed.

"Just a minute," I said.

Axyl looked at us both through narrowed eyes.

"No more shouting," he said, just in case he had not been clear, I suppose, and then left.

Fryn'gh also made to leave, but again I caught his arm.

"Wait, wizard."

The ungodly creature rolled his eyes.

"I'm a mage, not a wizard."

I looked at him blankly.

"Do I care?" I answered. "No wait," I said hurriedly as the irate wiz — mage — turned away. "Look," I was talking quickly now. "Even with the best healer in the land Hazzor is going to die if we leave him and he can't possibly travel."

"So you say, Saahni, but even if he let me try, I don't have the skills to heal him. I can make him look better, but that's the best I can do."

I released him and stepped back a pace.

"But you can do some healing — you healed me."

"Aye, and you know how much sleep and food you needed. If I tried to heal Hazzor, I'd kill him. His body would eat itself to try and find the energy it needed."

I nodded.

"But, what if you healed him a little bit? Enough to stop the blood loss if he's moved?"

Fryngh turned and looked thoughtful. Then he shook his head.

"It wouldn't work," he said, "I just don't know enough. If I overshot... I'm not even sure I *can* just heal only a little bit."

"What if I told you exactly what the wound

needed to look like? Could you do it then?"

"Honestly, Saahni, I just don't know." The mage looked worried. "Nine hells, priest, I've nearly killed him as it is, and I don't want to finish the job."

Tentatively, I touched his arm. "There is a difference between an act of fear and an act of hope — regardless of the outcome." Stupidly I could not resist adding, "Re'a sees the secrets of all our hearts — "

"Give me strength!"

Fryn'gh stormed out of the shed. I was left once again to contemplate my own folly.

Chapter 16

The rest of that afternoon was miserable. I was cold and wet, and it was no comfort to know that both were entirely due to my own stubbornness. I had relinquished my cloak in a fit of compassion that I now regretted, but I could not take it back. The others were all dry but, despite my attempt to make the mage use his magic on Hazzor, I was damned if I was going to benefit from the loathsome stuff merely for my own comfort. So, I sat cold and wet, chewing gentian bark in the hope that even unprepared it would keep the chills at bay. Given my luck this tennight, it would probably poison me.

For no very good reason that I could see, I was now expected to keep a constant watch on Hazzor (it was not as if he was going anywhere). Ranyl, on the other hand, kept flitting in and out like a fidgety ghost. Thorn had left to find some rabbits or some such and I was worried about how long she was taking. When I said something to Abe, he said something facetious about missing her too. He was unusually quiet, though, which worried me as well. Nobody was saying anything very much and the silence was not a comfortable one.

I had already checked the spy's wound and found it beautifully clean, for which I gave myself a pat on the back, but it was a nasty cut, narrowly missing his vitals, and there was still a strong risk the wound would become poisoned — especially with those accursed corpses in the corner. I decided to tackle Abe on this.

"Can we not move them?" I asked, nodding towards the bodies.

"Ah Sahnithi, my darling', I didn't think a healer of your qualities would be squeamish," was the reply.

I pursed my lips.

"It's not about whether I'm squeamish but about whether they'll produce poisonous odours. I really can't see that it'll make any difference if they're, say, in that shed beside us. If the W'shten get that close, they're bound to find us anyway."

The big outlander narrowed his eyes thoughtfully, and then smiled, "And are you going to help us move the bodies then, love?"

I glared ... and then smiled as sweetly as I knew how.

"Naturally I'd love to help, but it's dangerous to touch dead bodies and then live wounds."

"Dangerous?"

"Death spreads," I said simply. "An open wound is vulnerable to it."

"Well then," said Abernast, "it's just the three of us."

"What?" Fryn'gh looked startled.

"He's too used to wearing skirts."

I blinked. It wasn't like Axyl to be spiteful. Abe caught my surprise.

"Don't mind him, Sahnithi, sugar, Axyl likes to be in a fight or not in a fight. He doesn't like all this sneaking around."

The barbarian grunted. Abe stood up from where he had been crouched and thumped the mage on the back so that the young man nearly fell.

"Come, my young buck, we'll be done before you know it."

I sat cross-legged in my own little puddle and rested my head on my hands, with a frown. Awake now, Hazzor smiled weakly.

"You're wasting your concern, you know, Saahni."

"I know, I know, you're going to die anyway," I snapped. "Doesn't mean I have to like it."

"Your solicitude is touching."

I pulled a face and added,

"Besides, I've not given up yet."

All I had to do was get the blasted, godforsaken mage to agree to my plan. Who would have thought it would be so difficult to get a magic user to use magic? More for the sake of talking than anything, I voiced my problem.

"I need Fryn'gh to help me but he won't listen to me."

"Imagine that." I looked a question so he went on, "The mage won't listen to the priest who won't even accept a simple drying spell from him."

A thought stuck me and I lifted up my head.

"What if you asked him instead?"

The spy shifted and grunted with the discomfort of it. I moved to make him easy but he batted me away, hissing with the pain of the movement.

"Mother of the Blessed Lady, but you're stubborn!"

Hazzor did not answer but simply raised an eyebrow. I dug my fingers into my braids and tried again.

"Could you not ask him, Hazzor? He'd have to listen to you?"

That was the strategy he had used on me, after all. I had not forgiven the mage for forcing that healing on me. Perhaps this was payback.

("Vengeance is no solution, Kayt'an," my memory heard my teacher say. "It only turns the wheel anew."

Bah! I thought. Amtil Sahn had lived her whole life in Harset. What did she know of vengeance?)

I turned to the spy.

"Hazzor?"

"Tell me what you want me to ask, first."

"I want him to use his healing spell – "

"No."

That's what I'd said, but had anyone listened to me?

("Behave to others as you would have them behave to you, Kayt'an," Amtil had said.

Well, I thought, *I've already been done to. The standard has been set*.)

" — just a little, just to take you past the danger, so we can move you."

"Saahni, healing a strained knee left you unconscious for a day and famished when you woke. He'll kill me."

"You're going to die anyway," I threw back at him. "What have you got to lose? Anyway, he didn't just heal my knee, it was every bump and graze I'd picked up since your friend Reath," I fought to keep my voice neutral, "arrived in my village." Hazzor didn't answer. "I'm hoping I can guide him; explain to him when to stop."

"And just what do you know about helping a mage? Or about magic at all?"

"Hazzor, will you not give it a try? What have you got to lose?" I repeated. Then, unable to help myself I added, "The Readers tell us it is a grave sin to give up on life. It rejects Saen's great gift."

Hazzor snorted, and hissed again as the sudden movement of his diaphragm pulled at his wound.

"That was why Re'a killed herself, was it?"

I tutted.

"She didn't kill herself, she laid down her life. It's not the same. One is an act of despair; hers was an act of trust. She loved Saen and would give anything — "

"Alright! Haenid's tits, priest — "

"Saahni."

" — if it's a choice between talking to the mage or being sermonised by you, I'll talk to the mage."

He closed his eyes, ending the conversation. I put my head back in my hands and waited for the others to get back.

⊛

They were not long. I heard them talking long before they came upstairs. Thorn had met Ranyl on her way back with a brace of rabbits and a couple of pigeons. She had skinned and plucked them away from the village (that's what had kept her so long), and Ranyl was interrogating her to be sure she had hidden the remains well enough. It was Abe who had cut him short, asking the thief if he thought he, Abe, was in the habit of working with people who did not know what to do with a corpse of any sort. Ranyl had come back with a remark about people who could not decide where to leave their corpses.

Fryn'gh clearly decided to leave them to it and came up ahead. His hood must have come down while he was struggling with the bandit woman's body and his red curls were plastered to his skull. It made him look... almost vulnerable.

I, however, was ruthless. Seeing him come up alone, I crawled forward and tapped Hazzor on the shoulder. He opened pain-filled eyes, which he masked as soon as he saw me looking.

"Hello, Fryn'gh," I said pointedly.

The mage looked at me, surprised no doubt by my courtesy.

"Hello," he answered.

"*Saanhi,*" I supplied.

Not surprisingly he took no notice. I caught my patient's eye and raised an eyebrow. The spy sighed.

"Fryn'gh, the priest seems to think you and she, between you, can heal me," Hazzor slid his glance my way, "a bit."

The mage shook his head, impatiently.

"The priest isn't used to having to deal with reality. I've told her I can't do it but she won't listen."

So, we were talking about people in the third person were we? Well,

"The *wizard,*" I got a childish amount of pleasure in watching Fryn'gh twitch. I spoke again, before he could tell me again he wasn't one, "isn't used to taking risks for other people. The *wizard,*" oh boy, this was fun, "thinks he can define the world himself and knows no other power. The *wizard,*"

"*I am not a wizard!* You self-satisfied — "

"*Self-satisfied*? You *dare* to call *me* 'self-satisfied'? H'thetin *himself* would be considered self-aware next to you! I — "

I was not standing on the ground any more. Before I could identify the reason, beyond a certain tightness behind my shoulders, I was being shaken like a rattle. I bit my tongue and my mouth filled with blood. Just as I was convinced my head was about to leave my body altogether, I was dropped unceremoniously in a heap. Axyl turned his attentions to Fryn'gh who backed away.

"Oh no, sunshine, fair's fair."

My head was spinning. When did Abe come up here? However it was, Abe was now behind the mage — who found himself between a W'shten and a hard place. Axyl picked him up and applied the same treatment.

"Now, children, if you can't have a conversation without shouting I am going to have to cut out your tongues."

I blinked repeatedly to focus but, somehow, I doubted the pale bandit was joking. Those teeth were looking decidedly fierce. Axyl picked me up again like an old rag doll, holding Fryn'gh in the other hand. He brought us face to face.

"Say sorry, children."

Abe sounded revoltingly patronising and even in my dazed state, I could see the amusement on Hazzor's face. Thorn was too far across the room for me to focus on. I was livid — or at least as cross as it is possible to be with a bruised brain — and my tongue hurt, did I mention that? I spat blood. Axyl gave me another token shake.

"Thorry," I said, reluctantly.

"Sorry," said the godless red-head, sulkily.

"Thaahni," I added.

With one last assault, we were both dropped on the ground together.

"Now you children play nice while the grown-ups talk."

Oh now Thorn was playing too. Splendid.

"This is your fault," Fryn'gh hissed at me.

"*My* fault? You –" we both looked sideways at the four bandits who were still watching.

The mage sighed and said quietly, "Look if I try this, you will *owe* me."

"I will *owe* you?" The man constantly astounded me. "I will owe *you* for helping you thave the life of the man *you* thtabbed?"

I felt a little guilty, leaning on his guilt, but not much. My tongue really hurt. I stuck it out a bit, not as an insult, just to see if it still worked. I glanced up at the mage, belatedly realising he might have been offended, but his gaze looked inward.

"When I stabbed Hazzor, it was in alien circumstances with a weapon I'm not trained to use. I've never been in a fight before. I feel stupid and guilty but... If I kill Hazzor with magic, it'll be my *fault*. It's what I do. It's who I am. I can't afford to fail at it. Not here."

I looked at Fryn'gh with new eyes. We were both struggling to swim in strange waters. I looked over at the others — and they were the *others*. Thorn, Abe, Ranyl, Axyl and Hazzor were talking together. They were in their element, even Hazzor, wounded as he was. It was Fryn'gh and I who were struggling to keep up, in every sense. I leaned forward and tentatively touched his hand.

"Then let me pray for you first." When he reared like a startled foal, I added, "It's who *I* am."

The mage snorted and then to my great surprise nodded.

"But you'll owe me," he repeated. "I'll trust you this time, *Saahni*, but next time it'll be your turn to trust me."

I hesitated. Much later, when I looked back, I realised that even then he knew what he was going to ask of me. Perhaps at some level I guessed. The thought of having a debt of this order with a creature of magic felt tantamount to being indebted to the Dark Lord himself. What might he demand? I looked at the glove that hid the mark of my priesthood. Sacrifice or compromise? I looked at the wounded spy. He was exhausted, I could tell, but the stupid stubborn fool would chew his own arm off rather than admit it.

I nodded. I would pick up the pieces later.

"I'll go and say my prayers, then."

Chapter 17

It was a little while before I left the barn. First, Thorn insisted everyone ate, since she had caught and cooked the food. I had rubbed some therith juice on my tongue, but chewing was still tricky. I had perhaps managed ten hours both conscious and without any pain. I gave Axyl some fairly pointed looks but to no effect.

After we had eaten, I declared my intention to go to the temple and pray. Fryn'gh was studiously indifferent, but the four bandits looked at me like I had grown a second head. Fortunately, Hazzor was asleep. I doubted my ability to face him down. Abe tried charm.

"Sahnithi, love, much as I honour your religious sensibilities, the temple is a dangerous place for you to go. I'd hate to see what my compatriots would do to your pretty face if — when — they find you."

I could not help but see again the face of the priest who had minded the temple. I tried not to let the memory show.

"I'm more concerned about what they'll do to *my* pretty face after they've tortured you and found out where we are." Ranyl muttered.

"Hun'," Thorn answered him, "I doubt anyone'd notice."

"I'll be fine," I said. "I can hide if they come near."

"Sweetheart, last time you went to pray on your own, you didn't notice us until I had a blade at your throat."

"They didn't find me this morning."

"Saahni, that was chance, not skill."

I lifted my chin and answered Thorn,

"Or Re'a's grace."

The mage snorted.

Abe tried another tack.

"Well, Sahnithi, sugar, I'll grant you we're not going anywhere in a hurry. We'll stay right quiet and you can light your little candle here."

He smiled. I can only assume he believed it to be a winning smile. I composed my features into determination. (Hathil would have called it my mulish look.)

Thorn turned on the mage.

"Is this your doing? Are you *trying* to get the priest killed?"

"Tempting," answered Fryn'gh, "but no. Kayt'an *Sahn* and I have a ... plan. The priest thinks we need all the help we can get."

"A plan."

Thorn raised her eyebrows. Fryn'gh and I exchanged looks: both of us, I think, disconcerted to be allies and neither one of us happy about it.

Hazzor spoke before anyone realised he was awake.

"They plan to pool their expertise to try and heal me enough that I can travel."

His voice was worryingly weak. I went to check his face for fever, but again the dratted man batted my hand away, panting at the effort.

"Hazzor, you should rest," I told him.

This time it was he who tutted me. He took another breath.

"Send Ranyl with her."

He closed his eyes again.

"Damn," muttered Ranyl, "if Hazz's getting religion he must be close to death."

"Shhh!" Half the company hissed him quiet.

The little man shrugged.

"Just saying."

Abe wiped his mouth on the back of his hand.

"I don't like it."

"I'll be fine." I said with all the confidence I could muster. "If Re'a wills — " I lost eye contact with all of them. I tried another approach. "If we don't try to heal Hazzor, we'll have to leave him behind. If we leave him behind, our chances of completing this mission are miserable." Abe gave a grudging gesture of assent. "If I'm to work with," I didn't quite manage to keep the scorn out of my voice, "Fryn'gh, I must ask Re'a's blessing. When we are so near a temple I'm not doing it here. I have to give my all if I expect ..."

I did not know how to finish the sentence. What did I expect? That she would only listen if I went to her temple? That she needed a sacrifice of some sort before she would hear me? Perhaps it was I that needed the sacrifice to feel I was fit to approach her? I left the sentence hanging and finished instead,

"What have we got to lose?"

"Six lives," answered Axyl simply.

"Seven," Thorn corrected.

We all looked at Hazzor, whiter now than Abe.

"What the hell," Ranyl said. He pulled out one of his daggers and spun it on his thumb. "I can't stand being cooped up here anyway." He tossed the dagger and caught it. "I'm in." His brown eyes met mine. "But you owe me, priest."

"Saahni," I muttered, automatically.

The thief's thin mouth curled slightly.

"Saahni," he said.

I pushed my fingers into my braids. I already owed the mage, by his reckoning. Comparatively, a debt to a thief was nothing to worry about. I nodded.

"Fine."

The thief spat into his palm and held it out to me. I stared at the hand. The fingers were small but fine. There was a thin white scar running from his thumb to his palm. A globule of spittle lay in the centre of the palm, a trail leading to the blackened thumb. I looked back up into the thief's narrow face.

"He's waiting for you to shake it," Thorn pointed out.

"With what?"

Ranyl actually smiled.

I was wiping my hand on my skirt most of the way across the village. Thorn had retrieved my cloak, replacing it with her dry cloak, which was probably better for Hazzor anyway. The rain had picked up again and the light was starting to fade. Without Ranyl I do not know how long it would have taken me to find my way back to the temple, but Ranyl picked his way through the houses without hesitation. He moved like a shadow, making not a sound as he travelled. I was left with the fixed impression I was only able to follow him because he was making an effort to remember I was there.

As we neared the other edge of the village, he did start to disappear, returning, I think, only to check I was still heading the right way. Each time he appeared from nowhere I gave a little squawk. Each time, he gave a chuckle before vanishing again.

When we reached the temple, I remembered to take the deasil route around the building, puzzling Ranyl. I did not explain, figuring the first thing he would do, once he had left me, would be to circuit the building. He would find the dead priest soon enough.

Once again, I stepped through the broken door into the ruined temple. The candles were where I had left them. I walked among the broken statues, and tried not to think about the blood daubing the walls. At some point Ranyl left, but I did not notice. The space I had swept that morning was still clear and I stepped into it. For some reason my mouth was dry. I knelt and lit the candles. I took off my gloves and rested my hands, palm up, on my lap. I let the circles on my hand draw my eye round and round into eternity. *Re'a, saviour of the world, hear me.*

I said the hour, late though it was, blessing Re'a for her saving works. I prayed for the people whose statues lay around me — their lives, if not their bodies, as fragmented as the effigies. I commended to Re'a the soul of the priest who lay outside her temple.

Then, I lay my heart before my goddess and waited.

People often think prayer is easy. Until they try.

When I was young, I expected it to be like a conversation with someone hidden behind a wall. You would speak and she would answer; a little muffled, perhaps, a little hard to make out, but an answer.

Save me from the answers of the gods.

As part of my education, Hathil had once left me in charge of a baby for a day. The creature had done nothing but cry. When Hathil finally returned with the mother, my head was pounding and my stomach unbalance by lack of sleep. I was vocal in my expressions of disgust.

"It's the only way they've got of speaking to you," she said. "They cry when they're sick, they cry when they're cold, they cry when they're hot, they cry when they're hungry, they cry when they're lonely, they cry when they're bored. They cry to manipulate you."

"It's a baby!"

"He's a small person. They learn damn fast. He'll manipulate you to keep you fast by him as much as possible. Just because he's crying doesn't mean he's right."

When it comes to prayer, we are all babies, I think. We cry out our hopes and woes and fears with no comprehension of what the gods are saying to us. We have to be lifted bodily from our lives, fed, swaddled, stripped, cleaned or given foul tasting medicine, before we even notice that we have been heard. And, generally, that is not what we want. We just want to keep the gods near, listening, attending, while we lead our own lives.

As we had left the house, Hathil and me, the mother of the child had picked up the baby and held him. Even grumping and whinging, I could not help but see the harmony of mother and baby, and how the mother curled herself around the baby in her arms.

That was what I was looking for that evening in the vandalised temple. I cried out my heart before my goddess: my fear for Hazzor, for my country, for myself; my fear of magic and its consequences. And then, I waited. I waited to be held in the arms of my goddess, wordless, comforted.

It was full dark when Ranyl tapped me on the shoulder, some hours later. I jumped, as he knew I would.

"Did she hear you?"

"I don't know. I think so."

"Saen's balls, priest – "

"Saahni."

" – if you don't know, what the hell were the last two hours of grovelling in the dust for?"

"I never said she needed to hear me, I said I needed to pray."

Ranyl made a disgusted noise.

"Well, it's time we were getting back. We don't want Abe sending out a search party."

I got to my feet, stiffly. I licked my dry lips. At least my tongue felt a little better.

"Why not?"

"Because he'll never let me live it down if he does."

Both of us turned widdershins as we left the temple, and I noticed Ranyl looking uneasily over his shoulder. A thought stopped me in my tracks.

"What happened to the horses?"

"What?"

Last time I had been at the temple I had heard horses.

"The horses the W'shten patrol had, what happened to them?"

Ranyl stopped and turned.

"If you hadn't been so busy squabbling with the mage, you'd know."

I passed him a sour look.

"Know what?"

"Abe's hoping that with the horses we can get back off the roads."

"What about Hazzor?"

I had been thinking we would need a mount for the spy once we had him mobile. Abe had no plans that involved Hazzor being mobile. What was he up to?

Ranyl looked shifty ... shiftier.

"Saahni, that patrol will be followed up by people wanting to know what happened to them."

"I thought we were hiding?"

"Yeah. But we're going to have to run eventually."

"But — "

Ranyl's face closed.

"You want to argue, argue with Abe, but you should know."

"Know what?"

"That patrol will be missed."

I pursed my lips and shook my head, meaninglessly. I could only worry about so many things. I was not the strategist, I was the healer. My concern was the injured man.

"But you kept the horses."

"Aye. Come on, priest — "

"Saahni."

It was pointless, I know, but almost wholly reflexive.

"Can't stand here talking all night or you'll be too tired for your party trick."

He flitted off into the dark, returning from time to time to check on me.

Chapter 18

When we got to the barn, I moved swiftly to climb up to the loft. Again, I silently thanked Reath for my short skirt.

The others were sat in darkness, talking quietly. My arrival was greeted with an astounding lack of reaction. I greeted my fellow travellers and dripped over to see Hazzor. He had been asleep, but my cold hand on his brow woke him. He muttered a complaint and closed his eyes again. Fryn'gh joined me. His face looked tight.

"Are you ready?" I asked, keeping my eyes on his face, pale in the dark.

This was it. The room went silent. I could feel Ranyl, perched behind me.

The mage swallowed, audibly.

"What did you have in mind?"

I dropped my gaze back to the prone spy. I bit my lip. *Re'a shield me.*

"Could you show me what you ... see?"

"Only if you were a magic user or had any magic talent." I scowled, so the mage said, "What? Not my fault you're a blocked vessel."

"'*A blocked vessel?*'"

"Now, then, lovely Sahnithi."

Abe's undulating voice had a tone to it that brought to mind being shaken like a kitten. I sucked in air through clenched teeth.

"Well, then," I said with forced patience, "how long does it take, this healing? Can you do it slowly so I can watch Hazzor's progress?"

Fryn'gh scratched his chin, making a rasping noise across the stubble.

I listened to the rain and cursed it. I was so tired of being wet.

"Frankly, with a healing spell, I have very little control."

I dug my fingers into my braids, noticing that my fingers could now reach my crown. *What a sight I must look!* I sighed. We had to do this.

"How about I tell you what to look for, when to stop?"

The mage shrugged, one shouldered, and then he shook his head.

"Listen, when I do a healing spell, it's totally uncontrolled. I just give the target a ... boost, tell the body to get on with it, do what it takes."

Clearly, he did not like revealing so much.

I got up, walked to the window and looked out. I imagined where the bandit cart must still be lying by the road. It felt like this day was never going to end.

"When will they come looking for the dead patrol?"

"They'll set out first light, most likely."

I turned to check it was Abe speaking. The accent was his, but it was unlike him to be so terse. I could see little more than a silhouette, blurring into the wall he leant against. At first light, then, we'd also set out, with or without Hazzor. I wracked my brains. A long ago conversation with Hathil rose to the surface.

I turned,

"Alright. What if I slowed Hazzor down? Would it be easier to give Hazzor just a *little* boost, just a nudge?"

Fryn'gh crouched by the spy, still. In the dark, I thought he nodded, but was not sure.

"Mage?"

"*Yes!*" he said, impatiently, then, "maybe."

I heard a half-laugh, half-cough from my patient. It was his first contribution to a conversation that held his life in the balance. I waited to see if he was going to add anything but the spy did not speak.

"Well then."

I saw Thorn reach out and lay a hand on the mage's arm.

"It's got to be tried, Fryn'gh," she said.

Hurriedly I turned to my pack. *With gentian bark,* Hathil had said, *you have to be careful when the wound is severe.* How had I forgotten this? *Too much, and it can reduce the ability to heal.* It keeps the wound too fresh, too clean. So Hathil had said. I dug out the freshly ground gentian and demanded water for Hazzor to drink. I barely noticed who fetched it.

Gently, I lifted the little spy's head and held the cup of gentian-water to his lips.

"Here."

When the water touched his lips he pulled a face and pushed the cup away.

"Drink!" I could feel five pairs of eyes on us. I lowered my voice, trying to conceal my anxiety. "Please, Hazzor."

The injured man lifted his eyes to mine briefly, so I tried desperately to *look* all my appeal. He closed his for a moment, then nodded. Re'a bless him, he drained the cup without so much as a grimace.

"Give the gentian time to work, Fryn'gh."

The mage gave a brief nod, which I could only just see in the dim light.

I sank to my knees by the window. The rain beat out a chant on the roof and on the ground. I kept time with the clicking of my beads. *Please Re'a, please, please, please.* I was aware of Fryn'gh shifting about. I did not know if it was procrastination or necessary preparation. *Let him do it right, please, please, please.* I wished I could help. I wished I could tell him what to do, what Hazzor needed, what to look for. It was like watching a blind man paint. *Please, Blessed Re'a, please let Hazzor live, please.*

"Brother of my heart," I heard Abe say gently, after we had waited some half hour, "sooner it's done, sooner we know where we're at."

Oh, Blessed Three, if I ever earned any grace, any favour, please. I heard the mage draw a deep breath. *I will do anything, please, please let him live.* I heard Hazzor gasp.

"It's done."

"Sahnithi? Hun'?"

I swooped down on the hapless agent.

"Give me light."

"Damn you, priest, I'm exhausted!"

I threw my tinder box at the mage.

"Light!"

While I waited, I checked the rhythm of Hazzor's heart: weak but even, steady. His breath was sweet, though, which was worrying.

Somebody lit a torch.

"Help me lift him."

Axyl lifted the spy into a sitting position so that I could unwind his bandages. Hazzor did not as much as sigh. I took a cloth and wiped off the ointment that had covered the wound.

I was not sure whether to be sick or dance a jig.

Where Hazzor's gash had sat between hip and belly was now pink, new skin, which almost met. The stitches sat in a redundant pattern, like footprints in clay. I was astonished.

I checked again, his heart and his breathing. Still good. Only the sweet breath gave me cause to worry. I ran my hands over the spy. Again, I bit my lip. It was hard to tell, which was a good sign; his wiry body seemed solid to touch, but I had nothing to compare it with. We would know how much damage had been done when the spy woke, but I was confident now that he had suffered no major damage. *Thank you, Blessed Lady, thank you*. It would be tough though. The gash would still be present under the new skin. Any strenuous exercise (such as hiking across two countries with a bunch of bandits) would pull at the wound.

I remembered the mage, crouched by my side. His tension was almost palpable, even from where I sat. I nodded in the gloom.

"You did it."

A huge grin spread across the wiz — the mage's face. Even in the dark I could see the flash of his teeth. He jumped up punching the air.

"Yes! Yes! Oh, I am the BEST!"

I could not help smiling. Nor could I resist adding, "Thank the gods."

It was a gentle poke, meant in good will, but Fryn'gh turned on me.

"Oh that's right. Couldn't possibly be the mage's skill, no, praise the gods, 'cos *obviously* they were the ones who saved the man! Would you have cursed them, though, if I'd killed Hazzor, that's what I want to know."

I blinked, totally unprepared. Stupidly, I had thought the alliance would last at least a little while longer. *Fool that you are to expect a mage, of all people, to be open hearted!* Hurt, I snarled back,

"Heaven forefend an arrogant prig of a mage could see beyond his own *flailing* powers."

Axyl rose rapidly from where he had been crouched and the pair of us reined in our tempers.

"Fat lot of use you were anyway," hissed the mage.

I opened my mouth to reply but, checking Axyl from the corner of my eye, I thought better of it.

The mage stood and took a couple of steps backward.

"I've done here," he said. "I need to recoup my energies."

His clothes rustled as he brushed them down, dismissively, and in the flickering light of the torch I watched him groom his hair with his fingers.

"I need to go out."

"Well, sunshine," said Abe, cheerily, "don't go far." The mage gave a half-nod, half-shrug. "And Fryn'gh?" The mage paused on his way down the ladder. "Well done."

From my distance in the uneven light, I could not tell if he smiled. Neither did I care, I told myself: wretched, self-absorbed, hypocritical, narrow-minded puttock that he was. I frowned into my bag of wraps and bandages and returned to the task in hand. Fortunately, I had plenty of the wolf's heart. I also had some of Hathil's ointment left, but I would have to make some more soon. Hazzor would need strapping tight before we asked him to ride a horse, but I decided to leave him to sleep with just a light bandage. He clearly was not moving much.

"How is he, Saahni?"

Thorn's voice was soft in the half light and I could hear the worry.

I nodded, pointlessly.

"He'll need to be careful but, yes," it was easier to praise the red-topped *wizard* when he was not in the room, "Fryn'gh stopped in time."

I felt the tension drain from the room.

"Sahnithi, beautiful, I'm almost ready to kiss your sweet god's feet." I saw the teeth flash in the dark. "We'd better get some sleep." I heard him snort, "The *rest* of us had better get some sleep."

I looked around, puzzled. I could just make out Ranyl, curled up and audibly asleep in the corner.

"Who's on first watch?"

Axyl sat down with a sigh as he spoke.

Thorn gave a short laugh.

"Looks like the mage to me."

"Will he be alright?"

I was damned if I would admit I was worried about Fryn'gh but, well, I was — a little.

Thorn settled down for the night, stretching out by the wall of the loft.

"Frankly I'm too tired to care," she said.

I would have loved to follow her example, but as the three bandits followed Ranyl to the land of nod — apparently as easily and sweetly as babes — I was left wide awake. I stretched out next to Hazzor and listened to his breathing. My head ached and my eyes were ready to climb out of my skull for tiredness. *You must sleep.* As I tried to bully my body into somnolence, it fought back with a tension that started in the shoulders and spread down through my back to my legs. I began to feel sick with it. My legs wanted to get up and walk, but I was so tired I did not think I *could* move. Besides, if I was walking around, pointlessly, I was not sleeping. And I needed to sleep. Now. I almost shouted with frustration.

I fretted over the events of the day past and

worried about what needed to be done tomorrow. I listed the medicines I would need and reviewed the stocks I had in my bag. I considered moving some of them into the pockets in my jerkin that were still empty. I thought about the dead bodies below me. I thought about the dead patrol. I thought about the angry W'shten who would come looking for them. I wondered what food we had to feed Hazzor when he woke with his magic-induced hunger in the morning,

and I was walking in the woods near the Tharret. I could smell the wet mud on the banks of the river. Hathil walked beside me. As we went, she tested me on herb lore, pointing at plants and asking me to list the uses of root, stem and leaf or demanding I show her the black dock she had seen hidden behind the root of a tree.

"I can't do this, Hathil," I complained, "It's too difficult."

"Nonsense," she answered in her robust way. She smiled, "You're doing fine."

"But I want him in a bed, in a safe place, where I can control what he does and what he eats. If we run out of your ointment it takes hours to prepare more. We won't have the time. I — "

"List three places where you can find therith."

I sighed.

"Under brambles, amongst gorse and holly."

I hate therith.

"Where does gentian grow?"

"Shady, wet places."

"Where does — "

"I know, I know where these plants grow, but I don't have *time*."

"You have a well-stocked bag."

I dug my fingers into my hair.

"Kayt'an, when did you last braid your hair? A priest should look calm, measured and presentable at all times."

Amtil Sahn kissed me on both cheeks.

"I don't have the time," I repeated.

Amtil tutted.

"There is always time for the important things, Kayt'an."

"Where?" I asked, frustrated. "Help me!"

"You're doing fine," said Hathil, warmly.

Amtil took my hand.

"You are a priest of the blessed Re'a. You have all the help you need."

"But I'm doing terribly! Everyone thinks I'm a fool and Fryn'gh hates me — "

"And you care what a wizard thinks?"

Amtil raised her eyebrows.

"He's a mage," I corrected, guilelessly. I went on, "And I've got to keep Hazzor well and fit so he can play his part, and I *can't*."

"Yes you can." Hathil crossed her arms. "I've trained you well, Kayt'an."

"He killed the people of Harset, Sahnithi."

"Are you so sure you would not have done the same in his place?"

I felt the tears on my face,

"No!"

"No one knows what they're capable of, daughter, until they do it."

Hathil wrapped me in a warm embrace.

"You can do this," she whispered.

"I want to go home," I said.

Amtil tutted again.

"Your home is in Re'a's arms, and it's not your time yet. You have work to do."

"But I don't have *time!*"

I woke with a start. It was still dark. I listened. Then I held my breath and listened again. Silence, save the sound of the others' breathing. The rain had stopped.

Chapter 19

I sat up and checked on Hazzor as best as I could in the dark. Heart and breathing and brow were all as they should be. I hoped he would wake soon. I put my hand in my pocket for my candle to say the hour, and hesitated. First things first, I thought. I moved as quietly as I could to the hatch and took myself down. I sniffed: there was definitely a sickly sweetness to the air down here that would travel soon. At the door stood Thorn. I joined her.

She smiled at me.

"How's Hazz?" she asked softly.

I gave a smile and a shrug.

"I'm waiting for him to wake. I thought I'd look for anything left in the cupboards. He'll be hungry."

"Ranyl's your man for that kind of job." I opened my mouth to protest my competence, but Thorn went on, "Don't go far."

I nodded compliance and walked to the nearest house.

⊛

It was dark inside and I reached into my pocket for my candle, feeling a stab of guilt that I was planning to use it for such mundanities. I put it on the table and reached into my other pocket for my tinderbox. I swore. Fryn'gh still had it, wymns take him. I put the candle back and thought it served me right. I went by touch and smell around the kitchen. The flour bin had been knocked over, but there was still a little flour in the bin itself. I took a pinch. It seemed dry enough. I found a small container and took the flour with me to the next house. That one had been ransacked comprehensively, but in the next, with the help of Saen's new light (*first light*, I thought, thinking both of the searching patrol and my delayed duties), I found a little oil that had been missed by the looting W'shten. I took it and the flour back to the barn. There would not be time to cook it, but I doubted the spy would be in a state to care.

When I climbed back up to the others, they were already packing up the little camp.

"Sahnithi, honey! Any joy?" Abe greeted me.

I brandished my finds. Ranyl cocked his head in surprise.

"Well well, Saahni. First magic, now theft. We'll make a bandit of you yet."

It was not the complement he clearly thought it was.

"Bandits?" said Abernast as he scratched his unshaven jaw, "Who're bandits? We're just travellers, remember."

That interminable smile did another round. He was clearly feeling better today.

I ignored them both. Since the spy was sound asleep, I mixed my horde of flour and oil into a single pot and put it at the top of my bag. He was still asleep when everyone was packed and ready to go. Abe and Ranyl went to get the horses from their hiding place while Axyl lifted my patient so I could check the injury and bind it tight. It seemed to have healed a little more overnight, but the coming day would test any work his body had done.

I am not fond of horses so I viewed my mount with suspicion. There were only five horses and I was not surprised to learn the others thought it sensible I should share with Fryn'gh. We eyed each other with misgiving. He was obviously going to fight to lead. On the other hand I was eager to let someone else control the beast, so I volunteered to ride pillion, careful to sound grudging. Fryn'gh was surprised. He did a passable attempt at gracious, at which I smiled. *Ha!* I thought, and savoured the advantage.

I had been adamant it would do Hazzor no good at all to be thrown over a horse like a sack. While he still slept the bandits bound him behind Thorn so he sat up in the saddle, his head resting on the back of her neck. Her bow was strapped to the side of the horse. She simply smiled and said,

"Well, this is a new one."

Abe and Axyl mounted up. Not surprisingly, they had a horse each. I would not like to ask a horse to carry the pair of them. Abe took the reins of the fifth horse and nodded at Ranyl who promptly disappeared into the dawn murk. Abe kicked his horse and we all set off, back the way we had come.

I looked over my shoulder.

"What about Ranyl?"

What was going on?

Thorn flashed me a grin.

"He's doing what he does best," she said.

I was already uncomfortable, sat behind the saddle, but I gave Thorn the prompt she was after.

"Which is?"

"Deception and misdirection." She pointed behind at the village. "He's doing his best to hide our trail, to make it look like the patrol fought those bandits and lost."

"Is that plausible?"

Thorn shrugged.

"Any confusion is better than giving them an open book to read." She looked worried for a moment, and then gave an almost grudging smile. "And if anyone can pull it off, it's Ranyl."

Some little way back from the village, there was a gate into a field. The gate stood open and the crops in the field were already beaten down around the opening. Abe led us into the field and then on in single file. When we got to a point that seemed to me indistinguishable from the fields around, Abe stopped and dismounted.

"Breakfast," he announced.

Carefully, we untied Hazzor and laid him down on a bank while we waited for Ranyl to catch up. The rest of us crouched awkwardly in the mud and waited.

It was well past dawn so a candle was a little pointless. But still, I got out my beads and said my prayers while the others ate.

Axyl pushed some food my way.

"You should eat," he said simply.

"Aye, pretty Sahnithi, I've one gaunt woman travelling with me as it is." The horrible man flashed his accursed teeth at me. "Leave me with some curves to dream about."

I flushed scarlet and fumbled my beads. Wretched, despicable man! I cleared my throat.

"Today, I fast," I muttered.

Hazzor sighed. I went to his side and felt his brow. He batted my hand away and I smiled, ridiculously pleased by the gesture.

"Haenid's tits," said the big outlander delightedly, "the Yulid wakes!"

"Ranyl's on his way," the archer remarked, "Horoc."

"Horoc?"

The big barbarian's face cracked into a smile. "Got no tail," he explained, referring to the children's tale, warning of foolhardy courage.

I groaned. I reached for my bag and got out the pot of flour and oil. I took the portion of food offered to me and poured the mixture over it. Thorn wrinkled her nose. It did not look appetising, but it would be filling, I hoped. I stirred it as best I could with my fingers and held it near the fallen spy.

"Hazzor?"

His eyes flickered open and he stared at the grey sky, puzzled.

"Hazzor, here," I said, lifting him up to my shoulder as best I could and handing him the bowl. He winced as I moved him, but grabbed the bowl eagerly and ate with a determination that I remembered well.

I licked my own fingers while he ate and my stomach growled at the taste of food. *Not today*, I told my belly silently. I was enough of a burden on the group as it was, without taking more than my fair share. I had eaten this morning's breakfast the night before last, I reckoned. A fast would do me good, I told myself sternly.

Before the thief reached us, Hazzor had finished his bowl.

"More," he demanded, and he was passed his own portion of breakfast.

He finished that too.

"More?" he asked.

Ranyl was just arriving. We went through our packs and found between us a small dish of dry cheese and bread. Ranyl had a little jerky stashed away, which he handed over reluctantly. Hazzor ate it all. Finally he looked up, wiping his mouth and licking his hand.

"Saen's balls," he said weakly, hand on stomach, "I'm still hungry."

"Well, you've cleaned us out."

The thief, I thought, was still mourning his lost stash.

"I don't think you should eat any more, anyway," I added. "It'll put pressure on the wound."

I wasn't sure about that, but it might help him if he thought more food would set him back.

Abe passed Hazzor a water skin and the agent drank thirstily. He handed the skin back and said,

"Report?"

Abe filled him in and Ranyl told us how he had left the village.

"Hopefully," Ranyl finished, "they'll carry on through the village on the road to G'nered. If we're lucky it'll be a half day before they smell a rat and double back."

Reath's man took his weight off my shoulder. It must have hurt, but he didn't let it show. I tutted quietly but the spy ignored me.

"We'd best make the most of the time we have then."

I couldn't help fussing as Hazzor was helped up on to a horse. This time Ranyl rode with the injured man and Thorn hung her bow back on her back before climbing up into the saddle.

Abe paused next to me before mounting his horse.

"Look at her, Sahnithi," he said proudly, "I've known wychis less alert than her."

True, her eyes were scanning the horizon as she waited for the rest of us to be ready. I scrambled up behind Fryn'gh and the two big men sprang gracefully into their saddles.

"Are we ok?" the mage asked, cryptically.

"Oh aye, lad," Abe answered, "I'll let you know when we need you."

We set off.

The next couple of days were grim. The rain did not hold off for long. I argued for the importance of shelter, not only for Hazzor who suffered badly, but for the rest of us too. I dished out gentian against chills, but worried about Hazzor, to whom I dare not give any more. Ranyl declared he would rather risk lung-rot than chew the bitter herb. Thorn refused to light a fire, so I could not even brew a tisane. We sheltered in barns, when we could find an isolated one, but Hazzor would not let us stop in another village, particularly now we were in Ga'ared. The villages here would not be abandoned, and we would stand out even with one W'shten in our midst.

So we trudged on. The rain became the definition of my world, slowly turning everything to slurry. Fryn'gh dried us off when the water started to seep into our skin, but it still felt as though I was slowly dissolving. It wasn't long before I caved in to the lure of Fryn'gh's magic. It is astonishing how protracted, low grade misery corrodes the will. After a while, I just no longer cared. What did it matter? Even my prayers were generally just a mindless reflex, a thoughtless clicking of beads. After two days of riding in the rain, I had descended to a level well below your average fish.

⊗

Fryn'gh and I, stuck together on the same horse as we were, came to an uneasy truce. From my perspective, it was as much as anything because he was a useful source of information.

"I don't know why we didn't start out with horses," I muttered that first morning of riding.

"Horses are too easy to see, too noisy and leave tracks that are too easy to follow."

I looked at the mage in surprise.

"How do you know?"

"Because now we've got to get clear fast and we have to use them, I'm the one who has to hide us and muffle the noise. Ranyl and Abe reckon the rain should do some of the work for us as well as hide the tracks quicker."

"Oh." *When did this happen?* I was silent for a time. I shifted on the horse, uncomfortably. "I shouldn't have thought the W'shten'd have much truck with horses."

"How'd you reckon that?"

There was a hint of a sneer in the mage's voice, but little enough for me to ignore, so I was able to answer calmly,

"I thought W'shten is all marshland, hardly natural horse country."

"Around Shteriv, yes, but these days you'll hear W'shten bureaucrats referring to the Ga'ared lowlands as 'W'shten'."

I was surprised he knew so much. How did he know what W'shten bureaucrats said? I did not want to interrupt in case the red-head's fragile temper blew, so I said nothing.

"Besides, the W'shten built their empire with roads." I made an interested noise, encouraging him to continue. Fryn'gh obliged. "Sure. King Yr's great granddaddy — King Rashyr — bought vast amounts of stone from Ga'ared to build the harbour at Dar Tor. That's the basis of the family's wealth. But, King Rashyr also used the stone to build a road back into

Ga'ared. He *said* it was to speed up the importing of the stone. Better roads mean you can use bigger wagons and so forth."

I made another interested noise. I did not think the mage had ever spoken to me for so long without being rude.

He went on.

"Of course, with the roads, came soldiers to protect the road and before Firric — the then King of Ga'ared — realised, Rashyr was also offering protection to the lowland cities from the local bandits." Fryn'gh turned round and gave a wry smile, "Of course, the bandits were the peasants whose homes and livelihood had been destroyed by the W'shten road!"

Fryn'gh had to stop for a time to concentrate on helping the horse past a fallen tree.

When he'd finished I asked,

"So, that's how the W'shten took Ga'ared?"

"They never technically 'took' it. It's just a vassal state. Hersec, Firric's son, bowed the knee when Rashyr showed his hand: he controlled all of Ga'ared farmland. Slowly, slowly, Ga'ared is becoming about W'shten culture, W'shten money, W'shten soldiers, W'shten *roads*. So much so that Yr moved most of his bureaucracy to G'nered. Shteriv is really just a palace and a market these days." Fryn'gh made a wry noise, "It's a shame Yr can't manipulate his own family as deftly as he can his country."

"Oh?" After all the intrigue, it seemed strange to think of the W'shten king as a man with a family.

The mage shrugged,

"Oh, nothing."

He clammed up like a door in winter.

I was beginning to think I could no longer feel my bottom. Wanting to get the red head talking again, I said,

"So why doesn't Yr just do the same with Ttaroc? Why go to war with us?"

"Gayton's an ass but he's not stupid. Yr made a sally — offered to help Gayton keep order or something — and Gayton told him to get lost." Fryn'gh shrugged. "Could have been better managed, though."

"How do you know all this?"

"Because I haven't spent all my time studying fairy tales."

And then the bickering would take off again. As the day went on, though, occasionally the conversation would finish because of the rain, or because Abe or Hazzor called us to halt or be silent or duck or walk or hide or eat … but as Saen travelled across the sky it became not so terrible to be sharing a horse with the mage — or at least, the horse became the greater of the two evils.

Chapter 20

It was hard to say what time it was — the sun was a distant memory — but we had stopped near a village and Ranyl had gone foraging. What with my healing and then Hazzor, there was no food in our packs. Hunting was out — fires were impossible — so we were reliant on theft. I had ceased to care about the morality of it, or of anything, much.

I was mindlessly clicking my beads in token duty to my goddess when Thorn came down from a tree. She was a much better climber than me. Which is the same as to say, a bird flies better than a fish. The only witness to *my* attempt at tree climbing, thankfully, wasn't looking to see my blushes at the memory.

"They're coming," she said.

It seemed we all came alive again. We had gone a day and a half without any word of the W'shten, who were supposed to be following us, and I had assumed we had escaped. Now, fear cut through my rain-soaked apathy. To my surprise, it was an improvement. Apparently, I would rather be a frightened woman than an apathetic fish. Whether after two days I would say the same I was not sure. Variety, they say, is the spice of life.

"How far?" Hazzor was saying.

Remarkably, he was much stronger despite the travelling. I could hear the pain in his voice, but there was no doubt he held the reins again.

"Hard to say." Thorn tilted her head in thought. "Perhaps an hour behind us, maybe three. The rain fudges the distances."

"Dogs?"

"Can't see."

"Ranyl?"

Ranyl scratched his head through his cap, sniffed, and shook his head.

"Nah," he said, "they're too far."

"When?"

The spy was bright eyed, hard faced.

"When we can see them from horseback."

Abe snorted.

"They'll be on top of us by then, we'll be able to see for ourselves."

Ranyl snarled,

"Listen, milk-face, I'm good but I'm not a mage. If you can't see them, I can't see them. In this weather, they shift course, I lose them. I lose you. By the time I've found everyone, we've lost any advantage I might have earned us."

Axyl grumbled something under his breath. I knew how he felt.

"Then we'll just have to put as much distance as we can between us." Hazzor stood and hissed with the pain of the sudden movement. I was on my feet at once.

"Let me see."

"There's no time, Saahni."

I caught hold of his sleeve as he turned for the horse.

"How much time will we lose if your wound breaks open?"

The spy sighed, but came back under the meagre shelter of the tree. I looked up and a great drop of rainwater hit me in the eye. I wiped my face and called,

"Fryn'gh?"

I had discovered the mage was invaluable when it came to keeping Hazzor's bandages dry.

"I'm sorry, Saahni." Hazzor sounded remarkably unapologetic. "Fryn'gh has more important things to spend his energies on now. You'll have to manage as best you can without."

He unbuttoned his waistcoat and lifted his shirt.

I applied myself to removing bandages as quick as I could and handing them to Axyl — who was nearest — to keep dry while I checked the injury. Every time I saw it I could not help being amazed. Who would have thought it was only a couple of days ago that Hazzor was stabbed? It was not healing now as it would if he were resting, but the mage's magic had brought the spy's flesh to a point where it was able to hold on to the healing it had. I corrected myself — the mage's healing combined with my own arts. I praised Saen for the wolf's heart. It was stopping the wound from drying out, but also keeping the worst of the rain away. I frowned at it. It was not, however, getting visibly much better. I applied the last of Hathil's ointment and tutted as Hazzor pulled away.

"Don't be such a baby," I said ruthlessly.

I heard Axyl snort. Abe muttered something about cold women and out the corner of my eye I could see Thorn laughing into her coat. I took no notice, but pressed new wolf's heart on to Hazzor's side and reached out for the bandages. The spy sucked his teeth and tensed his stomach, but made no more attempts to escape my ministrations. I bandaged him as tight as I could and left him to sort his clothes out.

In warmer, dryer, safer circumstances, I may have found my healer's dispassion harder to maintain. Hazzor was not unattractive, and the body I was constantly handling was undoubtedly a fine example of its kind. As it was, I could have been handling raw meat for all the interest he aroused in me. Nonetheless, I found it hard to praise Re'a for the rain that kept me from making a fool of myself. I was barely on speaking terms with her. I was barely capable of speech.

Fryn'gh was waiting by the horse.

"You'll have to take the reins," was all he said, but his face was tense and his eyes were already distant.

I gritted my teeth and climbed ungracefully into the saddle. My wet clothes rubbed and grit from the mud created interesting little pockets where I was convinced I no longer had any skin. I was also sure a small army of insects had taken up residence in my scalp. My back, thighs and bottom hated me. The horse hated me, and I reciprocated. It tried half-heartedly to bite me as I climbed on and flicked its ears unhappily at the rain.

I held out a hand to Fryn'gh who mounted with as much grace as I had, and then I looked up to see, as usual, that the others were ready: waiting once again for the mage and me.

If I had thought it was tough going when Hazzor had been riding for stealth, it was nothing compared to the misery that was mine now he threw caution to the wind.

We pushed the horses to their limit, and they often stumbled, slipping in the mud. I let go of the reins of my horse. It was keeping up with the others and I figured it was better off picking its own path. I concentrated on holding on.

Fryn'gh behind me muttered to himself, holding on to me with handfuls of my cloak. Ordinarily, I would have complained, but I too was muttering,

"Re'a, Saviour of the World, hear us and save us."

The world of my faith was as muddied as the ground underfoot. How much could I keep asking? I was convinced that she had answered my prayers for Hazzor, but *O blessed Lady, this too, please, keep us ahead.* How much of her blessing had I earned? How much could I plead for? Was I being impudent, looking for her help when I had left the temple so far behind? Where was the sense in saving the spy only to hand us all over to the W'shten two days on?

And yet, how could she have done this to me? As the horses struggled and slipped through the fields and down the farm tracks running with mud, I cursed Re'a. I cursed the absent sun-god and cursed Farock Rha for his lack of justice. What had I done to deserve this? Time had blurred, but it had been more than a tennight of pain and fear and cold and sorrow and fear and self-doubt and now three solid days of rain. And fear. And rain — did I mention the rain?

Hazzor refused to stop until the sun began to set. When the horses had had enough he ordered us to walk. Or rather Thorn, Axyl, Abe and Ranyl walked; I slipped and slid and tripped, hanging on to the horse for dear life, who in turn kept trying to bite me. I did not blame it. I think I would have bitten it, if I could. Fryn'gh stayed on our mount, so as not to lose his concentration. Hazzor ought to have stayed on his horse, but got down and walked, his arm pressed to his side, slowly curling over his injured body. I bit my lip and glared at him, but if he felt my disapproval he gave no sign: stupid, stubborn man!

Thorn, I saw, constantly scanned the horizon. As the day wore on, there were fewer and fewer trees for her to climb. We could not know whether we were pulling away or if the W'shten were nearly upon us.

As evening fell, Ranyl spotted an old semi-ruined animal stall, tucked in a small fold in the land. Thorn, Abe and I pulled, pushed and slapped the horses to get them in — it was *very* small and, even with the rain, they were not keen. Fryn'gh crawled in and fell asleep. Ranyl and Axyl were busy disguising the pen with mud and some pieces of hedge, I think.

The horses took up most of the room. We camped at the back, where it was drier. We were knee to knee, shoulder to shoulder. I inched over to Hazzor.

"How is it?" I asked.

"Sore."

That he admitted so much spoke volumes. His breathing was shallow and when I put my hand to his brow, even after a day in the rain, he was sweating.

"It's alright," I lied, "let me have a look."

We went through the rigmarole again, the others trying to shift out the way while I unwrapped him. A horse breathed down my neck. It was not trying to bite me so I guessed it was not mine. I swore softly under my breath.

"What is it?"

I could not see much — not an awful lot of the evening half-light got into the stall and past the horses, but I could feel the wound had bled and it was hot to touch. I wanted to cry, so I swore again. It was not *fair.*

"*What*?"

I rubbed my face and dug my fingers into my hair. Then, I put my hands on my knees and tried to be Pastoral.

"It's fine, the injury's just opened a bit, that's all."

"Is it?"

I moved my head from side to side, as if looking for the best angle.

"Hmmm, and there's a slight infection."

Hazzor swore, too, and dropped his head back against the wall.

"You should have left me."

I saw a flash of teeth.

"Nay, Hazzor, son, we're all hoping to hide behind you when you explain to Reath what happened."

Hazzor gave a brief chuckle.

"I'd *rather* you'd left me, then."

Fryn'gh snored.

Axyl and Ranyl crawled in past the horses, which snorted and stamped in disgust. I rolled up the bandage — how had it got muddy? — and pressed the cleanest section to Hazzor's side. "Hold this," I told him and ferreted in my bag. I should have made more use of the pockets Reath had had made in my jerkin but somehow there had never been the time.

I realised the rest were discussing what Ranyl called the 'larder run'. I looked up.

"Get enough for another healing," I said.

I felt my belly growing tight at the thought but …

"Saahni, with respect — "

"'With respect' nothing," I said, senselessly.

I found the pestle and mortar and pulled them out. At least I had meant to. The pestle caught my pot of Collinsonia and tipped out the contents on to the floor. Seeds went everywhere. I swore, then I swore again, and then for good measure, I swore some more and threw the mortar onto the ground. I sniffed and pressed the back of my hand to my mouth. *O Holy Lady, don't let me cry.*

It seemed even the horses had stopped what they were doing to look at me. I made a valiant attempt to pull myself together. I picked up the mortar which, mercifully, was not broken.

"I can patch the damage today has done," I said with a miraculously steady voice, "but, tomorrow'll be worse. If Hazzor insists on pushing himself the way he has today, I reckon, give it a couple of days — at most — and he'll not be conscious." I took a deep breath, "With another of Fryn'gh's healing spells," after all this time I still tasted bile as I suggested it, "we might start late tomorrow, but we'll be able to move quickly."

"If we don't start first thing tomorrow, they could be on us before we move."

Hazzor's face was pale against the darkening evening.

"*Could*, as against *will* not be able to move at the pace you want to, Hazzor."

Hazzor stared at me, not a sign of his thoughts on his face. To my surprise, Abe weighed in.

"Hazzor, are you in the habit of barking after you've spent good money on a dog? Tell me why we've been carrying this priest, if we're not going to listen when she speaks as a healer?" Another pudhy grin. "Sure, she was sweet on the eye to start with, but frankly my imagination can do better, just now."

Suddenly, I became acutely conscious of my mud-splattered, soggy, and bedraggled state, and I cursed the W'shten. Silently, though — Re'a forbid I let him know he hit his mark. I concentrated on the mix I was intent on preparing. Digging out my lavender, therith, and, after a moment's hesitation, the gentian bark I had ground back in the abandoned village, I set to work while the others argued it out. After a time, Ranyl left. I realised the others were arguing practicalities and felt a cold relief. *They're persuaded*, I thought.

"It's not possible." I nearly spilt my ointment at the mage's voice. Saen *rot* that accursed mage in the darkest pit! Fryn'gh leaned on one elbow and scratched his head. "I can't. I just can't. I'm sorry, Hazzor."

Hazzor merely nodded, but it was Thorn who asked the question hammering in my chest,

"Why?"

"I can't heal Hazzor *and* hide us from the W'shten."

"Surely, you can?"

It was meant to be a statement but it came out a question. I knew so little of magic. I was ready to spit.

"I'm exhausted, Saahni. If I don't rest tonight, I *can't* do it again tomorrow."

It was Abe who answered.

"The question, then," he stopped and sighed, "the question is, which is more important — stealth or speed?"

In the silence that followed, I daubed my hastily concocted mixture onto Hazzor's injured side.

"Nraagh!" he yelled. "Will you not warn me, woman!" I opened my mouth to correct him, but he was ahead of me, "Saahni," he said.

He frowned, I think, and flinched for certain, as I laid fresh wolf's heart on the wound.

"Listen!"

Thorn laid a hand on Abe and we all stopped what we were doing. The horses stomped and sighed, but otherwise I could not hear anything. I strained my ears; still nothing. My heart was in my mouth, what had she heard? Had she heard other horses? I held my breath and listened again, could I hear horses far away as well as horses near? Then, I saw Abe's teeth flash in the dark and heard Thorn's answering laugh. I felt my own mouth stretch into a grin. I could hear nothing. The rain had stopped. I laughed.

"Praise the Holy Three!" I said.

Fryn'gh was still surly.

"I didn't hear you curse them for the rain."

I sighed, frustrated by his bloody-mindedness.

"No," I said, "but I thought it."

Hazzor cleared his throat. I was still pressing the wolf's heart to his side. I muttered an apology and brought out a fresh bandage to wrap round him.

As I tied the bandage, the spy said,

"That settles it. With the rain stopped, we lose the greater part of our cover." He turned to the mage, "Fryn'gh, I need you to heal me again."

The mage wearily shook his head.

"I tell you I can't, Haz, I'm sorry. I just don't have it in me."

I crawled awkwardly over to Fryn'gh. A horse stamped as I passed it, narrowly missing my hand. Must be mine, I thought.

"What do you need?" I asked the mage.

"Rest," he said, simply.

"We don't have time."

In reply, the mage simply shook his head again. I hesitated, and then took his hands in mine.

"Please, Fryn'gh." Still he shook his head. "Can you not give him just a little push?"

"You don't understand, Saahni." This close I could see he too was pale, his eyes red rimmed and watery. "This tired, I've almost no control. Doing a spell I'm not a master of could be disastrous."

"Fryn'gh — " Hazzor began, but Thorn shushed

him and crept over to kneel next to me.

"Fryn'gh," she said, "It's the same odds as last time, Kayt'an's right. Back in that barn, we didn't know it could be done, but we gambled and won. Tonight, you don't think you can do it, but if you don't try," she paused and I finished for her,

"We'll have to leave Hazzor behind."

"No," the spy corrected me. "If you leave me behind, you'll have to kill me. We can't afford for the W'shten to find me alive."

Chapter 21

The mage exploded. He huffed and puffed, and said we could not put that kind of pressure on him. I said I did not see the difference between this and the last time. He said that we had said, if he did not do this, he might as well kill Hazzor himself. Then, for some reason, I thought it was helpful to point out that the whole sorry mess was his fault in the first place.

At this point, Fryn'gh sank to the level at which I normally operated and shrieked,

"Shut up! Shut up, shut up, shut UP!"

For the second time that evening, the stall fell silent. The mage ran his fingers into his carroty fleece and pulled his knees up to his elbows. We all stared.

Hazzor was the first to break the quiet.

"Drop it," he said.

I could not see his face, but his voice carried no inflection. He could have been telling us to drop a packet, not the conversation on which hung his life. I forgot the poor man was doubtless in pain and I too lost my temper. Rolling back on to my heels, I straightened my back in ire.

"No!" I said, outraged. "That's not fair!"

When had Hazzor ever given me a break? From the day in temple, when he would cheerfully have killed me, to having a go at me in Marrett, to forcing me to accept Fryn'gh's magic, he had never cut me any slack. This was the first time the mage had wibbled, and the spy immediately backed off. I was too tired to see the conversation through the injured man's eyes. All I saw was the gross injustice. The entire world danced around this cynic's every whim, I told myself, while all my priorities and principles were stamped on without a moment's thought. I leaned towards the mage, ruthless now in my resentment.

"He is a selfish, stupid, self-absorbed scut who won't even *try* and save a life because he's," and I deliberately made my voice high pitched and childish, 'too tired'."

Fryn'gh's head whipped up and he shoved me backwards, barely giving me time to register his tears before I was among the horses' hooves. The horses snorted and skittered and stamped as I rolled, desperate to get away from them. I twisted and turned, seeking a path back to where I had been, but Axyl was in my way. He was leaning towards the horses, keeping me in amongst them.

"Are you satisfied now?" he growled.

I scuttled sideways and Axyl, thankfully, stayed where he was, letting me rejoin the people. He gave a dismissive snort, but all of my wrath was still focused on the mage.

"You could have killed me!" I hissed at him. "Have you absolutely no respect for life?"

Fryn'gh wiped his nose on his hand and snarled,

"I've more respect for human life than you have appreciation of humanity," he snarled. "Don't you ever let up?"

"Oh! So this is about me now?"

"I said, 'Drop it'."

Hazzor's voice rang out colder than ice now. Recklessly, I ignored him.

"Then why don't you prove you're better than me?"

"Yeah?" the magician, the dabbler in the occult, crawled over to me, Thorn moving out of his way. "And if I do?"

I smiled, grimly, in the darkness,

"You get to be better than me," I said.

"Fine," Fryn'gh said. Then, again, "Fine!" He wiped his face again and scratched his scalp, vigorously. He cleaned his hands on his trousers and said to Hazzor, "Ready?"

"Hold on!" I said, taken aback, while at the same time Hazzor pulled himself away from the mage, reflexively.

The mage flexed his fingers and breathed out slowly, clearly taking no notice of either of us.

"Just a very little!"

I reminded him, alarmed now about what he might do if his anger robbed him of the little judgement he had for healing.

Fryn'gh took hold of the spy. Hazzor gave a breathy grunt and slumped.

"There," the mage sounded empty, "satisfied?"

Thorn reached across Axyl to put a hand on Fryn'gh's arm.

"Fryn'gh?" she said, gently, but the mage just shrugged her off.

He inched his way back to his corner and curled up.

"Thank you," said the archer, but Fryn'gh did not look up.

"Just leave me alone," he said.

No one said anything.

I was left feeling distinctly shabby. It was a depressingly familiar feeling.

I said the hour while we waited for Ranyl to return. Abe would not let me light the candle so I had only my beads to help me pray. I counted off the joyful mysteries, mournfully, finding myself in stark contrast once again to my goddess. She had tended the weak; I picked on them. She lived in the light of Saen's love; I sat in dark soggy self-absorption. She sacrificed herself for the human race; I sacrificed others.

I thought about King Gayton, trying to galvanise the country to war, trying to keep his country — my country — distinct from the creeping W'shten influence. I thought how desperate the king must have become, how frightened of losing. I thought again of Challawin and Hazzor's mission, and how I'd despised and hated them in their ruthlessness. I curled up, back to the wall of the pen, head on my knees. *Every day you can see the way back and suddenly a door shuts behind you and you have become a monster,* Hazzor had said to me that morning, which seemed so long ago. What would I not do if I thought the end worthy enough? Only two days ago I had agonised about asking the mage to do magic. Tonight, I had forced him to against his will. How many steps between this and ordering the death of a village of strangers? I was no longer so sure I was so much better.

Re'a, Saviour of the world... I could not finish. What? Guide me? Save me? I lifted my head and stared bleakly at the horses. *Re'a, Saviour of the world,* find *me.*

It was late when Ranyl returned. I had not been able to bring myself to check on Hazzor. Nobody asked me to and I wanted to pretend the events of the evening had not happened. Either the spy was a little better or his wound was healed and his muscles wasted — possibly his organs too. He was breathing deeply and evenly so I believed the latter was unlikely, but frankly I did not want to find out any sooner than I had to. Tomorrow was soon enough.

The thief had got his hands on some cheese, to our delight. I was mostly past the point of hunger, though. I ate a little and then curled up to try to sleep.

I was back on the hill back home. Again, the temple was gone as was the statue of my goddess. Again, I was surrounded by the broken statues of my village. This time, the statues bore the marks of violence I had seen in the temple in H'th Iriq. This time, I stood. This time, there was an axe in my hands.

"It wasn't me!" I called into the emptiness. I looked at the axe. "It isn't mine!" I dropped the weapon and called out again, "Blessed Lady, where are you?"

I turned, and turned again, and saw that the statues on the ground were not those of my erstwhile flock, but of Axyl and Ranyl, Hazzor, Abernast and Thorn, broken and bloody. In front of me was a savaged statue of Fryn'gh, which still cried, and I wept with it. I dropped to my knees.

"Re'a!" I wept, "Blessed Lady?"

Somehow the axe was in my hands again and, no matter how I tried to throw it away, I found it still in my own grip.

"Re'a," I was weeping freely, "Saviour of the world," I was so lonely here, surrounded by symbols of my own folly, "redeem me."

I was woken next morning by horse breath. It was snorted hot and smelly at point blank range and I opened my eyes to a vision filled with horse nose. "Nyagh!" I said, surprised, and scooted backwards on my elbows, bumping into Abe. Before I could blink, the bandits were all rising to their feet, crouched under the low ceiling, weapons in their hands. Ranyl, who was the only one short enough to stand straight, said,

"What is it?"

I cleared my throat and sat up, sheepish and still sleepy.

"Umm," I cleared my throat anew, looking for an explanation that would not make me look a fool. I could find none. "The horse startled me."

Thorn turned her gaze on me.

"The horse," she repeated.

In the dim pre-dawn light, I could just see her mouth twitch.

Axyl grunted and dropped back down to his heels.

"Sahnithi, sweetheart," began Abe, palely visible in the dimness, "remind me to find you a room in an inn tonight."

"Ha ha," I answered wittily.

The only ones who were not awake were Hazzor and Fryn'gh. Fryn'gh was snoring so I reckoned he was simply sleeping off his exertions of the day before. I turned from him guiltily and walked on my knees to the sleeping spy. As before I checked breath, heart beat and forehead, and was relieved to find all these signs encouraging. I ran my hands over his limbs, which seemed much as they had two days before. I was cheered still further. I caught Axyl's eye and the big barbarian came and lifted Hazzor up for me so I could remove the bandages. I folded them up and removed the wolf's heart, using the big leaves to wipe off the ointment I had made last night.

As I looked at the little spy's midriff, my mouth hung open. Where, yesterday, there'd been a nearly healed cut, inflamed and slightly bloody, there was now a thin pink line. My stitches sat like some child's game, abandoned in the ground long after the players have been called in. Stiffly, I pulled over my bag and took out my little knife to cut the threads and remove them. Thorn looked over my shoulder and whistled. The ligatures, once removed, left behind six pairs of little holes where the flesh had healed around the thread. I ran my thumb over the holes and snatched my hand away, expecting the spy to flinch in his sleep. He sighed a bit, perhaps, but that was all.

Ranyl, too, whistled quietly.

"Saen's balls," he said, his face unusually open for a moment, wonder writ large until he caught me looking and composed his face to its habitual cynicism.

"Ranyl, quit admiring Hazzor's belly for a moment, hey," Abe's familiar slow undulating tones imposed on our admiration of Fryn'gh's work, "and go and check the horizon for us, no?"

Ranyl grabbed some breakfast from his cache and shouldered his way past the horses who were starting to look decidedly fed up. Axyl handed out bread and cheese to the rest of us, keeping a sizable portion for the sleeping spy. I took my ration and sat to eat it, chewing over, not only my food, but the relationship between wickedness and wellbeing. How could something as obviously wicked as magic cause such healing? I finished my breakfast and turned my thoughts to my prayers, feeling vaguely guilty I had not prayed first.

Before I had finished, Ranyl returned. When he

reached us I saw his dark face was pinched and his thin lips were pressed tighter than usual. I knew what he had to say before he spoke.

"They're close."

"How close?"

Thorn's face mirrored the thief's. Ranyl shrugged.

"Less than an hour, I'd say, and they're already moving." He looked grim — grimmer than usual. "But, if I can see them, they'll see us pretty well as soon as we move." He glanced at the two sleeping men, "When we do move, that is."

Chapter 22

A horse snorted and stamped, and all four bandits turned towards the sound. They did not seem startled, just thoughtful. Odd, I thought, those horses have been there all night and suddenly the beasts have caught their attention. I stared too, hoping to notice something interesting.

It was Thorn who spoke first.

"How far are the marshes?"

Abe nodded.

"Ay Toris is about," he tilted his head slightly, "oh, 10 miles from here."

Thorn raised her eyebrows.

"That close?"

Abe shrugged.

"Probably."

"Ey Torese?" I asked, still looking at the horses, still puzzled.

The W'shten raised his eyebrows at me.

"Ay Toris," he said, apparently correcting me. "It's where we're going, Saahni."

"Oh." I nodded, intelligently. "I thought it was Dar Toris?"

I could see Ranyl shaking his head sadly. Even Axyl was suddenly studying the wall beside him.

"Ay Toris, Saahni, is where we're going *next*."

Abe patted me on the head as though I were a child, and then turned back to his comrades. "We mustn't be followed there. Dar Tor is where we are heading."

Curiously, Thorn, Abe and Axyl were now looking at Ranyl. I cast a quick look at the horses just to make sure we were done with them for now. They seemed the same as they had last night. Less tired, perhaps, more ticked off. There was a lot of tail flicking going on and my horse was decidedly tight-lipped, like a disgusted old lady. Wary of that mouth, I checked the distance between me and the horse before I turned to Ranyl. Ranyl was somehow doing a very good impression of a nocked arrow, poised and sharp. His mouth held the usual suggestion of a cynical smile.

He nodded, slowly.

"And how am I to find you again?"

Had I missed something, I wondered, helplessly.

"We'll wait at Ay until tomorrow."

Abe hadn't taken his eyes off the thief.

"And how am I supposed to find this particular collection of mud people?"

Thorn gave a slow grin,

"You could always knock on the door of the first village you come to and ask."

"A ha ha ha," said Ranyl, looking not at all amused.

None of us were paying any attention to Fryn'gh so we were all surprised, I think, when a bored sounding voice said, "I can always make a signal."

I say we were all surprised. I was the only one who jumped. Perhaps no one noticed. Certainly, everyone's eyes were now on the mage.

"Go on," said Abe.

"A signal in the sky above us like ..." the mage seemed to be searching for an example.

"Like a wychi?" suggested Thorn.

"Not in the marshes," said Abe. "A sohra, perhaps?"

"I don't know what that looks like," said the mage, rubbing a hand over his face.

"Doesn't matter, I can show you. The point is does Ranyl, here?"

"Aye," said the thief, simply.

Abe nodded. He added, by way of explanation, "Sohra are sociable birds," he glanced at Thorn and flashed a grin, "just like me, honey." Thorn gave him a smile and the outlander carried on, "They don't last long on their own. A single sohra will stand out nicely, without being," he paused as he chose his word, "obvious."

"Single sohra, gotcha," said Ranyl, tersely. "When?"

"Midday, each day."

I didn't like it when Abernast was this succinct. It did not bode well. Besides, I was starting to feel invisible. I laid a hand on Thorn's arm.

"What's going on?"

Thorn looked my way, tension written on her face, the scar looking darker against her paler skin.

"Ranyl will take the horses and try to redirect the patrol again."

I glanced back to Ranyl who was taking a few bits out of his pack and tucking them in assorted pockets about his person.

"Is that safe?"

Ranyl bared his yellow teeth in his fox's grin and said,

"If I wanted safe, I'd have stayed home minding pigs."

"We're not going to wait for him?"

I looked back and forth between Ranyl and his comrades. Thorn shook her head.

"Let's get these horses out, then." Abe put a hand on my chest as I began to move. "Sahnithi, sweetheart, I've seen your way with horses. Stay here with Hazzor, no?"

I sat down again and turned to my sleeping patient, saving myself another view of Abernast's grin.

As the bandits applied themselves to turning the horses in the small, small space, I heard a softer sigh under the snorting and stamping of the mounts. Hazzor was starting to surface. Wary of the turning animals, I crawled awkwardly over the spy to reach for Ranyl's sack, which held the stolen food. Hazzor grunted and tried to turn, rolling himself into my skirt. I hissed through my teeth and pulled my skirt back, narrowly avoiding getting my hand trodden on. I grumbled under my breath as I retrieved the sack and sat back down.

"It's not their fault, you know."

The mage spoke quietly.

"Doesn't mean I have to like them, though." I turned to him as I answered and handed Fryn'gh some of Ranyl's stash of food. He nodded his thanks and I continued, "I'll be glad to be rid of them." He shrugged indifferently and I felt compelled to add, "I'm sorry ... you know?"

I felt the blood rushing to my face. To cover my discomfort, I brought the sad tangle that had been braids down in front of my face and made a pantomime of patting them to see if there was enough un-mud-caked hair to plait. There was not. In the silence of Fryn'gh's not answering, I seriously considered following Thorn's example and taking a knife to my hair. My scalp itched abominably. I heard the mage sigh. I folded my hair back and looked up.

Fryn'gh was not looking at me, but he cleared his throat and said,

"Makes us quits, I suppose."

He paused. He clearly had more to say so I bit my tongue to keep from jumping in. He sniffed.

"I forced magic on you, you forced me to do magic."

He shrugged. I shifted uncomfortably. It had been a long time since I had been this vulnerable in apology offered and returned. I smiled a little wryly and offered out my index finger in a gesture from childhood.

"Peace?" I said.

Fryn'gh suddenly smiled a bright smile that lit up his grime encrusted face.

"Peace," he answered and touched fingertip to fingertip.

"About time," a sleepy voice commented, "though I reckon Ranyl'll be keeping a book on how long it lasts."

"Hazzor," I smiled, relieved to have the distraction, "how'd you feel?"

"Hungry," he answered.

I passed him what we had and the spy applied himself to it. He did not speak while he ate, and remembering, still, the all consuming nature of that post-healing hunger, I did not try to speak to him.

By now the horses were outside and we had the pen to ourselves. I took a deep breath. All this air, just for the three of us: what luxury!

Fryn'gh leaned over a little and gestured to the determined eater.

"How'd I do?"

I shrugged.

"Hard to tell. No harm done, I'm fairly sure, but the damage is all inside now. I've no way of knowing what remains."

I rubbed my face and stuck a few loose strands into the morass that was my hair.

"Normally, I'd have time as a guide, but..." I hugged my knees and looked up at the mage's worried face. I offered a fleeting smile and shrugged. "I'll know more when he tries to move."

Fryn'gh nodded and brushed the last of the crumbs off his fingers.

"I'd better go and see if they want any help."

I was left with the horse shit and the spy.

I sniffed and got out the gentian bark. I began to chew grimly, mirroring the urgent mastication of my companion. I comforted myself with the thought that we were heading for a village. A fire, I thought, and — please Re'a — a bath.

Eventually, the remaining bandits and Fryn'gh returned. Hazzor was just finishing gorging, though he was examining Ranyl's bag thoroughly, just in case.

Abe strode — as best as a tall man can stride in such a place — across the pen and knelt beside the spy.

"Thank the gods, Haz, you're awake. We've got to leave this place. The patrol is nearly upon us."

It was as if someone had flicked a switch. Gone was the food obsession, Hazzor was again all purposeful — Reath's man.

"How near?"

"Too near, buck. Less than a mile."

The spy swore and rose to his feet. Quickly, we gathered up our possessions and left the stall. I dithered over the Collinsonia on the floor, but Hazzor practically dragged me away.

"No time, no point," was all he said.

Outside Ranyl was still waiting with the horses. Once we had scurried past to hide in a ditch near the animal pen, Ranyl took off, leading the horses, stamping and turning over our tracks, into the distance. I watched him go.

"Will he be alright?"

"Shh!"

Already, we could hear the patrol's horses coming and the odd shout of a soldier. We crouched in the ditch. The water came up to my hips. How lucky, I thought, that we have been living in mud for the last four days. We blend in beautifully. The bandits pulled the weeds and grasses around the ditch to cover us while Fryn'gh and I cowered. The horses were louder now. I could hear individual voices. We all crouched still, so still, thigh to thigh and knee to shin. I buried my fingers in the walls of the ditch and rested my head on my hands as though I could somehow burrow into the mud. I felt sick. I was so tired of being afraid. Visions of a mutilated priest filled my mind and I started to shiver. Fryn'gh sneezed. I started to curse myself inwardly. *I should have given him some gentian, I should have thought, exhaustion and rain lead to ...*

My own immediate danger began to override my fears for the mage. The horses were close, so close. I closed my eyes tight shut. *Merciful Re'a, Saviour of the world* (breathe out) *save us*. Suddenly and pressingly, I realised I had not relieved myself after waking. I was conscious of every splash and rippling of the ditchwater. I may have whimpered a little.

At last the horses were getting further away rather than nearer. They were following Ranyl away from us.

Next to me, I felt Fryn'gh relax and I started to move but Axyl held me down. My bladder was screaming at me.

I waited until the W'shten were a little further then, "I have to pee," I hissed.

I heard Hazzor sigh.

"Then pee," he said.

"I am not peeing here!"

I was indignant at the idea as fear took second place to the demands of my body and the small dignities to which I still clung. To my astonishment, Thorn started to laugh, quietly. Hazzor cursed. Slowly — far too slowly as far as I was concerned — Abe stood. After a pause — far too long a pause — he relaxed a notch.

"If our elegant priest needs privacy, gentlemen," I could not see the grin but I knew it was there, "I suggest we withdraw to the ground floor."

Axyl snorted and even Fryn'gh sniggered, but I did not care. I watched carefully — I would not put it past Abe to peek — and when it was clear I sorted myself out. Oh, the bliss.

I climbed up to join the others who had already forgotten the joke and were watching the horizon.

As soon as Hazzor figured they were far enough away, he gave the order to march. After, that is, asking sarcastically if anyone else wanted to "make themselves comfortable". Comfortable was not the word I would have chosen. As usual Fryn'gh dried us off and, as usual, that dried the mud into our clothes. I asked why he could not get the mud as well as the water out of our clothes, and the wretched man had the gall to look at me — again — as though I were stupid.

It was Thorn who answered as we crept around the edge of the field, keeping as low to the ground as we could. It was hard work on the stomach muscles and I watched Hazzor anxiously.

"Mud is made up of too many things, Saahni. Fryn'gh doesn't know exactly what it is, so he can't shift it."

I sighed and kept walking.

Interlude

Ttarah unwrapped her bandaged hand. Her fingertip was not *there, but* was *there still in her mind's eye, and in some corner of her imagination she couldn't explain. She made a fist, and the action made her flinch. So much tenderness for one small spot.*

There wasn't much missing, but it was still a violation that had taken her breath away. Without permission, without warning, Lord Reath had severed the tip of her little finger and left again, leaving her father to offer what explanations he chose, which were few.

A prince was promised. All was well. Honour was restored. It was a small sacrifice. She should be pleased.

Gayton had been trapped in his own deceit. To hide his daughter's 'shame' he had invented the curse; but now none would marry a woman warped by hideous magic. Now, apparently, a solution had been found: a new deception to hide the old.

Reath presented her father with many solutions. Ttarah was astonished by many of them, and by her Father's blithe acceptance of plans that would make a normal man flinch. If she had a tenth of Reath's influence — the princess curled herself round her healing hand, protectively — she would end the war that had created so much madness.

If she had a tenth of his influence, she would still have a whole hand.

Chapter 23

It was slow going. The rain had stopped but the mud was still an ever present hazard, which threatened alternately to suck at our feet and hold us stuck, and slide away underneath us like ice. I worried constantly about Ranyl. He was not what I would call pleasant company, but I had eaten, slept and suffered alongside him for what was beginning to feel like a lifetime. I poked that last thought again. I supposed it was a lifetime — my lifetime as this new creature, Adventurer Kayt'an. I smiled briefly at the thought, and then went back to worrying about Ranyl.

The morning wore on and — I had not thought it possible — the ground under our feet became increasingly waterlogged. In fact, more and more of our time was spent wading rather than walking. To my surprise, as the ground grew wetter the grass grew longer. I took to walking close behind Axyl so I did not have to wade through grass as well as water. As Saen approached his zenith unseen behind the clouds, we came to a river. Here, the grasses grew nearly as tall as me. At least, I thought, we will be hard to see or to follow in these wetlands. Abe crouched down and dipped his fingers in to the water. He sucked his fingers and grunted happily. He stood up tall and scanned the horizon up and down the river.

"There!"

I peered in the same direction. Lately, I had begun to feel as though my eyes were being drawn from their sockets. The horizon was so far away it made the land look empty and unending, unyielding in its featurelessness. Some two miles, perhaps less, down river I could see houses clustered at the edge of the water. There was something odd about the shape of the village but, from where I stood, I could not see what it was.

We headed down river and as Ay Toris hoved into clearer view I saw that it did not edge the river but spilled out into the waters. The houses —

"Abe, are those houses *floating*?"

He grinned at me.

"Welcome to the Steriv Marshes, Sahnithi, love."

I boggled.

"It's so ... empty," I said.

"Empty?"

Abe was a pantomime of outrage. In a caricature of the proud father, he pointed out the flowers as we walked. Low, almost heathery plants grew around us in the long grass, interspersed with really rather pretty purply flowers that Abe called lavender. I told him it was not lavender. I told him I had lavender in my pack and would gladly show him the difference, but he simply patted me on the shoulder and told me I was not in the Western Reaches now. I snorted, disparagingly. Abe pointed up at some birds circling over our heads. *Sohra*, he said. He told me they spent the whole day in the air, eating the insects that filled — and I do mean filled — the air of the marshes.

"Where are the fields?" I asked.

Abe pointed at the river,

"There," he said.

I looked at him as though he had gone quite mad, which I thought he had. He had an excuse after all: we had all had a very trying few days. His annoyingly white teeth made another appearance.

"In there, Sahnithi, darlin', lives more food than you would get from a field full of sheep or cattle."

"Fish," I said, unimpressed.

"Fish, yes, and also crayfish — "

"That sounds like another fish."

Abe ignored me. He was, very nearly literally, in his element.

"There are beautiful shrimp, sahnithi, and snails as big as my hand..." he looked at his own hand thoughtfully for a moment, "as big as your hand, anyway. Terrapins make the fisherman wary of his fingers and toes," he waggled his fingers at me gleefully, "and fierce dragons patrol the waters."

The big man glowed. Here was an outlander who had returned home. He put his hands on his hips and surveyed the waters for a moment, a new smile on his lips.

"My toes are going to be growing fins and patrolling these waters themselves, if I don't get them dry soon," Axyl grumbled.

The pale man turned and slapped the barbarian heartily on the back.

"Come then, brother, let's not let this priest delay us further."

I would have complained at this injustice, but the morning's march had been hard going. I was as keen as any to rest, and the closest thing to a dry place I could see was the village ahead.

Eventually, we were opposite Ay Toris. It was the most extraordinary place I had ever seen. Each building was made of an arch of woven ... material, thinly painted with a muddy cover. The arch seemed to be sewn on to a floating platform. Usually, there was only one arch per platform but, occasionally, there were two. Each arch was filled at either end by heavy-looking, colourful curtains. The platforms seemed to float in formation, but I could not see what held them together. The whole effect was surprisingly bright and cheerful in such an underwhelming landscape. Between the houses were a score of little flat bottomed boats. Children leaped from boat to boat and from platform to platform, shrieking and laughing. Men and women sat cross legged on the lips of the platforms busy with their hands and their tongues, companionable and industrious.

Abe stood on the banks of the river and shouted.

"Pelani!" He shouted again "Pelani, hee!"

We saw hands raised in greeting on the other side of the river, and I could hear an echo of the cry, 'Pelani' travelling round the village. In a short span, there was a movement outward and a boat headed towards us. In it was a man so pale I could have mistook him for a ghost. He made Abe look colourful. Nonetheless, the family-likeness was clear. The stranger was long-limbed, but more angular than Abernast. As he drew near, though, I saw a familiar grin stretch across the newcomer's face.

"Abernasti!" he shouted with glee, "Abernasti, hee!"

Abe jumped into the little boat, which rocked wildly. The stranger promptly swept his foot through Abe's legs, tripping him, and followed this a punch, which launched the big fighter into the river with a splash.

Instantly, Thorn and Axyl had weapons in their hands. Hazzor danced forward to control the boat. Behind me, Fryn'gh swore softly and at length.

"Saahni," said Thorn between nearly closed lips, "have your bow ready."

"My bow?"

I had it with me, of course, but it was not strung, and it was under my pack. A familiar dread filled my veins. Once again, I was being called on to fight. I ought to stand my ground; I ought not to take part in bloodshed. I was a priest and a healer. I ...

My dithering was interrupted by Abe's surfacing from the waters with a whoosh. He stood in the shallow river and roared.

Pelani — was that a name or a function? — put his hands on his hips and laughed heartily. My mouth hung open and I could see uncertainty bloom on the faces of Thorn and Axyl.

"Abe?"

Thorn lowered her knife.

Abe shook his hair like a dog, and also laughed. He reached up to the man in the boat, open-handed, clearly looking for a hand up to the boat. The boatman laughed again and shook his head, speaking incomprehensibly. Abe grinned wryly and held his hands out in an open gesture as he stepped towards the boat.

They looked like friends; they were certainly family. Thorn and Axyl still looked wary, but Hazzor had stepped away from the boat. The boatman directed a question at Hazzor who answered smoothly but, before the spy had finished speaking, our W'shten leant his whole weight on the side of the boat. The boat tipped sharply and now both men were in the water.

Once more, the bandits on the shore stood poised, ready to fight or flee, but Hazzor stood with his arms folded, a queer look on his face. Was he *jealous*?

men's relat.?

Meanwhile, from the village, I could hear shouting and cheering. There was now a crowd of the children clustered in a boat floating this side of Ay Toris. The two men in the water wrestled and laughed. First one and then the other would be held under; one determined and heavy and the other moving like a fish — dexterous and slippery. The six of us stood among the reeds, puzzled spectators, embarrassed and awkward.

Eventually, Hazzor must have got fed up with the performance as he said something that sounded like, "Abernasti, Pelani, hrat celly den?"

The two men stopped and stood: their faces held matching expressions of sheepishness. Both flashed revoltingly white teeth at us and both waded out of the river. Abe, I noticed, took an opportunity when his twin's back was turned to give him shove, which Hazzor promptly rebuked like a bored parent. I could not help smiling as the two grown boys climbed out of the water, both now cheerfully unrepentant, and pulled the boat to us. Under Hazzor's direction, we all got in the boat. Abe and his cousin chatted in their heathen language, occasionally throwing playful punches, and we reached the village of Ay Toris without further drama.

We were welcomed into the village as if we had been longed for. There was much jabbering and hugging and smiling and kissing and laughing. It was almost overwhelming. After days of weary trudging through the rain, these bright smiles and fulsome greetings made me more tired than ever. Thorn, it seemed to me, was getting even more attention. The locals seemed to be falling over themselves to pat her hand or her cheek and hug her. Abe was jubilant, hugging and kissing with the best of them, and he kept introducing family to us. "Sahnithi, darling', meet my cousin Pelan," or "my aunt Rhossa," or "my uncle Ghen," — he seemed to be related to nearly the whole village.

The floating platforms were surprisingly stable. We were taken to a large open platform or '*tuy heold*' where we were greeted by someone who behaved like an elder, but was a little child, surely no more than ten. The little queen appeared to welcome us solemnly, and then engaged Hazzor in conversation. At the end of this, the girl sent off her seniors as if errand runners. I felt my eyebrows rise, but I said nothing; nothing loud enough to hear, anyway. As I stood and waited for someone to explain what was going on, rugs and cushions appeared and were spread out.

"Yecho, yecho," said one of the cushion bearers to me, gesturing me to sit. I looked at the beautiful cushions and replied by showing the man how muddied and begrimed my clothes were. He shook his head and waggled his hands. "Tononi nyth. Yecho."

I glanced at Hazzor and Abe, and seeing them already seated I gratefully folded up. Close up I saw the fabric of both rugs and cushions was not woven or embroidered but painted. As everyone sat, I realised there was a fire in the middle of the platform. I stared at it for a few moments and blinked a couple of times. Fryn'gh was sat near me and I caught his eye. I nodded at the fire and mouthed "magic?" but he shook his head. I was mystified.

Hazzor leaned forward.

"Delaena asked if we wanted to eat or rest first." He grinned, uncharacteristically toothy, "I'm afraid I answered on my account." His glanced flicked at Fryn'gh. "I'm famished."

I did not complain as my own stomach rumbled at the thought of food. A distant voice reminded me that I should pray before I eat, but the food came too quickly. It was a form of bread, hard and unleavened, which was served with honey and cheese. It was a welcome meal and I ate hungrily, our hosts smiling and nodding at every mouthful. It would be rude to delay my meal, I told myself, and promised Re'a I would pray afterwards.

After our meal, we were separated, Thorn and I herded off with some women, while the others were taken to another side of the village. I shouldered my way over to Hazzor as he was lead away.

"What's happening?" I asked anxiously.

"A wash and a change of clothes," said the spy calmly.

Then, his eyes darkened and he took my arm.

"Keep your palm hidden, and your arm," he said, referring to the ritual scarring of my left arm. I opened my mouth to object, but as always he spoke without waiting, "The W'shten believe the priests of Re'a are witches." Again, I tried to speak. Again, he took no notice. "They may stomach your prayers, if you are discreet, but *Kayt'an,* Keep. Your. Hand. Hidden. They will kill us all if they think we have brought a witch into their village."

He held my eyes until I nodded, and then he released me.

I stomped off after Thorn, grumbling to myself. What, in Saen's name, were we doing in this place that was so dangerous in the first place? It was not my fault I was here, anyway — I stepped uncertainly into a boat and out again — it wasn't as if I had volunteered! I should ask Hazzor why Reath chose me in the first place, that might quiet the man. Surely Reath planned his team before he planned the mission? What were we at? The question had not overly bothered me for the last few days as we'd trudged through the rain and I'd been all taken up with Hazzor's wound; but the puzzle now demanded my attention, and I had no answers.

Washed and in clean clothes (oh the bliss), I asked to borrow Thorn's knife. I had had enough. One of our companions, whose name I had discovered was Keas, looked in horror when she saw my intent.

"Nen!" she exclaimed, and made to stay my hand.

I nodded my head vigorously and pointed at Thorn's shorn head.

"Clean," I said, and pointed at the matted pelt that used to be my hair. I pulled a face to help my meaning and said, "Dirty," and stuck my tongue out in a child's pantomime of disgust.

Thorn merely shrugged. Then, she seemed to change her mind and held out her hand for the knife.

"Here," she said, "give me the knife so I can at least make a decent job of it."

Keas saw that Thorn intended to help me and her eyes opened wide. She seemed ridiculously upset by the idea. *"Nen!"* she had her hands up to her face now, wide eyed and even paler.

Thorn and I exchanged mystified glances. Keas fled the *tuy heold*, and the two of us watched her leave; felt her leave, too, as the platform bobbed slightly.

"I always did say the W'shten were an odd lot," remarked Thorn. She raised an eyebrow, "Are you sure you want to do this?"

I took a deep breath and nodded.

My hair has always been my vanity. I have lovely hair — when it is clean and groomed — straight as hung flax and the colour of the sun. Amtil chose me for my hair or, at least, she had said my hair was a sign I was a blessing from Saen.

When I was younger, Amtil had used to wash and braid my hair. Then, it had been the fashion to weave ribbons and beads through the hair, and I had begged Amtil to do so for me.

"A priest has no need for baubles and fripperies," the old priest had said, sternly.

"I am not a priest, Sahnithi."

"But you will be."

"Maybe," I had quibbled, "if Re'a wants me, but maybe not." I had looked up to try to coax my mentor, "Please, Sahnithi? All the other girls wear ribbons."

"And if all the other girls ran about naked or filled their hair with sticks?"

I had sighed, frustrated.

"Sahnithi, please, just a couple of ribbons? Just so they won't laugh at me, Sahnithi, pleeease?"

"So what else will you do, Kayt'an, to stop the girls laughing at you?" Amtil put down her brush and swept my hair out of my face with her fingers. She held my head as she spoke to me. "If you stand straight before the Holy Three that is all that matters."

I had rolled my eyes. I tried sophistry,

"But you said no one can stand before Farock Rha. You said everyone falls short. You said ..."

Amtil's eye's had narrowed dangerously and I tailed off.

"If you spend your time worrying about being laughed at, Kayt'an, you will be pulled hither and thither all your life. You will not be able to stand anywhere."

I tried another tack.

"But it looks pretty, Sahnithi."

"Your hair is the ornament Saen gave you. Do you need more?"

My face had fallen into a sulk. Amtil combed my hair with her fingers again, almost stroking me like a dog. Her voice was softer when she had said,

"Kayt'an, your hair is beautiful. It is so like Blessed Re'a's hair. You should not spoil it."

I had sniffed. The old priest picked up the brush again, and began to work ruthlessly through the tangles.

"Your hair is a sign, child. What if your friends cut their hair off? What will you do then? Will you cut off the sign that called you to priesthood?"

Apparently, Sahnithi, yes.

Thorn was quick and thorough. She had nearly finished lopping off the matted braids when Hazzor arrived with Abe close behind. The *tuy heold* bobbed deeply and we both looked up. Thorn and I were sat on a colourful rug, in the thick green over-shirts and short brown leggings the villagers wore. Instead of gloves, which no one here wore, I had pretended an injury and my marked hand was bandaged. Bandages, likewise, hid the H'mariq scars on my left arm.

Save one quarter, Thorn had cut my hair down to the length of a finger joint. There was a great pile of my hair beside us. Abe looked horrified and even Hazzor looked stunned.

"Oh hell," said the spy.

Chapter 24

It seems, in this corner of W'shten, a shorn head is a sign of mourning. When a close relative or near friend dies, the bereaved cut off their hair and sit and wail for a day or two.

Alternatively, when a person walks into a village and cuts her hair off, she is predicting the death of the village. Usually it is an act of war. Just occasionally, mystics do it as prophecy or a warning. I had done it because my head was itchy.

On the plus side, my head now felt great. Strangely light and naked, but also free.

Hazzor had sat with Thorn and me while Thorn glumly finished the task she had started. Abe was busy trying to reassure Keas. At least I now understood Keas' distress. She had been trying to stop me pronouncing a terrible future for the village.

Damn W'shten, why could they not speak a sensible language?

Sickness crept into my stomach as I thought of the last time I had cursed a village. Was I to become some sort of plague, Destroyer of Villages? *I should be shut in a box*, I thought, *for the safety of the world.*

I remembered Reath's mocking words, a lifetime ago, *'What a great creature you are, that the world moves on your action or inaction.'* I bit my lip. I was being foolish.

"I should have just let them burn you."

Hazzor's words brought me back to myself with a start. He looked strange in the simple clothes of these people. Like a green cat. As my last lock fell to Thorn's blade, the little man looked up. His face was back to its usual impassiveness. He stood smoothly and went and spoke slowly to Keas. Periodically, both of them and Abe looked at me and Thorn. As Hazzor spoke, Keas' face became more sorrowful and she looked at me with eyes that were deep pools of pity. If I had let my own sorrows rise, I could have drowned in them. By the time Hazzor had finished speaking, tears were running down her face and her eyes were wide with anxiety. She nodded and left the little platform.

Abe turned to the spy.

"Haz, chuck, you've missed your calling. I felt my own heart wrench at that tale."

I narrowed my eyes, suspiciously.

"What tale?"

Hazzor's mouth twitched.

"I told her that some three days ago, despite your best efforts as a healer you lost your lover — Thorn's brother, by the way — to fever. I told her you've been mad with grief and it's only with rest and food that you've been able to accept his fate and mourn decently."

My mouth hung open for a moment. Ire, never far away from me, kicked in.

"You said *what*?"

Thorn, behind me, chuckled earthily.

"We are of course accompanying Thorn and Abe back to Abe's father's family for a wedding."

This time it was Thorn's turn to open her eyes wide. Abe's grin was wide and triumphant.

"Have I not always said, beautiful Thorn, that one day I'd be your rose?"

"Unfortunately, there are those on both sides who would see an end to the match, so we're being pursued and need to proceed with a degree of stealth."

Thorn was the first to speak.

"A romance. Haz, you've turned this whole pudhy mess into a romance?"

"Aye, my heart, who'd have thought Reath's man had so much poetry in him?"

I held my hands up as if to call a halt to something.

"Did we have to lie to these people?" The three of them looked at me as though I had asked whether we needed to breathe. "Couldn't you just have said it was a mistake?"

I faced three pairs of eyes united in amazement at my stupidity.

Hazzor clasped his hands behind his back and nodded. He began to speak, his tone dripping with sarcasm,

"I see your point, Kayt'an — "

Reflex kicked in before thought. "Sa — " I began.

Quicker than I thought possible, Hazzor crossed the platform, grabbed me by my shirtfront and plunged my head underwater, before I could even finish speaking. I coughed in surprise and watched a great bubble of air leave for the surface of the water. My nose and throat seemed to swell with my need to breathe. Frantically, I beat on my attacker's chest, kicking reflexively with my feet. *Sweet Re'a! He's killing me!* I could see little through the water but the pale oval of Hazzor's face above me. I grabbed his wrists and shook my head, desperate to raise my face above the waterline and reach the air above.

As quickly as it happened, it was over. I was on my feet again, water running down my chest and shoulders, gasping for breath and coughing.

Hazzor stepped in close to me: eye-to-eye, nose-to-nose.

"Next time, I *will* drown you." His grey eyes showed nothing, no pity, no anger. "It will be a quicker death for you, and may just save our lives." He let me go and stepped back a little. "Do you understand?" I was still gasping for breath so he shook me once and repeated, "Do you understand?" I nodded. Still close to me, he spoke so quietly I had difficulty hearing. "If they even suspect you for a priest, you will die horribly. If they suspect we knew, we will join you. If we manage to persuade them we didn't know, we will simply be abandoned in these marshes without a boat or a guide." He shook his head disgustedly, "Will you ever see this is more than just an exercise for your pride and piety?"

Stunned by this display of anger and hostility, my bottom lip trembled and I sniffed. I gritted my teeth. I . would . not . cry.

"People's lives depend on this. More than just you and I."

His eyes were stone. I pushed my chin up briefly. It was not a nod — that would be to acknowledge too much — but Hazzor could take it as assent, if he wished.

Thorn, as usual the first to take pity on me, pushed Hazzor aside.

"Kayt'an," she spoke my name hesitantly, "what truth could we tell them?"

"We could tell them it was a mistake, tell them I'm a stranger to their culture."

"Too weak," said Abe: succinct, for a change.

"Well, then, we could tell them my village has died. I'm in mourning for them." With the memory of Keas' pitying eyes, I felt my throat tighten. I looked at Hazzor, defiantly — he, after all, had been a significant instrument of those deaths — "That much is true."

"Too vague." Thorn gave an embarrassed shrug. "I'm sorry, Sa -" she coughed, hurriedly, "Kayt'an, but why would you come all this way and wait nearly half a moon to mourn your village? And then we'd have to explain why they all died." She shook her head. "It won't do."

Hazzor made to straighten the skirts of a jacket he no longer wore and frowned, irritably. "People believe in romance more than they believe in any god," he said. "Give them vague truth and they'll look for the holes in it. Give them a ballad and they will work hard to believe it." He straightened the oversized shirt instead. "It gives Abe a good enough reason to be asking his kin to help without involving them knowingly." The abominable man looked at me with a raised eyebrow. "Unless you have a better plan that also includes a creditable explanation for why I have just sold them such a tale?"

I scowled. I hoped Hazzor's knife wound was pulling under the skin. *Drat the man. Who did he think he was to treat me so?* Abe flicked his eyes upward for no apparent reason. I looked up too; glad to have an excuse to look away. Above us the sky was still grey. High in the sky flew a solitary bird, swooping and circling. I guessed it was the sohra for Ranyl. It was past midday. The mage had remembered his duties, but I had completely forgotten mine.

"I have to pray," I said.

"Of course you do."

Hazzor's sarcasm was heavy. I stepped back towards him again.

"I am still ..." I hesitated. I did not want another dunking for saying the word out loud. "I am still the same as I was."

Both Abe and Thorn looked away for some reason, but Hazzor held my gaze. His face was full of bitter amusement.

"Kayt'an, look at yourself. Your own mother wouldn't recognise you."

Indignantly I answered,

"I've only cut my hair."

The spy only raised his eyebrows sardonically. He turned to the W'shten,

"Abernasti, hee. We've got wedding plans to arrange."

Abe smirked and Thorn rolled her eyes at me as they stepped off the *tuy heold*.

They left me to my prayers.

I prostrated myself on the platform. Any who saw me could assume I was prostrate in grief if they wished. I breathed out slowly and stared at the weave underneath me. It was less than comfortable to lie on. That suited me. I had had three days of glorious mindlessness, in which I could think only of the next step and whether I had the strength to take it. Now, Hazzor had given me back my stick and I proceeded to beat myself with it.

'You've made the decision not to die. Now your soul belongs to Reath' That's what Hazzor had said to me. Well it was not true. I might be late to say the hour, but I was still praying, still trying to be the priest I was called to be.

Wasn't I

'Kayt'an, look at yourself. Your own mother wouldn't recognise you.'

He was right. I was dressed now, not as a priest, not even as a Ttarcine adventurer, but as a W'shten marsh-dweller. I had cut off the braids of my womanhood. I mixed with heathens, atheists and magicians. I had not kept the feast. I realised with a jolt that I had said no prayers this morning and my midday prayers were late. Habits and opinions formed over all my years with Amtil were dissolving into the marsh ooze.

I was losing myself in lies. I was lying about who I was, lying about what we were doing, even lying about why I had cut my hair, by all that is holy! I was going to have to leave my prayers and fabricate grief for a man who did not exist, when I had all this real grief that I must not mention. In my mind's eye I saw Karl sneering at me for a hypocrite.

I put my hands to my head looking for my braids, to bury my fingers, and found none. I bit my lip. I did not know whether to laugh or cry. I linked my hands behind my head and sighed.

I served Re'a, and through her Saen, the Father of Truth, but everything I did or said was false. What was I becoming? Truly, I had no control over my life anymore.

Re'a, Saviour of the World, find *me.*

As I measured my prayers by my breath, I tried to place myself in my goddess' arms. Just as I felt myself reaching a calm place I felt the *tuy heold* dip. I cursed under my breath. Was it Abe come for a laugh or Hazzor come to enmesh me further in his fictions?

I refused to be drawn and kept my eyes shut.

There was another dip of the platform. I sighed.

The platform dipped again. This was beyond a joke. Now, three of them had come to disturb me when they knew I was praying. Was I never to be left to my devotions? Not even when we had nothing to do but wait for Ranyl? The remembrance of him made me offer a quick prayer for his safety. He was a thief and a scoundrel, but he was risking himself for our safety. I was just beginning a whimsical meditation on Ranyl being a figure of Re'a when the *tuy heold* dipped a fourth time.

I looked up, puzzled, were they all coming to look?

Three W'shten women were seated on the platform around me. A fourth had just joined them. They carried a beaker and a jug and one — Keas — held a blanket. I sat up, startled, and they gathered around me, crooning. Keas wrapped the blanket round me. She took my hand and patted it gently, her eyes still full of boundless pity. They had come to comfort me.

Oh, it just kept getting worse! Having no words to tell them I did not want comfort, but fearing any misleading gestures, I was forced to sit there passively while they patted and stroked me as though I were a baby. I was only grateful none of the others were watching. Were they? I looked round anxiously, but I could not see them. I was acutely aware of the pattern from the deck on my face. I put my hands to my shorn hair self-consciously, which only put the women into a lather of maternalism.

I found a cup pressed into my hands and I drank a sweet tea. As I drank, my comforters made approving noises and my back was rubbed. I wanted to tut — this was ridiculous — but these women meant well. More, well, my still-wet head was a potent reminder of Hazzor's likely reaction if I put our welcome at any further jeopardy.

As the tea warmed me, I began to relax. One of the W'shten women pulled out a child's toy from the folds of her clothing and held it out to me. Perplexed, I took it. It was a little cloth dolly. I stared at it dully. Did they genuinely think I was simple or was there a purpose to this, some new ritual of grief Hazzor had not thought to mention? I hoped the magic unravelled in his belly and the wretched little man bled to death. This was His Fault. I hated Hazzor. From the first moment I had met him he had wanted to kill me and now he was set on humiliating me.

I suddenly realised the little dolly was made just like him. Odd. I shook the Hazzor-doll viciously. Wretched man! I threw it to the ground and it lay there crumpled and helpless. Was he bleeding? Had I actually opened the wound? I did not mean it; it was an accident. *It always is*, said the monster within. I picked up the doll again. I did not mean it. I did not want him hurt again. I clutched it to me. All the fear I had felt for Hazzor's life rose up and overwhelmed me, all the guilt over my actions and lack of action. Karl, Fris'an , Ranyl, Hazzor, Fryn'gh, all danced around me variously beaten, bloody, and weeping. I was gripped by fear and guilt and grief and loss. I thought my heart would stop beating; there was so little room in my chest. Tears welled up in a flood that threatened to drown me.

In the distance, I felt someone stroking my head.

I curled up around the doll and wept like a child.

Chapter 25

Keas and her friends stayed with me until nightfall when I was finally cried out. The tears had come and gone in waves. Every time I had tried to pull myself together someone poured some fresh tea and I would lose myself again. All the while my comforters patted and stroked and sang and crooned.

As darkness began to draw in, the overflowing well of emotion finally dried up. I was exhausted and empty. The women washed my face and eased the doll out of my grasp. As I reluctantly handed it over, I saw it looked nothing like any of my travelling companions. How had I thought it looked like Hazzor?

I was thirsty so I reached for a beaker of tea, but Keas batted my hand away, speaking sternly. I looked up, surprised, and she smiled at me.

"Nythi veheru, sesri. Zaeni sepandth."

I looked at her blankly and she pointed at the horizon. I followed her pointing finger to where Saen must have been behind the clouds. I was astonished the day was so far gone. I ran my fingers into my hair, sheepish at my total loss of control, but the women just smiled at me.

They stood, and Keas held out her hand to me.

"Kayt'ani, hee."

I smiled back but shook my head.

"Just a minute on my own," I said, reflexively, reaching for the beads that live in my pocket.

The women shook their heads at me and tutted softly, but left me.

I had no pocket. I had no beads with me, no candle, no emotion left and precious little thought, but I said the hour that evening in the marsh more peacefully than I had since I left H'th Iriq.

As I finished my prayers, I saw Abe heading my way. He hopped gracefully from the neighbouring *tuy heold* to my own. He flashed his teeth at me in the waning light.

"Well, now, darlin', — "

"No," I said. I was almost — *almost* — too drained to care, but not quite.

"No? Sweetness, you're — "

I drew myself up, getting awkwardly to my feet. Ignoring the stiffness in my limbs I said, chin high,

"Abernast, I am not your love, your dear, your darling or any kind of sweet thing. Do I make myself clear?"

I did not think it possible but the heathen's smile actually grew.

"Clear as the crystal waters of my home, sunshine."

I gave him a long look. I looked into the murky waters around us and frowned.

"Speaking of sunshine," I said, "does the sun ever shine here?"

"Now, my precious flower — "

"I'm. Not. Yours."

Abe's grin stretched a little further. He continued as if I had not spoken,

"— we've not seen the sun since before we left Ttaroc.

"The womenfolk are worried about you, Kayt'an. You'd best come to dinner."

Abe led me back to the central platform where we had first been fed. Most of the village seemed to have gone back to their own business. The little girl who had acted as though she was in charge was just leaving. It seemed just Abe's family who were playing host.

The *tuy heold* was again strewn with rugs and cushions, and Axyl, Fryn'gh, Thorn and Hazzor were already comfortably sat. Keas and some other familiar faces had remained to eat with us. I looked at the spy with narrowed eyes. He actually seemed to be making small talk. Perhaps Fryn'gh's magic had affected him more than we had thought. Keas smiled when she saw me. She seemed genuinely pleased to see me, and I felt my heart lift slightly in response. I smiled and waggled my fingers in an uncertain greeting.

At the sight of Abe, the pale man who had first met us — Pelan? — grinned the family grin and greeted his cousin with the now familiar,

"Abernasti, hee."

"Hee, Pelani."

Abe sat by his cousin, drawing me down next to him. He threw a casual arm around me and pressed his other hand to his heart.

"Pelani, heth Kayt'an, sesri mu."

The coxcomb sighed heavily, and his cousin reached across to pat me on the knee, consolingly. I stared at that knee, embarrassed by the pantomime. Abe grinned again (I hoped his teeth would rot and fall out before the man turned forty), tightened his hug and said,

"Sister, this is my cousin Pelan."

He patted Pelan on the chest a few times in case there was any doubt about the identity of his cousin. Hazzor leaned forward a little.

"Pelan has been good enough to say he'll lead us through the waters to Dar Tor."

I nodded and thanked Pelan, who pressed a fist to his chest in answer. I turned back to Hazzor,

"Why can't Abe take us, though, if this is his home?"

Abe shook his head sadly.

"Alas, sister-mine," there was just the slightest stress on that 'mine'. I narrowed my eyes, but the fighter continued innocently, "I have been gone too long."

Pelan asked a question, which his cousin answered. Pelan barked a laugh and punched his heavier image vigorously in the arm. He spoke to me at length and Hazzor gave a crooked smile. Fryn'gh grumbled under his breath and Thorn elbowed him sharply. While Hazzor translated for Pelan — some remark about Abe never having been able to navigate the marsh — I looked at the mage and thought how well he looked here.

Before I could frame a polite question about the mage's ancestry, the food arrived and, unsurprisingly, it was fish. What I did not expect was the flavour. I nearly spat out the first mouthful, but Hazzor was watching with a baleful eye so I forced it down. Once my mouth had got over the shock it was actually — not pleasant, pleasant is too uneventful a word — exhilarating perhaps; like trying to eat a comb of honey with the bees still on it. Hungry, I cleaned my bowl and looked around anxiously for a drink.

Pelan noticed me looking and picked up a jug to pour a drink for me. Before he did, he caught his cousin's eye and the two of them grinned, positively wickedly.

Thorn's curiosity was piqued. She poked Abe with her foot.

"What's the joke, Abe?"

Abe glanced back at his cousin who nodded with a smirk.

I waited for the drink that Pelan had poured, but he seemed to have forgotten all about it, leaning back holding the cup to his chest.

"Well, beautiful Thorn," began Abe with the mien and tone of one beginning a story, "you know of Haenid?"

"Only from your curses," answered the archer, but she placed her chin in her hand ready to listen.

"Ah, well Haenid is the Mother of the World," he said. I snorted, I could not help myself but, thankfully, no one took any notice. "Well, Haenid had a daughter by Rh'onyn — therein lies a tale that will keep for another night. This daughter of Haenid and Rh'onyn was a beauty, so the legends say, with shining teeth and hair like silk. Eyes had she, like the sea at night and breasts like — "

"I get the picture," said Thorn, dryly. "She was pretty, now tell the tale."

Abe shook his head sadly, but continued, "Now this gift from Haenid, Ethil by name, swore that no man would touch her that did not also carry divinity in his blood." I managed not to tut and was proud of myself. Abe leaned in gleefully. "There are many tales of Ethil, but there is one that she was once shipwrecked and found herself at Shteriv. The king then was Dav' Yr, the father of our kings. Dav' Yr welcomed Ethil into his home and cast a lecherous eye upon her."

This time it was Thorn that snorted. Fryn'gh leaned in, enjoying the story's opening sally. Axyl promptly leaned forward too, and stole the last of his dinner. I grinned into my hand and tried not to look. Our story-teller went on,

"Of course, the king would not dare anger the gods by attacking a guest, so he called Ethil to him."

Abe caught my eye and smirked. Pelan, watching his cousin tell the story, grinned broadly. Despite my growing thirst, I was drawn in.

"'Do, you, accept my hospitality and welcome, love,' "

"He did not — "

Abe held up a finger at Thorn's interruption, raising an eyebrow. She stopped speaking, reluctantly. He smiled, triumphantly.

" '*love,* '" he repeated. "'but take anything that's *mine*, and give me anything I choose in return.'

"Ay, well, the divine creature agreed, thinking no harm, but that very evening the father of cunning kings set his trap. Ethil sat down to dine on *dhis'ruy*." Pelan caught the name of the dish we were eating and, like his cousin, seemed to be able to stretch his grin indefinitely. Abe grinned back. "She ate it hungrily and when she'd finished she looked around for her drink." I had a sudden boding feeling. Dry mouthed, I looked at the cup still in Pelan's hand with suspicion. "But Dav' Yr had ordered all the wine and all the water to be hidden, save one jar only. Ethil ran through the palace her thirst growing with each step," *I know how she feels*, I thought, "searching high and low for something to douse the fire on her tongue." Pelan took a slurp from his own drink and waggled his eyebrows at me. I was beginning to take him in a similar dislike to his cousin. "Finally, the god-born beauty arrived at Dav' Yr's chambers. There, beside the king's bed, was the only jar of wine in the palace. Ethil, parched beyond all bearing, took the wine and drank it down, the wine dripping from her chin as she drained the jar.

"'Ah, sweetness,' said the king behind her, 'so you quench your thirst from my jar,' " Abernast leaned in to me for the punch line we could all see coming, leering, "'now I quench my thirst from yours.'"

The whey-faced fighter roared with laughter and we all joined in — with varying degrees of enthusiasm. I thought Axyl would fall off his cushion he laughed so hard. My amusement was severely curtailed by the knowledge that I now *really* wanted the drink that Pelan was holding expectantly.

Resigned, I held out my hand for the cup and the laughter around me renewed. Pelan half held out the cup and spoke with a leer. It did not take a linguist to understand him. It was Keas's reaction that took me by surprise. Poor man, Keas berated him forcefully until the fisherman managed to stammer out an apology.

I looked to Hazzor, bewildered by the change of tone. Unruffled, the spy smoothed his beard and said,

"Pelan apologises for speaking out of turn, he assures you he was only trying to lift your spirits." When I looked blank he added, evenly, "On account of your being in mourning, you and Thorn."

Oh hell, I thought. *What do I do now?* While I sat there feeling awkward, Keas gave Pelan one last clip around the ears and stood. She took the cup from him and crossed the short distance to where Abe sat. Abe scooted out of her way hastily as this explosive woman sat down beside me. Gladly, I took the drink from her and she patted my hand, murmuring soothingly. While I drank, Abe spoke to her, clearly adding his apology to Pelan's.

I was touched. We were total strangers, foreigners from a country W'shten was at war with, yet they treated us with a consideration I had rarely had even from my own. I said something of the kind to Keas and Abe — with a glance at Hazzor — translated.

"You are guests," Keas answered through Abe, "and unlike the kings of old," here Keas gave Abe a poke, "we look after our guests. Besides," she leaned over and planted a big kiss on the pale warrior's cheek, "It's been so long since we've seen our Abernast." To my vast amusement, our pale companion began to look distinctly rosy. Keas opened her hands towards Thorn. "It is a delight to welcome his bride and her friends." Now, it was Thorn's turn to be uncomfortable, but she tried to look gracious and I began to relax.

The evening turned out well.

Not long after this, I asked Abe where I was to sleep. Keas led me to her archy-tenty-house: her *tuy*. My bag was there ahead of me, my washed clothes folded neatly next to it. She insisted I took her bed, to my embarrassment, and asked to see my hand. She pulled at the hand I had roughly bandaged and I pulled it back alarmed.

"No, it's alright," I said, hoping to make myself understood. I wriggled my fingers and smiled. "No pain, see?" Keas frowned and reached again for my hand.

I felt panic rising up and my heart beat painfully in my chest. I looked at the bandage round my hand. I could almost feel the circles on my palm burning through. I tried again to deflect her. I pulled my bag toward me and opened it for her to see.

"I'm a healer," I said. I pulled out bandages and my empty pot of ointment.

Keas seemed to understand, but still did not look happy. I pantomimed tiredness and climbed into her bed. She nodded slowly and drew some blankets onto the floor, pulling closed the door cover.

I lay in the dark and stared at the roof of the *tuy*. I had no doubt we would have go through all this tomorrow. A woman like Keas does not take no for an answer. I chewed my lip and worried. She would not rest until she had treated my hand. Then she would see the marks of Re'a. Even if by some miracle Keas did not take exception to my priesthood, Hazzor would probably drown me anyway. I stifled a sigh.

I wondered where Ranyl was sleeping. Was he safe? I tried to imagine him in the costume of these marsh folk and smiled into the dark. Somehow colour and Ranyl did not fit together.

I wondered where all the others were. Were we all spread out in different *tuy*? I could not see Hazzor liking that. It did not seem very ... defensive. Still — I thought of the spy relaxed on the cushions on the central *tuy heold* — he appeared at ease here. Then I remembered the dunking he had given me, and wondered if he ever fully relaxed.

Circling around, my mind came back to Keas. I listened to her breathing. I was almost certain she was still awake. I sighed. Keas immediately turned and asked a question.

"I'm fine, Keasi," I said, assuming she had asked the obvious question. She settled again. This was ridiculous. She was worried about me, and her worrying worried me. I wiped my face with my right hand, feeling the bandage run across my jaw. I stared in the dark at my hand, which I could barely see in front of my face. I traced the bandage round my hand with my fingers.

Around my hand. I blinked, suddenly seeing clearly in the dark. I turned to my bag in the dark and rummaged for the small sharp knife I kept wrapped in cloths.

"Kayt'ani?"

I bit my lip. I muttered something reassuring into the dark and lay back again. This would have to wait until my nurse slept.

I returned to my contemplation of the ceiling. Despite the worry, my heart felt curiously light. There were problems that needed solving, and problems that would have to find their own solutions, but for the first time in too long I felt that Re'a smiled upon me.

I fell asleep and slept dreamlessly.

Chapter 26

I woke with a start. It was still dark. It was impossible to know how far away dawn was. I was wide awake, but from experience I knew that meant nothing. It was time I had another go at implementing my plan. I took the bandage off my hand and tucked it under the thin pillow where I could find it easily in the dark. Moving carefully, I reached over to my bag. This time Keas' breathing stayed slow and regular. I found the little bundle that kept the knife's edge from fumbling fingers. Slowly, quietly, I withdrew the bundle and unwrapped it. I took the knife in my hand and felt a knot in my stomach. Deliberately, I recalled my sister priest, dead beside her ransacked temple. I carefully drew from memory the battered face, the twisted limbs, the eviscerated torso. I reminded myself this was my alternative. Then I stuffed the binding clothes into my mouth and dragged the knife across my hand as if stripping the flesh from a fowl.

Holy Lady give me strength!

I buried my face in the pillow and tried not to shout. My breath came raggedly and tears flowed silently, as my whole world revolved around my self-inflicted pain.

After a moment or two of intense wretchedness, I realised I was bleeding on the bed. I bit back a curse.

This would need explaining in the morning. I took out the now severely depleted stock of wolf's heart and therith, and held them in my good hand while my right dripped slowly down my wrist and on to the sheets. I did not know how I would replace this stock. I decided to do without. The cut hurt like hell, but it was not supposed to be severe. I figured it should heal reasonably quickly on its own, as long as I kept it clean. I wiggled my fingers. Good, no damage done. I breathed out in a slow sigh of relief. I re-wrapped the wound, tighter this time, now the bandage actually had a job to do. Carefully, I hid the little knife back in its cloths and buried it in my bag.

Cradling my hand, I lay back in the bed and wondered whether it was worth going back to sleep. I closed my eyes and gave it a go, but my hand throbbed abominably. So I lay there and I listened to the strange noises of the wetlands, chirping and croaking and rustling. It was not long before I gave up my attempt to sleep. I moved the curtain slightly and watched the starless sky, waiting for the light to change.

"If Saen loves us, why does he leave us each night?"

I was a child still, newly apprenticed to Hathil.

"Saen is a god. Who can fathom the mind of a god?"

Amtil still tucked me in at night and woke me each morning to say the hour with her. I yawned.

"Hathil says that without the darkness we don't love the light."

"What do you say, child?" Amtil had already started to tense slightly when I started a 'Hathil says' conversation. Undaunted, she had learnt caution.

"I think it's cruel to leave us. I hate the dark. But Hathil says, if we always have everything we want we don't appreciate it as much."

Amtil nodded slightly.

"We are creatures of appetite and appetites wax and wane. But do you love your mother more because you see less of her?"

I thought about it. I missed her terribly but there was awkwardness between us. The memory of my scorning her was still hot and painful. I envied my brothers and sisters who had stayed at home, together. I doubted I would ever quite be one of them in the same way again. I shrugged.

"I don't know."

"The good gods are not like sweeties to be saved as treats, Kayt'an. If I beat you daily, would you love my kindness more?"

"Maybe?"

The thought was alien to me. Amtil never needed to beat me. Her cold disapproval was always more than enough.

"But would you trust it?" Amtil thinned her lips slightly as I shrugged in response. "We love good things instinctively, child. There is no joy without the Three."

I opened my mouth to argue, but thought better of it. I returned to my principal grievance.

"So, why does Saen leave us?"

"Does Saen leave us?"

I looked at my teacher, uncertain as to her sanity.

"It's night time, the sun goes down. You say only Re'a can follow him."

Amtil smiled a humourless smile.

"Just because we can't see him, doesn't mean he isn't there." I groaned and rolled my eyes, flopping back into bed. "Come Kayt'an," she said, "come rejoice with Re'a at the new day. Hathil will have much for you to do today, I'm sure."

I smiled grimly as I watched the sky. I certainly had not seen Saen for some days now. I might still trust he was there, but nothing matches the comfort of the sun on your face. Overcast was better than rain, but I *longed* for the sun. I narrowed my eyes, was the sky a little lighter to the East? I waved my hand in front of my eyes. Flapping it about hurt, but I was sure there was a clearer silhouette than there had been. The day had begun. I sat up to say the hour, relieved.

I reached for my clothes to dig my beads out of the pocket of my jerkin. The candle I left, thinking it was pushing my luck, but my movement disturbed Keas who must have been starting to surface. She sighed and coughed. I froze and she settled again, but I knew it would not be long before my self-appointed nurse and protector woke. Carefully tucking my feet under me, I began silently to recite my prayers. When I had finished, I had time to pray for Ranyl's protection and was just starting to pray for the success of my deception when Keas greeted me.

"Zaeni vystet, Kayt'ani, vyst dobre," she said, sleepily.

Aiming for good will, I took a stab at repeating it back to her. She beamed in response, her teeth flashing in the dark.

"Dobre, dobre," my nurse said and patted my knee.

As she rolled out of her blankets, I decided to plunge in and get this over with. I cleared my throat. I wriggled the fingers of my bandaged and, now, decidedly painful hand.

"Umm, Keas, er I think I slept on my hand? It seems to be bleeding again." I shifted the covers to expose the soiled sheets, though as yet the light did not show the blood. "Umm, sorry, Keas, I've, er," I patted the bloody bed, rubbed my fingers together, and said, uncertainly, "I've spoiled your sheets?"

Keas followed my gesture and leaned forward to feel the sheets. Finding them damp she tutted and drew back the curtain to the door. The early morning light exposed a dark pattern on the sheets. She tutted some more and began to rebuke me. If I had showed her the cut before we slept, I inferred, this would not have happened. I made suitably apologetic noises. Keas lit a lamp and unwrapped my hand. I was careful to rest the palm of my hand on my lap while she huffed and tutted at me like an indignant hen.

"Yecho," she said sternly, before marching out of the *tuy*.

I examined my hand by the light of the lamp and was quite pleased, in a perverse way, with my work. I had made a flap of skin, which looked messy — not like a simple knife wound — but should heal easily if bound down again. I made a fist and winced. Ah well.

Keas returned with man who was astonishingly dark. His skin was almost leathery, and his hair and eyes were both black. I blinked several times in surprise. Where had this man come from? He most certainly was not local. They were jabbering away when they came in the *tuy* and, without even a by-your-leave, the man took my hand and poked at it.

"Gragh!" I said, and tried to retrieve my hand but to no avail.

This new man — I had not seen him until now (where had he been?) — held my hand like a vice. With a voice like gravel, he sent Keas away and, irresistibly, inexorably, he turned my hand over.

I stopped breathing. This man, this dark man, who held my hand in his, and with it my life, still did not look up.

"Well," said the man in my own tongue.

Still, I did not breathe, though the muscles in my stomach were starting to ache. I said nothing. It is hard to talk when you are not breathing. Also, I had nothing to say. *He* traced the lines on my palm with his index finger and my blood ran cold. Not looking up, he said,

"I wondered what you were hiding. This," he turned my hand over again, briefly, "was not here yesterday." He traced his hand across the cut, making me gasp and renew my attempts to retrieve my hand. I began to breathe again, but shallow breaths quickly drawn, as if my lungs had suddenly shrunk.

"This on the other hand," he turned my hand back, not seeming to notice the pun, "this is old."

He renewed the tracing of my mark. I felt sick, really, really sick. Every warning Hazzor had given me was reverberating through my mind.

Finally, he did look up. The dark eyes that met mine were full of ... amusement. My breathing slowed, but I did not relax, neither did I speak. I was still frightened. I still could think of nothing useful to say. He waited a while and then said,

"Are you not going to explain what a priest of Re'a is doing in the W'shten marshes?"

I shook my head, my heart hammering in my chest. My gut spasmed.

At last, he released my hand, and I clutched it back to my chest, palm twice hidden in my fist against my breastbone. Visions — so carefully rehearsed in the night — of exposed organs and broken limbs, danced grotesquely in my mind.

I could not hold this man's eyes. As the morning light brightened in the *tuy*, I found myself staring at the stubble on his chin. It was dark like his hair, but there were holes in it. The beard, that is, not his chin. Odd, I thought, vaguely. *He* rocked back on his heals and laughed quietly.

That was when I was sick, right in his lap. Well, mostly his knees really, and a little up his thighs.

He stopped laughing.

"Kayt'an, sweet sister?"

I never thought I would be pleased to hear that lazy drawl. I could have kissed the man. Not now of course, not when I was wiping vomit off my chin.

"Keas here reckoned you might need a translator?"

He ducked in and I watched him take in my bleeding, un-bandaged hand clutched to my chest and the healer man knee-deep, so-to-speak, in sick. The two men — one so pale, one so dark — eyed one another.

Abe's face hardened and, suddenly, I was afraid not so much for myself as for this strange man who knew so much.

Hard faced, but smiling he spoke.

"Hrat den, Lecyel?"

Lecyel rose slowly to his feet.

"Your friend bleeds and I need to bathe."

He reached into a box-like case I only now noticed, and drew out some clean bandages and a little pot. He held both out to Abe. Abe made no move, but remained blocking the doorway as if by accident.

"You can use the old bandage to clean the wound," he said, as if he hadn't noticed that Abe stood like an ancient guardian in the exit. I sat, rabbit-like, between the two.

Finally, I mustered the will-power to speak.

"What will you do?" I said.

The healer looked back at me, eyes still light with humour.

"Bathe," he said.

Lecyel took a step towards Abe who, slowly, took his offering and stepped aside. The dark healer left.

Abe looked at me.

"Kayt'an, sunshine, I have never known a woman for getting herself into trouble like you, *sister*."

Chapter 27

"Saen's balls, woman," I opened my mouth, reflexively, to correct him and Hazzor glared at me, "what were you thinking?"

This was grossly unfair, and I said so. We were on the platform the men used for their ablutions, on the opposite side of the village. We spoke quietly through gritted teeth, watching for any who might be coming to wash.

"Can *you* not tell the difference between a wound that's hours old and one that's had a day and a night to heal?"

I said that I could. I had intended to go on and say I was a trained healer while Keas was not and it was not full light when I let her see my hand, but Hazzor, naturally, did not let me finish.

"Then why, by all the Wyrms in Shael, did you think no one else would?"

Again, I tried to make my point about darkness and people not trained in the healing arts, but to no avail — wretched, horrid, Hazzor! I thought he would be pleased at my cunning, but all I got was another verbal assault. And my hand hurt, not that anyone cared. I asked what he thought I should have done.

"Kept your hand hidden."

"Ah, Hazz, buck, this is Keas we're talking about."

I had not expected Abe to come to my defence, but it was, I thought, a fair point well made. Hazzor was checked for a moment in his charge, but only for a moment.

"Well, you should have thought of *something*."

"I *did*, I cut the back of my hand to stop her looking at my palm."

"So she calls a healer, of course."

"But *I'm* a healer, Hazzor, why should she call for another?"

"Because you were hurt and bleeding all over her bed. It's what normal people do."

"And what would you know about normal people, Hazzor?"

"More than you, it seems."

Oooh, the Dark Lord's wyrms were too good for that bitter ingrate!

"You need not abuse the priest," a gravelly voice interjected.

I practically swallowed my tongue and even the spy spun on a shrekna and stood, like a coiled spring, as Lecyel climbed from his boat to the *tuy heold*. I was holding my breath again and had to force myself to exhale.

"Abe," said Hazzor in a measured voice, "see what Fryn'gh is up to will you?"

So the spy feared magic, did he? As Abe moved away, I eyed the stranger warily. Hazzor was doing his inscrutable thing. We both waited for the healer — the *other* healer — to speak. He had, I noticed, changed his trousers.

When nobody spoke for a while, curiosity got the better of me and I said,

"That ointment you gave Abe, Lecyel, what was in it?"

Lecyel smiled.

"Ah, priest," (Hazzor winced slightly, though I think only I saw) "we have common ground you and I."

There followed an interesting conversation about leaves and roots and oils; although, marigold and mallow were described to me with the healing properties of their various parts. I was keen to learn, depleted as my own stocks were. When the healer invited me back to his *tuy* to take some samples, Hazzor stepped in, physically putting himself between Lecyel and me.

"You'll forgive me, sir, if we don't trust you."

The swarthy stranger still looked amused.

"I think your priest does."

Hazzor's face darkened a shade.

"We'd be grateful, sir, if you didn't mention Kayt'an's calling. You understand the risk to her — and us — if others in this village know what she is."

Lecyel took a step closer to the spy, a merry twinkle in his eye.

"You'd best take me with you, then, or you'll only worry."

Hazzor raised his eyebrows.

"To Abe's wedding? You'd have to ask him."

"You're not a wedding party."

"You're mistaken. Perhaps the grief of our party has misled you."

Hazzor's tone was even. I looked from one man to the other. One guarded, the other apparently diverted by the exchange. I felt the platform tip slightly, once, twice. I glanced over and again was relieved (twice in one morning!) to see Abe arrive, with Fryn'gh in tow. Lecyel chuckled. It was a warm, friendly sort of laugh.

Judging from Hazzor's expression you would have thought he had cackled like the wicked wizard from a story.

"Just the man," the healer-man smiled. "Abernast, I have never been to an international wedding before; may I tag along?"

The big man's grin split his face, and he slapped Lecyel heartily on the back, but his eyes were still those of a killer. I scooted over to Fryn'gh. He eyed me warily.

I tried a pleasant sally to ease my own anxiety.

"Good morning, Fryn'gh. Sleep well?"

I got a snort for a reply while Abe was extending a cheery invitation to Lecyel. The *other* healer thanked Abe courteously, and climbed back into his little boat. He paused before pushing off.

"Should your minder change his opinion of me, little priest — "

The diminutive was too much for me and I got as far as, 'Saa — ' before Hazzor clapped a hand over my mouth.

" — anyone in Ay Toris can bring you to my *tuy*."

I would have smiled, but I was still gagged so I wiggled the fingers of my good hand in what I hoped was a polite way. Lecyel laughed again and paddled away, but it was a moment or two longer before the spy released me. I expected another dressing down, but Hazzor just shook his head and called me a stubborn renwit. He had an expression on his face I could not read and his eyes followed the little marsh punt out of sight.

Then, Hazzor turned to Fryn'gh and raised his eyebrows in a question.

The red-head shrugged.

"More than none, less than some."

To my astonishment, the spy nodded as if the mage had made sense. I looked suitably sceptical. Abe was more verbal in his derision.

The mage curled his lip at us.

"I mean he's got some magical affinity, but no skill, I think. I'm guessing any magic he manages he does by instinct, probably doesn't even think it's magic, probably thinks it's luck. He's got more than no magic, but not anything measurable."

I turned to Abe and Hazzor.

"We're not really inviting him along are we?"

Abe's eyes were still glittering.

"If a man wants to tag along where he's not wanted when he holds a secret they want kept quiet, well," he smiled, "I call that suicide, don't you? The man's obviously suffering."

I opened my eyes wide,

"You can't just kill him!"

There I had been, worried about being supplanted and maybe left behind, and they were plotting murder.

"Be grateful it's not *your* life," said the spy. "It is a fine balance between the difficulty of clearing this up, and the difficulty of finding another healer we can use, this far into W'shten."

He flicked the tails of the coat he was no longer wearing, and stepped gracefully from the platform.

I was sat with Thorn outside Rhossa's *tuy* chewing on what they called breakfast or '*sidani*'. I chewed slowly. Fish for breakfast is lovely. Pickled eels, on the other hand, I was less sure about. I was still worrying at the problem of Lecyel.

"Do we know where he's from? I mean, maybe, he's got no reason be a threat? If he's not from round here, what does he care what we're up to?"

Thorn leant back against the arched structure behind her.

"Kayt'an, give it a rest. It's done. There's nothing we can do. Lecyel saw your secret and Hazzor can't leave him wandering the marshes knowing there's a ... well, knowing we're not who we say we are. Too much depends on it."

We were speaking softly and in a language no one around us spoke, but still Thorn moved her lips as little as possible as she spoke.

"He seems so nice."

Thorn gave a look full of amusement and did not bother to answer.

"Can't we just ... lose him somewhere?"

"We'll have Pelan with us remember. He'll not leave someone behind. Not unless he knows he's dead."

"You can't just murder someone because they're *inconvenient*."

"Not just inconvenient, Kayt'an, dangerous. With what he knows, he can get us all killed."

I chewed my lip.

"Why, by all the Dark Lord's arts, did Reath pick me for this when I'm such a danger to everyone?"

"That question has crossed my mind." Thorn had a twinkle in her eye but it did not make me feel any better.

"I don't even know what we're doing here!"

It was nearly a wail, but Thorn went on as if I hadn't spoken.

"Look, *sister*," her mouth twitched, briefly, "this sort of life is dangerous, we risk our lives and people around us get caught up in it." Thorn turned to look straight at me. "Think of it this way, how many people will die or lose their livelihoods if we don't stop this war?"

"Come on Thorn! There are seven of us. How can seven people stop a war?"

Thorn shrugged.

"One well-placed, well-trained little old lady pinned down the four of us. Now, we work for the king." She leaned back against the *tuy*. "The right force, Kayt'an, in the right place... You believe Re'a changed the world, right?"

"She died in the process," I said, dryly.

"I didn't say we'd survive. But, hey," my friend grinned, "we're only trying to save one country, so maybe we'll live to tell the tale!"

"Lecyel won't."

The morning was wasted by my drifting around the village aimlessly. The strange healer's stock called to me, but I could not trust myself not to warn him.

I watched the children play. I watched the bandits check their weapons for water damage. I watched Fryn'gh do party tricks to entertain the villagers. I watched Pelan getting three boats ready, filling them with supplies. Hazzor had vanished, as had Lecyel. I watched the fish in the water and birds fishing. I watched the sky and waited for midday. I got in everyone's way.

Eventually, I decided I needed to see the local healer — I had stocks to replenish and not the skills to fend for myself in this strangely busy wilderness. I figured I probably had time to visit and return before I needed to say the hour. In fact, I thought to myself, pleased, I could say the hour there. In Lecyel's *tuy* I would not have to worry about hiding myself. We did not need to talk about anything other than herbs. I convinced myself my motives were pure and sound and set off.

I found a guide by the simple stratagem of saying, 'Lecyel?' to a man in his boat, who then took me where I wanted to go.

Lecyel lived a little apart from the rest of the village, which was, I assumed, why we had not seen him on the first day. Abandoning my resolve, almost in my first breath, I asked him why.

Inviting me to sit, he answered,

"The village is a nice enough place, but very noisy. I have space to think here." He handed me a warm, sweet drink and said, "I know most cultures have forms of respect for their priests. Tell me, how ought I to address you?"

I think I saw a challenge in his smile, but it may have been my imagination.

I sipped at my drink. Normally, it would have been lovely to have someone *seek* to give me the courtesies I was due, but these were not normal times and this was not a normal man.

"You're very kind," I said, giving Lecyel the benefit of the doubt, "but Hazzor would rather my title wasn't used 'til we are back in Ttaroc again. He fears someone might overhear."

"Your Hazzor is a deeply suspicious man, but you needn't worry. I understand the need for discretion. Here in my home, though, you are safe."

I smiled and told him again he was very kind. I took another sip of my drink and changed the subject.

"I was hoping you might let me re-stock some of my supplies from yours. I don't know how much longer we'll be on the road and, um, my friends can be accident prone."

Lecyel laughed a deep throaty chuckle that was infectious. I laughed with him and relaxed. I was right, I thought, this man was a healer, a good man. So when he said,

"They are not the only ones," and took my injured hand, I found myself blushing.

Flustered, I tried to retrieve my hand, but he held it tight. Keeping his eyes on my face he slowly unbandaged my hand and, ridiculously, I blushed furiously. Embarrassment created its own vicious circle. I flushed because I was discountenanced and was further abashed because I was blushing. I stared out of the doorway and tried to gather some composure. I was being absurd. I covered my embarrassment by drinking deeply from my cup.

I changed the subject back. "I was, um, also wondering if I could say my prayers here Lecyel, um, where I'm not overlooked?"

The dusky man held onto my hand still as he assured me I should treat his home as my own.

"Though you need not worry about supplies. As I'm coming with you, I'll bring some with me."

Suddenly, I was relieved that I was already blushing.

Lecyel checked my hand over, quite unnecessarily in my opinion. It was a humdrum cut, recently tended. Before he replaced the bandage, he turned my hand over again and examined the palm. He stroked it with his finger and I felt decidedly uncomfortable. I suddenly wished I had mentioned to one of the others where I was going.

"How are they made, these circles? It looks more like a birthmark than a tattoo."

I tugged at my hand, futilely. "It's a miracle," I muttered.

'Miracle' is not how I'd have described it at the time, but I was feeling suddenly uncommunicative.

"I think it's now time to say my prayers, sir."

"Of course, Kayt'an."

He bandaged my hand again, running his fingers over mine in a most unsettling way. His touch was dry and smooth, and I wondered how his hands were so soft.

To distract myself, I asked,

"What are you doing so far from home?" Then, I thought that might be rude, so I added, "If you don't mind me asking."

His eyes were warm as he said,

"I'm happy to answer any question of yours, Kayt'an, but what makes you think I am far from home?"

"Oh!" Again I was on my back foot. "Umm, I ... well I, your skin?"

Lecyel laughed again, and again I found myself laughing with him.

"I tease you, Kayt'an, sorry. I am from far away, beyond the Circle Sea, you are right."

My hand was bandaged by now, but he still did not release it and I decided to let it rest in his hands a little longer. He stroked my fingers as he spoke. I could not hold his eyes and did not want to watch his hands, so I watched the movement of his jaw as he spoke. I wondered what those little bare patches of his beard would feel like if I touched them. I watched the corners of his mouth curl.

"I am a traveller, like yourself, an explorer. My skills make me welcome wherever I choose to pause for a time." He pushed my sleeve up a little and ran his thumb across my wrist. I shivered. He reached up to my shorn head and ran his fingers through my hair.

"Why did you cut off your hair, Kayt'an?"

I licked my lips and found myself staring at this strange man's mouth.

"I, umm ..."

My mind had gone blank. What had Hazzor said?

Hazzor! I had a sudden and vivid memory of being half-drowned by the angry spy. Lecyel cupped his hand round the back of my head and pulled my mouth towards his, but I pulled away, startled. I scrambled back, thoroughly confused about all but one thing. Hazzor was going to be livid that I had come here.

Lecyel looked puzzled.

"Kayt'an?"

"I, umm, er ..."

I seemed to have lost all ability to speak and my legs felt unaccountably weak. I lurched through the door of the *tuy* and looked around for a means to leave. I was holding on to the door of the *tuy* for balance when I felt a soft hand cover mine and another on my waist.

"Kayt'an come inside, you shouldn't be troubled. You're safe here."

I felt very strange and the greater part of me wanted to relax and stay, but an insistent voice hammered in my mind, *Hazzor's going to be bloody furious about this.*

"Cy'wri, hee!" I managed.

I had to get back before he found out.

Chapter 28

Cy'wr heard my hail and took me back to the village without comment. In the little time it took to return my legs recovered, but my hands had started shaking. *What* had just happened? It made no sense to me. I shook my head. I was becoming hysterical over nothing.

As I wandered across the village, disorientated, I saw the lonely grey bird circling above. *It must be midday*, I thought dully. I sat down, suddenly. I had to say the hour I thought, and then to my complete surprise, I vomited.

"Kayt'an?"

I jumped. Hazzor was crouched next to me. He actually looked concerned. I was touched but puzzled.

"Kayt'an are you alright?"

"Fine," I answered. "Why do you ask?"

He looked at me, his face unreadable.

"You've just been sick in the river."

I could taste it in my mouth, sweet and bitter, but I had no memory of being sick. I did feel wrong, though. Not any kind of ill I had ever felt before. Just ... wrong. *I mustn't tell Hazzor*. I frowned.

"I'm fine," I repeated.

The spy nodded slowly.

"Where've you been?"

Mustn't tell Hazzor.

"Nowhere," I said, quickly, "just ... "

I tailed off. *Where had I been?* I decided attack was the best form of defence.

"You're a fine one to talk! I haven't seen you since this morning."

"What have you eaten?"

Is he interrogating me? The cheek of it! I sat up straighter. (*Why am I sitting?*)

"It's alright, I haven't been rude. I ate the nasty fishy pickle they gave me. Is there time for me to say my prayers before lunch?"

"What have you drunk?"

"What is this?"

The little spy was clearly born to be suspicious, but this was getting silly.

"What have you drunk?"

Hazzor looked as though he could keep asking the same question all day if he needed to.

"She alright?"

Axyl had come over and seemed to want to join the cross-questioning.

"I'm *fine.*"

"She was sick just now."

"Don't be silly!" I said, and gave a little laugh.

Both men frowned at me. *Hazzor's going to be bloody furious about this.* I put my hands to my head.

"Do we fetch the healer, what's his name?"

"Lecyel."

"No!"

I was adamant. *Don't tell Hazzor.*

"Kayt'an, you're not well."

Hazzor was looking concerned. I was surprised. *That's not like him.*

"I'm fine," I said.

I stood up and swayed. *Where had I been going?*

The spy took my elbow. I felt suddenly tired. I put my head on Hazzor's shoulder. It was a nice height for the purpose.

There was a conversation going on over my head. I took no notice until I heard the word, 'Lecyel'. I stood up straight again.

"NO!" I shouted.

Don't tell Hazzor — Why not? I could not fathom what was going on in my own head.

"Kayt'an," Hazzor was speaking in a Very Calm Voice. "Kayt'an, did you go to see Lecyel this morning?"

Mustn't tell Hazzor. Don't tell Hazzor!

"No!" I laughed again, with forced gaiety, and shrugged casually. "Why would I want to go to see Lecyel?"

Had I been to see him? I felt so vague.

Hazzor and Axyl exchanged glances. Hazzor pointed into the sky, up and away from Axyl.

"Is that a pig?"

Instinctively, I followed the spy's finger and my jaw exploded.

I woke up back in Keas' *tuy*. She had changed the sheets, but was nowhere else in evidence. I groaned and hugged my poor jaw. Three, I thought to myself, or was it four?

"How are you feeling?"

"Three."

"Kayt'an?" Thorn sounded worried.

"Abe's hit me once and Axyl's knocked me out twice."

"Kayt'an, I'm sorry, but Hazz didn't know what you'd do next."

I sat up wincing.

"What kind of an excuse is that? I rarely know what people are going to do next, but I don't go round knocking them out."

Thorn grinned.

"Would you know how?"

I smiled, ruefully. I rubbed my jaw again and stretched my neck.

"Ugh!"

The archer leaned forward.

"Do you know what happened?"

I thought back, and shook my head.

"Apart from Axyl hitting me again."

"Fryn'gh says you were enchanted."

"Enchanted!"

Blugh! My gut twisted at the thought.

"How? Who? *Lecyel?*" I said, "Why?"

Thorn's face went carefully neutral.

"Fryn'gh reckons you were drugged first, which is why you were sick, by the way — "

"I was sick?"

" — then it only took a very little magic to compel you. Neither the drug or the weak magic would show much, but the two together would have been pretty potent."

Thorn's face was still carefully neutral, but she took my hand. I snatched it back again, though I could not think why. My head ached horribly. I had plenty of lavender oil in my bag, so I reached for it and dabbed it on my forehead. Thorn stayed where she was.

"Is he still coming with us?"

Thorn nodded.

"Aye, but he'll not get far."

A silhouette blocked the door for a moment as Hazzor came in. Thorn looked up.

"Ranyl back yet?"

The spy nodded and perched lightly on the bed next to me.

"He's drying out as we speak." Hazzor looked at me, head tilted. "How do you feel, Kayt'an?"

I narrowed my eyes.

"My head hurts abominably."

Hazzor's mouth twitched at one corner.

"Kayt'an, did your mother never tell you not to go off with strange men?"

"Funny." I did not laugh. "Thorn's telling me you think I was ..."

I did not want to say the word. I searched for another that would do, but Hazzor supplied it for me.

"Compelled, yes."

"Why?"

"Classic symptoms. You were suddenly vague and muddled. I didn't think you'd been drinking so you were either ill or enchanted." The spy shrugged. "Since you couldn't — or wouldn't — tell me what you'd eaten and drunk, I got Fryn'gh to check you over. He said there was a simple weave, which he's removed. Do you remember anything?"

"I *mean*, why was I ... compelled?" The thought was not a nice one. What might I have done while under Lecyel's influence. "*Was* it Lecyel?"

Hazzor nodded.

"Seems the most obvious candidate. As for why he compelled you?" He frowned. "That's where I'm worried. I don't know, and we don't know whether you've already done it or whether it was something he wanted done later."

Later? Dear Re'a! My eyes widened.

"Do you mean I might still ..."

Thorn shook her head.

"It's alright, Kayt'an. Fryn'gh says the weave was simple and he's unpicked it. If you haven't done — whatever it was — you won't do it now."

"But I might have already done it."

I felt sick again. And people wonder why Saen condemns magic.

"What do you remember?"

I do not think Hazzor had ever spoken for so long without lecturing me. Both he and Thorn had matching solemn expressions. A thought struck me.

"Will Keas get Lecyel again?"

I was not sure how I would face him.

"I told her you have a habit of passing out."

Reath's agent had not even the flicker of a smile on his face. A 'habit of passing out' indeed! People keep hitting me, he means. I refused to rise to the bait. He went on,

"A little rest, I said, and you'll be fine. What do you remember?"

"You're repeating yourself."

I saw Thorn hide a smile, but Hazzor merely raised an eyebrow.

"That's because you still haven't answered my question. What do you remember?"

I did not want to think about it. I shrugged and shook my head.

"Kayt'an, try. If you've sabotaged us somehow I need to know."

There was another silhouette at the door and Abe squeezed in. He grinned at me merrily.

"Hey, little sister, how are you feeling?"

I decided the familial endearments were no better than the sweet-talk.

Hazzor wasted no time on either.

"Well?"

The big man shook his head.

"He's gone. Either Kayt'an's done something we're gonna notice and soon or he knows he's been rumbled."

Thorn swore. Hazzor simply said,

"Tell Ranyl he's going to have to dry out on the move. We're leaving."

The others burst into determined activity. But I sat still. I was conscious that my supplies of herbs were low. I had stocks to replenish and not the skills to fend for myself in this strangely busy wilderness. I figured I probably had time to visit Lecyel's *tuy* and return before anyone was ready to leave.

A sudden wave of *oddness* washed over me like an echo in my mind. I shook it off. It was probably better if Hazzor did not know what I intended. I could almost hear him telling me we could not trust the man or his herbs, but still, I felt decidedly peculiar, as though I had doubled myself. I decided activity was probably my best course.

I found someone to take me to his home. His name was Cy'wr. He gave me a funny look, but agreed and we paddled out to the healer's *tuy*.

As we pulled up, I wondered if I ought to enter Lecyel's home uninvited. I brushed aside the thought. Not only had he assaulted me in some way, he had, in front of witnesses, offered to give me some of his stock. I was only taking him up on his offer. I nodded to myself, and I stepped inside the arched building. I felt like an army of ants were marching up and down my spine. On the little table I could not help but notice there were two cups, one still full. I took a sniff and my head swam. I sat down suddenly. Again.

Again?

Memories rose up from the darkness of my amnesia and I reeled. I had been here before. The memories were jumbled and blurry, but I had been here. Lecyel un-bandaging my hand. Lecyel with his hand on my waist. I stared at the cushions he had sat on. What had happened? The thought rose, unbidden. *Hazzor must not know.*

Shaking the feeling — there was nothing I could do about it — I rummaged through Lecyel's stocks, feeling no compunction now but wanting to distract myself. I found the leaves and roots he had described to me as well as a pot of ointment that smelt like the stuff he gave to Abe — the scent of it seemed to crawl out of the pot and down my arm. I gathered up some other samples out of idle curiosity — Hathil might find a use for them in her studies — and then I left.

My relationship with the other children in my village had never been an easy one. Believing that you are uniquely special is rarely a fortuitous grounding for friendship. Add to that the little time I had to play and the fact that, even physically, I was apart from the village; my successful sorties into the world of juvenile group play were few and far between. I gained an extended vocabulary of insults and taunts but, outnumbered as I was, I usually came off worse. I did not care, of course. What did I care what they thought?

Still, one evening, as I was approaching adulthood, I met Talin, Anid and a few others in the woods. I had been sent by Hathil to gather black dock before the dew settled. They had jumped, startled at my arrival, and then Talin had called me over.

"Kayt'an, come and join us, come on."

The others had sniggered and I had hovered, doubtfully, at a distance.

"What're you up to?" I had said, wary of practical jokes.

Anid had giggled, and sneered,

"Oh leave her; she's not going to soil her *soul* with our company."

More sniggering.

I had tossed my head and declared,

"Don't want to know anyway. I've got more important things to do than sit around in the dust."

The others had been whispering and now Talin said,

"No, really, Kayt'an, come and join us, tell us what you think."

Even then I had had a very fine opinion of my own wisdom so I had not been able to resist stalking over to see.

"What've you got?"

"Ruid's got hold of some of Ra'an's scrumpy."

"And you've been drinking it?" I was scandalised — and deeply curious. "What's it like?"

Ra'an's scrumpy had a reputation that filtered down even to our level. It was said to be lethal, which could not be true because I had never been called on to prepare anyone for burial afterwards. Still...

"Try it for yourself."

Ruid had a sly look on his face, which made me hesitate anew.

"What's the matter, Kayt'an? Scared?" Anid sneered.

I sat down in the circle and reached for the jar.

"Bet I can drink more than you can."

I do not think any of us remembered who drank the most that evening, though I still remember the reception I got when I finally crawled back to Hathil's that night. I had not dared go back to the temple.

The next morning I thought I had died and was being slowly consumed by the Dark Lord's wyrms. I thought they were chewing through my eyes into my brain and somehow they had shat in my mouth on the way.

Coming out of Lecyel's *tuy* reminded me of how I felt that morning. Not only did my head ache abominably — may Axyl rot with the dark wymns — but I felt that I had somehow lost part of my mind. I was disorientated without being dizzy and, just as my memories of that evening were decidedly piecemeal, I could not put together any sensible recollection of what had apparently happened only this morning.

I got back into the little boat and Cy'wr took me back to the heart of the village.

Again.

I sat with my bag full of herbs I might never use, wearing a strange assortment of marsh-wear and my adventurer's outfit, and waited for the others.

Chapter 29

As it turns out, they had been waiting for me on the south side of the village where the boats were ready for us. After they had waited a while, Fryn'gh was sent to find me, which only took time because he looked for me round Keas' *tuy* while *I* was waiting on the central platform where we had eaten. Naturally, everyone blamed me.

"Where in the nine hells have you been?"

The spy was tight lipped and looked pale.

Hazzor must not know.

"Are you alright, Hazzor? You look pale. Is your side pulling?"

The last thing I wanted was damage under the skin where I could not see it. I was worried about muscle damage. *Damn magic!* I had no idea what stage his wound was at.

"Don't change the subject."

"Who cares where she's been? I thought we were in a hurry."

Ranyl looked well, I thought, considering. He was the only one of us still wholly dressed as a Ttarcine, though his clothes were barely recognisable through the mud. He had lost his cap, his dark hair was plastered down with silt, and his hands and face were covered in grime. Still, his manner was as brooding as it ever was, but his eyes were bright and alert when he flicked them at me, disdainfully, so I gave Re'a a brief prayer of thanks for his safe return; one less person to worry about.

Ranyl nodded towards the middle boat where — surprise, surprise — Fryn'gh was already climbing in. With a sigh of resignation, I followed, reminding myself we had made a pact and, now, I owed the mage twice over. But for him unpicking the weave, I would still be under Lecyel's thrall.

"I care."

Hazzor was standing by the last boat, barefoot in his short baggy trousers, completely failing to look like a local man. (How was this man a spy?)

"Kayt'an was placed under a compulsion this morning. 'til I know why, I want to know everything she does."

"Fine," the thief climbed into the little vessel, going around behind the spy, "but you were in so much of a hurry that I didn't get a bath, so if it's not too much trouble can we talk as we go?"

Hazzor did not turn — though I would not like Ranyl walking behind me like that — but he did climb in, wrapping imaginary coat tails around him as he sat.

I threw my bag in beside Fryn'gh's, awkwardly climbing after it. A small crowd of children who had gathered to watch us depart giggled as I tripped and landed gracelessly. The whole boat rocked.

"Watch it!"

Fryn'gh swore as water splashed up the side and on to his bag.

"Well, it was hardly *my* fault that someone left their stuff lying around in the middle of the boat."

The nascent quarrel died as Axyl approached our boat. Fryn'gh and I smiled mirror smiles and sat quietly either end of the vessel. When Axyl threw in his bag and armour and climbed in after us, though, neither of us stayed quiet.

"Holy Lady, save us!" I gasped as the water sloshed over the side of the boat.

The mage merely swore and drew his feet up hurriedly. The watching children laughed with merry abandonment as the three of us Kept Very Still Indeed, matching expressions of alarm on our faces. Hazzor raised his hands in an expression of exasperated dismay.

Of the others, only Pelan was still standing on the *tuy heold*. He gestured with his head as he spoke, while Abe translated from the boat in front.

"One of the little ones will have to move into this boat."

As I turned to him — carefully — an indignant expression on my face, the whey-faced fighter simply said,

"His words, *sesri mu*, not mine."

He smiled, sunnily.

As I opened my mouth to tell him I would rather chew off my own arm than voluntarily share a boat with him, the alternative presented itself to me: interrogation by Hazzor from the boat behind. In an instant I found my words transformed into,

"Very well."

I was given some satisfaction in the astonishment writ large on Abernast's face.

Carefully — very carefully — I stood up and stepped out on to the *tuy heold* and down again to join my so-called brother. I ignored the hand he offered and sat down in the pointy end of the boat. I hoped that since I was one of three — one of three in a boat that was not sinking, that is — I would be excused rowing. My hand still throbbed somewhat.

Pelan climbed in after me and I gave the spy a cheery wave, which he ignored. When Pelan sat down by me and patted my knee like an amiable uncle I gave him a measured look. I had not forgotten it was he who encouraged his cousin to tell lewd stories at my expense. I sniffed.

We set off. I had expected to be in a boat with two grown men egging each other on in silliness, but I had underestimated them both. Once we were moving, Abe turned back into a bandit, alert and vigilant. His cousin concentrated on guiding the little water-born train. Behind us — facing me — Axyl and Fryn'gh were talking quietly, and I could see Ranyl curling up to sleep while Hazzor and Thorn rowed. I wondered how Ranyl had managed to shake off the patrol. After a moment, I voiced the thought.

"Ah, sugar," I glowered to no effect. I had a nasty feeling this was a battle I had lost. "Leading people astray is something Ranyl loves almost as much as killing. He'll have led those soldiers a merry dance and then slipped off the horses when he reckoned they'd not see. Child's play to such as he."

I nodded politely. The boats floated down the river. It would have been quite pleasant but for the insects, and the strange creatures slipping in and out of the waters, and the possibility that Lecyel was out there, and the risk of being brutally slain if we were caught. I leaned back in the boat and listened to the sound of the paddles dipping in and out of the water.

I sat on the grass hill of my temple. The wind blew my hair about and the sun shone on my face. The temple was behind me and below me was my village. I smiled. All was well in my world. Acting on impulse,

I got to my feet and walked down the hill. I sang a hymn as I walked. As I reached the village I thought it strangely quiet. I walked into the village square and it was empty. Doors hung on their hinges and the forge was cold. In the distance I could hear someone calling me, but I turned and turned and could see no one. My home was empty.

Suddenly, I was in the woods to the west. My clothes and hair caught in bushes and trees as I walked, calling for Hathil.

As I opened my mouth to call again, she was before me. But, before I could speak, she lifted the cup she held and threw its contents in my face.

"Brrah!" I shook my head.

"Much as I'd love to leave you to sleep, sweetness, Hazzor won't have it."

Abe held out his hand to help me up. I scowled at him and wiped my face. My head felt thick with sleep. Around me the others were moving purposefully. It seemed Pelan had found us a little island on which to camp. When I failed to move, the fighter reached down and grabbed my forearm in his hand.

"Come," was all he said and pulled.

It was stand up or be dragged up; so I stood and followed the bandit out of the boat.

While the others set up camp, Hazzor sent Thorn and me to shoot eels. We waded barefoot into the shallow water and waited, bows drawn. To my surprise, it was surprisingly good fun, and before long we were giggling like children, shushing each other and gasping with laughter. I gave a victory yell every time I caught one, but we were a pantomime of dismay when the eels slipped away just as the bow twanged. Needless to say, Thorn caught far more than me, but I was not completely useless with the bow and it was more about patience than aim.

After a time Ranyl came to join us.

"Hazzor wants to know whether we get to eat or were you planning on playing all night?"

Thorn threw an eel at him, but the thief spoilt the effect by catching it, smugly. Gathering our spoils, we headed back to the camp.

Somebody had obviously decided a small fire was an acceptable risk. Whether that was because Ranyl had done such a good job or because explaining the exact nature of the risk to Pelan created a whole new problem, I did not know. Taking myself aside, I said the hour while Pelan prepared the eels. The cloud cover had broken a little and the setting sun lit the sky with Saen's colours. The great expanse of sky, instead of being oppressive, became breathtaking. I gave thanks for our salvation and gloried in Saen's beauty.

Then I ate.

As I was chewing the surprisingly good eel, Hazzor — who had sat next to me to my disquiet — leaned over and said conversationally,

"So, Kayt'an, where were you earlier?"

I stared at the spy over my remaining eel.

"Don't you ever let up?"

His colour, I noticed, was worse. Rowing, I figured, would not be good for a wound in the stomach muscles. I pursed my lips.

"How's your belly?"

"No. Full of eel. Where were you?"

Don't tell. I blinked. Why should I not?

"I don't want you rowing tomorrow," was all I said.

"Will you row in my place?"

Every time I thought I could warm to the man, he turned me back round again — wretched, stubborn man! I flexed my hand and sighed. I nodded. Hazzor raised an eyebrow.

"So, either you really don't want me to row or you really don't want to tell me where you were. Fryn'gh!"

The mage looked up from his mumbling.

"What does a man have to do round here to get five minutes to concentrate on his own stuff?"

Hazzor ignored him.

"You told me you'd shifted the compulsion."

Fryn'gh blew out through lose lips. He sounded like a horse. It suited him. He looked at me, or rather through me.

"There's nothing magical left."

The spy frowned.

"Why won't she tell me where she's been?"

"I am *here* you know."

I scowled at the pair of them.

"Where were you?"

Don't tell Hazzor. I rubbed an eye that hurt suddenly.

"You're being unreasonable. Wasn't Ranyl going to tell us a story of Ygrin?"

The mage scratched his fleece-like hair.

"Well?" snapped Hazzor.

"I'm thinking. The compulsion's gone, so she'll not — "

"It's rude, you know, you talk about people like they were a cat or something."

" — do anything against her nature," continued the mage as if I hadn't spoken. "But there may be something that took root while she was under his influence."

"*Took root?*"

Hazzor frowned.

"You think she might still be following Lecyel's compulsion?"

"Hello? I'm sitting here." I began to wonder if they remembered I was sitting with them. "I'm fine. I'm not under any compulsion from anyone."

Fryn'gh examined his fingernails.

"I think there might be an idea lingering, almost certainly something that doesn't conflict with her own preconceptions."

"Like not telling me where she's been."

"Like not telling you where she's been."

Hazzor's eyes rested on me thoughtfully. "Kayt'an, where have you been?"

He mustn't know. I looked from spy to mage and back again. By now the others had stopped their conversations and I felt seven pairs of eyes on me. I wrapped my arms around myself and shrugged. I drew breath to speak but could not think of anything to say. Suddenly ashamed — though of what I could not tell — I got up to be by myself.

Quick as a cat, Hazzor stood also.

"Oh no," he said, "while you've got secrets from me you stay where I can see you. Is that clear?"

His grey eyes gave nothing away.

I lifted my chin under his scrutiny.

"You should sleep," I said. "I think that wound is bothering you."

I wrapped myself up in my cloak and lay with my back to the fire. I could hear the others talking softly. I heard my name once. I did not care. They could think what they liked. What did I care what a bunch of bandits and spies and wizards thought? I sniffed and waited for sleep to claim me.

Chapter 30

The next morning was uneventful. We all rose according to our usual patterns. I was up a little before dawn ready to offer my day to my goddess. I was doubtful about how good a sacrifice the day would prove to be. *It is a lot easier*, I thought*, to lead a holy life when you are not constantly cheek-by-jowl with a bunch of folk who are determined to set you off your path*.

I had woken decidedly grumpy.

As I say, we rose according to our pattern.

Once in the boat, I unwrapped my hand carefully. Hazzor had insisted I sat in the boat with him and Thorn. She had laughed and told Ranyl it was because he still stank of horses. Ranyl had stalked off to the front boat to take my place, muttering about injustice. I thought a thief not in gaol ought not to complain about injustice, but I had kept silence, wisdom for once ruling my tongue.

"How is it?"

I glanced at Thorn as I wiggled my fingers. I made a fist. It stung and pulled a bit but no more.

I pulled a face.

"It's healing nicely."

Thorn raised her eyebrows.

"Why the long face, then?"

I felt a smile stretch reluctantly across my face.

"I was hoping not to have to paddle."

She laughed.

"Just for that you can have first shift!"

We set off down the waterways. By the time we stopped for lunch, my arms *ached*. Axyl, bless him, had paddled alone from time to time to give Fryn'gh a break. I do not think the big barbarian even broke into a sweat. He was an astonishing man. I could see why he led the life he did. I said as much to Thorn, but it was Hazzor who answered me.

"He had a wife and children once — a prosperous business, too, for that matter."

I was quite taken aback.

"Axyl?" I looked at the enormous mountain of muscle and tried to imagine him bouncing children on his knee. I failed. "What happened?"

Hazzor answered in a perfectly neutral tone.

"His village exiled him."

My jaw flopped down, quite of its own accord. Thorn, I noticed, was taking care to put all her attention into stowing the oars, but it was clear from her expression this was a sad story with which she was already familiar. I directed my puzzlement at her and she responded.

"A Ga'ared raid killed his family many years ago," she said.

This was nonsense. I did not know what to say. Of course, that did not stop me speaking.

"But why would — "

"Axyl, when things get heated, he — " she hesitated, and then shrugged.

"He forgets who his friends are," finished the spy.

Apart from necessary breaks (when I waded into the water behind the long reeds and unidentified creatures investigated my feet), we spent the whole day in the boat. Even when we stopped for lunch (last night's meal was less pleasant when revisited cold), we stayed in the blasted boats.

I kept telling myself it was better than horses. At least the boats did not bite me.

Thorn took shift at midday, so the boat moved silently through the reeds while I said the midday hour. Saen was still mostly out of sight behind the clouds, but it was possible to see his whereabouts in the sky. I had no idea how Pelan could tell where we were. Not only was one patch of the waterways identical to the next, but it was impossible to see more than ten yards ahead. I prayed fervently to Re'a that we were not just going around and around in circles.

After I had said my prayers, I dug in my pack and found the little pot of ointment Lecyel had given Abe, and which Abe had given to me. Even without opening it, I could smell the sweet sickly scent of the balm. I opened the pot and poked, lightly, the greenish-black salve. It was greasy to the touch. Hazzor looked up and asked me what it was. I told him and began unwrapping my hand.

"You're not going to use it."

I noticed there was no question in his voice. Typical! Well, two could play this game.

"I am," I answered, steadily.

He paused in his work and held out a hand.

"Can I see?"

Stupidly — *stupidly* — I held out the little pot, which he promptly took from my hand and dropped in the river. I sat there with my mouth hanging open like a fly-trap while the spy leaned over and took the oars from Thorn. She gave me a look which said I should have known better.

"Well, what did you expect?" she said.

"That was mine!"

I was not indignant: indignant was coming, but had not made it past astonished yet.

Hazzor looked at me evenly.

"Lecyel has betrayed you for certain, and us probably. Yet you want to use the ointment he gave you — an ointment whose ingredients you don't know — on your injured hand?"

He shook his head and said no more. Indignant arrived at last.

"You brought me on this trip as a healer. How am I supposed to look after you all if I know nothing about the local herbs and tonics?" I heard my voice rising in pitch so I took a couple of deep breaths before I continued. "We don't know what Lecyel did," I bit my lip, nausea rising, "but, he was the healer for Ay Toris. Have you asked whether he was trusted? Have you asked how long he was there? I can't be expected to just walk away from the knowledge and herbs that he had." *Don't tell him any more!* I stopped, bewildered, and shook my head. "I ... " I managed and then ground to a halt, unaccountably tongue-tied.

Hazzor did not lose so much as a stoke paddling.

"Two years," he said, "and yes, they trusted him. Apparently, he was very helpful when a couple of young women went missing, and again last year when another woman disappeared. Unfortunately, though, all his help was to no avail. They found none of them."

He paddled quietly for a couple of moments, watching me like a cat watches a mouse hole. I bit my lip and said nothing.

After a while, I busied myself mixing a new pot of ointment from my own stocks. I had another pot of Lecyel's salve burning a hole in my bag, but I dare not experiment with it now. It just sat among my healer's stocks and looked at me. *Hazzor mustn't know.*

As we came to the end of the day, the world around us began to change again. The boundary between water and dry land became clearer, and there were animals on the land that I recognised — cows mostly. One cow came right up to the water's edge as we passed and gazed at us with curious eyes. I laughed at her and waved at her sisters.

"If you'd keep both hands on the paddle, we'll be less likely to hit the bank," Hazzor remarked with his usual dryness.

I huffed at him, and then mentioned my surprise at the change in landscape.

"Yr'th Ra drained the marshes near Steriv to improve the port."

"So we're nearly there?"

Hazzor gave a small smile.

"All but."

Not long after, Pelan pulled the boats into the bank just south of a little village that sat among the cows. It was a blessed relief to leave the boat. My legs ached with inaction while my arms and back were complaining bitterly about endless repetition. I was torn between flopping down onto the grass (short, normal, *proper* grass) and running a quick lap of the field. I chose to flop. Fryn'gh, I noticed, chose to pace about.

Pelan was gesturing westwards to Abe and Hazzor, and the three were chatting merrily and nodding. Finally, Pelan gave Abe and then Thorn a great enveloping hug and, with a farewell salute, Hazzor strode off to the west. The others followed and I scrambled to my feet to catch up.

I could hear the sound of the sea in the distance. Further south, I could see a tower dominating the horizon, surrounded by a huge town. The tower was the most graceful thing I had ever seen, tapering up into the heavens like a finger pointing to the gods.

Fryn'gh saw me looking.

"Quite something, isn't it?"

"I've never seen anything like it!"

The wretched mage smiled, patronisingly. I rolled my eyes.

"I suppose you've seen a hundred cities," I said sarcastically.

"Only Hethin and Steriv. And Ephatha."

"Ephatha's not a city," I muttered. Then, "You've been to Steriv before?"

The mage looked a shade uncomfortable.

"I went to study under Regnik for two years."

"In Steriv?"

"Yes in Steriv. Why not?"

"We're at war."

"We weren't then."

"Oh," was all I could find to say. Then, "Didn't they have teachers in your own tower?"

The mage had the effrontery to look pitying.

"Did your teachers really believe they could teach you everything?"

I sniffed, dismissively.

"You don't have to travel to find Re'a."

"Oh? And she talks to you direct, does she?"

Impudent puttock.

"Kayt'an — "

"*Saahni,*" I said smugly. Pelan was behind us now and I could reclaim my dignity.

Fryn'gh rolled his eyes and said something like 'hpha'.

"Why don't you know what Lecyel's herbs do?" I did not answer so he went on, "Aren't there great mysteries of faith you want to explore?" Then he could not help himself, and added, "Or are you content to peddle fairy tales?"

"Better beautiful tales than wickedness that ruins faces and kingdoms in one breath!"

"Well, if you're going to judge a whole class of scholars — "

"*Scholars?*"

" — *scholars* by one rogue, there's no talking to you."

We walked on in silence.

Dusk began to fall soon after, but Hazzor wanted to keep going. We could see Dar Tor on the western horizon, and the spy figured we should be at our destination before full dark. I drew my beads from my pocket and mumbled as we walked. Both Fryn'gh and I tripped from time to time, but I swear the others must have the sight of owls in the dark. Hazzor was right, but only just. We were perhaps as much as ten minutes from full dark when we approached the farm house.

A dog ran out to investigate us, noisy and suspicious. As it barked and snarled, running little darts of aggression at us, Hazzor called out,

"Heanahi! Hee!"

The door opened; a golden rectangle framing a woman's silhouette. She gave a curt command to the dog, who ran back to heel, and waited for us to draw near.

When we were near enough, I saw she was beautiful; graceful and bright and fair-of-face and I wondered what a woman like her was doing in a farmhouse in the middle of nowhere.

"Welcome," she said, and I was relieved she spoke Ttarcine. In fact, as we filed into her house, I saw she did not look like a W'shten.

"You're Ttarcine!" I blurted, and she smiled bitterly.

"My father was, and he gave me his face. These days I'm neither fish nor fowl. Neither welcome nor trusted this side of the border or that.

"Come, sit, eat. I've a stew ready and plenty of bread."

"How did she know we were coming?" I whispered to Ranyl.

"Don't ask, don't tell," he muttered quietly.

"You've a message for me," said Hazzor conversationally, though I wondered if it were a little discourteous to jump to the matter before we had even eaten her food.

The woman nodded.

"From a friend," she said.

"A good friend?"

"Good enough."

Hazzor stretched out his legs in front of him.

"Madam, thank you for your help in this. It's most welcome."

"Our friend thinks this will end the war."

"Let's hope so."

The farmer brought out a supper she somehow had ready for seven. I had no idea what was in it, but it was recognisable and I loved it. As I began to nod over the last of my stew, Heanah led us to a back room that she had covered in an assortment of bedrolls and cushions and blankets.

"I'm sorry, but this is the best I can offer you. If there's anything else you need, just let me know."

We said not at all, it was lovely, and she left us. Hazzor stayed in the front room with Heanah while the rest of us lay down for the night. In the dark, while the spy could not see, I fetched out my spare pot of Lecyel's ointment. What harm could it do? I anointed myself and flexed my hand. I felt a little better already, I thought. I lay there listening to the sound of their voices until I heard the stairs creaking and Hazzor come in. By the time he was still, I was asleep.

Chapter 31

I awoke after a dreamless sleep refreshed and alert. Even the usual morning recollection of my losses did not hurt like it usually did. I felt bright-eyed and bushy-tailed. Here we were, at last. We had travelled far to accomplish this task of Reath's, which would make all my sacrifices worthwhile. At last I was to find out what all this had been *for.* This was It, and I was Ready.

I went outside to say the hour. The dog, so fierce last night, had clearly accepted us as guests. He wandered over to greet me, pressing a now amiable nose into my hip in a demand of a fuss. Saen lit the sky in an array of pinks and reds, and I thanked Re'a in good heart for reconciling us to him. Once I had recalled her saving acts, I begged Re'a's assistance in our Task. It must be one she would bless, I argued. She had brought the war between humanity and Farock Rha to an end. Surely, ending this war would please her?

I got to my feet and headed back to the house. I paused in the doorway as the smell of breakfast assaulted my senses, and the dog seized his opportunity to push past.

"Ohar! Wretched hound!" Haenah grabbed the dog by his sizeable collar and hauled him bodily outside again, giving his rump a smack as she released him. "You know better!" she told him sternly, and shushed me in the house before closing the door behind me. "Wretched hound," she repeated, fondly.

Around Haenah's fire, the others were eating breakfast with enthusiasm. I sat down and took my portion, thankfully.

"Where's Hazzor?" I asked.

Ranyl shrugged and it was Fryn'gh who answered.

"He went to Steriv."

I looked at him wide-eyed with astonishment.

"But he'll never pass as W'shten!"

The mage looked a trifle smug.

"Magic doesn't only *ruin* faces," he said.

"A good disguise is safer than an illusion."

Ranyl barely looked up from his food as he spoke. Fryn'gh snorted.

When I asked Heanah what she knew, she refused point blank to share, telling me Reath had given her the message for Hazzor, and only Hazzor, and she was not one to cross the master spy.

In the end, we had the morning to ourselves. Fryn'gh sat under a tree in the farmyard, muttering to himself. Axyl and Abe sparred while Thorn practiced her aim with a target drawn on a barrel. Ranyl disappeared and I, I played with the dog.

Hazzor returned on horseback while I was saying the midday hour. I looked up from my prayers to see him dismount with a face so grim I did a quick review of my morning. Satisfied that this time it was not me that had caused his ill humour, I closed my prayers and got to my feet.

"Hazzor, hee!"

The little man looked my way with a flicker of a smile.

"Hazzor*i*, hee," he corrected me, "but close enough."

I drew near.

"Greetings, Saahni."

As we walked towards the house, I watched him out of the corner of my eye. He did not look a happy man. The others saw us approach and also headed for the house. Even Ranyl appeared out of nowhere.

Haenah came out, and took the horse while the seven of us went in.

"Spill, then," said Thorn, "why so grim?"

"We lost more time than I'd realised getting here," the spy replied. "We've only got one day — two if you count what remains of today — to plan and execute our mission."

The bandits received this information stoically. I was still blissfully in the dark, but Fryn'gh protested,

"I'm not ready."

"Then get ready."

The little man's face was unyielding.

"Hang on," I looked from Fryn'gh to Hazzor, "are you saying *he* knows the plan — the big, mysterious, we'll tell you when we get there plan?"

"Saahni, this is not the time for childishness."

"You *knew.*" The ginger nonentity looked back at me defiantly. "How come he got to know?"

"ENOUGH!" Hazzor's already grim expression was now black. "Kayt'an Sahn, if you cannot contain your petty rivalry, we may all die. It is too late to replace you. We all depend on you being able to lift your sight above your own status and piety," he spat the words, "for *two days*. Do you think you can manage that?"

He was practically snarling.

I was silenced. No one else moved or spoke.

"Right, Fryn'gh, you go and sit in a hole and get yourself ready."

The mage scrambled to his feet and left the room.

"So, sunshine, what's the plan?"

Despite the shouting, Abe was looking relaxed and his slow drawl seemed to ease the tense atmosphere in Haenah's front room. Hazzor nodded.

"Tomorrow is the last day of Prince Vasht-Yr's hunting trip in the marshes to the north."

"The ones we've just come from."

Ranyl looked less than impressed.

"Nearer the coast. There's word there's a dragon. The prince wants its head."

"So?"

"We need to isolate the prince from his guard, kidnap him and take him back to Ttaroc."

Even Abe looked stunned.

"And how were you reckoning we can do this?"

The spy gave his half smile.

"*We're* not, Abernast."

"No?"

"You are." As the big man's jaw dropped, the spy added, "At least you're the one who's going to draw the prince away from his men."

"Oh ay?' The whey-faced fighter looked decidedly sceptical. "And how're I doing this?"

Hazzor leaned forward, elbows resting on his knees.

"It's well known that the prince resents his role in the royal household. Big brother, king-in-waiting, is rather the golden boy and Vasht-Yr has been playing up more and more. The fact that the body guard has been increased — they know Reath's up to something — plays in our favour. With such a heavy retinue Vasht-Yr will almost certainly try to slip away, if only to prove that he can. He's a talented lad — that's why my master wants him. You, Abernast, will be waiting. Once he's a little apart, you lead him further away. Kayt'an will prepare a drug for you to dose him."

"I'll do what? Pardon me?"

Hazzor continued as if I had not spoken.

"I'll be waiting with Axyl to help you get him back to the farm where Fryn'gh *will* be ready."

"That sounds well and good," Ranyl spoke up, "but Yr's not just going to let his son wander around the marshes on his own. If 'it's well known' the boy's kicking over the traces he'll have men watching for it."

"Ay and I'll have you watching for them. Find them, Ranyl, and put them out of our misery."

The little thief narrowed his eyes as he considered the plan and nodded.

"Can we go back to my making a drug?"

Axyl tapped his foot.

"What about all these guards who've lost their prince? They're not just going to sit down and wait for him."

"Thorn and Kayt'an Sahn will keep them busy."

"Thorn and Kayt'an Sahn will *what*?"

I looked at the spy in disbelief.

"How are you expecting us to keep them 'busy', Haz?"

Thorn leaned back lazily as she spoke, long fingers fiddling with the embroidery on the wall.

"I was thinking a game of hide and seek should entertain."

"Hmm." The archer gave a humourless smile, "I'm just not sure everyone will play."

"You have to make them think you are a force to be reckoned with."

"Kayt'an and me."

She did not look convinced.

"What else do you want?"

Thorn shook her head and sighed.

"Well, it's your party. I wasn't fancying the journey back anyway."

"Well, just make sure you stay alive long enough for us to get the prince away. We'll wait back here 'til sunrise."

I was fed up with being ignored.

"Will somebody *listen* to me?" I slapped the floor with my hand. "I am not a poisoner, nor am I a killer. I can't fight and I won't drug this prince."

Hazzor regarded me with his slate eyes.

"Saahni, you and I need a word."

He got up and left. Working to keep my ire hot, I followed him.

"What do you think will happen if you don't play your part, Saahni?"

"That's not the point," I exclaimed hotly, utterly fed up with being brow-beaten and patronised.

"It's exactly the point. You agreed to this, you came with me to do *this*. I have dragged you, carried you, pushed and pulled you across two countries while the moon has vanished from the sky and now you tell me you *won't*?" The spy glared at me, his grey eyes dark, and his whole body tense with suppressed energy. "If you fail us, we will all die and the war will go on." He actually sneered at me. "You tear yourself apart over your imagined guilt for your village, but you condemn untold numbers to death without blinking."

Now your soul belongs to Reath.

I fled the thought, stoking the anger. I was better than this. I stepped forward to be almost nose-to-nose with the man.

"How dare you talk to me about guilt for the village you helped kill!?" I was not entirely sure that made sense so I moved on quickly. "I came under protest. I said at the outset that I'd not poison anyone. I'm a *priest*, not a killer. I don't care what you're doing; if it depends on murder it's wrong and I'll not be part of it."

Hazzor pushed his hands into the pockets of his long coat.

"Who said we were murdering anyone?"

The solid ground I thought I was standing on shifted and I lost my mental footing.

"What?"

The spy regarded me with his usual unreadable expression.

"We're not murdering the prince, we're kidnapping him. We need him safe and well."

"Oh."

I ran my fingers through my shorn hair. I still felt the need to resist, to fight this slippery man's influence, his belief that he commanded me ... but I had lost the absolute that was so easy to defend. Hazzor still held the ground I had stepped into, still stood fast, and the small space between us suddenly seemed *too* small. I stepped back and averted my gaze. I saw Fryn'gh sat under the tibbith tree, muttering, and was reinvigorated. I stepped back into the battlefield.

"You may not be planning to kill him, but you'll ensorcel him."

I thought I had a winning hand again, but Hazzor, may he rot for eternity, gave a satisfied nod.

"And Fryn'gh needs you to put the prince in a suitably ... receptive frame of mind."

The wretched, overblown, contemptible little man took my breath away. He wanted me to do to Vasht-Yr what Lecyel had done to me. My mind flicked to the contents of my bag, taken from Lecyel's *tuy*. I probably had the wherewithal to do it, too.

I snarled, "You must be *joking*!"

The spy narrowed his eyes, triumphantly.

"And I thought you were a woman of your word, Saahni."

Once again the ground beneath me shifted and I leaned back a tad, uncertain.

"What do you mean?"

"You owe the mage, Saahni. When he used magic to aid your healing — twice, mind you — against his judgement, you acknowledged the debt." When I did not respond he prompted, "Didn't you?"

He could not have heard. He was three quarters dead at the time. *How* did he hear? Did Fryn'gh tell him? The dirty tattle tale! Again I gave ground, looking anywhere except at Hazzor, but my gall burned.

"*Didn't* you?"

I nodded, eyeing the ground at my feet. I did not want to see the spy's face.

"So, now, you help him with your skills. You'll make a sedative for Abe to give the prince so we can get him back to the farm, then Fryn'gh'll need something to make Vasht-Yr biddable. Then, you'll send him back to sleep for us. Won't you?"

It's funny how a question can sound like a statement. The spy had me in a corner of my own making. I hated Hazzor.

"And, Saahni?" I looked up. "You'll go with Thorn and you'll help her or do I have to recall for you your debt to Ranyl?"

I did not see how a debt to Ranyl meant me shooting W'shten guards for Thorn, but I was confident Hazzor could make it so. I wanted to spit. The bitter irony was that both these debts were because I had wanted to save the life of the man now hounding me. I turned on my heal and marched off. I had to review the contents of my bag.

And maybe get some archery practice in.

I spent the rest of the day playing apothecary: altho, marigold, mallow and all the rest needed to be ground and mixed, and tested. There was not much we could do until the prince's hunting trip in the morning. Haenah, bless her, was test subject for me. I knew Lecyel had had the herbs to make the drug Hazzor wanted — something to make people 'biddable' (we had yet to find out how 'biddable' I had been). I dropped various mixtures on her tongue and she told me how she felt. The drug Lecyel had used must have kicked in quickly for it to be used like it had been on me, but I had to leave enough time between each test to stop them blurring. It was a very frustrating afternoon.

After hours of waiting and testing and sniffing, I opened a little bottle I had picked up that had lain at the back of Lecyel's store. Tentatively I raised it to my nose, and my head reeled. Hairs stood up at the back of my neck: just out of reach was a memory I could not grasp. My stomach flipped. This bottle was what I needed, already mixed. I thanked Haenah and told her I was done.

I held the bottle in my hand and stared at it. What was I becoming?

Chapter 32

I studiously avoided Hazzor for the rest of that day and went to bed early, conscious that we would have to set off before the morning hour. Not only would I be poisoning someone, I would be starting the day badly. Both the priest and the healer in me were offended. In a small act of rebellion, I applied some of Lecyel's lotion to my hand, which was not healing as well as I would have liked.

I tucked into the corner of the back room, and stared at the ceiling long after the others had come in to sleep. I feared what the morrow would bring. I was afraid I would fail at my designated tasks.

I was afraid I would not.

I dreamed I was on the temple at H'th Iriq. I was helping the local priest sort out her things on the roof. I found her bucket of candle stubs where I had left it.

"Shall I melt these down for you?" I asked the priest.

She looked at me with her one eye.

"I have no need for them now."

"It seems a shame to leave them." I think my sister smiled at me, but it was hard to tell. I put down the bucket and touched her twisted hand. "You should have run, Saahni."

"I stood by my Lady." The priest pushed back in a piece of intestine that was escaping. "Can you say as much, Saahni?"

"There was no one left to serve."

"You've left more than just your temple, Kayt'an Sahn."

I shook my head vigorously.

"Saahni, no. I have worked hard to stay with my Lady. I have kept the hours — "

"When it suits."

"I have worked to stay true to her Way."

"Charity? Patience? Loving all Saen's children?"

I would not be bullied by a dead woman.

"Can you tell me you were all that?"

"I died for Re'a."

I answered angrily, "I choose to live for her."

The dead priest sagged pitifully.

"Do you belittle my death, Saahni?"

We were down inside the temple, kneeling face-to-face where Re'a should have stood. I tried to help my sister-priest tuck her leg under her, where it belonged, but it persisted in jutting out to the side.

"I can't tell my way forward, Saahni. I walk a path someone else has mapped for me."

"You always have, Saahni." The broken priest cocked her head to one side. "Amtil Sahn, Hathil, Reath, Hazzor — always, Saahni, always others have mapped your path."

"I have no choice! I've never had a choice."

"Then what is your life worth?"

I watched as blood ran down the priest's chin.

"Worth?" I asked.

"Saen gave you the gift of life, Saahni. What have you done with it?"

The next morning Thorn shook me awake and I sat up in the darkness, forcing my eyes to stay open. Around me the others were rising and I could hear Fryn'gh complaining that *he* did not need to be up this early because he was not coming on the trip. Curse him. I reached for the thick, warm skirt and Thorn stopped me.

"Sorry, Saahni, we're back in our marsh clothes today."

I grumped. One day in a skirt, and then I was back in trousers and bare feet again.

Abe had asked how we would follow Vasht-Yr's expedition without being seen. Hazzor told us the rumours Reath's agents had started were very specific about where the dragon was. We would wait for the prince to come to us.

I was less than reassured.

It was cloudy and there was no starlight as we set off along the coast. Hazzor led the way with a lantern, but he kept its light dim and half-shuttered. I picked my footing along the bank and listened to the sea dragging the sand up and down the beach like some child-giant's toy. As the sun started to rise, the bank sank down and met the reeds. Once again, we were wading through mud and water as Hazzor led us to the 'dragon's den'.

The trap, apparently, was to be set on a little mound, an island.

"Abe," the spy commanded quietly, "you wait here. Reath's confident Vasht-Yr will want to get here before his entourage. You'll have only a short window to lead him away before the rest catch up.

"Axyl, stay with Abe, out of sight if you can. He may need another pair of hands.

"Thorn, Kayt'an — "

"*Saahni,*" I hissed.

" — I suggest you wait to the south of here for the guards."

He looked at Ranyl and simply nodded. In the blink of an eye the thief had disappeared.

Hazzor turned to the rest of us. "I'll be waiting on the bank," he finished and, without further ado, he turned his back on us and headed back the way we had come.

When Saen had risen, he found me crouched among the reeds waiting for Vasht-Yr's retinue. Thorn was like a coiled spring behind her bow, wiry and poised. I had my bow strung and ready, but my heart was not in it.

"Thorn," I whispered, "I don't think I can do this."

The archer gave an exasperated sigh.

"Saahni, this is not the time for second thoughts."

They were not second thoughts; they were first thoughts.

"I can't kill these people."

Thorn took her eye off the horizon to say,

"Then don't. Just fire arrows in their direction when I tell you to. We want them to think it's an attack. We want them to come after us. The more people we can pretend to be, the better. We could have done with Fryn'gh, ideally, but not to worry. We'll just run about lots and fire lots of arrows. Oh, and we mustn't get the prince's attention."

I looked at her, horrified at the idea. I was clear that killing others was wrong, but I was far from keen on being killed either. I *knew* that my life was not more important than theirs, but I *felt* differently.

All I said was,

"And then what?"

My companion brushed some crawling thing off her leg.

"Once we've given Abe long enough we disappear."

I nodded, vigorously.

"And how do we do that? Once we've got a whole retinue of body guards following us, that is."

Thorn gave me a cheery grin.

"We drop down in the mud and hope they don't find us."

I tried to envision a band of angry guards failing to find us after we had spent a significant portion of time aggravating them and drawing their attention to us. I failed.

"We're going to die, aren't we."

The archer slapped me on the back.

"Nah. We'll be fine."

Re'a, Saviour of the world, have mercy on me.

Not long afterwards, Thorn tapped me lightly on the arm and pointed. The prince was coming. He was armoured, riding a horse and carrying a great spear, bigger than the horse. His helmet rested on the pommel of his saddle. He was riding fast through the marshland, looking over his shoulder often, grinning with mischief.

As he passed, I could not help but whisper,

"He's just a boy!"

Thorn didn't even bother to sush me.

Almost on his heels came more riders with some servant-types running alongside. I felt a moment's pity for the servants as they struggled to run in the mud, but it was fleeting. Thorn led me behind them, and fired a dart at the nearest horse. It reared and kicked, causing the horses either side to shy. Quickly, the horses were calmed and the party continued after their prince — until Thorn shot another dart and another horse reared. This time they stopped, and there was some discussion among the riders. A guard walked round and checked the horse. Thorn shot him with another dart and the man clutched his face. I was confident that whatever he was shouting would not have been said in front of his mother. He pulled the dart and brandished it at his companions who all started shouting.

I tensed, ready for most if not all the body guards to charge our way.

They didn't.

The riders launched themselves after their prince instead and the servants did their best to run after them.

Thorn swore. She stood and fired in earnest at the departing escort, felling three runners in quick succession, but the rest did not even pause. In a couple more heartbeats, the runners disappeared into the reeds.

I crouched beside Thorn in the reeds, torn between dread and relief. Nobody was trying to kill me, but we had bought hardly any time for Abe.

"Come on!"

The wiry woman grabbed my shoulder, and followed the running men and horses. Amazingly, she still managed to fire from time to time. One shot winged a rider who must have been a quarter of a mile off. Another crippled a runner. Thorn stabbed him mercilessly as we overtook him. I just concentrated on keeping up. Still the riders pulled away, and the runners kept on ahead of us, hardly visible among the grasses. Thorn was shouting frantically — somehow

— as she ran. I could barely stand, so short of breath was I, let alone talk or shout.

In the distance, we could hear more shouting as the riders caught up with Vasht-Yr. Thorn had stopped shooting — even for her it had become a lost cause — and she ran in earnest. I started to flag and she pulled away from me. Not only was my breath burning in my chest and throat, but every step slipped and slid beneath me. My calves and thighs screamed, and I fought to keep running though I barely knew why. I doubted I would be any use in a fight. Soon, I could not see anyone else and I was running — staggering rather — towards the shouting, hoping rather than knowing that I was heading in the right direction. *Re'a, Saviour of the world, guide me.*

I could hear screaming, hoarse and raw. *Holy Lady, who* is *that?* I veered, aiming for the awful noise and, sooner than I would have guessed, I found myself on the island where Hazzor had left us.

I dropped to my knees. Whether it was the bloody chaos in front of me or my sheer inability to hold myself upright once I had stopped running I do not know. Heaving for breath, I stared in horror. In the centre of the mound, Axyl whirled and danced, a screaming butcher carving weeping red gashes in the arms, legs, faces and chests of the men, women and horses around him. To my left, Thorn crouched ready to loose arrows at any opportunity. Beside her, Abe savagely attacked the armed servants trying to stop her. Horses kicked and screamed, soldiers shouted and moaned, and over and through it all Axyl screamed and howled as he carved his way through the prince's escort. The ground was black with gore, and the guards slipped and tripped over the bodies of their fallen comrades. It was as though someone had opened a door to the Dark Lord's own Pit.

In no time, it was over. The island was littered with the dead and mortally wounded. At their centre, Axyl was collapsed in a heap, sobbing and panting for breath. Abe, I noticed, approached him cautiously before kneeling beside him and speaking quietly. Thorn laid down her bow and attended to a fallen figure I had not noticed until then. I dragged myself to my feet and went over to see. As I picked my way across the battleground, I slipped in the blood-soaked earth and fell. I swore, weakly. Feeling like I was lifting lead weights, I brought my hands underneath me to push myself up.

I discovered I was laying on the arm of a woman whose eyes still rolled while the blood pumped from her throat.

"Gah!"

I scrambled away into the spilling intestines of a horse. Heaving and retching, I spat bile into the gore and struggled to find an empty space where I could get purchase on the ground. I shouted again, rolling and sinking further into hysteria, as I covered myself in the vital fluids of the bodies around me.

A hand grabbed my upper arm and hauled me to my feet.

"Haenid's tits, woman, are you *completely* useless?" I stood gasping and retching. I considered correcting the W'shten's address, but decided in my current state I would have to work hard to carry it. "Go and check on the prince. I hit him pretty hard, but he had a nice, soft landing."

On legs that felt as though they had more in common with the eels I had had for yesterday's breakfast than with anything human, I wobbled and staggered over to Thorn. I sat beside her and looked blearily at Vasht-Yr. There was a nice bruise developing on his jaw (it matched one I sported on my own), but I could see no other signs of harm. This close, I could see the boy must be barely more than sixteen. There was a slight down on his cheeks and, poor soul, there was a pimple between his brows that looked decidedly sore. I checked for his heart beat, and found it strong and rhythmic. I pushed his hair out of his eyes and patted his chest as though reassuring him.

"You'll be fine," I said to him.

Then my stomach spasmed again, and I had to turn my head.

"Well then," said the big fighter, "job done. Last one back cooks breakfast."

Chapter 33

Hazzor was less than impressed with our account when we caught up with him. Thorn offered the opinion that it was his plan, not its execution, which had been faulty. The prince had failed to escape his escort.

The spy glared at her.

"A missing prince could have been anything, including the tide or the prince's wilfulness. A slaughtered bodyguard, on the other hand, means they are going to come looking for kidnappers."

"Oh well, we're so sorry we pulled the prince out of the ruins of *your* plan."

Thorn was unscathed, but I had never seen her look so irate.

"There was nothing wrong with the plan, Thorn. All you needed to do was distract the prince's guard for ten minutes but no, apparently, that was too much trouble."

"Listen, you, I did everything you asked of me, so don't — "

"I reckon they knew."

Ranyl chewed on a piece of grass. He had been waiting for us with Hazzor on the bank, shamelessly declaring he had felt superfluous.

"They didn't even think about checking out Thorn. Someone knew."

Hazzor halted his stride for a moment and stared at the thief, his face a careful blank.

"If we could keep moving, buck?" Abe's usually soft voice was strained. They'd sunk Vasht-Yr's armour, but the prince was still a well-muscled young man and Axyl was in no state to help carry anyone. "I'd be grateful if I could put this lad down sooner than later."

Hazzor nodded, and we continued on down the sea bank in silence. The spy's face wore a frown and I noticed no one was looking my way.

"Hey!"

I ran in a series of jerky lurching strides to catch up with Hazzor. My legs still felt wobbly, and I must have turned my ankle during the frantic rush across the marsh. It hadn't hurt at the time now it did. A lot. I reached out for the spy's sleeve with a hand that still shook.

"It wasn't me, you know."

He ignored my hand, keeping his own hands in the pockets of the jacket he was wearing over his marshland clothes.

"Wasn't you what, Saahni?"

"I didn't warn anyone we were coming." Why I cared so much what he thought I did not know, but I was earnest in my attempt. I gave a short, unconvincing laugh. "Who would I have told?"

"Would you have known if you had told someone, Saahni? Would you tell me?"

Damn Lecyel and damn all magic!

"I'm not a traitor, Hazzor. I wouldn't do it." I pulled at his jacket some more. "Fryn'gh said I'd not do anything against my nature. I'd not have gone to the W'shten."

"Not even to save lives?" The spy's expression remained neutral. "Not even to save a man from being enchanted?"

I let go of Hazzor's sleeve. Truth told, it had not crossed my mind to try to get out of my predicament by informing the authorities. I did not even know who the authorities were. Hazzor was right, though. If I could imagine my trying to rescue the prince by such means, so could everyone else.

I trudged alongside the others as they carried the prince back to the farm. It was going to be another long day, long beyond all bearing. *Holy Re'a, saviour of the world, have mercy on me.*

Haenah was waiting for us when we returned and Ohar greeted us with great enthusiasm, as if he had never doubted our intentions. We trod wearily down the path while Ohar jumped and sniffed at Vasht-Yr and tried to lick Axyl's wounds as he stomped along behind us.

Fryn'gh had prepared an area for his *ministrations,* and looked pale and tense as he directed the prince into the space marked out for him. He received the news he would have to hurry because troops might be coming for us, with a worsening pallor and with a noise that I — were I less charitable than I am — might have called a squeak. He pulled at his hair and stared into the middle distance.

While Fryn'gh was quietly panicking, I took the two fighters aside to mop up their wounds. Abe had a nasty bruise on his cheek and a knife wound on his arm that needed stitches. Axyl, on the other hand, looked like a pillow that had had a close encounter with a naughty puppy. It was hard to see what was holding him in one piece. I shook my head in wonder, stitching him back together as best I could. Thorn followed us in.

"I told you he gets carried away," she said.

Abe was examining my work on his arm and seemed satisfied.

"You didn't tell me he becomes deranged!"

As I tended to Axyl, the big barbarian was nodding off despite his efforts to stay awake.

"If you've dealt with the worst, Sahnithi, sweeting, you'd best let the man sleep. No one's going to want to be the one paddling the boat Axyl's asleep in."

The truth of this was inescapable, so I dismissed the barbarian who simply curled up where he was like an enormous dormouse.

I shook my head again and let my gaze return to the mage who was circling the still unconscious prince, muttering.

The W'shten clapped me on the back.

"You'd best go find out when he wants your help."

It is funny how that was exactly what I did not want to do.

Warily, I approached Fryn'gh and his victim. From my bag, I slowly drew a potion I had mixed earlier. The mage held out his hand for it, but I was reluctant to hand it over.

"What are you going to do to him?"

Strange that this was the first time I asked.

The mage drew something from the pocket on his belt. He had the grace to look embarrassed and said,

"You don't need to know."

"I *what*?"

"Can you open up some skin while he's still unconscious?" The mage spoke quickly, not answering, "Just over the bottom couple of ribs on the left hand side of his chest? I don't need it deep, just big enough to fit this."

He waved something small and white at me, about the size of the tip of my little finger.

I looked at the mage incredulously.

"Now you want me to cut him, too?"

Fryn'gh sighed.

"Look, if I do it, he's far more likely to notice it and wonder. A neat job will be dismissed as some patching up done while he was out." As I continued to stare, he rolled his eyes and said, "Fine! For the spell to work Vasht-Yr needs to be touching this." The red-head waved the thing at me again. "I could tape it to his body and shield it, but there'd be a risk of it getting knocked off and it'd mean another weave to set up. Safer and easier this way."

I gazed in horror.

"And you want me to help you?"

The mage gazed at me levelly.

"Why do you think Hazzor has dragged you all this way instead of simply buying potions from an apothecary?"

"I'm a healer. People who fight get hurt. Hurt people need a healer. I've proved my skills," my voice sounded dull and lifeless in my ears. "I'm not a sorcerer. This isn't *me*."

"You owe me."

This was too close to the conversation I had already had with Hazzor. I scowled. Fryn'gh scowled back.

"You said you'd trust me," he said. "I said I would trust you, but you would have to trust me later. This is later." When I did not answer, he continued to push. "I cannot see the difference. You *urged* me to use magic to save Hazzor for the sake of the mission; I need you to help me use magic for the thing that *is* the mission. It is still the same magic, still the same purpose."

This must be how the Dark Lord draws you in, I thought. First, you use a wicked means to achieve an unquestionably good end and, then, the next time the good end is moved a little further away. Instead of saving the life of a man who can end the war, you are asked to help enchant a man to end the war. Once you have stepped off the plateau and used magic, it is so hard to find a level place to stand again. How near, how immediate, did the end have to be in order for it to justify the means? *How far down this path will I slide?*

I took one more step downwards. I handed Fryn'gh the vial.

"Thank you Saahni."

Re'a, Saviour of the world, find *me.*

I took another step down the slope.

"If you rub this on his temples," I handed the mage the pot I had found among my looted herbs, "it'll keep the boy confused and sleepy. One drop of that and a dab of this on here," I gestured, "will probably mean you can tell him to go to sleep."

"*Probably*?"

"If you wanted perfection, I should have had more notice about what you wanted," I answered, sharply. I drew a breath slowly and then added, "I can't just keep adding potions one on top of another. I don't know how they'll react to each other." I shook my head, half apology, half rejection of my own act. "At the very least he'll have little or no recollection of the time he spends under the salvis."

I conducted the little operation Fryn'gh had asked of me, and then I left the mage to his work and went to sit under his tibbith tree. I stared glumly at the cloudy sky. The mud and gore began to dry on my skin and it itched abominably. Ohar came to keep me company. He tried to apply himself to cleaning my arms and legs, but I wasn't having it. He put his big, brindled head in my lap and sighed heavily. I leant against the smooth tree trunk and scratched Ohar behind his ears to his evident enjoyment. He stretched out his legs and splayed his toes. *Well*, I thought, *at least I have one friend.*

The rest of the morning passed slowly. I watched Saen reach his zenith, and for only the second time since I had left Harset I deliberately did not say the hour. I really was not sure I could still call myself a priest. I vividly remembered the morning Hazzor instructed me to pack the poisons in my bag.

'Each step is so simple, so small, so reasonable. Every day you can see the way back and then suddenly a door shuts behind you and you've become a monster,' he had said that morning, so very long ago, it seemed. *'You've made the decision not to die. Now your soul belongs to Reath.'*

I had been so sure that I was better than that.

But I had packed the poisons, nonetheless.

Haenah called us to lunch.

Hazzor was waiting when I came in to the house. He smiled into his beard as Ohar had another attempt at sneaking into the house behind me. I had no idea why the hound had decided I was his ticket into his mistress's home, but it did me no favours with the lady. This time Haenah chose to remind me that the dog was not allowed in.

"I didn't bring him," I muttered weakly, but truth be told I had grown fond of the animal and would probably have fed him half my food if he had come in with me.

I caught the spy's eye and smiled reluctantly.

"You should keep a dog, Saahni."

"She'd spoil it rotten."

Haenah's frown eased.

Save Axyl, the bandits rolled in, apparently without a care in the world, laughing and jostling one another. Ranyl had been bitten by a blood-sucking marsh worm and was now the butt of some decidedly ribald humour. I chewed on my food and watched, wondering how these killers were so at ease with themselves.

Last of all, Fryn'gh, pale and withdrawn, trudged in.

Hazzor greeted him with a nod.

"Is it done?"

The mage nodded and sighed.

"I'm exhausted."

As he sat down, Haenah handed him a plate of bread and cheese and he took it doubtfully.

"You'd best eat up. You've a long day ahead." Haenah turned to Hazzor, "Where'll you be heading?"

The spy shook his head.

"The less you know the better, Haenah."

He did not say there was a traitor among us, but his eyes flicked my way and I noticed he was not the only one. I concentrated on my cheese. More words would get me nowhere.

Interlude

The Princess stood while her ladies in waiting hung clothes on her like some seamstresses' dummy. They chattered like magpies and the room hummed with their excitement. The king had ordered a ball. With all to the east of the capital descending into ruins, and the West beginning to fear bankruptcy, the king thought a party would restore morale. Ttarah's mouth twitched in the ghost of a smile. As her face moved so did the scars. She felt them shift and refuse to fold on her cheek. She didn't like smiling.

As usual, the ladies in waiting had not come in until she was in her underclothes and veil. Her new veil, she had to admit, was very pretty. The usual exchange of opinions with the seamstress had not gone her way. J'lid had, for once, prevailed and Ttarah had to admit the effect was striking. She ran the corner of it through her fingers and felt the bumps and knots of the threadwork. It was an effort of will not to run her hand over her face, to feel the bumps and knots of that threadwork. She swallowed the bitterness, and answered the twittering flattery of Lady Esta.

Ttarah had heard no more about the prince who was supposed to marry her. She assumed she would be told who he was before the wedding day. Perhaps this new drive towards making her fashionable was to draw her in a new marriageable light in the minds of the people. In her own heart, hope warred with doubt. It was more enticing than she could admit to have someone of her own, an ally in the seething morass that was palace politics; but she instinctively mistrusted any plan that had Lord Reath at its heart, as this one most assuredly did. She had never yet known him work for her *benefit.*

Chapter 34

We set off soon after we had eaten, the prince presumably being carried on a pallet. I say presumably because, for all the world, he looked like a roll of carpet. I could not help staring, and when we arrived back where Abe had arranged to meet his cousin, he was equally nonplussed. The cousins chatted for a while, but Hazzor — whose expression had been almost universally glum since the kidnap — began to frown. I watched his eyebrows inch nearer and nearer one another, like two shy but fascinated caterpillars, and felt my chest tighten in response.

I sidled over.

"What's going on?" I asked.

"Pelan wants us to return to Ay Toris to show off the rug."

The caterpillars were almost touching now. Hazzor joined in the conversation his tone conciliatory. I could not help noticing that the more conciliatory Hazzor's tone, the more emphatic Pelan became. As I watched they came to an impasse. Pelan stood in his boat and grinned cheerfully at his prospective passengers. I confess I did hope Abe found his cousin's teeth every bit as exasperating as I found his. In the distance, we heard a bell begin to ring followed by another and another. I looked over my shoulder at the tower on the horizon. It seemed they had noticed the prince was missing. The muscles tightened in the spy's jaw, and he spoke again, resignedly.

"N'dihodo celly den. Dali pak."

He nodded to the rest of us, and we climbed into the boats.

Pelan wanted to travel with the new rug so, since Fryn'gh wanted to travel with the prince, I found myself in the middle boat again, with Axyl and Thorn. I eyed the water level anxiously, but once Axyl put his armour with Hazzor, and his bag in the first boat, I began to hope we *might* not sink.

Of the rest of the day, there is little to say. Hazzor said little to anyone. I was consumed by my own inner angst, and Fryn'gh was wrapped up, so-to-speak, in his 'rug'. Even the banter among the bandits was limited, assigned as they were across different boats with people who were not talking, did not speak the same tongue, or were asleep.

Hazzor had brought food from Haenah so we stayed in the boats all night. I confess, I hardly noticed. Despite my earlier intentions, I found I could not keep not saying the hour. I had started before I had remembered my doubts, and continued because sheer habit kept me moving through the words. They are words I love, but they brought little comfort that day. I was not the woman I wanted to be. I was not the priest I wanted to be. I felt divorced from myself and from Re'a.

I must have looked even glummer after I had said the hour because Thorn was moved to ask again, why 'the long face'. I took a deep breath and said simply that I had participated in magic, which is forbidden.

"You know," she said in return, "for a priest of Re'a, you don't have much to say about forgiveness."

That night, we once more anchored the boats and slept curled up between the benches. When I say, 'slept', I mean something that passed for sleep, but was hardly restful. Axyl screamed and whirled through my blood-soaked nightmares, friends and family falling beneath his axe, while the priest of H'th Iriq asked me what I'd done with my life.

The night left me feeling stiff and even more out of sorts. The day ahead felt very long and, when I said the hour, it felt like a mockery of what my life had been. I did not recognise what I saw when I leaned over the boat's edge and caught my reflection. I wondered if she liked what she saw.

"Are we nearly done, Thorn?" I asked, as I took the paddle from her that afternoon.

"Done what?"

"Done dancing to Reath's tune."

She shrugged.

"When this is done, we start something else." She smiled at me, suddenly cheerful. "Pray to your god that next time it'll be drier, hey?"

I smiled, dutifully. Is that what lay before me now? One task after another while I slid further and further down Reath's path?

"I don't want to," I whispered.

"Hmm?"

"Nothing."

Thorn frowned.

"Saahni?" When I looked up she did not quite catch my eye. "You wouldn't betray us?"

"No!" I was indignant. "Thorn, I promise I don't know what happened — maybe they were just extra cautious? Hazzor said they were anxious."

The archer nodded but she did not say anything more.

It was nearly time for the third hour when we arrived back at Ay Toris. One small, colourless child, her feet dangling in the water, saw Pelan arrive and gave out a joyful shriek. Almost falling into the river in her excitement, she yelled,

"Hee! HEE! Pelani, hee!"

Within moments the *tuy heold* was covered in children all shouting and waving, jumping and laughing. Where they had all come from, and how they had got here so quickly was anyone's guess. For a moment I actually wondered if they had been hiding in the water.

They were delighted with the 'rug' and brightly curious. Every time a child climbed into the boat to poke it, Fryn'gh twitched violently. Abe gently fended off one child after another. Eventually, Axyl took pity on the mage, and waded through the diminutive W'shtens to hoist Vasht-Yr over his shoulder and take him to the relative safety of the village's central platform. This left Abe trying to keep the little dears out of Axyl's bag and the armour he had left behind, and I saw at least one blade disappearing up the sleeve of a sexless imp. I wondered if the prince would be any safer surrounded by W'shten adults. Fryn'gh was nearly as pale as the locals. Hazzor was not looking much better.

Soon the adults arrived, and Thorn and Abe were hugged and kissed and hugged again. There was much patting and coy looks directed at Thorn, who did her best to play her part but Abernast was obviously having more fun. I soon tired of the pantomime. The unrelenting company was getting to me. I needed solitude and I knew where I could find it: I figured I had time to visit Lecyel's empty *tuy*, and return before dinner was ready. It was probably better if Hazzor did not know what I intended. I would go quietly, say the hour, and return before I was missed.

I climbed up into the healer's *tuy* for the third time. It had not escaped me that each time I came here I had intended to pray, but I was determined this time I certainly would. After all, what could possibly stop me? Candle stub in one hand and fumbling for my beads with the other, I ducked around the unusually plain curtain into Lecyel's abandoned home.

It was not abandoned.

There, lounging on his bed, sat the missing healer. The candle slipped from my hand and fell to the floor. He was *not* supposed to be here! Because of him I had a gaping hole in my memory, hiding Rea only knew what — or at least only Re'a and Lecyel. Because of him, Hazzor and most of the others no longer trusted me. *Hazzor. Hazzor is going to be livid that I have come here!* I should leave, I thought, and I should leave *now*.

"Kayt'an," said the man.

Despite the wyrms crawling in my stomach, I found myself smiling. This man, I knew, this healer was my friend. Still, I knew I should leave.

Lecyel smiled back, his eyes — as ever — alight with amusement. He gestured to the pile of cushions and despite myself I sat. He handed me a cup. Dazed, I took it. It was almost certainly poisoned — with the same poison I had fed the prince — but somehow I could not instruct my hands to ignore the offer. I held the mug curled against my chest and felt its warmth spreading. I sat rooted to my place, entranced already by the predator in front of me.

The dark man sipped at his drink and smiled some more.

"Why so suspicious of me, Kayt'an?"

Uncertain, I shook my head.

"You poisoned me." It was hard to speak. "Lecyel, you poisoned me and then you enchanted me."

"Oh Kayt'an," he gave a low laugh, "no. Who told you I did such a thing?" He laughed again — deep and gravelly. "I'm not a mage. If anything, you enchant me." He spread out his arms. "Look at me, Kayt'an, would I be living out in the marshes if I was capable of such things?"

I opened and shut my mouth a few times. Every instinct told me to believe him though my judgement still screamed at me to leave.

"Who told you you were — what was it? — poisoned and enchanted?"

"Umm ... Hazzor," I managed, eventually. Then, more confidently, "Why do I not remember what happened?"

Lecyel leaned towards me.

"Kayt'an, oh Kayt'an," he was all compassion, all cordiality, "you simply banged your head." He rested a hand on the table. "I'm very sorry I didn't realise how dazed you must have been. It was most remiss of me, and me a healer, too."

He shook his head sadly: overcome, it appeared, by his own lack of perspicacity.

What a fool I had been! I had been confused, disorientated and sick. Of course, I must have hit my head! Hathil would be ashamed to own me as a pupil.

Colour rose in my cheeks. How rude I had been on such a base, groundless assumption! I hung my head and stammered an apology. My friend leaned closer, and touched my cheek with the back of his hand.

"I'm used to mistrust," he murmured, sadly. "I look different, I speak differently, I have secret knowledge ... But you, Kayt'an, priest of Re'a, I had hoped you would be different."

I wanted the floor of the *tuy* to open up and drop me into the marsh.

I took a sip of my drink to cover my embarrassment, forgetting my caution. It was hot and sweet and good. I took another sip.

Smiling, the dark man held out his hand for mine.

"All forgotten now, my priest. How is your head?"

I muttered something about it being fine. I was fine, increasingly fine. There was a hint of unease in the corner of my mind, but it was fading fast. Everything was just fine. I gave Lecyel my hand.

"I'm so glad. I was mortified you hurt yourself in my home."

A thought wandered lazily into my attention.

"You went away."

The healer shook his head sadly.

"Kayt'an," there was rebuke in his voice and I blushed. "I had to gather supplies for my stock. Besides, your friends clearly did not want me with them. I decided it would be less embarrassing for all if I just waited for your return." He smiled again, warmth again shining from his eyes. "Are you interrogating me?"

I dropped my eyes. I had nothing to say. I felt, rather than saw Lecyel begin to unwrap the bandage on my hand.

"So, mistress priest, now that you trust me," he looked at my cup in what seemed to me to be a pointed fashion, so I drank deeply, "tell me, Kayt'an, that carpet Abe carries, is it truly a wedding present?"

I shook my head.

"No? I'm all curiosity."

He finished unwrapping my hand and held my hand, palm up. He trailed a finger across the marks of my priesthood.

"What is it?"

This was not my secret, I knew it. It was Hazzor's.

Hazzor.

Bright in my memory, I saw his face next to mine, thin lipped and pale with anger. *'We are trying to stop a war and you want to risk everything for what?'* My breath quickened. I must go, I thought, and tried to pull my hand back, but the healer's hand tightened on mine.

"Kayt'an?" He was all concern, all consideration. "Kayt'an, did you use the ointment I gave you?"

I panted, fought to bring my mind under my control. Why was I here? What was I doing? *Hazzor's going to be bloody furious if he finds out.* I shook my head, trying to clear it.

"Finish your drink," my companion's voice was deep and hypnotic, "you'll feel better."

Automatically, I glanced at my drink. The cup sat in my free hand, warm and inviting. There really was very little left. It seemed rude to leave it. I swallowed it down. The remnant was thick and gloopy with honey and ... something else. Panic rose — and died. *Everything* was just fine. Lecyel was my friend, of course he was, and I could trust him with anything. I felt a little warm as some things occurred to me with which I might trust him.

"Kayt'an," his voice seemed to live inside me, "do you trust me?"

Again, he ran his fingers over my palm. I could barely lift my eyes from his fingers' dance. I was comfortable and very relaxed. I nodded. He smiled again.

"Tell me about the carpet."

So, of course, I told him everything I knew.

Lecyel's smile grew, and I was happy to have pleased him.

"So where are you taking the prince?"

I did not know. My heart sank.

"Never mind, Kayt'an, I will come to you. Be ready for me at dawn in," he considered for a moment, "four days."

I was puzzled. If I did not know where we would be in four days, how did he? I voiced my question, anxiously. In answer, the healer turned my hand over. Oozing from the cut on my hand was a thick, black discharge. I was puzzled and mildly surprised. This was not what I expected. I intimated as such.

Lecyel, eyes on mine, lifted my hand to his mouth and I felt him trail his hot, wet tongue across the injury. Before he closed his lips again, I saw a line of the black pus melting into his mouth. I watched his throat move as he swallowed the corruption issuing from my hand. I smiled. He moved my wounded hand to his belly.

"I feel you now," he pressed my hand against his stomach and groaned slightly, "here. I can find you anywhere."

He stroked my face and I leant into his hand.

"Little priest, tell me about your companions. When I bring soldiers to retrieve Yr's princeling, they'll need to know what to expect."

Eagerly, I disgorged my little experience of the

bandits. I told him how far and how well Thorn can shoot, and how Axyl in a frenzy had fought off nearly the entirety of the prince's bodyguard. I told him of Ranyl's skill at hiding. I told him everything I could to be sure there would be no surprises for Lecyel's men. All the while I talked the strange man's smile grew.

When I had finished he kissed me, and I tasted on his lips the pus from my hand mixed with honey from his drink.

He drew his thumb down my jaw line, and leaned forward to whisper in my ear, "Go back to your companions now, little priest." This man who filled my world thought for a moment. "Hazzor will want to know where you've been. Tell him you went to bathe."

I hated to contradict my dear friend, but at this point I felt it was worth pointing out that Hazzor did not trust me since the kidnap had gone awry.

There was an expression on Lecyel's face that in my addled state I could not read.

"Surely not?" he said quietly, and smiled another slow smile. "Give him this," he rummaged in a pocket and brought out a scrap of paper. "Tell him you found it on the ground at the farm. Now go," he withdrew his hand from my face and I sighed with disappointment. "Forget you came here."

A thought floated up from the darkness of my mind. I had come here to say the hour in private, as my friend had invited me to. It felt important that I should. I mentioned my desire, tentatively.

The dark man rested his hand on my knee and gazed long into my eyes.

"Kayt'an, listen to me, Re'a knows your needs before you ask. She knows how difficult it is to pray just now. I'm sure she doesn't need you to stop and pray — it only causes conflict. Everything's alright."

I knew that it was so.

I left the *tuy,* and headed back in Cy'wr's boat to the village. I headed for the sounds of celebration and the probable location of my companions.

Chapter 35

I was on the village's central *tuy heold*. I wound my way through several jubilant W'shtens before I found Fryn'gh. I sat down beside him with a sigh. He was far from my first choice as a companion, but Thorn was in the middle of the party with Abe and the child-matriarch while the mage was hanging back out of the way. I thought I ought to make conversation with Fryn'gh.

"What's going on?" I asked.

"What does it look like? Now shut up, I'm concentrating. Damn those children!"

Someone put a plate of food in my hand and I poked it around a bit. I really ought to make an effort to talk to Fryn'gh, I thought, feeling a vague echo in my mind.

"What's going on?" I asked.

The mage just glowered at me. I raised my eyebrows, but said nothing further. *Honestly! And the Tower wonders why the Readers of the Lady Re'a think magic belongs to the Dark Lord.* Fryn'gh had been surly to begin with but now he was just rude. Ranyl came and dropped down beside me.

"Kayt'an! Where've you been? Haz's been chewing bees over you." The thief's mouth twisted in what I had come to know as a smile. "You should try some of this pirvo."

He pressed the cup into my hand and I felt a sudden wave of nausea. I must have eaten something that disagreed with me, though I could not think what. I could not, come to think of it, remember sitting down, nor where I had been. This did not, to my vague surprise, feel like a problem, but I know this kind of thing worried Hazzor. *Hazzor must not know where I have been.*

"'s good stuff," said Ranyl, misinterpreting my hesitation.

The thief rose, a tad unsteadily, back to his feet and departed again, presumably to replace his cup.

After a while — and a few sips of pirvo — I began to relax and my stomach settled. Hazzor clearly had not seen me. I began to feel tired and realised, with an unspoken oath, that I would need the spy to find out where my things were, and where I was to sleep.

I got to my feet and looked around. Once I was looking for him Hazzor was unmissable. He was back in his long jacket, waistcoat and trousers, looking thoroughly out of place. He was looking directly at me: so much for him not seeing me. When I saw he was watching, I turned and headed away from the celebrations and, predictably enough, he followed me.

"Is there any point my asking you where you've been?" he asked without preamble.

"I bathed," I said, without hesitation.

He was visibly surprised. "I'm all astonishment." He raised his eyebrows. "Though you put back on the grubby marsh-wear, I see, rather than your normal clothes."

"I have no normal clothes," I snapped back. "Somebody in Marrett threw them away."

Truth be told, though, I would feel very strange in my clothes of old. It felt like an eternity since I had worn my priest's skirts. I was not sure they would still fit.

Hazzor was nodding.

"I'm curious. Where did you find a private place to bathe?"

I glanced around me. Where had I bathed? The world shifted and twisted under me and my legs felt suddenly inadequate. His hand steadied me and I was grateful.

"Too much pirvo," I muttered.

"I can smell it. Kayt'an."

"Ssssah," I said, before I managed to stop myself.

"Given your lack of conviction keeping secrets ... " He narrowed his eyes a fraction. "Some secrets, anyway — it'd be better if you stayed sober."

"Here," I handed the spy a scrap of paper I had in my pocket. "I found it on the ground. Forgot to tell you. At the farm."

"What's this?"

"I'm going to bed." Dignity is hard to achieve when you are three parts drunk on two sips of pirvo and being held up by a man you are trying to impress, but I had a fighting stab at it. "Do you know where my things are?"

Thorn raised me at dawn the next day, excusing herself to Keas who had still been asleep.

"Come on sleepy head. No time for prayers now, we've got to get moving. Haz wants to be clear of the Ga'ared lowlands before Fryn'gh collapses completely."

I grabbed my things together and we set off.

I was glad when we cleared the wetlands. Saen shone high in the sky. I will not say the land further west was dry, but it was dry enough that boots actually worked. I pulled mine out of my pack and did my best to dry my feet a little before pulling them on. They had admirably survived the soaking they had received and I was galvanised to pull out the jerkin as well. I looked up, dressed half-and-half as I was, and found the others — save Fryn'gh who had eyes only for the prince — watching me with puzzled expressions.

"What?"

"Sahnithi, *sesri mu*, I'm filled with doubt."

The wretched man was clearly teasing but I could not resist giving him what he wanted. "Doubt?"

"Sahnithi, don't tell me that all our adventures have tarnished your sweet faith? Sweetheart, I'm relying on your Re'a to get us through."

He waggled his eyebrows at me, but I refused to be bated. I gathered he was surprised I had not insisted on everyone stopping while I said the hour. Well, I was wiser than that now. Re'a was a peaceful goddess. She would not want me to cause unnecessary conflict.

"I'm alright. It's Fryn'gh you should worry about."

Indeed, I was beginning to worry. He was very pale, as if all his colour had leached into his red hair, and beads of sweat stuck to his forehead. Axyl and Abe were fully engaged carrying the 'rug' so it fell to Ranyl and Thorn to balance the mage between them as he slipped and tripped and slithered — barely upright — down the tracks between the fields.

It was Ranyl who filled me in.

"He's holding two spells at once. It's a lot to ask. Give it another couple of days and he'll be able to drop the illusion. He'll be better then."

"Why does he have to wait 'til then? There's no one here but us."

The little thief shrugged.

"You never know who's looking."

Hazzor was still looking at me strangely, and when we set off again he dropped behind to walk alongside me.

"Saahni, do you know what this is?" He was holding a scrap of paper. I shook my head. He walked a little further before answering, "It's a note, promising information."

I felt I should contribute.

"Ah," I said, wisely.

"In W'shten."

Now something more emphatic was clearly required of me.

"W'shten?"

I gave it as much emphasis as seemed decent. Hazzor seemed satisfied.

"You say you found it at the farm."

I was at a loss. Had I? I shrugged. It seemed a safely ambiguous gesture. The spy thrust the fragment back in his pocket, leaving his hand thrust deep inside the pocket. He did not look a happy man.

"Saahni, it seems I owe you an apology."

This was new. I tried to look gracious. Hazzor sighed, and looked away, back the way we had come.

"I near as anything accused you of being a traitor.

"In my defence, I'd hoped it was your involuntary betrayal because this," he shook his head, "this is so much worse."

I was now totally at a loss so I ventured nothing. After a while Hazzor picked up his pace again and I was left struggling through the mud on my own.

I stared at his back. The conclusion of our non-conversation was, clearly, that I was no longer distrusted. I smiled to myself. That felt nice. I watched Abe and Axyl carrying the 'carpet' and bit my lip. It was time I found out what, exactly, I had assisted. I was less worried about my part in the sorcery — everything was fine, I knew — but still, it would be good to check it was nothing I would really regret.

I lurched and slid through the mud to catch up with the spy again.

"Hazzor?"

"Hmmm?"

"What exactly did Fryn'gh do to Vasht-Yr?"

I was subjected to a long, scrutinising look. Then Hazzor nodded.

"You're right. It's only fair you should know." His lips twitched a couple of times. He stared straight ahead. "It was a love spell."

He gave me a sideways look. I snorted in disgust.

"That's impossible."

"Not impossible — difficult."

"You're telling me we can bewitch this boy into falling in love."

I snorted again. It was patently ridiculous.

"Let's say we can make him decidedly susceptible."

"Are you telling me," I could hear my voice rising, and noticed Thorn dropping back a step or two. Working at keeping my voice level, I continued, "that we have come all this way, gone through all this," I became shrill, "to administer a love potion?"

To my surprise, the spy actually smiled. "Not just any old love potion. Vasht-Yr has been primed to perceive Princess Ttarah as the most beautiful woman he's ever seen."

I was so taken aback I slipped in the mud and would have fallen had Hazzor not caught me. For a moment, I thought he was going to laugh.

"Princess *Ttarah* ? Princess cursed-by-the-mage-Beurth-and-now-hideous Ttarah?"

"Brilliant, no? You've got to admire Reath's sheer bravado. We take her up to the hills near Hethin. Wake the prince up in time for him to rescue her from another attack by 'Beurth'."

"Beurth is dead. He was caught and killed ... Wasn't he?"

Hazzor shrugged.

"This will be some criminal Reath has lined up for the part. The prince will think he's killed Beurth himself and broken the spell. When Princess Ttarah unveils for him, and he sees the face of his dreams, the combination of his heroism and her beauty — as he sees it — ought to see him head over heals."

"How are we going to account for his waking up in another country? And for the fact that no one else thinks she's beautiful?"

This was by far the silliest plan I had ever heard.

The spy's lips twitched some more. I was beginning to fear he was drunk.

"He'll be so disorientated by the drugs you've given him, he'll believe anything we tell him. As for the princess, she's to have an attack of modesty. No one but her husband will be allowed to see her face. No one will ever see she is unchanged."

I opened and shut my mouth a couple of times.

"Husband?" I managed.

"Their marriage will give Gayton the bargaining chip he needs. Not to mention also giving us some of the scheming brilliance of the Yr dynasty in the person of a son who's desperate to escape the shadow of his elder brother."

The spy actually smirked. Thorn had dropped back enough to hear and added,

"Don't forget the plausibility of romance." I thought I detected a hint of asperity in her words. I did not think she had overly enjoyed being Abernast's romance for Hazzor.

"But," I stammered, "but it's all a lie!"

Hazzor shrugged. "Who's to know? Are you planning on telling anyone?"

There was a flint in his eyes again.

"No! But ... *poor* Princess Ttarah!"

"She gets a husband who thinks she's the most beautiful woman in the world, when until recently she thought she'd be lucky to get a husband who'd even look at her."

I looked at him and Thorn. I could not think why I was worried. Everything was just fine.

Hazzor walked us hard that day. Since setting out at sun-up, we had barely stopped for lunch and kept going again until it was practically full dark. My thighs screamed, my back was unhappy and my feet *ached*. I fell asleep almost before I had finished eating and slept dreamlessly until Ranyl kicked me awake in the morning.

"Come on. Re'a's gunna have words with you if you keep sleeping late like this."

He chuckled at his own humour, and left me scrambling to shove my possessions into my pack and lurch after the others.

I could not help noticing as the day wore on that my companions were keeping some small distance from me. They were still chatting among themselves but — after we had stopped for our frugal midday meal — no one really spoke to me again.

It was alright, though. Everything was fine.

Come the evening Ranyl found an abandoned herdsman's shack for shelter — and more to the point somewhere dry to sit. I flopped down, weary. Another day of hard walking had left me drained and bone-tired. Everyone else was engaged in setting up for the night, however, and I felt my idleness. I was on the receiving end of Hazzor's sharp tongue often enough without giving him extra opportunities. For once I actually had time to pray, but it seemed to me — I don't know why it hadn't occurred to me before — that I could advance my gods' cause far more by being helpful. I asked what I could do. Everyone stopped what they were doing and stared at me. Even Fryn'gh flicked a glance my way before returning to his internal battle.

"What?"

Why is everyone being so odd?

Abe and Hazzor exchanged glances. Hazzor cleared his throat.

"Are you not going to say the hour this evening, Saahni?"

I shrugged and shook my head.

"There are more important things. I don't want to be a nuisance. Everything's alright."

I felt curiously queasy. Surely, that was what they had been telling me all this time?

This time, the two mismatched men turned to Fryn'gh, but the mage had attention only for his own mental efforts. The spy scratched his beard.

"Saahni," he said with slight emphasis. "We're crossing enemy country, carrying the kidnapped prince of this country who is known to be missing. Our mage is fully occupied with maintaining the enchantment he's placed on him along with the illusion that the prince is, in fact, a carpet. If, for example, we feared hostile magic, there'd be nothing we could do." Unconsciously, he rubbed his knife-wound. He was still paler than I would like. "I don't think I'd be able to sustain a fight, so we've only two warriors and an archer if we're found." (I noticed he didn't count me in his list of assets.) His expression was the immovable one I'd begun to associate with grave concern. "*How* is everything alright?"

I was puzzled at Hazzor's agitation. (Inferred agitation, that is. He was displaying none.) What he said was true, of course, but — well — everything *was* alright. I could not explain it. Perhaps it was my faith finally reaching my heart. I wondered if I had reached a new instinctive level of faith. Everything was alright because Re'a already knows our need before we ask. She will never abandon or forsake us, the Readers say. I liked the thought and shared it. It was received with universal expressions of scepticism.

"I'd love to believe you, Saahni," Thorn was frowning and really looking very worried, "but only three days ago you were beating yourself up about your failure as a priest. How have you suddenly reached this new..." she searched for an acceptable word, "plateau?" she said at last.

I could not say.

For the rest of the evening, I was left in a little island of my own. None of the others sat near me or spoke much to me, but all gave me worried looks from time to time. Only the mage was indifferent, absorbed in his own thoughts. I was, to be honest, surprised it did not bother me more.

Chapter 36

That night I again slept almost dreamlessly, and woke up rested and cheerful in the pre-light of dawn. I had the feeling that I *had* dreamed, but I had no recollection of it. I was awake before anyone was moving, so I slipped outside the shack to change out of the grubby marsh-dweller clothes I was so sick of, into the warm clothes Reath had given me. When I returned to the cabin the others were moving, but Hazzor took surprisingly little notice of my reappearance.

"No dawn prayers, Saahni?" he asked.

I was getting slightly irritated by this constant harping on about my spiritual discipline.

"How do you know I wasn't saying them outside?"

"Were you?"

I considered lying to the spy, but decided there was no need. It was none of his business. I changed the subject instead.

"When are we off?"

Hazzor did his inscrutable thing again.

"Not yet."

To my surprise, he walked stiffly over to Fryn'gh. The mage did not look as though he had slept at all. Abe looked colourful by comparison. Even Fryn'gh's hair seemed to be fading and drooping. Hazzor patted him gently on the cheek and clicked his fingers less than an inch from his nose. The mage practically growled and tried to turn his back, but was stopped by a scarred hand.

"Fryn'gh," said the spy gently, "let the illusion go, we've got bigger problems."

"Hazz?"

Abe was clearly startled. As one, the four bandits turned and looked at me.

Fryn'gh sighed and slumped. Apparently, he did not need asking twice. As I watched, the rolled carpet melted into the shape of a recumbent prince, and I wondered how I could ever have mistaken him for anything else.

"Saahni," the spy had pulled a scrap of paper from his pocket. "Where did you go when we got back to Ay Toris?"

"I bathed," I said, automatically.

Hazzor nodded a couple of times in a manner that lacked conviction.

"A bath," he said evenly. "Then can you tell me how your arms and legs are still crusted with mud and gore?"

The man was a fool. Of course I had bathed.

"Nonsense."

He saw conspiracies everywhere, I supposed. It comes with the profession.

"Really."

In four short steps, he was standing right in front of me. He unlaced the sleeve of my shirt and revealed my arm. I stared at the dried mess encrusting my forearm and elbow. I could not understand it. I had bathed, I was sure of it.

"This is what you needed me for?"

I tore my eyes away from my arm, and felt slightly sorry for the mage. He not only looked unbelievably drained, he sounded it too.

"Yes, she's compelled, clearly. What do you want me for?"

My arm was brandished at Fryn'gh, which I felt was out of order, but I was too baffled to say anything. I *had* bathed.

"Unpick the weave."

The spy was starting to sound distinctly terse.

Fryn'gh rubbed his face with both hands before he spoke.

"Hazzor, this love spell — " I snorted, despite everything, I could not help myself. The mage gave me a filthy look. "This love spell," he repeated more slowly, "is more difficult than anything I've ever done before, and casting it five days before it's completed is, in and of itself, slowly turning my brain to cheese. The *reason* I was sustaining a simple illusion all this time was because I didn't reckon I'd be able to start it once I'd done any significant time holding this weave. It's been more than two days. I couldn't unpick sparkle dust."

Nobody said anything for a minute or two, and then Ranyl drew a blade from his sleeve.

"I say we eliminate the risk."

"Ranyl!"

The little thief suddenly looked like a knife himself — hard and sharp, and with only one conceivable purpose.

"Don't worry, Saahni, you'll not feel a thing."

I tried to step backwards, but Hazzor still had hold of my arm.

"That's not a big comfort, Ranyl."

Hazzor was staring at the hand at the end of my captured arm. The bandage had come loose and Re'a's mark was visible on the heel of my hand. With his free hand, he pulled at the bandage to reveal the three interlinked circles.

"How did you come by these, Saahni?"

It was such a *non sequitur* it was a moment or two before I replied. Then I managed,

"It's a mystery."

"I was told it's a miracle. Re'a marks her priests mystically."

What could I say? Memories of the night I received the mark usually brought the threat of tears. I figured a nod would do.

"Then pray, Saahni."

"*What*?"

The man who had grumped and moaned about the practice of my religion since the day we set out now *told* me to pray? Wyrms take him, *I* was the priest. *I* would decide when I needed to pray!

"No."

"No?"

"NO. I don't *need* to pray."

"Who told you so, Saahni? Where did you go?"

"I ... I ..."

I really did not feel well. The nausea rose in my throat and I began to suspect I might swoon. Somehow, though, I did not reach out for my Lady for help. That was odd. I needed to sit down. Hazzor released my arm as my legs failed me.

"It's none of your business," I managed, weakly.

Vaguely, I noticed I was still relatively calm, which impressed me. I was surely much more in harmony with the Holy Lady than I had been. The old me would have lost her temper by now. *Well done me!*

Hazzor sank down to his haunches to face me.

"*Pray.*"

The mage snorted, half heartedly.

"This is ridiculous. Hazzor, you've been sucked into the fairy tale. Invoking a long dead criminal is not going to solve anything."

"'Invoking a long dead criminal'?" I was still calm. Fryn'gh did not know any better, of course, but I could not in good conscience let that pass.

"You heard me."

"Praying is entering into the mind and will of the divine, surrendering to the love that holds creation. Not 'invoking' anything. And Re'a was *not* a criminal."

Everything was still fine, of course, and yet in a perfect world I would not need to have this conversation. The mage simply snorted again. Hazzor simply urged,

"Saahni, pray for me."

"Hazz, you're wasting your time and ours."

The mage's voice was strained and faint, but still managed to convey the smug certainty with which he always addressed matters of faith. Oooh, I hoped I would get to see his face when he stood before the Throne of Grace. If resisting Hazzor meant agreeing with Fryn'gh, well — I would not side with the poxy wizard-man against Hazzor in this, not for anything.

"Sure, I'll pray," I said, though it was strangely difficult to get the words out.

Praying, or not praying: it was of no great moment ... but I suddenly was not entirely sure I *could* pray. When I neither moved nor spoke, Hazzor reached into my pocket and retrieved my beads. He took my hand and wrapped it round the beads.

"Pray, Saahni."

I took possession of the beads and tucked thumb and forefinger into a pinch around the first bead. *Re'a, Saviour of the world, have mercy on me.* Words I had spoken over and over and over since I was a little child, yet astonishingly difficult even to think, today. *Re'a, Saviour of the world...*

⊗

I was reminded of learning to say the beads as a child. *Re'a, Saviour of the world, have mercy on me.* I had resisted, complaining that the prayers were tedious.

"Repeat the prayer over and over, Kayt'an, until the words stop having a meaning of their own. Then, they'll become a path to Re'a."

Re'a, Saviour of the world, have mercy on me.

"Saahni, you are making no sense. This is ridiculous." I had thrown down the beads and stuck out my bottom lip. I had not wanted to be there, doing that, I had wanted to be at home, avoiding my mother's chores.

Re'a, Saviour of the world, have mercy on me.

Amtil had sighed and muttered to herself.

"Come," she had said at last.

She took my small hand in her bird-like one and led me into the temple.

"This does not need to make sense. Does a kiss make sense? We are reaching out to Our Lady and she is waiting for us."

She knelt beside me in front of Re'a.

Re'a, Saviour of the world, have mercy on me.

"Kayt'an, say your prayer now."

"Re'a, Saviour of the world, have mercy on me — Saahni, this is no better."

"Again."

"Re'a, Saviour of the world," I puffed out my cheeks, "I feel too silly." My priest and mentor made no response. I sighed. "Have mercy on me."

"Again."

Re'a, Saviour of the world, have mercy on me.

"Saaaaahni," I whined.

"She listens."

"Then she must want to hear something *interesting*."

"It's not about her listening to something interesting, Kayt'an. It's about you listening to her."

"How can I listen if I'm talking?"

"The words keep you concentrating on her, instead of daydreaming."

Re'a, Saviour of the world, have mercy on me.

In my memory, the afternoon was spent in diminutive rebellion while Amtil made me say the prayer over and over and over.

In the dream of my memory — *Re'a, Saviour of the world, have* mercy *on me* — the statue of Re'a looked at me. She *saw* me. I stopped breathing. She said,

"Kayt'an."

Her voice cracked something inside me and I felt pain leak out of my heart and into my chest and stomach. I fell onto my face, tears bleeding from my eyes.

"Kayt'an," she said again, and although I could not see I knew she had crouched down beside me.

I felt her stroke my head. The crack widened and the pain became a flood. *Oh dear life it* hurts. *Re'a, Saviour of the world, — O Lady — have mercy on me.* Memories began to follow the pain. I remembered fleeing Lecyel's *Tuy* the first time, my mind full of fear lest Hazzor should find out where I had been. I remembered going back, not once but twice. *Oh Holy Lady.* "Kayt'an, do you trust me?" he had said. "Do you trust me?" *No!* I should have said, *no — you are a liar and a philanderer!*

Gracious, merciful Lady! I tried to hide from the memories but there was nowhere to go but the floor of the temple. I remembered telling him all the secrets with which my friends had trusted me. I remembered handing them over to this man, this so-called *healer*. I remembered — *Oh Holy Lady make it stop* — I remembered the feel of his tongue on the back of my hand. I had put his poison on my hand, despite all Hazzor's warnings — I had been so *sure* I knew better. I had been stupid and careless, and all the time I had thought I was being *clever*.

The guilt I felt at the death of my village paled into nothing compared with this betrayal of my companions. That seemed so long ago. I perhaps might have stopped it, but I did not *cause* it. This was something else.

I curled into a foetal-ball, and gasped and sobbed and choked.

"Saahni?" Re'a held me and stroked my hair. "Saahni — Kayt'an — hun', it's all right."

No — not Re'a, I realised, Thorn. I filled my fists with her skirt, and sobbed and choked. *Re'a, Saviour of the world, have mercy on me, have mercy on me.*

"It's alright, hun'."

"No," I managed sniffing and panting, "No it's *not* alright."

"Saahni?" Hazzor's impassive expression was calming, but I was all turmoil.

I had to speak. I had to warn them, but — well, if Ranyl had been ready to kill me before this, he was sure to do it once I spoke.

Then I thought, perhaps Ranyl is right. I pulled myself into a sitting position. Now I could see Abe and Axyl standing behind Thorn with matching expressions of concern. Ranyl was nowhere to be seen. Hazzor waited, patient as a stone. Under his eye, I pulled myself together piece by piece. Abe passed me a handkerchief. I took it gratefully and wiped my face and blew my nose. With great gasping breaths, I brought my breathing under something like control. I combed my hair back with my fingers — finding room in my mind to enjoy the ease of it.

Seeing me calmer, Abe leant back against the wall of the hut while Axyl perched on the shepherd's bed with the unconscious prince. Neither took their eyes off me. Thorn stayed on her knees by my side, managing to do a fine impression of a particularly fierce mother hen. I could not look at Hazzor.

After a couple of minutes the spy spoke again.

"Well?"

"Where's Ranyl?"

Prevarication was my friend. Or so I thought.

Hazzor was having none of it.

"On his own business. *What happened?*"

"I saw Re'a." Hazzor raised his eyebrows. Fryn'gh snorted in the background. I was hesitant so I backtracked, "Well, sort of. In a dream. I think." I was conscious I was not making much sense but urgency drove me on. "Hazzor — " I stopped suddenly, my new memories flooding my heart with remorse.

My voice trembled and my eyes filled. I covered my mouth and closed my eyes for a moment. Behind me I heard the mage sigh. My back straightened. Nasty, pasty-faced pox of a creature. How dare he sigh at my distress! I took a deep breath and opened my eyes again. The spy could have been waiting for the moon to rise for all anyone could see.

"Yes?" he prompted.

Another deep breath. "Hazzor," I spoke quickly now to get it over with, to speak the dreadful words and be done. "I'm sorry, I've betrayed you all." *Don't stop here, but oh, Re'a give me strength!* "I went to Lecyel's *tuy* and he was there and I told him everything and he said he could find me anywhere and he's coming with soldiers — he said four days. I didn't mean to. I'm *sorry*."

I stopped before the fragile pieces of my self-control deserted me again.

There was silence in the shack.

Then Axyl said,

"Shit."

Everyone else seemed to think Axyl's comment covered it because no one else spoke for a while. Hazzor did not move, did not appear to blink, but his eyes turned inwards.

"Hazzor must have broken the compulsion by getting her to break the prayer block." The mage must have felt my own account needed expanding. "Must have been a background piece of conditioning, probably not intended and therefore weaker." I could not see him but I could hear the smirk in his voice. "Like a secondary infection. Once that was broken the rest of the compulsion followed."

He sniffed, clearly pleased with his explanation, which — frankly — *I* did not hear anyone ask for.

"Never mind *how*, buck," Abe linked his fingers behind his head and stared at nothing, intently, "What in Hother's hairy dark pit of an *arse* are we going to do?"

Chapter 37

Hazzor puffed out his cheeks and blew out a sigh. He ran a hand across his face and back again.

"*How* can Lecyel find you?"

I took a deep breath, then said very quickly and quietly,

"The ointment he gave me left a poison in my hand, which he ... ate. He said it linked me to him."

I watched the muscles in the spy's jaw work for a while before he said impassively,

"The ointment I particularly told you not to use. That ointment."

I closed my eyes and nodded. I heard him sigh.

Thorn took my hand — my still bandaged hand — in hers, but her usually bright eyes were dark.

"Haz, what do we do?"

The whole room looked at the man who still had not moved significantly since I had woken. It was a while still before he spoke.

"I can see only three options. Either we surrender, or we kill Kayt'an Sahn ..." Hazzor's expression still had not changed, and he held my gaze with his slate eyes that told me nothing. My mouth was suddenly as dry as parched bones. I swallowed, trying to revive it, and waited for the third option.

"Or?"

Abe was not as patient as me.

"Or we send her as far away from us as we can. Give her a lie to feed Lecyel. Hope it buys us some time."

At this moment Ranyl knocked and entered the shed.

"What'd I miss?"

"Either we all die, or Kayt'an dies, or both."

Another time I would have to thank Axyl for his succinct analysis, but I was too shocked to speak.

"No brainer, then," said the little thief cheerfully and he pulled out his knife.

It filled my vision.

Hazzor gestured with a lazy hand.

"Wait." Finally, his face deigned to show some emotion: he frowned. "If we can get the lie right, there may be a small chance our priest could survive."

I was staring at Ranyl's knife. I heard Hazzor's words but the little hope they offered failed to get past the vision of my death.

"I don't know that I can lie to Lecyel."

After all, I had willingly poured everything I knew into his ears. How could I manage to control what I said to him?

"Fryn'gh, will Lecyel be able to tell that the weave's broken?"

"Hard to tell. With the very little magic he has, probably not, but he's damn skilled at compulsion. He may instinctively know something's wrong."

Probably *not. Oh. Good.*

The conversation continued over my head. One thought filled my mind. *Traitor. I'm a traitor and I'm going to have to die.*

"So, it might work?"

Unlike the spy to be optimistic, I thought, idly.

"It might."

"Saahni listen to me." I tried to focus on what Hazzor was telling me. "You need to get as far away as you can. With a following wind and little rest, you might reach H'th Iriq — when is Lecyel coming, did he say?"

"Dawn tomorrow."

The spy shrugged briefly.

"Do what you can, but a village looks more deliberate. Get there. Tell Lecyel you're waiting for us to come back, we've just left you for a couple of hours to ..."

He trailed off and was lost in thought again.

"How about another raid?" suggested Thorn.

"Too easily checked. No. We need something more vague."

He tapped his finger on the floor. Then, suddenly, his eyes refocused.

"Got it. Tell him we sent you ahead. Tell him the prince slowed us down — that'll ring true, he's known to be headstrong. Tell him I was due to make a meeting in H'th Iriq with Reath. He'll stay for that. The chance of getting his hands on Reath," a smile flickered across the spy's face, "is not one he'll let pass in a hurry."

"You want me to lie?"

Ranyl swore.

"Haz, I still say kill her quick and painless and have done. It'd be kinder."

Hazzor ignored him.

"Saahni listen to me. The longer we can delay Lecyel and his men, the better our chance of success."

I still sat in front of his crouching form. The skirts of his coat, I noticed idly, were resting in the dust around his feet. As Hazzor dropped to one knee, and leaned towards me, I watched them sweep up a small ridge of dust, which formed a throne around him.

"Remember what's at stake. If Lecyel stops us, Gayton's best chance for a decent settlement is dust and ashes. This war will go on until the whole of the Eastern Territories has been razed to the ground and the Western Reaches are penniless." Briefly his hand rested on my knee — so briefly I was not entirely sure I had not imagined it. "Saahni, what did you tell Lecyel about Fryn'gh?"

"What?"

It seemed like another of Hazzor's *non sequiturs* and I was thrown.

With infinite patience, the spy repeated himself and added, "You said you'd told Lecyel 'everything'. He'd have wanted to know our strengths and weaknesses. How much does he know about what Fryn'gh does?"

I shrugged.

"I didn't mention Fryn'gh."

"You didn't — " the spy gave a short gasp of laughter and ran his hand over his face again. "Kayt'an Sahn, I never thought I'd live to see the day I was grateful for your narrow mindedness."

I opened my mouth to protest — '*narrow minded', indeed!* — but the look in his eye left me in no doubt I stood on very shaky ground to be complaining about insults.

"And he, Lecyel, he never asked you about our mage?"

I shook my head. Something like a smile crept across the spy's face, like a trout just visible beneath the water.

"Hazzor, my buck, with the greatest respect to the mage," Abe gave a brief nod to Fryn'gh behind me, "I don't think he's going to make a huge difference."

The smile rose closer to the surface.

"If Lecyel doesn't know we've got an illusionist, if he thinks the carpet illusion was woven in Dar Tor, he's got a harder job guessing what we've done. Saahni you must, *must*, not tell him how Vasht-Yr has been enchanted. If Yr discovers what we've done it's a piece of simplicity to smuggle in a mage to dispel the weave. Vasht-Yr, instead of being an ally against his father and brother, will turn from his wife in horror. The marriage settlement will be annulled and the prince will do everything he can — if I've read his character right — to destroy us."

"I wouldn't blame him," Thorn muttered.

"But — " I struggled to keep up, "but if Fryn'gh can see what's been done to me, can't Yr send a mage to see what's been done to his son?"

"It'll be too late." Fryn'gh sounded smug from where he sat, though I could still hear the strain. "Once he's met Princess Ttarah, the weave completes. The rest of the spell is tiny — just keeping the prince from noticing that what he sees day-by-day is not what he saw then. Since most people only see what they already know is there, it takes only a very little to keep his eye inwards. You'd have to know what you were looking for to see it."

I turned to see the mage.

"Surely, he'll notice sooner or later?"

The mage preened.

"It's a damn good weave. Held in place by a token. His imagination will supply the passage of time but, basically, every time he sees her, he'll see that first illusion."

"As long as no one suspects," repeated Hazzor.

I sat on the floor and tried to gather up the events of the morning. I felt like a cloth that had been wrung out so many times holes were beginning to form. I hugged my knees to my chest. Hazzor was trying to create some hope out of the destruction I had wrought. But it all relied on me not falling for the healer's charm this time. It relied on my being able to tell a convincing lie. It relied on me pretending to be complaisant in the presence of a man of whom I was — when in my right mind — terrified. The tears that had been held at bay for a little while spilled over again.

Another wave of self-pity and loathing threatened to overwhelm me.

"I can't." I sniffed. "I'm sorry, but I can't do it."

My chest heaved as sobs threatened to grip me again.

I expected to see flint-eyes filled with bleak disdain. I couldn't bring myself to look.

I heard Fryn'gh suck in air through his teeth.

"Well, I could have warned you that a priest is bound to let you down when it counts." I began to turn to retaliate, before realising I deserved it. I had let everyone down. "After all," he continued, "what can you expect from the follower of a creed that bases everything on a failed prophet who just gave up."

This time, I was answering before I had time to think anything.

"She didn't give *up*. She gave *herself* — sacrificed herself." I sneered, antipathy to everything represented by the mages' tower overriding anything merely personal. "As opposed to the principles of magic, which care nothing for anything or anyone except the prestige and skill of the trumped up conjurers who practice it!"

Fryn'gh's eyes narrowed and he panted with effort.

"'As opposed to' the priests of Re'a who *never* consider their own dignity — *Saahni*."

Oooh the scut! I had had it with people pushing me around and telling me who I was.

"That's right!" I retaliated, "You can't defend your own so you attack the selfless dedication of — "

There was a hand on my arm.

"Saahni," said Hazzor gently, "if you provoke Fryn'gh any further, he'll lose his concentration."

I felt almost dizzy being pulled back from my anger to the pathos of the present moment.

"Sahnithi, why do you think Reath recruited you?"

He had said something about someone else dropping out, I thought, but the conversation had been so long ago, and I had not wholly paid attention to it at the time. I shook my head, my mouth an ungainly trap for flies. Hazzor's mouth twisted up into his crooked smile.

"You are the most stubborn, bloody-minded, irascible person I know. Don't think about what Lecyel might do. Think about what he has done. Get angry. Stay angry. It's your best chance of survival. It's our best chance of success."

I decided now was probably a bad time to point out that anger is a betrayal of Re'a's compassion.

So I gathered my things, and I left.

Chapter 38

Hazzor told me I would have to walk hard to reach H'th Iriq in time. Ranyl pointed me in the right direction, and told me how to keep my line true. Axyl gave me a pat on the back that almost dislocated my shoulder, and Abe wrapped me in a suffocating bear hug. Thorn patted my cheek and told me I would be fine. She grinned and told me Re'a must be on my side so what did I need to worry about?

Then she laughed.

I hoped she spoke true. I did my best to follow Ranyl's instructions. I stopped to rest only when I really had to, and I walked on by the light of the moon. I began the journey in prayer, walking to the click-click of my beads; but by the end of the day I was so tired I had to pour all my effort into putting one foot in front of the other. Eventually, I found a road and realised it was the same road those bandits had come from, a lifetime ago, before Hazzor was hurt — before I made a pact with magic. I looked to my left and, sure enough, I saw the shape of the village on the horizon ahead of me. I followed the road and the stars to H'th Iriq and before the night was at its deepest I was walking past the cart, which still sprawled by the roadside.

I was footsore and so, so weary. I limped past the barn, past the house from which I had taken flour for Hazzor, past houses indistinguishable to me, back, back to the temple.

I steeled myself and circled the building to find the dead priest, now incomplete and alive with the life her dead body fed. Despite myself, I retched and looked away. I had meant to say something, make some kind of peace with a woman to whom I had never spoken except in my own mind, but I could not face her. I hoped she forgave me; that she would hold my hand if I had to endure what she had. I hoped she would not hold it against me that I was dying, not for my goddess, but only for my country. No, not the country, not even my friends, though I hoped what I was doing would salvage some good for them. No. I was here because it was where my own folly had brought me.

Still, I hoped she would keep me company all the same.

I went to her room. I tripped on a pile of books that had already been kicked over. Sitting among her things, even when they were reduced to chaos, was like coming home. I could almost imagine myself as I had been last time the moon approached her fullness. I found her thread box, and I lay down to get a few hours of sleep before I faced Lecyel. I was too tired to be frightened. Too tired to be anything. I closed my eyes and prayed for sleep.

For the remainder of the night I tossed and turned, drifting in and out of sleep. I found myself at Amtil's deathbed.

"Shhh, Sahnithi," she had said. "Re'a will walk with both of us. Death comes to all of us eventually, Kayt'an. It is senseless to run in fear of it."

"Does it hurt?" I had asked, but she had become Abitha, her eyes rolling while the blood pumped from her throat.

"Not at all," said Abitha. "Everything's just fine."

I tossed and turned and tried to warm myself at a cold forge. Karl stood at his anvil, hammering a sword, his lip bleeding down onto his chin.

"Is it beneath your dignity to raise a sweat for the village you tell me you serve?"

"But the forge is cold, Karl."

"You know nothing of real life, Saahni."

I became angry with this ghost who had pursued me for so long.

"Damn you Karl! I've been living 'real life' for nearly a moon's whole cycle. I've been poisoned, punched, kicked, kissed, ignored, scorned and half-drowned. And it's led me back here. And I think I'm going to die."

As I watched, I realised that it was not Karl's lip that was bleeding. It was the dirty great trench that had been cut through his face so not just blood but also a viscous grey matter oozed out.

"Come share in the fun then, *Saahni*."

I stood in the dark and screamed for Amtil. Lecyel sat before me, lounging on his bed.

"Everything's just fine, little priest."

I woke, and groped for my dead sister's thread box. I could see the threads, but not distinguish between them yet. I was groggy for a moment before I remembered where I was and why.

Sweet Re'a, I was nearly sick. I wanted to go back, to apologise to Karl, to ask, to beg for help restoring the temple. I wanted to stay in the village or hide in the woods with Fris'an, or return to the village by another way, never to have met Reath. I wanted to be lying in my own bed in my own temple in my own village, not here.

I did not want to face again this man, the very thought of whom scared me almost to insensibility.

'Think about what he has done. Get angry. Stay angry.' Easier said than done. I had spent most of my life angry, it seemed, but, now I needed it to hide behind, it was nowhere to be found.

Searching for distraction in the darkness, I put my hand in my pocket for my candle stub only to discover I had lost it somewhere along the way. I put out my hand and checked under the bed, where I might put a spare candle for the night. Nothing. In the end, I simply picked up one of her books off the floor and held it. I smelled the pages and fingered the binding. 'For freedom Re'a has set us free. Stand firm, therefore, and do not submit again to a yoke of slavery.' That was one of Amtil's favourite passages. Slavery comes in lots of different forms, she would say. I prayed Re'a would keep me from Lecyel's thrall. She had released me from it, after all — whatever that damned wizard might say.

I took a deep breath and glanced again at the thread box: one black thread, one white. It was dawn. I rose from my sister-priest's bed and smoothed down my skirt, put on my jerkin and combed down my hair with my fingers. I left her books as tidily as I could, and walked through into the disordered temple. I stepped over the broken and defaced statues and stood in the space I had cleared some ten days ago.

I did not want to

die, but the alternative was to live apostate: a coward and a traitor. I still hoped Re'a might be merciful and let me live, but most of all I needed her to help me help my friends, who loved her not. I needed my goddess of truth and love to help me be angry so I could deceive a man I hated and feared. I needed her to stay with me as I walked away from her.

I knelt in front of the statue that was not there, and waited.

It was time.

Epilogue

Princess Ttarah stood at the top of the hill and watched her hero approach. The wind caught at her skirts and pulled at them like a child wanting to be elsewhere. She knew how it felt. She, too, was impatient to be gone. Anywhere else was better than this place, but failing that she wanted to get this over with. The prince slid off his horse and stood for a moment, bewildered, on the slope below her. She ought to be excited. Her heart, she told herself, should be fluttering. This was her rescue, her handsome prince. Without noticing, she began to trace the lines and ridges on her face for the thousandth time. How many times had she read the story and envied those other princesses their Happy Ending?

But her fairy tale was just that, a tale for children. No, not even that. It was a pantomime, a farce, directed by her father's liege man, Lord Reath. He stood below the tree-line, watching. Next to him stood the archer who, just in case, kept her sights on the man whose hand trembled on Ttarah's arm.

The villain beside the princess sweated and his breath was short. He was a criminal, chosen by lot from those who'd accepted the doubtful mercy of a quick death at the hero's hand. The palace had done their best with him, but they had not been able to fix *his broken teeth or nails. As the principal boy staggered up the hill drawing his sword, his hand looked neither swift nor sure. The princess wondered if 'Beurth' had changed his mind.*

Apparently, no. He remembered his lines, and began to wave his hands in a magical way.

Like one in a dream, the princess watched her prince swing his sword in an arc that reached its apex in the condemned man's neck. The blade sliced through bone and muscle, down into the villain's chest. The poor man spasmed. Ttarah watched, horrified, as blood poured from his mouth and neck. He dropped to the ground, blood pumping onto the grass.

Vasht-Yr looked up and into her eyes and smiled. It really was a charming smile, despite the gore that had splashed across his face. The princess resisted the temptation to ask for a cloth but, as instructed, held out her remaining whole hand. He took it in his, and she felt the magic spark between them. Happy Ever After, *she thought. She wondered what he saw.*

Lord Reath said it did not matter that he had never seen her face, that she should be grateful just to be loved. He was wrong. The princess knew it did matter, and she was not grateful.

As the magic bound the two of them together, Ttarah looked into the prince's glazed eyes.

If a man never knows my face, never sees the scars life has drawn upon me, *Ttarah thought*, how can he ever really know me?

The Tangled Web

A Priest's Tale: Book Two

The fragile threads of peace are held in the hands of a princess who has reached the end of her patience – and of her docility.

On the border sits the King Yr of W'shten and his army.

In Ttaroc, the Mage Tower and the Temple of Re'a are drawing up their own battle lines.

And in a village temple a young priest kneels, waiting to discover if she will see another day.

Spring 2014

Mages

Ghyr wraith	creature summoned by mages
Beurth	the mage blamed for cursing Princess Ttarah
Ceruine	a mage of legend
Dtan	an illusionist
Erlene	a healer
Fryn'gh	recruited by Lord Reath
Hetti	an apprentice mage
Myri'a	a seer
Regnik	Wi'shten mage
Salek	a senior mage of the Mage Tower
	summoner
Talithys	a senior mage of the Mage Tower

Title: Sahn
Honorific: Saahni
Familiar honorific: Sahnithi

Priests of Re'a

Amtil   priest of Harset
Bath'an   priest of Hethin
Gath'ar   priest of Talishead
Heth'e   priest of Talishead
Renid   priest of Hethin
Sissith   high priest of Hethin
Yrith   priest of Ephatha

Things religious

Ashi cymbals	W'shten military rite
H'mariq	solemnities of the death and liberation of Re'a
Holy Book of Sam'th	religious text
Ladlas	marriage feast of Saen and Re'a
Lament of Dhun'ir	religious text
Psalms of Aelithin	religious text

Creatures of myth and legend

Horoc	figure of foolish bravery
Yulid	beast
H'thetin	famed for his hypocrisy
R'thyn	beast
Dhan'ret	Ancient king, sold humanity to the Dark Lord
Greth'l	fairytale paragon
Ygrin	legendary hero

Bandits

- Abe/Abemast — recruited by **Lord Reath**
- Axyl — recruited by Lord Reath
- Dan'an — an independent bandit, not friendly
- Ranyl — recruited by Lord Reath
- Thorn — recruited by Lord Reath

Kings

- Ttarcine
- W'shten
- Gayton — King
- Ttarah — Gayton's daughter
- Dav Yr — Father to the Yr-dynasty
- Rashir — Great grandfather to Yr
- Vasht-Yr — Yr's son
- Yr — King
- Yrth Ra — Grandfather to Yr
- Ga'ared
- Firric — Rashir's contemporary
- Hersec — Firric's son

Herbs:

Altho
Alvia
Black dock
Butcher's broom
Collinsonia
Echusa
Gentian bark
Ginger
Haenid's Heart
L'thoren's flower
Mallow
Marigold
Motherwort
Mustard

Nailwort
Nettle
Oakmoss
Old man tree
rattlegrass
Salvia
Therith
Thyme
Troll-flowers
Willow
Wolfsbane
Wolfsheart
Yellowfin

Flora and Fauna

Badger-fox	small, bear like mammal
Ishet	reptile
Linnit	bird
Occaris	fruit tree
Sohra	marsh bird
Thorn berries	small, sweet fruit
Tibbith	tree
Wychi	bird of prey

Geography (cont)

Ga'ared hights	
W'shten (adj W'shten)	

Tharret		river
	Ay Toris	borderlands with Ttaroc and W'shten
	G'nered	Neighbouring state to Ttaroc
	Steriv	marshland village
	Tuq	Second city of W'shten
		capital of W'shten, port
		river

Hethin

J'lid	seamstress
Lady Esta	lady-in-waiting to Ttarah
Laeni	beggar child
Temple	focal point of the priests of Re'a

Geography

Ttaroc (adj Ttarcine)

Arwn	Kaytʰan's country of origin
	river
Arwnstone	mountain trading post
Ephatha	Second city of Ttaroc
Feris Bek	port
Fhy mountains	geological feature
Harset	Kaytʰan's home village
Hethin	capital of Ttaroc
Hitʰ Jraq	border village
Hethron valley	geological feature
Koile	river
Marrett	trading post
Natt	river
Rastʰin hole	hamlet
Talishead	village

Harset

Abitha — miller
Anid — Kayt'an's sister
Cylla — Anid's friend
Enrith — baker
Essin — villager
Fris'an — villager
Frith — Fris'an's cousin
Hathil — healer,
Heleg — carpenter
Jani — child

Karl — smith
Letty — Wrenik's wife
On'rith — Karl's friend
Ra'an — villager
Ruid — villager
Sarai — Talin's sister
Seuki — weaver
Talin — Abitha's apprentice
Talith — Kayt'an's mother
Wrenik — smith

Ay Toris

Keas	matron	
Cy'wr	boatman	
Pelan	cousin to Abe	
Rossa	Abe's Aunt	
Ghen	Abe's Uncle	
Delaena	child-elder	
Lecyel	healer	

Ephatha

Mage Tower — Both the building that houses the mages of Ttaroc and the policital system of the Ttarcine mages

Wizard's Staff	an inn	
Watering Hole	an inn	
Graent	noble	
Raena	noble	
Juliaen	apothecary	
Frith'a	servant in the Mage Tower	
Yan	servant in the Mage Tower	

Talishead

Daeny	widow	
Zach'ar	thatcher's assistant	

18010758R00236

Printed in Poland
by Amazon Fulfillment
Poland Sp. z o.o., Wrocław